London Churches
Step by Step

By the same author

London Churches
Step by Step

CHRISTOPHER
TURNER

faber and faber

LONDON · BOSTON

First published in 1987 by
Faber and Faber Limited
3 Queen Square London WC1N 3AU

Photoset by Parker Typesetting Service, Leicester
Printed in Great Britain by
Butler & Tanner Ltd, Frome, Somerset
All rights reserved

British Library Cataloguing in Publication Data
Turner, Christopher, 1934–
Outer London Step by Step.
1. London—England—London—Guide-books
2. London (England)—Description—
1981—Guide-books
I. Title
914.21'04858   DA689.C4/
ISBN 0-571-138987-6

Contents

Introduction

This book is written for all who appreciate art and architecture and are fascinated by England's rich history as embodied in its churches.

London is defined here as the vast area covered by the London boroughs. Although one hundred and thirty-two churches are included, a selection has, of course, had to be made and I appreciate that not everyone will agree with my choice. However, few medieval or Georgian churches have been omitted and the most important Victorian examples are also described. Although technically London churches, Westminster Abbey, St Paul's Cathedral and Southwark Cathedral are not included because they are three of London's great sights and have already been fully covered in *London Step by Step*.

The ancient parish churches of what were once small villages occupy much of this book and it is astounding that so many have survived virtually unchanged whilst great residential, and sometimes industrial, areas developed around them. Some have already been featured in *London Step by Step* and *Outer London Step by Step* but the information about these has been greatly expanded, and many completely new churches added, so there is little duplication.

To assist the reader in selecting which churches to see, an initial paragraph briefly describes their main attractions. A short history follows and then the visitor is led, by explicit directions, around the exterior followed by the interior of the church. Each point of interest is described precisely as it is reached. Your eye is the TV camera and this book the explanatory commentary.

Visiting many London churches is not a simple matter as they can be difficult to find and are frequently locked because of vandalism. For these reasons I have given precise directions for reaching them by public transport and, unless they are open 10.00 to 16.00, a telephone number, usually that of the vicarage or rectory, is included so that viewing arrangements may be made in advance. If there is another church of interest nearby, means of proceeding to it by public transport are detailed.

Good exploring!

Christopher Turner

Acknowledgements

For their kindness and help I should like to thank the numerous incumbents and church officials who have advised on and checked the contents of this book. The Information Centre at Church House, Westminster and the Council for the Care of Churches both gave invaluable assistance.

Useful Telephone Numbers
Please note that when telephoning from outside the London area, the prefix 01 should be dialled.

General
Church House Enquiry Centre   222 9011
National Information Centre   730 3488
City of London Information Centre   606 3030

Transport
London Transport   222 1234
British Rail   928 5100
Victoria Coach Station   730 0202
Riverboats   730 4812

London churches – a brief history

This summary outlines the major events that have shaped London's churches. How the different parts of the church and its contents have been affected by these events is described at the end of this book in 'Church buildings and their contents'.

Christian worship was first officially permitted in the Roman Empire by Constantine the Great's Treaty of Milan in AD 313, and between then and the departure of the Roman legions from Britain in 410 some churches would certainly have been built in England. Physical evidence of their existence, however, is inconclusive. Almost two hundred years, the 'Dark Ages', elapsed before Christianity returned, with St Augustine's mission of 596. Churches were built, mainly of wood, but work was interrupted in the eighth and ninth centuries by the Danish invasions. Many London churches appear to have been founded in the tenth century and, although far from numerous, some Saxon work survives.

The Norman conquerors quickly surveyed the country, publishing their findings in the Domesday Book of 1087, and our earliest record of many churches is contained within its pages. The City of London, however, was among a few areas that were excluded. Much rebuilding of Saxon churches now began; the Romanesque style was continued, but in a more robust form, and stone was generally used. The Normans founded a great number of monasteries and their period is sometimes called the 'age of abbeys'.

In the mid twelfth century the lighter, Gothic style, distinguished by the pointed arch, arrived from France. Initially, it merged with Romanesque to provide Transitional style buildings, which still incorporated some Romanesque features. However, Gothic was fully established by the late twelfth century and in its three consecutive phases of Early English, Decorated and Perpendicular remained the dominant style in England until the Renaissance.

During the reign of Henry VIII, the Italian Renaissance at last began to affect English design but its Classical themes were employed only as decoration to what remained basically Gothic forms. The result was an unsophisticated mannerism, which lasted throughout the Elizabethan, Jacobean (James I) and Carolean (Charles I) periods.

The Reformation of the Church in the sixteenth century was instigated by the pope's refusal to allow Henry VIII to divorce Catherine of Aragon. The King, although remaining a Catholic, declared himself supreme head of the church and denounced any interference from the papacy. All seven hundred monasteries were dissolved by 1540 and their properties, which included land occupying a quarter of the country, seized by the Crown. Some monastic churches were kept to serve as parish churches, e.g. St Bartholomew-the-Great, in the City, but most were demolished.

Parish church interiors altered dramatically throughout the religious turmoil of the next twenty years, when zealous Protestantism and Catholicism alternated with the reigns of Edward VI, Mary I and Elizabeth I. The most significant change was the disappearance of statues and paintings, regarded as idolatrous, and the colourful interiors of Gothic churches were lost for ever.

Very few churches were built between the Reformation and the Restoration of the monarchy – a period of more than two hundred years. In the early part of Charles I's turbulent rule a few were constructed, including Inigo Jones's St Paul, Covent Garden, England's first Classical church. However, the Civil War, followed by Oliver Cromwell's Protectorate, again put a halt to new church building. Much that had been spared at the Reformation was now destroyed by the Puritans, stained glass, particularly in London, being a prime target for their iconoclastic enthusiasm.

The great impetus for new church building in London was created, of course, by the Great Fire of 1666. Before this catastrophe, which destroyed two-thirds of the City, there had been one hundred and seven City churches. Of the eighty-six destroyed by the fire, fifty-one were rebuilt, plus St Paul's Cathedral. Fortunately, a genius, Sir Christopher Wren, was available to accept overall responsibility for this work and he personally designed most of the buildings. A tax on London's coal, which was brought to the capital from the north by boat, was levied to pay for this massive operation. The Classical style was now established, although, to give variety to his steeples, Wren sometimes returned to Gothic inspiration. Most of the medieval 'needle' spires had been lost long before the Great Fire, as they were generally of timber, clad with lead and prone to destruction by lightning.

Carving and plastering skills were approaching their zenith and, happily, Wren had no difficulty in finding outstanding craftsmen to decorate his churches.

In the early eighteenth century, London was spreading apace and more parish churches were needed. To provide them, Queen Anne's Fifty New Churches Act was passed in 1711. However, only twelve were eventually built and six of these were designed by Nicholas Hawksmoor. His work and that of Thomas Archer, together with some late Wren buildings, provide the few London examples of English Baroque, a more sober version of the Baroque style then in vogue on the Continent. In the 1720s, a reaction set in, led by Lord Burlington, and the 'purer' Palladian style (Classicism) was revived. Most London churches until the reign of Queen Victoria were now built in this style, and resembled Classical temples with the addition of a tower and steeple which originated as Gothic features. Frequently, this tower 'grew' incongruously behind a severe Roman or Grecian portico and caused great controversy.

The Gothic Revival of the early nineteenth century was followed by revivals in practically every other style, including Romanesque, Renaissance and Queen Anne.

Emancipation in 1829 soon led to the 'Oxford Movement' of

Keble and Newman which opposed liberalization of the church. 'Ritualism', now known as Anglo-Catholicism, gained favour and as the century progressed, churches were acquired, or newly-built, for Catholic and Anglo-Catholic worship; features and practices not seen in England since the Reformation reappeared.

A Victorian desire to open up a clear view of the chancel to the congregation led to great changes in the interiors of existing as well as new churches. Galleries, screens and box pews were removed and pulpits lowered and relocated from their central position. Stained glass, of varying quality, became *de rigueur* even, for the first time, in Classical buildings. Much restoration took place in which, unfortunately, genuine Gothic features were often removed or 'improved' by inferior craftsmen.

Church building in the twentieth century has produced relatively few masterpieces, partly perhaps because adequate funds have not generally been available, as in the past, and partly because the traditional skills have become harder to find.

Second World War bomb damage to churches was particularly severe in central London. However, many City churches had already been demolished because they became redundant when residents left to live elsewhere and parishes were combined following the Union of Benefices Act of 1860. At the outbreak of the Second World War forty-nine City churches still existed and although many were badly damaged during the Blitz, thanks to skilful restoration only eight have been lost completely (St Mary Aldermanbury being dismantled and re-erected in Fulton, Missouri, USA).

Eighteen Guild Churches were established by Act of Parliament in the 1950s. These relieved some City churches of parochial responsibilities. They were assigned other complementary functions instead. Although small, and often irregular in shape owing to the re-use of medieval foundations, the City churches as a group still provide outstanding examples of late-seventeenth century English art and architecture that are unmatched elsewhere in the country.

After the war the population of many outer London areas expanded and new churches were built. In some cases a completely new and much larger structure was added to an existing parish church, usually involving the demolition of one ancient wall and complete re-orientation.

England's ancient churches, although primarily places of worship also, without doubt, form, collectively, a major part of the country's greatest architectural heritage. They demonstrate our history, beliefs and artistry over a thousand-year period. Fortunately their importance is now appreciated by Christians and non-Christians alike, but many are in mortal danger. Declining congregations, development of ethnic, non-Christian communities, escalating maintenance costs, theft and vandalism, all pose a threat to their existence. Many of the less important will undoubtedly go and others will be adapted to secular use, but it is to be hoped that some means of preserving most of them, as functioning churches, will be found before it is too late.

Elements that may be found in a London church

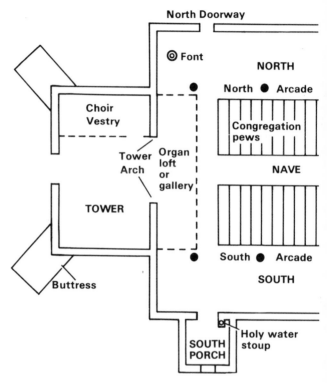

Notes.

1. Features connected with Catholic worship
   were not incorporated in post-Reformation
   churches. Some, however, may be found in
   those built specifically for Catholic or
   Anglo-Catholic worship since the 19C.
   These include from west to east:
   Holy water stoup, Rood loft stairs, Squint,
   Easter Sepulchre, Aumbry, Sedilia, Piscina.

2. The positions of the pulpit and lectern may
   be transposed.

3. Transepts are only a feature of major churches
   or cathedrals, they may have their own aisles.
   The area formed where they meet the nave and
   chancel is called the crossing.

4. The font usually stands near an entrance but
   its position varies.

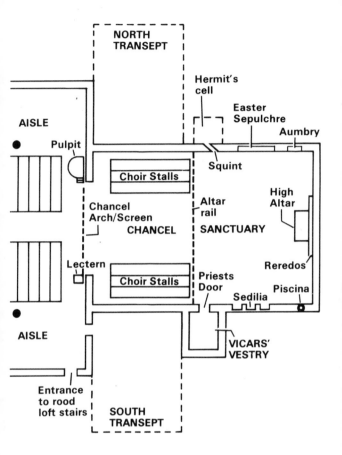

5. Vestries may be built on either side of a church.

6. Not every church possesses aisles; in larger buildings they may continue around the sanctuary forming an ambulatory.

7. Chapels may be built in any position around a church, many originating as private chantries in pre-Reformation buildings. A long eastward extension to a church, stretching behind the sanctuary is a retrochoir, often serving as a Lady Chapel dedicated to the Virgin Mary.

8. Some churches retain north and south galleries at upper level.

**Elements of a nave's side wall
in an important church**

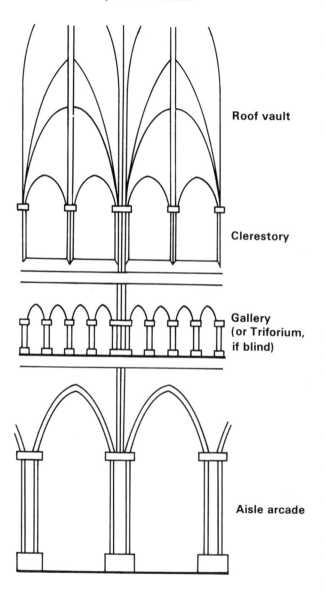

Roof vault

Clerestory

Gallery
(or Triforium,
if blind)

Aisle arcade

The City of London

This is 'the square mile' where London originated. Practically all its medieval buildings were destroyed by the Great Fire of 1666 but a few churches survived around the north-east periphery of the city wall. Most existing City churches, however, were designed, after the fire, by Sir Christopher Wren and these provide an oustanding example of late-17C craftsmanship. Few are open at weekends and visits are best made mid-week between 10.30 and 16.30. The nearest Underground stations are indicated for each church and their positions shown on the two maps that follow.

All Hallows-by-the-Tower
All Hallows-on-the-Wall
St Andrew-by-the-Wardrobe
St Andrew Holborn
St Andrew Undershaft
St Anne and St Agnes
St Bartholomew-the-Great
St Bartholomew-the-Less
St Benet's Welsh Church
St Botolph-without-Aldersgate
St Botolph-without-Aldgate
St Botolph-without-Bishopsgate
St Bride
St Clement Eastcheap
St Dunstan-in-the-West
St Edmund-the-King
St Ethelburga-the-Virgin
St Giles-without-Cripplegate
St Helen Bishopsgate
St James Garlickhythe

St Katherine Cree
St Lawrence Jewry
St Magnus-the-Martyr
St Margaret Lothbury
St Margaret Pattens
St Martin-within-Ludgate
St Mary Abchurch
St Mary Aldermary
St Mary-at-Hill
St Mary-le-Bow
St Mary Woolnoth
St Michael Cornhill
St Michael Paternoster Royal
St Nicholas Cole Abbey
St Olave Hart Street
St Peter-upon-Cornhill
St Sepulchre-without-Newgate
St Stephen Walbrook
St Vedast
Temple Church of St Mary

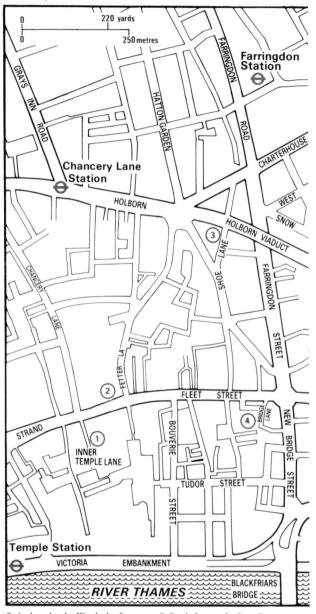

St Andrew-by-the-Wardrobe **9**
St Andrew Holborn **3**
St Anne and St Agnes **12**
St Bartholomew-the-Great **8**

St Bartholomew-the-Less **7**
St Benet's Welsh Church **10**
St Botolph-without-Aldersgate **11**
St Bride **4**

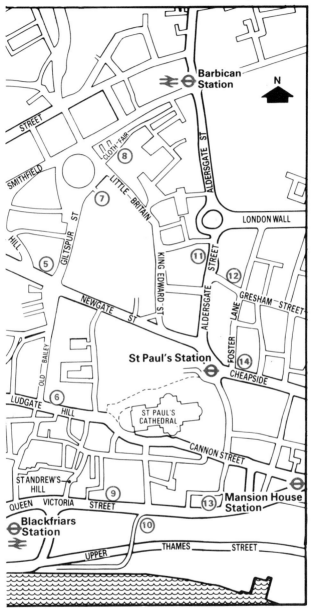

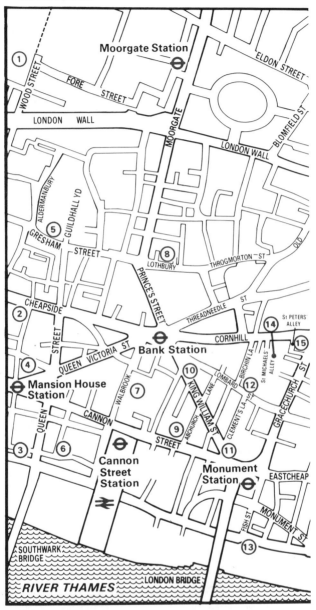

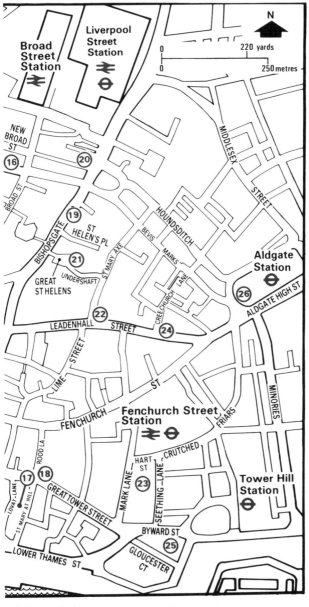

ALL HALLOWS-BY-THE-TOWER

Byward Street

*Tower Hill Station,
Circle and District
lines.*

Although gutted by bombs in the Second World War, much of interest remains within this ancient church. There is Roman and Saxon work and one of London's most beautiful pieces of carving, by *Grinling Gibbons*. Brass rubbings may be made.

All Hallows' was first built by the Saxons in the 7C, shortly after the foundation of Barking Abbey in Essex. The abbey owned land nearby and probably built this church for use by its tenants and visitors from the monastery. Until recently it was known as All Hallows Barking. Traces of Roman buildings existed on the site and some of their bricks and tiles were re-used. Aisles, added in the 11C, were rebuilt in the 15C. The chancel was renewed in the 14C. In 1645 the headless body of Archbishop Laud was buried here immediately following his execution; this was transferred to Oxford at the Restoration. John Quincey Adams, later to become sixth president of the United States, married at All Hallows' in 1797; he was the son of the second president, John Adams.

An earlier west **tower** was destroyed by the blast from an explosion in a nearby ships chandlers' premises in 1649. Reconstructed in 1659, it was the only major new building work in a London church during the Commonwealth. From the top of this tower, the diarist Samuel Pepys records watching the Great Fire spread perilously close. The church was saved, however, by Admiral Penn, father of William, the founder of Pennsylvania, who ordered the demolition of surrounding buildings, thus halting the blaze.

Its **steeple**, by *Mottistone* 1958, was the first newly designed example to be built in the City for two hundred years.

The walls of both **aisles** survived the bombing.

The **east gable**'s design was inspired by Henry VIII's Great Hall at Hampton Court.

Also surviving the bombing was the two-storey north **porch**, built by *Pearson c.*1885.

•● *Enter from the north porch. Proceed ahead and turn R beneath the organ to the Brass Rubbing Centre.*

Remains of a Saxon doorway L, from the original 7C building, were discovered after the bombing. This had probably been the main entrance to the church. Roman tiles were incorporated in the top of the arch but the red brickwork dates from the 17C.

All Hallows' possesses outstanding medieval brasses; rubbings may be made.

The **vestry**, now subdivided, is reached through the north door from the Brass Rubbing Centre. Embedded in the wall, L of this door, is an 11C pillar. Apart from fragments in the crypt, this is all that has been discovered from the Norman church.

●● *Leave the Brass Rubbing Centre and proceed to the* **baptistry** *in the south-west corner of the church.*

Viewed behind a glass screen is the prize possession of All Hallows', its font cover, carved, almost certainly, by *Gibbons* in 1682. This is judged to be one of the most exquisite pieces of carving in London. For this work, which comprises more than one hundred pieces, the carver was paid £12, according to the churchwarden's accounts.

The modern font was made of Gibraltar limestone by Sicilian prisoners during the Second World War. An earlier All Hallows' font, in which William Penn was christened in 1644, is now at Christ Church, Philadelphia, USA.

●● *Return to the nave.*

In the **west gallery** is the organ; its case is a copy of the *Renatus Harris* original that was destroyed in the war.

Fronting the gallery is the coat of arms of Charles II.

Three 18C Lord Mayor's sword rests stand in the bays.

All Hallows' possesses three outstanding wooden effigies of saints. Against the third column from the west, on the north side facing west, is St James of Compostela, 15C.

Facing this, protected by a grille, in a wall alcove that probably once formed the entrance to the rood loft stairs, is St Anthony of Egypt, 16C.

The wall monument to Hieronymus Benalius Bergomi, d.1583, commemorates an Italian parishioner.

The founder of the Toc H Christian Association, 'Tubby' Clayton, was for many years the vicar of All Hallows'; he is buried in a tomb chest R that bears his bronze effigy.

The pulpit, *c.*1670, came from St Swithun London Stone.

●● *Continue to the north aisle's* **Lady Chapel.**

On the north wall is the restored tomb chest of Alderman Croke, d.1477.

Standing on the chest is a casket containing the 'Lamp of Maintenance'. This was given in 1922 by the patron of the church, the Prince of Wales, who became Edward VIII and later the Duke of Windsor, to commemorate his friends who had died in the First World War.

In the centre of this chapel are the four Tate panels, a 15C painted altar-piece, originally in five sections. This was made for the Royal Chantry Chapel which stood to the north of the church and was separated from it by the road. The chapel had been built in the mid-13C as a Guild Chapel dedicated to the Virgin Mary, but Edward IV acquired it in 1465. No trace of this building survives. The panels that disappeared in

1547 were rediscovered in the 18C but the central panel was missing. The kneeling figure depicts Sir Robert Tate.

All Hallows' possesses seventeen brasses dating from 1389 to 1651; they are located around the east end of the church.

At the east end of the south aisle is the **Mariners Chapel**.

The lectern incorporates rails of Sussex iron from the earlier Jacobean pulpit.

At the east end of the chapel, the ivory figure of Christ is believed to have come from a 16C ship of the Spanish Armada.

Against the third south aisle column from the west, facing west, is the wooden effigy of St Roche, 1510.

•● *Ask to visit the* **crypt**.

The main crypt was only formed when the foundations of All Hallows' were strenghthened in 1926. Two Roman tesellated pavements and a detailed model of Roman London are exhibited.

The three Saxon crosses, discovered after the Second World War, are London's most important Saxon finds.

Now linked with the modern crypt at its east end is a small crypt, beneath the sanctuary, which was created in the 14C when the chancel was rebuilt. This was originally the vicar's private burial ground but its altar now contains a columbarium (tiers of niches for cinerary urns).

The mensa (stone altar table) came from the crusaders' castle at Athlit, below Mount Carmel.

ALL HALLOWS-ON-THE-WALL
Dance the Younger 1767

London Wall

Open daily but closes 13.00–14.00.

Liverpool Street Station, Central, Circle and Metropolitan lines.

This is London's only surviving building of importance by George Dance the Younger who called it 'my first child'. It is now the headquarters of the Council for the Care of Churches but some services are still held within.

The first recorded All Hallows' was built on a bastion of the Roman wall in the early 12C and rebuilt in the 13C. Although this building escaped the Great Fire owing to protection by the adjacent London Wall, it deteriorated and was replaced by the present church. When laid out, the street of London Wall was extremely narrow and remained so until 1965. In medieval times All Hallows' was renowned for its numerous hermit cells. The Carpenters' Company holds its annual election here, a tradition that has continued for over 600 years.

Ahead, the west door was for long the only entrance to the church. Immediately west are remnants of London's ancient wall.

•● *If closed, return eastward and apply at the first door L (83 London Wall) to enter the church.*

The simplicity and spatial balance of the interior had an important influence on Dance's pupil, John Soane. It was restored by *A. Blomfield* in 1891 and again by *Nye* in 1962 following extensive bomb damage.

The most important internal feature is the coffered ceiling which is an exact reproduction.

When constructed, the church was surrounded by buildings and it is only lit, therefore, by high-level lunette windows.

The **west gallery** slopes to the south as does the lintel of the west door; this was caused by settlement which took place before the south wall was restored. It accommodates the organ, made *c*.1885 and transferred here from Islington Parish Hall in 1968.

Fronting the gallery are the arms of George III.

On the south side, beneath the west gallery, is the font which was brought from St Mary Magdalene Old Fish Street. Its bowl is late 17C but the stem is modern.

Paving the nave's central alley are the original squares of black marble and white stone.

Unusually, the pulpit can only be reached from the vestry. This was a three-decker until 1891 but never seems to have possessed a canopy.

Above the **sanctuary** hangs a chandelier, the body of which is dated 1766. It is an amalgamation of two pieces and was presented by a parishioner who almost immediately went bankrupt.

Behind the altar is a copy of the painting by *Pietro da Cortona* in the Church of Conception, Rome. It was made by Dance's brother.

In the south-east corner of the sanctuary is a Lord Mayor's sword rest brought from All Hallows' Staining in 1891.

ST ANDREW-BY-THE-WARDROBE
Wren 1695

Blackfriars

Blackfriars Station, Circle and District lines.

Gutted in the war, much of Wren's interior has been reproduced and there are some fine 17C and 18C furnishings.

St Andrew's, first mentioned *c*.1244, was probably founded much earlier. It was completely destroyed by the Great Fire and only the tower and walls of the rebuilt church survived the bombing. 'Wardrobe' refers to the Great Wardrobe where many of the monarch's possessions were stored and which stood behind the church from the 14C until destroyed by the Great Fire.

The weathervane on the tower's south-west corner came from St Michael Bassishaw (demolished in 1900).

◗ *Enter the church.*

All three **galleries** have been rebuilt but, unfortunately, the aisles beneath those on the north and south sides have been enclosed to provide vestries and offices.

The late-17C font and its cover came from St Matthew Friday Street.

In the west gallery is an 18C chamber organ.

The Stuart arms came from St Olave Old Jewry.

Stained glass in the west window is 18C and illustrates the conversion of St Paul.

The pulpit is late 17C.

ST ANDREW HOLBORN *Wren 1690*

Holborn Viaduct

*Chancery Lane
Station, Central line.*

This is the largest parish church in the City to be rebuilt in the late 17C. *Wren* was responsible for encasing the tower, in which some medieval detailing survives, but apparently only supervised the re-design of the body of the church.

A Saxon church, recorded in 951, was rebuilt by the Normans, and again in the 15C. This building escaped the Great Fire but had become dilapidated and was rebuilt under Wren's supervision. The medieval tower, however, was retained although Wren re-faced and heightened it in 1704. It was in this church that Benjamin Disraeli was christened, age twelve, in 1817. This was arranged by his father in a fit of pique, after he had been fined for refusing to act as a warden in the Bevis Marks Synagogue. St Andrew's, restored by *Seely and Paget* in 1961, is now a Guild Church.

The church was erected on the summit of Holborn Hill and only assumed its apparent low level when Holborn Viaduct was consructed in 1869.

Embedded in the **north wall** is a 'Resurrection' stone which was once part of the entranceway to the burial ground; more than 3000 parishioners died in the Great Plague.

When the **tower** was refaced by *Wren* in 1704 he also heightened it. Originally, the structure was surmounted by weathervanes supported by pineapples.

The statues of schoolchildren at the base of the tower came from the parish school nearby.

•● *Enter from the north porch. Turn R and proceed towards the chancel.*

The 18C pulpit, organ and font were brought here from the Foundling Hospital at Berkhamsted. The organ had been a gift from the composer Handel to the original hospital.

The reredos, *c.*1730, came from St Luke Old Street.

•● *Return to the west end of the* **nave** *and pass the font.*

In a niche R is the 18C tomb of Thomas Coram, creator of the Foundling Hospital.

•● *Continue ahead.*

Some 15C vaulting remains within the **tower vestibule**. This was revealed during renovations made to the organ and its case in 1872.

ST ANDREW UNDERSHAFT *1532*

St Mary Axe

Aldgate Station, Circle and Metropolitan lines.

This is a rare example of a City church that escaped both the Great Fire and significant bomb damage. There is ironwork by *Tijou* and an unusual 17C monument, to John Stow.

St Andrew Undershaft gains its name from the Cornhill Maypole, which stood higher than the church steeple, when it was erected every May Day outside its south door. Student riots in 1517 ended its use, but the pole (or shaft) was hung on hooks in the wall of nearby Shaft Alley. A sermon against pagan practices was given in St Paul's Cathedral in 1550 and a mob, inspired by piety and drink, chopped up the shaft and burnt it. St Andrew's was first recorded early in the 12C and again in 1268 as 'St Andrew juxta Aldgate'. The body of the church was rebuilt early in the 14C and again in 1532.

The **tower** was rebuilt in the 15C and its three lower stages survive. Its upper stage was rebuilt in 1883.

•● *Enter the church from St Mary Axe, by the door at the end of the path.*

Internally, major restoration took place in 1634, 1726 and 1876.

The roofs of both aisles are original 16C work.

Specimens of heraldic glass in some of the aisle windows commemorate important contributors to the cost of the 16C rebuilding; evidently more pieces survive, awaiting insertion.

At the east end of the **north aisle** (L of the door) is the monument to John Stow, d.5 April 1605, by *Stone*. Stow's *Survey of London* valuably describes the capital in detail before the Great Fire. At a service held on or near to 5 April each year, the Lord Mayor of London replaces the quill pen on the monument. He also presents a copy of the *Survey of London* to the author judged to have written the best essay about London during the year.

•● *Proceed westward along the aisle.*

The wall monument west of the door commemorates Alyce Bynge, d.1616.

On the same wall, facing the pulpit, is the huge monument to Lord Mayor Sir Hugh Hammersley, d.1636.

The tracery of the west window of the **nave** was restored in 1876 when it was transferred here from the east window, together with the 17C stained glass depicting rulers of England. Much of the remaining glass in this window, particularly the heraldic pieces, are 19C work. A fire at this end of the church in 1976 necessitated some restoration. The five monarchs featured are Edward VI, Elizabeth I, James I, Charles I and

William III. Originally, the last section featured another king, probably Charles II or James II. The original feet were kept but do not quite fit the new figure.

Below this window stands the font made by *Stone* in 1634; its cover and rails are later.

A tablet on the west wall of the **south aisle** commemorates the painter Holbein, d.1543. He is reputed to have been a parishioner.

•● *Proceed to the* **nave**.

On the spandrels of both arcades are monochrome paintings illustrating scenes from the life of Christ. These were executed in 1726 and represent all that is left of the grisaille work at St Andrew's. The remainder was removed from the chancel and between the clerestory windows in 1875.

When the nave's panelled roof was rebuilt in 1950 the original 16C bosses were replaced.

The third corbel from the west on the south side is dated 1532.

The pulpit is late 17C.

It is believed that the altar rail of 1704 is a rare example in a London parish church of the work of *Jean Tijou*, the great French ironsmith.

On the north wall of the **sanctuary** is the monument to Sir Thomas Offley, d.1582, his wife and three sons.

The organ and its case, south of the sanctuary, were made by *Harris* in 1696.

ST ANNE AND ST AGNES   Wren 1680

Gresham Street
(373 5566)

Open irregularly.

St Paul's Station,
Central line.

Almost completely rebuilt after bomb damage, the church's unusual Greek cross plan is of great interest. Several 17C furnishings have been acquired from other churches.

First mentioned in the 13C as St Anne-in-the-Willows, that church is known to have had Norman features. Its present double dedication, unique in the City, is referred to in 1467. The building was restored many times but only a section of its 14C tower survived the Great Fire.

A short **tower** was added to the body of Wren's church by *Colin c*.1714. Its weathervane is in the form of a large 'A'.

•● *Enter from the south-west door.*

The plan of a vaulted square within a square was inspired by Nieuwe Kerk, Haarlem, Holland. Wren also used this format at St Martin-within-Ludgate and St Mary-at-Hill.

The original west doorcase of 1683 survived the Blitz.

Above this are the arms of Charles II which came from the bombed St Mary Whitechapel.

The font is a modern copy (omitting decoration) of that of St Mildred Bread Street, the original cover of which it possesses.

On the north wall, the crown above two mitres symbolizes the monarch's supremacy in the Church of England.

Three of the pulpit's panels came from the pulpit of St Augustine Watling Street.

Flanking the original reredos are paintings of Moses and Aaron, from St Michael Wood Street.

ST BARTHOLOMEW-THE-GREAT

West Smithfield

*St Paul's Station,
Central line.*

St Bartholomew-the-Great, together with St John's Chapel in the Tower of London, possesses the capital's most significant Norman interior. It originally formed the chancel of a once much larger monastic church.

Fronting West Smithfield is the mid-13C **gateway** which once led directly into the church. Its detailing was renewed in 1966.

The timber superstructure, much restored, was added in the 16C and served as the rectory.

◆● Proceed through the gatehouse to the churchyard.

The path follows the approximate position of the south aisle of the long 13C nave, presumably built in Early English style, which once stretched to the road. A low wall R is all that remains of the south wall of this aisle.

Rahere, a courtier of Henry I, recovered from a fever and in gratitude erected a church and hospital dedicated to St Bartholomew in 1123. The church formed part of the small Augustinian Priory of St Bartholomew and Rahere became its first prior. Only the chancel and ambulatory were completed in his lifetime. The transepts and crossing were added in the mid-12C and the nave completed in 1240.

Miraculous healings were reported and on 24 August, St Bartholomew's Day, the church was filled with sick people. From earliest times the priory church had possessed rights of sanctuary (no one could be arrested within its precincts). These, however, as elsewhere, were eventually terminated by Richard III. At the Reformation, the long nave was almost entirely demolished. However, much of the remainder was spared to provide the parish with a new church, as the building then in use, which lay to the north of St Bartholomew's, had become unsafe. A large tower above the crossing had been taken down before the Reformation. Prior Fuller, who had held office for seven years, submitted to the King in 1539 and received a pension. Although St Bartholomew's escaped the Great Fire, by the 18C it had become run down and was occupied by industrial squatters. Much restoration and rebuilding was carried out by *Aston Webb* in the late 19C. The church was undamaged by bombs.

The brick **tower** with its lantern dates from 1628. Uniquely, it houses five bells that pre-date the Reformation.

The west **porch** of 1893 is entirely the work of *Webb*.

•● *Enter the church.*

Originally, the interior was painted throughout with red and yellow zig-zag stripes, a characteristic Norman motif. Some restoration had taken placed in 1789 (*Dance*) and 1791 (*Thomas Hardwick*) before the major 19C work of *Aston Webb*.

The **nave** is entered directly but only one bay remains. This is mostly occupied by the organ, made in 1763 and restored in 1931. It was brought here from St Stephen Walbrook in 1886.

•● *Turn immediately L and R through the choir screen to the* **crossing**.

The choir screen, designed by *Webb* in 1867, was decorated by *Frank Beresford* in 1932.

Pointed north and south crossing-arches are believed to be mid-12C and, if so, represent the earliest known appearance of the Transitional style in London.

The **north transept** had been partly demolished to accommodate a forge in the 18C and was open to the elements. Because of this, much of the stonework in the church has been damaged. The transept was entirely rebuilt by *Webb*, albeit as a foreshortened version.

•● *Continue ahead through the* **chancel**.

Massive, typically Norman piers support a gallery.

The clerestory windows above were remodelled in Perpendicular style in 1406.

The wall monument R commemorates Percival Smallpace, d.1568, and his wife, d.1588.

Facing this is the monument to Sir Robert Chamberlayne, d.1615.

The oriel window, protruding from the gallery, was built for Prior Bolton in 1515. His punning rebus on the stonework depicts an arrow (bolt) piercing a barrel (tun). From this window, the prior could observe mass without leaving his lodgings.

The decorative tomb of Rahere, the founder, stands L of the altar. Although Rahere died in 1144 his present tomb was made *c*.1500. An opening at the rear permitted pilgrims to make offerings from the ambulatory.

Arches at the east end of the **gallery** are blind, in the manner of a triforium. They had been mostly demolished in 1406 when this wall was rebuilt but were restored in the 19C.

•● *Turn L and follow the ambulatory clockwise to the* **Lady Chapel** *behind the altar.*

The original semi-circular apse was lost when the Lady Chapel was added to the church in 1331; this was heavily restored by *Webb* in 1897. A printer set up his press in the chapel and in 1724 employed Benjamin Franklin, who was to become the renowned American statesman; it later became a fringe factory.

Only the windows at the extreme east end of the north and south walls are original. The sill of the latter formed a sedilia.

The wrought-iron screen is by *Gardner*, 1897.

•● *Continue around the* **ambulatory**.

Two wall monuments in the south ambulatory commemorate James Rivers, d.1641, and Edward Cooke, d.1652. The Cooke statue originally 'wept' in damp weather, owing to condensation, now cured.

The large monument to Sir Walter Mildmay, d.1589, and his wife, commemorates The Elizabethan Chancellor of the Exchequer who founded Emmanuel College, Cambridge.

•● *Proceed to the* **south transept**.

Like the north transept, this was rebuilt by *Webb* who foreshortened it. The original was destroyed by fire in 1830.

•● *Turn immediately L.*

The early-15C font, in which the painter Hogarth was baptized in 1697, is the only medieval example in a City church but its cover is probably 17C.

On the east wall is a small memorial tablet to Elizabeth Freshwater, d.1627.

•● *Continue ahead to the 13C door L at the west end of the church; this leads to the* **cloister**.

The east section of the cloister of 1406 was rebuilt in 1928 and is all that remains of the original four.

•● *Proceed ahead towards the south end.*

The blocked 15C door L originally led to the monastic chapter house which was destroyed by fire in 1830.

At the end L is a 13C doorway, originally another entrance to the chapter house.

•● *Exit from the church. R West Smithfield. First R Cloth Fair. Proceed ahead to view the* **north façade.**

This north façade of St Bartholomew's is its most interesting. First seen are traces of Norman and 13C work. Most of the church has been refaced with flint.

The 19C **north transept** by *Webb* is followed by the low wall of the **chancel's aisle** which *Webb* also rebuilt.

The upper-level brickwork is 17C but the brick house with its turret is 16C.

Some buttresses supporting the **Lady Chapel** at the east end of the church are 14C.

•● *First R St Bartholomew Lane passes the east end of the Lady Chapel. First R, follow the south façade as far as possible.*

ST BARTHOLOMEW-THE-LESS

West Smithfield

*St Paul's Station,
Central line.*

St Bartholomew's, although mostly rebuilt in the 19C, retains its medieval tower and vestry.

The church, founded nearby as the hospital's chapel *c*.1123, was transferred to its present site in 1184. It was known as the Chapel of the Holy Cross until the Reformation when it became the parish church of the hospital. St Bartholomew's was rebuilt in the 15C. Within the shell of the medieval church *Dance the Younger* created a wooden octagonal interior in 1793. The body of the church was completely rebuilt in 1825 by *Thomas Hardwick* who closely followed Dance's plan. Restoration, following some Second World War bomb damage, was completed by *Mottistone* in 1951. Inigo Jones, father of English Classical architecture, was baptized in the earlier building in 1573.

The **tower** and west end are 15C.

•● *Turn the L handle to the left, push hard and enter.*

Within the vestibule beneath the tower are Perpendicular features.

•● *Turn L to the* **vestry.**

The stone floor is original 15C work.

On the north wall are carved angels holding shields. They stood outside the south wall until 1823. The lower, probably 16C work, is that of Edward the Confessor and incorporates the arms of England and France.

Against the west wall is the 16C altar tomb of Elizabeth Freke, d.1741, and her husband, John, a surgeon, d.1756.

•● *Enter the* **nave.**

The iron roof is decorated with a plaster rib vault.

Corner chapels 'square up' the otherwise octagonal plan.

At the east end of the north wall is the monument to Thomas Bodley, d.1613, founder of the Bodleian Library, Oxford, and his wife, Anne.

The **sanctuary** was remodelled by *P. C. Hardwick* (grandson of Thomas) later in the 19C. Tracery was then added to the upper parts of the windows.

ST BENET'S WELSH CHURCH *Wren 1683*

Queen Victoria
Street
(723 3104)

*Open by appointment
only apart from
Sunday services (in
Welsh).*

*Blackfriars Station,
Circle and District
lines.*

St Benet's possesses one of Wren's least altered interiors and most of its original fixtures and fittings survive.

The church is first mentioned in 1111 as 'Sancti Benedict super Tamisiam' (above the Thames); by 1275 the dedication had been corrupted to St Benet, Woolhithe. Following the Great Fire, the nearby Paul's Wharf was used for landing Portland stone for the rebuilding of St Paul's Cathedral. By then, the church was known as St Benet, Paul's Wharf and this remained its name until recently. The medieval St Benet's was

rebuilt after the Great Fire but the lower 12ft of
its tower was re-used, although encased.
Restoration took place in 1836, and again in 1946
by *Godfrey Allen* although, miraculously, there
was no bomb damage. Baynard's Castle stood
nearby to the west, until destroyed by the Great
Fire, and St Benet's royal connections were,
therefore, strong. By tradition, Edward IV was
proclaimed King in the pre-fire church in 1461
and in the vestry of the same building, Lady Jane
Grey was proclaimed Queen in 1553.
Shakespeare refers to the bells of St Benet in
Twelfth Night, Act V, Scene 1. Henry Fielding,
the author of *Tom Jones*, married his second
wife, who had been his first wife's maid, at St
Benet's in 1747. The Metropolitan Welsh
Episcopal Church moved here in 1879, thus
saving the building from threatened destruction,
and St Benet's is now a Guild Church; services
are held in the Welsh language.

The church is an early example of Wren's 'Dutch'
style, with its neat brickwork, stone dressings and
carved festoons.

Its roof on the north side is hipped.

The north wall continues 16ft below ground level
(1987) but it is planned to excavate, thus
restoring this façade to its original appearance.

Enter from the west door.

The ceiling at the base of the **tower** is formed by
the pulpit's old canopy.

Above the internal doorcase are the
exceptionally fine carved arms of Charles II,
presented to St Benet's by the King.

Immediately ahead is the poor box.

At the west end of the **north aisle** is the original
font with its cover.

*Proceed along the central alley of the **nave**.*

Attached to the first pew on the north side is a
beadle's staff of 1729.

Although the congregation pews have been
reduced in height they were never box pews, but
many were curtained.

Stone flooring was laid in 1946; the floor level is
now approximately 6ft 9ins. higher than that of
the medieval building.

Inserted in the floor is the tombstone of Mrs
Delarivier Manley, d.1724, author of *The New
Atlantis*, England's first recorded 'best-seller'.

The original **galleries** are rare survivals in the
City, but restoration was needed at the north
gallery's east end after a fire in 1971.

The first shield, the Pallium of Canterbury,
displayed on the north gallery's front, represents
ecclesiastic law and the third, the Court of
Admiralty's fouled anchor, represents civil law.
Both these courts formed what was known as
Doctors' Commons, whose members occupied
the north gallery until 1867. A speciality of this

legal institution was the provision of facilities for quick marriages.

Between them are William IV's arms, painted in 1837 and incorporating the escutcheon of the Kingdom of Hanover, a rare example in this country. Queen Victoria was unable to succeed to the Hanoverian throne as only males were permitted to do so.

Thirteen banners of the members of the nearby College of Arms hang from the galleries. This has been their church since 1555 when they first occupied premises nearby. The fourteenth banner is the Duke of Norfolk's.

Supports of the pulpit's canopy were used to form the face of the reading desk in the **nave**.

A communion table stands at the east end of the **north aisle**. Allegedly this is one of the furnishings from the pre-fire church that had been presented by *Inigo Jones* and rescued from the blaze.

•● *Proceed to the* **sanctuary**.

The altar rails are also believed to have been saved from the pre-fire church and, again, had been presented by *Jones*.

On both sides of the sanctuary are the pews belonging to heralds of the College of Arms.

The three sanctuary chairs were presented by Sir Leoline Jenkins, later Secretary of State to Charles II, in 1683.

The outstanding carved altar, made *c*.1660, is probably Dutch.

North of the reredos, a tablet commemorates John Charles Brook who was killed when the ceiling of the Haymarket Theatre collapsed in 1797 during a performance attended by George III and Queen Charlotte.

The reredos is original.

South of the reredos, on the east wall, is the small memorial tablet of 1878 to Inigo Jones, the father of English Classical architecture. He was buried beneath the sanctuary of the pre-fire St Benet's in 1652, in the same vault as his parents. Nothing survived of Jones's memorial which had depicted some of his buildings; the plaque, however, repeats the inscription that it bore.

•● *Return to the* **nave**.

Part of the original three-decker pulpit, by tradition the work of *Gibbons*, has survived. Inscribed on a panel is 'CR', possibly the royal cypher of Charles II, and 'Donum [given] 1683'. This may indicate that the King presented the pulpit to the church. Its stairs, stem and base are modern.

At the south-east end of the church is the unusual monument to Mark and Alice Cottle, 1698.

On the south wall, towards the west end, is the oldest surviving monument at St Benet's, that of

Sir Robert Wyseman, Dean of the Court of Arches, d.1684; his portrait medallion is exceptional.

ST BOTOLPH-WITHOUT-ALDERSGATE *1791*

Aldersgate

*Open Monday–
Wednesday and
Friday 10.30–15.30;
Thursday 12.30–
14.00.*

*St Paul's Station,
Central line.*

St Botolph's well preserved late-18C interior is a unique example in the City.

This St Botolph's is one of three that survive in the City; originally there were four, all situated outside the wall, as Botolph was England's patron saint of travellers. It is now a Guild Church. The church was founded *c.*1050 and rebuilt in 1350. Protected by the London Wall, St Botolph's survived the Great Fire but fell into disrepair, necessitating rebuilding.

Initially, in 1754, only the north and south external walls were re-built, the major work taking place between 1787 and 1791 under the direction of *N. Wright* who was responsible for most of the present interior.

Aldersgate was widened in 1829 and the east wall had to be moved back. It was rebuilt, probably by *J. W. Griffith*, in 1831.

A tablet, R of the churchyard gate, commemorates John and Charles Wesley. John was converted whilst walking along Aldersgate in 1738 when he felt his heart 'strangely warmed'.

Enter the church from Aldersgate by the door R on the east side.

Against the wall, immediately R, is the bust of Elizabeth Richardson, d.1699.

The Lord Mayor's sword rest ahead is late 18C.

All the box pews were renewed in 1874.

The pulpit is late 18C.

The east window's 'Agony in the Garden' was painted by *James Pearson* in 1788.

Other windows are late 19C or post-war.

Baroque plasterwork decorates the ceiling which is coffered above both apses.

St Botolph's three **galleries** are original and the organ case above the west gallery, by *Green* 1778, was rebuilt and extended later.

Proceed to the **south aisle***.*

On the east wall is the tomb of Dame Ann Packington d.1563.

Against the south wall, west of the door, is the monument to Elizabeth Ashton, d.1622.

Exit from the church, turn R and proceed through 'Postman's Park' to the Watts Cloister at the west end.

This park combines sections of the old churchyards of St Botolph, Christ Church, Newgate and St Leonard Foster Lane. It is much used by weary postmen from the large post office building nearby in Edwards Street – hence the name by which the park is popularly known.

The Watts Cloister was built in the late 19C at the expense of the painter G. F. Watts, who wished to commemorate heroic acts of self-sacrifice by ordinary members of the public. Plaques describe these and name the 'unsung heroes' who died. Many are extremely moving.

ST BOTOLPH-WITHOUT-ALDGATE
Dance the Elder 1744

Aldgate High Street

Aldgate Station, Circle and Metropolitan lines.

Although designed by Dance the Elder, much of the interior decoration is the late-19C work of *Bentley*. Some 18C furnishings survive.

The church was probably founded in Saxon times, although first referred to in 1115. Rebuilding and enlargement took place in 1418 but much of this work was replaced early in the 16C. Until the Reformation, St Botolph's was within the jurisdiction of the Augustinian Priory of Holy Trinity and services were conducted by one of its canons. Holy Trinity lay just within Ald Gate and was the City's most important monastery, apart from Westminster Abbey. The church escaped the Great Fire but gradually decayed and was completely replaced by the present structure designed by Dance. Daniel Defoe, author of *Robinson Crusoe*, married in the earlier building.

•● *Entered directly is the **baptistry** which was formed in 1965 following a fire.*

The Renaissance-style font cover is 18C.

Flanking the door are busts of Robert Dow, d.1612 and Sir John Cass, d.1718, by *Winter*, 1966.

The alabaster monument, made in 1570, commemorates the burial here of Thomas, Lord Darcy and Nicholas Carew, both executed by Henry VIII in 1538.

•● *Proceed to the **nave**.*

Most of the interior, including the ceiling, was redecorated by *Bentley* in 1889.

The altar is sited, unusually, at the north end.

The organ above the west gallery, by *Harris* 1676, is London's oldest and its early 18C casing is reputedly by *Gibbons*.

The pulpit of 1745, together with the 18C altar rail and Lord Mayor's sword rest, comes from the previous church.

On the east wall is a late-17C figure of King David from St Mary Whitechapel.

ST BOTOLPH-WITHOUT-BISHOPSGATE
James Gold 1729

Bishopsgate

Liverpool Street Station, Central, District and Metropolitan lines.

Although St Botolph's survived the Great Fire and Second World War bombing, little within pre-dates the Victorian era.

The church was first recorded in 1213 as 'Sci Botulfi exa Bissopeg' but had been founded during the Saxon period, probably when

Erkenwald, who did much to develop Bishopsgate, was Bishop of London. The medieval St Botolph's survived the Great Fire, which spared Bishopsgate, but it was demolished in 1724. Rebuilt, the church has undergone no less than seven restorations. Edward Alleyn, Elizabethan entrepeneur and founder of Dulwich School was baptized in the previous church in 1566 and John Keats, the poet, in the present church in 1795.

The **tower** is placed, unusually, at the east end.

To increase the light a **dome** and lantern were added in 1828 by *Meredith*.

The north-east **chapel** was a 1928 extension.

• *Enter the church from the south door.*

The pulpit and wooden lectern are original 18C work.

An 18C Lord Mayor's sword rest faces the pulpit against the choir's north column.

The organ at the west end was made in 1764 but much rebuilt in 1912.

• *Exit from the church.*

In the large churchyard stands the former church school built in 1861. The figures of charity school children were made of Coade stone in 1821 for an earlier building.

ST BRIDE *Wren 1678*

St Bride's Avenue

Blackfriars Station, Circle and District lines.

St Bride's, the journalists' church, possesses Wren's highest steeple. Although its internal restoration disappoints, post-war excavations in the crypt give a unique demonstration of the development of a City church from Saxon times.

St Bride is a corruption of St Bridget, the dedication, unique in London, by which it was known until the early 19C. Excavations have revealed work which may indicate a Roman church on the site. However, the earliest clear outline is of a 6C Saxon building with a simple nave and chancel. This was probably destroyed by the Danes, as it was rebuilt in the 10C with an apse. A fire in 1135 led to rebuilding by the Normans and this is the first church to be recorded. A larger St Bride's, constructed in the 15C, had a nave with a north aisle and a chancel with north and south chapels. Its tower, from which the curfew tolled, was detached and lay to the south. The building was entirely destroyed by the Great Fire and the interior of Wren's replacement was later gutted by bombs, everything being lost. Restoration by *Godfrey Allen* in 1957 was preceded by excavations of the foundations which now form the crypt. England's principal court, the Curia Regis, sat within St Bride's in 1205. St Bride's was the first church to use the Common Prayer Book. Burials here have included Richard Lovelace (pre-fire) and Samuel Richardson in 1761. Samuel Pepys was christened here in 1633.

The restored exterior is faithful to Wren's original. Outstanding is the **steeple**, Wren's tallest and judged one of his most successful. It was completed in 1706 and suggested to William Rich, a local baker, the tiered format of wedding cakes which still remains popular in England. It was partly destroyed in 1764 after being struck by lightning. Allegedly, Benjamin Franklin advised George III that its replacement should end in a point but the King insisted on a blunt end. Contemporary satirists made much of this dispute between 'good, blunt, honest King George' and 'sharp-witted colonists'.

•● *Enter the church from the north door.*

Many consider this to be one of the least successful internal restorations of Wren's churches. Before the Second World War the galleries and box pews remained but they have not been replaced.

The font cover's design is based on early ideas by Wren for St Bride's steeple.

Opposite the entrance, in the south-west corner, are figures of charity children made *c.*1711. It is possible that they came from Bridewell Hospital (the former royal palace) nearby, but they more probably stood outside the Charity School in Bride Lane.

The reredos was designed by *Allen* and based on Wren's work in the Chapel Royal at Hampton Court. A parishioner, Edward Winslow, later governor, was one of the Pilgrim Fathers and this serves as a memorial to them. South of its plinth, a plaque commemorates Winslow.

•● *Descend to the* **crypt** *from the west end of the church.*

This was opened to the public in 1953.

Immediately L is displayed a party dress of Susannah Rich, wife of William, the wedding-cake baker.

Foundations of earlier churches are revealed, together with explanatory displays and artefacts discovered during the excavations.

At the east end is a Roman tessellated pavement *in situ.*

St Bride's well, which gave its name to Bridewell Palace, once stood in the south-east corner.

ST CLEMENT EASTCHEAP *Wren 1687*

Clements Lane

Monument Station, Circle and District lines.

This, now the City's smallest parish church, escaped serious bomb damage and retains many original fittings, mostly the work of the master carver *Jonathan Maine.*

The church is first referred to in a Charter of 1067. By the 14C it was called St Clement Candlewickstrate. Before King William Street was built, in the 19C, Eastcheap stretched further west as far as St Clement's. Complete rebuilding of the church was necessary after the Great Fire and Wren used brick with stone dressings, although later the structure was rendered. St Clement's, like its Strand namesake, claims to be the 'Oranges and Lemons' church of the nursery song. It has more justification as Spanish oranges were once sold nearby alongside old London bridge.

➥ *Enter the church from Clements Lane by the west door. Proceed to the* **nave**.

During the alterations by *Butterfield* in 1872 the south gallery was removed and the east end remodelled. Only slight bomb damage occurred and this was repaired in 1954.

General redecoration, with much new gilding, took place in 1968.

The ceiling was restored in 1925, and modelled on the original.

At the west end is the organ by *Renatus Harris*. Much of the front of its case is original but with some enlargement.

The centrally placed font, at the west end, is an original piece by *Maine*.

Against the north wall is the pulpit with its canopy also by *Maine*.

The doorcases are original and that in the north-east corner is judged exceptional.

Unfortunately, the original reredos, in the **sanctuary**, was divided into three by *Butterfield* and reassembled, with a new centrepiece, by *Comper* in 1933.

The east window was altered by *Butterfield*.

In the centre of the south wall of the **nave** is the coat of arms of Charles II by *Maine*.

Below this are carved breadshelves.

Flanking these are benefaction boards.

ST DUNSTAN-IN-THE-WEST   *John Shaw 1833*

Fleet Street
(607 2865 or 405 1929)

Open Tuesday and Thursday, other days irregularly.

Temple Station, Circle and District lines or Chancery Lane Station, Central line.

The statues that embellish the exterior of St Dunstan's are its greatest historic attraction.

The church, judging by its dedication, was probably founded in Saxon times but is first recorded in 1185. It was initially monastic but passed to the Crown in 1237. However, in 1386, St Dunstan's was acquired by the Abbey of Alnwick, Northumberland, and remained in its possession until the 15C. The Great Fire stopped short of St Dunstan's but alterations carried out in 1701 weakened the structure which eventually had to be replaced. The medieval building was orientated conventionally, east to west, but the present church had to be built further north on the old churchyard, to permit the widening of Fleet Street, at which time it was re-orientated north to south. Minor bomb damage was repaired in 1950 and St Dunstan's became a Guild Church in 1953. Orthodox services are held on Sunday in Romanian and other 'oriental' churches make use of it north-east chapel. The Earl of Strafford, executed in 1641, was baptized in the earlier church.

Shaw based his design of the **tower** on All Souls Pavement in York but added pinnacles.

The clock was the first public example in London to include a minute hand. It was made for the previous church in 1671 as a thanks offering for its escape from the Great Fire. The two savages, possibly Gog and Magog, who strike the bells on the quarter hour, are part of the clock.

When St Dunstan's was rebuilt, its clock, with the figures, was transferred to Hertford Lodge, Regents Park, which was later renamed St Dunstan's Lodge. Subsequently, Sir Arthur Pearson acquired the house where he founded St Dunstan's Organization for the Blind. (The saint had no connection with blindness.) Viscount Rothermere returned the clock to St Dunstan's in 1936 where, for the first time, it embellished the present building.

Below the clock is a memorial to newspaper baron Lord Northcliffe, by *Lutyens*, 1930. The bust was made by *Lady Hilton Young*.

The statues of most interest, however, came from the old Ludgate, once the most important western entrance to the City. The gate was rebuilt in the Elizabethan period and stood until 1760. 'Lud' in Old English meant the back or postern. Above the small **east porch** the statue of Elizabeth I, by *Kerwin*, 1586, from the gate's west face, is the oldest public statue of an English monarch. The inscription below is modern.

•● *Enter the east porch via the gate to the courtyard.*

Within L are 16C (?) statues of the mythical King Lud and his two sons, from the gate's east face.

•● *Return to Fleet St R and enter the church from the west porch. Proceed clockwise.*

Unusually, the high altar is at the north end.

Most of the monuments came from the previous church.

At the south end of the west wall is a framed bust commemorating Cuthbert Fetherstone, the King's Doorkeeper, 1615.

In the second bay L, the monument above the door is to Hobson Judkin Esq, 'the Honest Solicitor'.

The 19C iconostasis (screen) was brought from Antim Monastery in Bucharest, Romania, in 1966.

Within the chapel behind the screen, the stained glass window commemorates Izaak Walton, author of *The Compleat Angler*. Walton was an officer of the church 1629–44: 'Scavenger, Quistman and Sidesman'.

The high altar, altar rails and reredos have been made up from 17C Flemish woodwork.

The iron Lord Mayor's sword rest, facing the

pulpit, was presented to the church in 1785 to celebrate the English victory over the Scots at Culloden.

On the east wall, north of the vestry door, is a monument to Alex Layton, d.1679, 'ye famid swordsman'.

ST EDMUND-THE-KING
Wren or Hooke (?) 1679

Lombard Street

Bank Station, Central and Northern lines.

Although damaged by bombs, St Edmund's retains many of its original fittings, including an exceptional font cover.

The church, founded *c*.1000, was bestowed on the Priory of Holy Trinity, Aldgate, by Matilda, consort of Henry I, early in the 12C. St Edmund's first rector was Daniel the Priest, 1150, and the church was then known as St Edmund Grasschurch; it stood within London's grass market which supplied hay for horses. Uniquely in the pre-fire City, the church appears to have been orientated north–south as is its replacement. For long believed to be the work of Wren, it now seems possible that the body of St Edmund's was designed by his assistant, Robert Hooke. Restoration, following bomb damage, was completed by *Tatchell* in 1957.

The **steeple** was added by *Wren* in 1706; its spire was originally decorated with flaming urns.

•● *First L George Yard. Proceed to the rear of the church.*

The 17C iron gates and railings L originally enclosed the old churchyard.

At the north-east end is the **vestry**, rebuilt with an additional upper storey by *Tatchell* in 1968.

•● *Return to the south front and enter the church.*

The original font with its rail, L of the entrance, has an exceptional cover decorated with gilded figures of the Evangelists which unfortunately is now rarely displayed.

Although the interior was remodelled in 1864 and 1880 much original woodwork remains, including the wall panelling. Redecoration took place in 1968.

Unusually, the organ case is divided. On its southern section are the Stuart arms transferred from St Dionis Backchurch.

Churchwardens' pews flank both sides of the south entrance.

The pulpit is sumptuously carved.

The altar rail is original.

On the original reredos in the **sanctuary** are paintings of Moses and Aaron by *Etty*, 1833.

Flanking the reredos are fine doorcases.

The east window, brought from Munich, commemorates Edward VII's eldest son, the Duke of Clarence.

The lectern in the **nave** was made up from 17C panelling.

Fixed to a pew on the east side is a Lord Mayor's sword rest of 1753.

Three royal funeral hatchments on the east wall are, from north to south, those of Princess Charlotte, d.1817, only child of the future George IV; Queen Victoria's father, Edward, Duke of Kent, d.1820; and George IV (?) d.1830.

ST ETHELBURGA-THE-VIRGIN *1411(?)*

Bishopsgate
(588 1053 or
588 3388)

*Open Tuesday and
Thursday (or,
alternatively, on
Saints Days)
10.30–16.00.*

*Liverpool Street
Station, Central,
Circle and
Metropolitan lines.*

From this rare medieval City church, the smallest to survive, Henry Hudson took Holy Communion in 1607 before setting sail for America on his first search for the North-West Passage, a voyage commemorated in the names of the Hudson River and Hudson Bay.

This, the only English church dedicated to St Ethelburga, a 7C abbess of Barking, presumably had a Saxon foundation, but is first recorded in 1250 as St Adelburga-the-Virgin. In 1273 the name was spelt Edburga. The Puritans deleted '-the-Virgin' from St Ethelburga's dedication in the mid-17C but reference to her purity reappeared after the Restoration. A late-12C or early-13C rebuilding in Early English style appears to have taken place and some of the stonework from this structure was incorporated in the present church. Although no clear records exist there are indications that this was built in 1411. St Ethelburga became a Guild Church in 1954.

Today, the appearance of the **west façade** is very different from that which existed for more than 350 years prior to 1932. Then the church was entered via an ancient tunnel-like wooden porch, flanked by two shops, built in 1570 and 1613 to provide additional revenue for the parish. Both had an upper storey, originally separated by a balustraded gallery but subsequently linked, and most of the front of St Ethelburga's, including practically all the west window, was hidden. In 1932, Bishopsgate was widened and, in spite of protests by conservationists, the shops were demolished. The wooden porch was also dismantled, but fortunately its sections were kept and may now be seen, reassembled, in the Museum of London.

St Ethelburga's doorway and window are original early-15C work but the window tracery has been almost entirely renewed.

Stone rubble was used to build the structure and this is now revealed on the Bishopsgate façade, following the removal of rendering which had probably been applied in the 18C.

St Ethelburga's once possessed a tower with a needle spire but this was replaced in 1775 by the present **bell turret** surmounted by the old weathervane which had originally been fixed to the spire.

•► *Enter the church.*

Although St Ethelburga's has a medieval structure, most of its interior was remodelled by *Ninian Comper*, 1912–14. Surprisingly, considering the building's age, there are no monuments of particular interest.

Inscribed on a stone set in the floor in front of the entrance is the Latin motto 'Bonus Intra Melior Exi' (come in good, go out better) which was taken from an ancient temple at Aesculapius.

•● *To view the west window (otherwise hidden by the organ) ascend the* **gallery** *stairs in the north-west corner.*

Incorporated in this window are three pieces of 15C glass.

•● *Descend to the* **nave.**

The organ, made in 1912, was encased by *Comper* who also designed its gallery. Prior to this, a west gallery, erected in 1629 for 'the daughters and maidservants of this parish', had survived until 1862.

Experts have disagreed on the age of the font but it is now believed to be 19C work. Around its bowl, inscribed on brass, is one of the longest known palindromes (reading the same forward or reversed). It is in ancient Greek and roughly translated means 'As well as cleansing my body, cleanse me of my sins'. The font cover was made in 1686 and came from St Swithun London Stone.

The ceiling of the church was renewed in 1953 following some bomb damage; at the same time the building was redecorated and its stained glass refitted.

On the north wall is a painting of Christ healing the beggar, attributed to the 16C Flemish painter *Peter Coeke van Aelst* and presented to the church in 1931.

Set in the wall is part of a quatrefoil from a 15C(?) stone canopy.

All tracery from the side windows has been removed.

Three of these windows incorporate stained glass, commissioned from *Leonard Walker*, 1928–30, to commemorate St Ethelburga's most famous parishioner, the 17C explorer Henry Hudson. On the north side, in line with the pulpit, Hudson is shown cast adrift; this window was donated by citizens of the British Empire in 1930.

Opposite, on the south side, the most easterly window, donated by United States citizens in 1929, shows the explorer sailing up the Hudson River.

The most westerly window, also on the south side, represents Hudson taking Holy Communion at St Ethelburga's in 1607 and was presented by the Hudson Bay Company in 1928. Hudson was accompanied in the church by eleven members of his crew and the chalice used during the service is almost certainly that which the church still possesses, dated 1560.

It is known that St Ethelburga's once possessed a chapel dedicated to St Katherine and this probably stood at the north-east end beside the chancel.

The screen separating the chancel from the nave, the parclose (subsidiary) screen separating it from the south chapel, the altar candlesticks and standards and the flooring were all designed by *Comper c.*1913.

In the **sanctuary**'s north window are pieces of 17C heraldic glass.

Stained glass in the east window is by *Kempe*, 1878. One of the saints featured is St Ethelburga, the daughter of King Ethelbert and Queen Bertha of Kent, who assisted St Augustine's mission to England in 596. She was not the saint to whom the church is dedicated and her inclusion was presumably an error. The window itself replaced a round-headed example similar to that surviving in the south chapel.

Inserted in the south wall of the sanctuary is an original early-15C piscina.

➡ *Proceed to the* **south chapel**.

Originally the Lady Chapel, this is now dedicated to St George and incorporates the First World War memorial.

On its south wall is another 15C piscina, contemporary with that already seen in the sanctuary.

The chapel's east window also incorporates some 17C heraldic glass.

➡ *Proceed through the east door to the* **vestry**.

The vestry was added to the church on part of the old burial ground in 1904.

➡ *Continue to the rear garden.*

St Etheburga's garden, with its covered loggia, is a popular lunchtime resting place for City workers; it occupies part of the old burial ground. Strangely, no burial stones have survived.

ST GILES-WITHOUT-CRIPPLEGATE *c.1550*

The Barbican

Open Sunday 07.30–18.00, Monday–Friday 10.00–14.00, Saturday 14.00–17.00.

Barbican Station, Circle and Metropolitan lines.

This large church, rebuilt at the height of the Reformation, escaped the Great Fire but was gutted in 1940. Well restored and retaining some ancient monuments, St Giles is of historic interest owing to its connections with Shakespeare, Milton and Oliver Cromwell.

St Giles's stood outside Cripplegate, the oldest known gate in London's wall. A 'crepel', Saxon for an underground or covered way, is believed to have run from this gate to the Barbican watch tower. The church was allegedly founded by Alfune c.1080; it was first enlarged and then completely rebuilt in the 14C. A fire in 1545 necessitated further rebuilding which was completed during the reign of Edward VI, a rare period for churches. Most of the structure

survives from this building, albeit later refaced, but pre-Reformation details suggest that some earlier work may have been incorporated. Edward, the illegitimate son of William Shakespeare's brother Edmond, was baptized in St Giles in 1606, almost certainly in the presence of 'the immortal bard'. He only lived for a short time and was buried here in 1607. Oliver Cromwell married in the church in 1620.

The east window, in Perpendicular style, is entirely the work of *Godfrey Allen* who completed the post-war restoration in 1960; it replaced an oval 18C window.

Originally the **tower** possessed a spire, but this was replaced by the present cupola in 1683 when the tower was heightened by *John Bridges* who used brickwork instead of stone. The lantern is a post-war copy.

The pitch of the roof was reduced and the clerestory extended in 1791.

Refacing and castellation of the **south aisle** took place in 1869.

The **north aisle** was treated to match its southern counterpart in 1904.

•● *Enter the* **north aisle** *by the north door facing the lake.*

Immediately R, on the north wall, is the bust of Sir William Staines, a Lord Mayor of London, d.1807.

Ahead is the 18C font and its cover, brought from St Luke Old Street.

Also from St Luke's is the organ of 1733 (reconstructed 1970). This occupies the large **loft** specially built for it by *Cecil Brown* in 1969. Its case of 1684 came from St Andrew Holborn.

•● *Proceed eastward along the* **nave**.

Much of the structure of both the 16C arcades survived the bombing; repair work is obvious.

Stone 'musician' corbels supporting the roof at the east end indicate the original extent of the chancel which was reduced by two bays when the clerestory was extended in 1791.

In the north-east corner is the dilapidated bust of Thomas Busby, d.1575.

The present chancel arch was erected in 1869.

In front of the altar rail is a tablet marking the burial place of Milton, d.1674. It had been rumoured that Milton's grave was vandalized in 1798 and some of his bones sold as souvenirs.

The tracery of the north and south (blocked) windows in the **sanctuary** is probably original.

On the south wall of the sanctuary the piscina and two-seat sedilia were possibly retained from the earlier building. Incorporated in the sedilia arch are re-used Roman tiles.

The chancel floor was raised in 1888, which is

why the piscina and sedilia now appear to be set too low.

Attached to the south pier, at the entrance to the choir, is an exceptional 18C Lord Mayor's sword rest.

The lectern of 1888 survived the bombs.

In the south wall is a blocked door which originally led to the rood loft stairs.

A monument commemorates Margaret Lucy, d.1634. She was the grand-daughter of Sir Thomas Lucy who reputedly threatened Shakespeare with prosecution for stealing his deer. Sir Thomas is also believed to have been the prototype of Justice Shallow in Shakespeare's *The Merry Wives of Windsor*.

John Speed, d.1629, historian and mapmaker, is commemorated by a wall monument restored in 1971.

On the sill above are busts of (from L to R) Defoe, Milton, by *Bacon the Elder*, 1793, Bunyan and Oliver Cromwell.

The statue of Milton, further west, was carved in 1904 and originally stood in the churchyard; it is based on a contemporary bust carved in 1654.

•● *Exit from the church R.*

Remains of the London wall can be seen.

ST HELEN BISHOPSGATE   *13C*

Great St Helen's

Liverpool Street Station, Central, Circle and Metropolitan lines.

This medieval building, once partly a nunnery's church, possesses the finest early-17C woodwork in central London, together with more monuments than any London church apart from Westminster Abbey and St Paul's Cathedral.

St Helen's is dedicated to the mother of Constantine the Great, who, in the 4C, became the first Christian Emperor of Rome. By tradition, Helen discovered the True Cross. The present St Helen's parish church was created at the Reformation by linking two churches that had existed side by side since the 13C. Divided by a shared wall, the buildings had provided the parish church and the church of a nunnery. St Helen's parish church, probably founded in Saxon times, was first recorded in 1150; it was rebuilt in the 13C. A nunnery became established within its grounds *c*.1210 and it is believed that the nuns erected their church on the north side, shortly after St Helen's had been rebuilt.

The **nuns' church** L, London's only surviving example, was originally slightly longer but the **parish church** R was soon extended westward, thereby lining up the two buildings and providing the existing double frontage.

Both windows in the 13C west façade were formed in the 15C.

The bell tower is 17C.

The doorway L was formed *c*.1500 and the entrance doorway R *c*.1300. In the latter, the door itself was made *c.*1635.

•• To view the south façade, follow Undershaft, ahead.

The south doorway is dated 1633.

Blocked 13C lancet windows were revealed when adjoining houses were demolished in 1966.

It is believed that the **south transept** was built early in the 13C at the same time as the westward extension of the parish church. Its east extension was built in 1374.

A **rectory** and **offices** were added in 1968.

•• Return to the west front and enter the church. Descend the steps and proceed L towards the nuns' church (or nuns' choir).

All except one of the existing arches in the dividing wall were formed *c.*1480 but they may have replaced even earlier openings as the chancel's east arch is 14C. Wooden screens between them were removed in 1538 when the nunnery was dissolved.

Some timbers in the tie-beam roof, built *c.*1480 to span both churches, are original.

*•• Proceed to the **nave of the nuns' church**.*

Behind the font of 1632 is a structure that appears to be of rusticated stone but is in fact of timber and forms part of the bell turret.

•• Turn R and follow the north wall.

The small 13C lancet window in the corner is the only example that was not filled or replaced.

Eighteen monuments were brought to St Helen's from St Martin Outwich in 1874. Outstanding is the canopied altar tomb of Hugh Pemberton, d.1500, and his wife Katherine. Bronze figures on the small plaque represent ten of their sons, others are lost.

•• Continue eastward.

The doorway, *c.*1500, leads to steps, once the night staircase to the nuns' dormitory.

Most of the stained glass in the window above is 17C.

*•• Continue to the **chancel of the nun's church**.*

The blocked doorway, *c.*1500, was the processional entrance from the nuns' vestry, but the function of the side recesses is uncertain.

On the wall, below the penultimate window, is the monument to Martin Bond, d.1643; he is shown in his military tent.

Nuns were able to view the altar through the angled slots of the squint at the east end of the wall, which was combined with the Easter Sepulchre, above, in 1525 to form a memorial to Johane Alfrey.

In front of the squint is the tomb chest of the founder of the Royal Exchange, Sir Thomas Gresham, d.1579.

•➡ *Turn R.*

All the east windows of St Helen's were renewed by *Pearson*, c.1893.

In the centre of the chancel, the tomb chest of Julius Caesar (Adelmare) by *Stone* (?) 1636 commemorates a Master of the Rolls and Privy Councillor of James I.

Beneath the east arch lies the tomb chest of Elizabeth I's ambassador to Spain, Sir William Pickering, by *Cure* (?) 1574.

•➡ *Proceed past this monument to the* **chancel of the parish church**.

This was remodelled by *Pearson*, c.1893, when the reredos, all the wooden screens and the floor tiling were completed.

The communion table is 17C.

Right of the altar against the second pier, the rare wooden Lord Mayor's sword rest, made in 1665, is the oldest in London.

In front of this is the tomb chest of Sir John Crosby, d.1475, and his wife.

The first rows of the choir stalls are mid-17C but the back rows on each side are 15C.

•➡ *Proceed immediately L to the* **south transept**.

Immediately R is a 13C lancet window that was opened up in 1966.

The organ L was presented in 1744. Until 1868 this had stood in a west gallery which was then removed.

The south window R is 17C.

•➡ *Continue ahead to the north section of the* **east chapel**, *now subdivided.*

Chapel of the Holy Ghost. The tomb chest of John de Oteswich and his wife, c.1500, is the oldest monument in the church.

The patterned floor tiles are 15C.

The 19C window incorporates seven roundels of 15C stained glass.

•➡ *Ask to see the south-east section, now an office but originally the* **Lady Chapel**, *R.*

The piscina and niches in the east wall are 14C.

In the south-west corner the seated female alabaster figure was possibly carved by *Colt*, c.1600.

•➡ *Return to the chancel and proceed L to the* **parish church**.

Immediately R of the steps is an 18C Lord Mayor's sword rest.

The Jacobean pulpit L is believed to have been made c.1615. Its canopy was made in 1640.

•➡ *Proceed ahead.*

Against the south wall, before the doorcase, is the large monument to Richard Staper, 1608.

The flamboyant south doorway L, *c*.1633, incorporates the Stuart coat of arms which is believed to have come from an earlier reredos.

Immediately past this doorway is the monument to a clothmaker, Sir John Spencer, d.1609.

In front of this stands the 17C altar table from St Martin Outwich.

The west doorcase, *c*.1635, although practically contemporary with that on the south side, has fluted Corinthian columns; these denote a greater Renaissance influence.

•► *Ascend the step L.*

Just before the west door is a late-18C poor box supported by a 17C carved beggar.

ST JAMES GARLICKHYTHE *Wren 1683*

Garlick Hill
(236 8839)

The church opens irregularly.

Cannon Street Station, Circle and District lines.

One of the most satisfying post-war restorations of a Wren church. Internally, much survived the bombing including the many outstanding 17C fixtures and fittings from St Michael Queenhythe.

St James Garlickhythe, first recorded in 1170, gained its name, according to Stow, from the garlic that was sold nearby on the banks of the Thames. The church was rebuilt in 1320 but completely destroyed by the Great Fire. Its replacement, extensively incorporating clear glass, became known as 'Wren's Lantern'.

The **steeple** was added in 1717.

During the restoration by *Lockhart Smith*, completed in 1963, the upper parts of the **walls** were rebuilt and the glass renewed. Most of the **tower** has been refaced. Originally a clock, surmounted by the figure of St James, projected from this at the junction of the first and second stages but it was destroyed by Second World War bombs and not replaced.

Unusually for a Wren parish church, the **chancel** projects from the body of the building.

•► *Enter the church.*

Within the **porch** are tablets commemorating Wren's rebuilding and the 19C restoration work.

An outstandingly carved Stuart coat of arms, displayed in the **vestibule**, was, together with other 17C pieces, acquired by St James's from St Michael Queenhythe (demolished in 1875).

The font is 17C but its contemporary cover is generally kept in the vestry.

Throughout the church St James's scallop shell emblem appears as a decorative theme.

The interior is the highest of all Wren's City churches and has been likened to a miniature St Stephen Walbrook without the dome.

Fixed to the churchwardens' pews at the west end are metal wig pegs.

The organ, by *Schmidt*, in the original west

gallery has been restored to its original condition although some amendments were made to its case.

Fixed to both front pews are 18C Lord Mayor's sword rests.

Surviving within the canopied pulpit (from St Michael's) is a wig peg, the only example in the City.

Within the **sanctuary**, the 'Ascension' painting above the reredos, by *Andrew Geddes*, was presented in 1815; it took the place of the original east window.

Both east doorcases (from St Michael's) which act as screens, are exceptional.

Two royal funeral hatchments are displayed on the south wall.

•● *Proceed, with permission, to the* **vestry** *which will be shown if convenient.*

In the vestry are kept the font's 17C cover and 'Jimmy Garlick'. 'Jimmy' is the mummified body of an unknown person that was discovered in one of the church vaults, probably early in the 18C; he is kept in a glass-fronted cabinet.

ST KATHERINE CREE *1631*

Leadenhall Street

Aldgate Station, Circle and Metropolitan lines.

St Katherine Cree was the City's last church to be designed in the Gothic style and is the only surviving church to have been built between the reigns of Henry VIII and Charles II.

Originally called St Katherine de Christ Church at Aldgate, its site had been the churchyard of the 11C Priory of the Holy Trinity, also known as Christ Church. 'Cree' is believed to mean 'Christ'. St Katherine's was founded by the prior in 1280 so that canon's services in the monastic church should not be disturbed by parishioners. The church, rebuilt in 1504, was demolished at the Reformation, apart from the lower stages of the tower. Rebuilt, St Katherine's escaped the Great Fire and suffered very little bomb damage. However, it had developed structural problems and was restored by *Marshall Sisson* in 1962.

On the **south wall** is a large sundial bearing the Latin motto 'non sine lumine' (not without light). It was originally dated 1706 in Roman numerals but this has disappeared.

The **tower**'s top stage was rebuilt in 1761, surmounted by a colonnade and cupola which replaced the 17C square turret.

•● *Enter from Leadenhall Street.*

Following its restoration in 1963, St Katherine's became the headquarters of the Industrial Christian Fellowship and, unfortunately, their 'temporary' offices in the aisles disfigure the interior.

The organ, in the west **gallery**, made by *Schmidt* in 1686, has been renewed. Allegedly, this was played by Purcell, Wesley and Handel. Its decorative 17C case, attributed to *Gibbons*, is outstanding.

The organ gallery and Corinthian capitals of the arcade's columns are the only Classical features of importance in the church.

The 17C stained glass in the **north aisle**'s west window, R of the organ, came from St James Dukes Place.

The south face of the most westerly keystone of the north arcade is dated 1630.

Against the north wall are the arms of Charles II.

Decorated bosses in the plaster-vault roofs of the nave and aisles bear the arms of City Livery Companies. Much of this work dates from the 1962 restoration.

•• *Proceed to the east end of the* **nave**.

A rare Carolean font of alabaster stands north of the altar. It was presented by the family of Lord Mayor John Gayer, *c.*1640. Allegedly, Gayer was confronted by a lion during a visit to Lebanon. He prayed and the beast passed by without harming him. This story is related at an annual service that is still held in memory of Gayer, who is buried between the font and the modern altar rails.

St James Duke Place provided the 18C reredos and also, possibly, the 18C pulpit.

The lectern was assembled from 17C joinery.

Allegedly, the rose window of the **chancel** represents the toothed wheel on which St Katherine was tortured during the persecution of Christians by Emperor Maxentius in 307. Its tracery pattern is reputedly modelled on the great rose window of Old St Paul's Cathedral. The 17C stained glass is original.

The monument commemorates Sir Nicholas Throkmorton, d.1570, after whom Throgmorton Street was named. He was Chief Butler of England and father-in-law of Sir Walter Raleigh.

The **south-east chapel**, founded by the Society of King Charles the Martyr in 1962. commemorates Archbishop Laud who consecrated the church in 1631. His alleged 'bowings and cringings' during the service were described by the Puritans at his trial as evidence of Catholic sympathies. In spite of being, under coercion, a signatory to Charles I's death warrant, Laud was found guilty and executed. His portrait on the wall is a copy of the original by *Van Dyck*.

A cartouche of 17C glass survives in the central window of the south aisle.

Behind the first column from the west on the south side is a stone section preserved from the medieval church.

•• *Proceed to the east end of the north aisle. A door leads to the churchyard, now a public garden.*

On the wall ahead is the Avenon doorway, dated 1631; this originally formed the Lombard St entrance to the churchyard.

●► Return to the church and proceed to the east end of the **south aisle**.

ST LAWRENCE JEWRY *Wren 1687*

Gresham Street

Bank Station, Central and Northern lines.

This expensively restored Wren church, copiously decorated with gold leaf, possesses what the late Alec Clifton-Taylor described as 'the most beautiful of the restored interiors of London'.

'Jewry' refers to the Jewish community that lived in the parish from the time of William I until the expulsion of Jews from England by Edward I in 1290. The church probably had a Saxon foundation but is first recorded in 1136. Its rebuilding after the Great Fire was the most expensive of all Wren's City churches; Charles II is known to have attended the reconsecration. Gutted by bombs in 1940, St Lawrence was restored by *Cecil Brown* and reopened in 1957 as the Guild Church of the City Corporation; once again no expense has been spared. However, the pre-war St Lawrence was renowned for its magnificent woodwork and what was judged to be one of Europe's finest small rooms: an exquisite north-west vestry with a painted ceiling by *Thornhill*. All this was destroyed, one of London's most grievous architectural losses in the Second World War. St Lawrence has been adopted as the church of the New Zealand Society.

Externally, the walls and tower withstood the bombs. The **east wall** is pedimented, providing St Lawrence's with the most Classical of all Wren's City church façades.

The west end of the church was originally hidden by adjacent buildings and its asymmetry concealed.

It was necessary to rebuild the tower's **steeple** and the replica is surmounted by a representation of an incendiary bomb supporting the original 17C weathervane, which takes the form of St Lawrence's gridiron emblem.

●► Enter the church from the west door.

In the **vestibule** is a north Italian late-16C painting of St Lawrence which survived both the Great Fire and the bombing.

The **chapel** beneath the tower was reopened for services in 1943 when the rest of the church was in ruins; it has been little altered.

The north-west **Trumpeter's Gallery** is occupied by musicians on ceremonial occasions.

In the centre of the **nave**'s west end, is the font of 1620 which came from Holy Trinity Minories. Its cover incorporates some wood from the bombed roof of the nearby Guildhall.

The congregation's pews came from Holy Trinity, Marylebone.

In the **north aisle** stands a concert grand piano that was presented to the church. It once belonged to the great conductor Sir Thomas Beecham.

As the City played a large part in the development of the Commonwealth, the north-east chapel is now known as the **Commonwealth Chapel**.

The memorial to John Tillotson, Archbishop of Canterbury, 1691–94, stands against the north wall of the **sanctuary**.

Attached to the Lord Mayor's pew (front, east end, south side) is an 18C Lord Mayor's sword rest, St Lawrence's only fixture to survive the bombing.

ST MAGNUS-THE-MARTYR *Wren 1676*

Lower Thames Street

Monument Station, Circle and District lines.

St Magnus's, little damaged in the Second World War, combines Wren period fittings with Neo-Baroque work by *Martin Travers* which is mostly connected with its adoption by Anglo-Catholics in 1920.

The subject of the dedication is a mystery as the church was first recorded in 1067 already dedicated to St Magnus, whereas the only St Magnus now known is the Norwegian Earl of Orkney, who was not canonized until 1135. When the buildings were removed from old London Bridge to widen the roadway, *c.*1760, two west bays of St Magnus's were demolished and the east pavement of the bridge was re-aligned to pass through the tower. Because of this, the north doorway is no longer positioned centrally. London Bridge has since been re-sited.

Parts of the wall fabric were re-used by Wren after the Great Fire.

The **tower** was added in 1706.

Although its clock is dated 1709, the year of the lord mayoralty of its presenter, Sir Charles Duncombe, it is believed to have been made earlier.

To reduce traffic noise in 1782, the north door was blocked and the windows reduced in size and remodelled to match the already existing circular window above the door.

Enter the **vestibule**.

Immediately R is a modern holy water stoup.

Three royal funeral hatchments are displayed: on the north side, Queen Charlotte, d.1818; opposite, Princess Charlotte, only child of the future George IV, d.1817 and Queen Caroline, d.1821.

Also displayed in the vestibule are bread shelves and two 17C chests.

Proceed to the **nave**.

The two box pews that survive on the north side are now used as cupboards.

Like the external clock, the organ in the **west gallery** was presented to the church by Sir Charles Duncombe. When made by *Abraham Jordan* in 1712 it incorporated the first known organ 'swell'. The case of 1670 is carved in the style of Gibbons.

On the north wall is a 19C Russian icon.

The most westerly window on the north side incorporates 17C heraldic glass featuring the arms of the City of London and the Plumbers Company; the latter, of 1671, came from the Company's old hall.

One of the City's most decorative Lord Mayor's sword rests is attached to the north pillar facing the pulpit. It was made in 1708 but the royal arms on it are early 19C.

In front of this is a modern Lord Mayor's seat.

The **Lady Chapel** on the north side was created by *Lawrence King* during his rearrangement of the interior in 1951.

●● *Proceed to the* **sanctuary**.

The 18C altar rails are of Sussex wrought iron.

Surmounting the original reredos is a Crucifixion scene carved by *Travers* who was also responsible for the bishop's chair on the sanctuary's south side; both were made *c.*1924.

The original pulpit, once a three-decker, retains its canopy.

Also created by *King* in 1951 is the **south chapel**.

Panels of the chapel's reredos originally formed part of the south doorcase.

St Magnus's original high altar stands in this chapel.

In front of the south-east door stands a mother-of-pearl crucifix made in Bethlehem.

At the south-west end is the **baptistry** with its marble font which was presented in 1683.

The painting of St John the Baptist is by *Alfred Stevens*.

●● *Exit from the church.*

The timber post, immediately L, came from a Roman wharf of AD 75 and was discovered nearby in Fish Street Hill.

Stones from the first arch of Old London Bridge, 1173, pave the churchyard.

ST MARGARET LOTHBURY   *Wren 1690*

Lothbury

Bank Station, Central and Northern lines.

Fortunately undamaged in the Second World War, St Margaret's is regarded by many as virtually a museum of Wren period furnishings, most of which came from long-demolished churches. Outstanding, is its chancel screen, one of only two fitted in Wren churches.

Many origins of 'Lothbury' have been suggested. In the 13C, the church was known as St Margaret

Lodebyre or upon Lodingberi and Loth may well be a corruption of lode which meant a drain leading to a stream; it is known that the Walbrook once flowed beneath the church although it does so no longer. First recorded in 1181, St Margaret's belonged to Barking Abbey until the Reformation and probably had an earlier foundation. It was rebuilt in 1440 but nothing survived the Great Fire.

Wren added the **tower** in 1700.

At one period, much of the façade of the church was hidden by shops built against it.

●● *Enter the church.*

A benefaction board, displayed R of the entrance, came from St Christopher-le-Stocks (demolished 1781).

The organ, in the west gallery, was made by *G. P. England* in 1801 and acquired from St Olave Old Jewry (demolished 1888).

Against the north wall is the outstanding bronze bust of Sir Peter Le Maire, d.1631, by *Hubert Le Sueur*; this came from St Christopher's.

The pulpit was made for St Margaret's but its tester came from All Hallows-the-Great (demolished 1894). All Hallows' pulpit itself was scheduled to come here but proved to be too big and went to St Paul, Hammersmith instead.

Facing the chancel screen, on either side, are two 18C Lord Mayor's sword rests.

The chancel screen, also from All Hallows', is one of only two in a Wren church. Wren was opposed to screens as they obstructed the congregation's view of much of the service. The only other example is in St Peter-upon-Cornhill. Originally the royal arms of William and Mary surmounted the screen and were double-faced but after the transference of the screen to St Margaret's these were removed and one face disposed of; the other was returned to the screen in 1969 and this time fixed to its face.

●● *Proceed to the* **sanctuary**.

The altar rail came from St Olave's, as did the reredos which was later Victorianized, but subsequently restored by *Tatchell*.

Flanking the reredos are paintings of Moses and Aaron, *c*.1700, from St Christopher's.

Both the 18C candelabras are from All Hallows'.

●● *Proceed to the* **south chapel**.

The south chapel is enclosed by a screen, designed by *Bodley* in 1891 when the chapel was created. It incorporates, at lower level, the altar rail from St Olave's.

Attributed to *Gibbons* is the late-17C font, carved to depict biblical subjects.

Busts are displayed of Mrs Simpson by *Nollekens*, 1795, and Alderman Boydell, engraver, publisher and Lord Mayor, by *Banks* and *F. W. Smith*, 1790, from St Olave's.

ST MARGARET PATTENS *Wren 1687*

Eastcheap

*Monument Station,
Circle and District
lines.*

Another Wren church that escaped Second
World War bomb damage, St Margaret's retains
much original 17C work.

By tradition, the name of the church derives from
pattens, iron-soled shoes, examples of which are
displayed on the south wall. However, it is more
likely that the true source was a Mr Patin,
benefactor of an earlier St Margaret's.
St Margaret's is first referred to in 1067 and this
was probably a small wooden building. Already,
in 1275, the church is recorded as St Margaret de
Patins. In 1530 the church had to be demolished
and its great rood was set up in the churchyard to
assist the appeal for money to pay for a new
building (hence the name of Rood Lane that runs
west of the church). St Margaret's was completed
in 1538 but destroyed in the Great Fire.

The **steeple**, Wren's third highest, incorporated
the only 'needle' spire that he designed in a truly
medieval style.

☛ Enter the **nave**.

Above the west door is a rare example of the
arms of James II.

On either side are London's only canopied
churchwardens' pews. The ceiling of one is
inscribed 'CW 1686' (difficult to decipher) and it
has been alleged that the 'CW' refers to
Christopher Wren. More probably it simply
denotes churchwarden.

A west gallery was removed in 1971.

Much of the surviving 17C woodwork is by
Cleere.

The organ case is 18C.

As part of the unfortunate alterations made in
adapting the church to provide a Christian study
centre, the north gallery was rebuilt and enclosed
as a lecture room; offices were built below at the
east end.

At the upper level on the panelling in the north-
west **Lady Chapel** (created in 1956) are wig pegs;
it was customary to remove wigs during hot
weather.

The font is 18C but its cover is 17C.

The two 18C Lord Mayor's sword rests are of
Sussex iron.

Against the most easterly north column is the
17C monument to Sir Peter Vandeput, merchant
and sheriff.

The choir stalls were made from the original
congregation pews. On the north side the front of
the central panel is inscribed 'PH 1709'.

In the **sanctuary**, the original reredos
incorporates a 17C painting, 'The Garden of
Gethsemane' by *Carlo Maratti*.

Attached to the original pulpit is a rare 18C
hourglass-stand of wrought iron.

The reredos in the **south-east chapel** is made up from a 17C doorcase.

On the south wall, at the east end, is the monument to Sir Peter Delmé, d.1728, by *Rysbrack*.

Nearby are two late-18C needlework panels illustrating respectively Pilate washing his hands, and Joseph with his brothers.

In the centre of the south wall of the **nave**, at upper level, is the gilded cross which once surmounted St Margaret's spire. It weighs ¾ cwt and is a copy of that of St Paul's Cathedral.

Below the cross is the painted coat of arms of Charles I, and the words 'touch not mine anointed'.

Further west, in a display case, is a pair of original pattens.

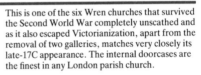

ST MARTIN-WITHIN-LUDGATE *Wren 1684*

Ludgate Hill

Open Monday morning; Tuesday to Thursday 10.30– 15.30; Friday afternoon.

Blackfriars Station, Circle and District lines.

This is one of the six Wren churches that survived the Second World War completely unscathed and as it also escaped Victorianization, apart from the removal of two galleries, matches very closely its late-17C appearance. The internal doorcases are the finest in any London parish church.

St Martin's is first recorded in 1174 but by tradition has an 8C foundation. Rebuilding took place in 1222 and 1437, however, nothing survived the Great Fire. Wren moved the church slightly further north but his crypt (not open) is almost half as long again as the present church and appears to follow the plan of the pre-fire building. Surprisingly, it is north–south orientated. Allegedly, King Cadwalla (mythical?) was buried in the Saxon church. Captain William Penn, founder of Pennsylvania, was married in the pre-fire building in 1634.

A wall plaque on the west side commemorates Ludgate, one of the gates in London's wall, which was linked with the church by a chapel dedicated to the Virgin Mary. St Martin's was the only 'gate' church situated within the walls. Others, generally dedicated to St Botolph, stood outside. In Saxon times the gate was known as Lutgate (back gate) but had gained its present spelling by 1253. Although the structure was rebuilt in 1586, like the other gates in the wall and most of the wall itself, this was demolished in 1760 to improve traffic flow.

The west end of the church is attached to a surviving part of the old London wall which continues briefly northward.

Wren placed his **tower** centrally on the south side to help deaden traffic noise. Its slender **spire** was designed to act as a visual foil to the dome of St Paul's Cathedral nearby.

●● *Enter the vestibule, turn L and proceed to the* **nave**.

Ahead is the font of 1673 with its Greek

inscription that reads both ways (as at
St Ethelburga's).

Above is a white marble pelican.

The organ, originally made by *Schmidt* in 1684,
occupies the west **gallery**. It has been much
rebuilt and incorporates some work by *Harris*.

Internally, the cruciform plan of the church is
reminiscent of St Anne and St Agnes.

In the north-east corner, on an iron chest, is a
church bell of 1693 that was presented to
St Martin's. No bells now ring at the church but
its old bells were possibly those referred to in the
'Oranges and Lemons' nursery song.

The pulpit is original but has lost its canopy.

The altar rail is also original.

In the 19C the floor level of the **chancel** was
raised.

On the east wall, north of the altar, is the
Ascension painting by *R. Browne*, 1720 (not
Benjamin West as has been alleged).

The reredos is original.

South of the altar are relatively modern copies of
paintings of saints made by a Belgian artist.

The double churchwarden's chair of 1690 is
unique in the City.

Along the south wall of the church, Wren built
the partitioned area with its ceiling to help
soundproofing. Originally a gallery stood above,
but this, like its north counterpart, was removed
in the 19C.

The three south doorcases are outstanding, that
in the south-east corner, with cherubs' heads,
being particularly reminiscent of work by
Gibbons.

High on the south wall are the Stuart arms, but
the shield has been repainted to incorporate
modern heraldry.

Visitors may be shown the north **vestry** if
convenient. Within are finely carved 17C
breadshelves.

The prized possession of St Martin's is a silver
replica of the old Ludgate, including its statues of
Elizabeth I and King Lud and his two sons; this is
surmounted by a figure of the Virgin and carried
in procession on important occasions. Obviously
this is kept in safety but may be seen by advance
request.

ST MARY ABCHURCH *Wren 1686*

Abchurch Lane
(626 0306)

*Open Wednesday
11.00–15.00 and
other days (except
Tuesday) at varying
times.*

Bomb damage has been painstakingly made good
and St Mary's interior is now judged to be the
least altered in any of Wren's churches. Its
reredos is the only fitting in a City church that is
known with certainty to be the work of *Grinling
Gibbons*.

Historian John Stow believed that Abbechurch,

Monument Station, Circle and District lines.

as it was formerly spelt, meant up, i.e. on a hill, but it may commemorate an early benefactor named Abbe. The church was first referred to in the late 12C. Nothing survived the Great Fire. Wren's building, badly damaged in the Second World War, was restored by *Godfrey Allen* and is now a Guild Church.

It is not apparent externally that the church possesses a shallow buttressed **dome**.

St Mary's brickwork was stuccoed, presumably in the late 18C or early 19C, but this has been removed.

The upper part of the **spire** was rebuilt in 1884.

•• Enter the church from the paved area, once the churchyard, on the south side.

All St Mary's doorcases, two of wood, one of stone, are original.

Above the south doorcase is fixed the coat of arms of James II.

Immediately L is the railed **baptistry**. Its original marble font by *Kempster*, 1686, possesses a cover of similar date by *Emmett* decorated with figures of the Evangelists.

Pews against the west, north and south walls of the **nave** are original and finely carved.

Against the north section of the west wall are two 17C poor boxes followed by a display cabinet containing fragments of everyday articles discovered around St Mary's. These include pottery, clay pipes and keys.

Above the vestry door in the north wall is a gilded copper pelican on its nest which served as the original weathervane of the church until it was replaced by a simpler vane in 1764.

The west **organ gallery** was once reserved for boys of the Merchant Taylors' school that originally stood nearby. Although the organ is new it has been built into a 17C case brought from All Hallows Bread Street (demolished 1878).

During post-war restoration, Victorian glass was removed and the floor lowered by 18in to its original level.

The domed ceiling is the only painted example in a Wren parish church. It was executed by *William Snow* in 1708 when St Mary's was 'beautified'. Badly damaged during the Second World War, the work has been faithfully restored by *Walter Hoyle*.

The pulpit, by *Gray*, 1685, is original and unusually retains its steps and canopy.

Facing the front pews are a carved lion and unicorn flanked by Lord Mayor's sword rests.

Within the **sanctuary**, St Mary's reredos, the largest and finest in a City church, is the only authenticated fitting by *Gibbons* that any of them possess. A letter from the great carver referring to it was discovered in a chest in 1946. Almost certainly the frame would have been made by assistants, whilst Gibbons himself carved the detailed work. Bombs shattered the reredos into approximately two thousand fragments which, after the war, were painstakingly and practically undetectably reassembled.

At the south end of the east wall is the monument to Lord Mayor Sir Patience Ward, d.1696, a Lord Mayor of London, and his wife, Elizabeth.

On the south wall is the monument to Edward Sherwood, d.1690.

Beneath the church, a crypt, probably 14C, was discovered after the bombing in 1940; it is not open to the public.

ST MARY ALDERMARY Wren (?) 1682

Queen Victoria Street/Bow Lane

Open Tuesday– Friday 11.30–15.00.

Mansion House Station, Circle and District lines.

St Mary's interior is the only example in a post-fire church to be rebuilt in Gothic style. Its plaster fan-vaulted ceiling is unique in London. The tower survived the Great Fire.

Aldermary may mean, as Stow asserts, that this was the oldest church in the City to be dedicated to the Virgin Mary, or it may simply imply that it is older than the nearby St Mary-le-Bow, originally called St Mary Newchurch. It has also been suggested that alder is a corruption of *altera* meaning 'the other' i.e. Mary Magdalene rather than the Virgin Mary. First recorded in 1080, St Mary's was rebuilt in 1518 but only its tower, added later, survived the Great Fire. The remainder was rebuilt on the old foundations, but why Wren adopted, for the only time, the Gothic style remains a mystery. A parishioner bequeathed a large amount of money towards the rebuilding but did not stipulate in his will that the Gothic style had to be retained. It has been suggested that Wren only played a supervisory part in the design of the church and that another architect, now unknown, was responsible. Milton married his third wife in the pre-fire church in 1663. Judge Jeffreys, the 'Hanging Judge', was buried in the present building in 1693 (there is no monument).

The **tower**, begun in 1530, remained unfinished until 1629. After the fire its upper part was rebuilt with balls and weathervanes surmounting the pinnacles. The present finials of gilded fibre glass were added in 1962 and are similar to those which, in the late 18C, had replaced Wren's work. These had been inexpertly renewed in 1876 and were demolished in 1927.

Two of the earlier finials stand in the churchyard.

Buttresses and pinnacles at the east end of the church were added to St Mary's rather plain façade in the 19C.

•➡ *Enter the church (generally by the west door from Bow Lane).*

Slight bomb damage was repaired, including the replacement of stained glass.

The west doorcase, attributed to *Gibbons*, came from St Antholin (demolished 1875).

The font, dated 1682, is surrounded by a balustrade which may be a re-used altar rail.

In front of the second column, R of the entrance, is a 17C poor box on a turned stand.

St Mary's is renowned for its fan-vault ceiling which is made entirely of plaster, the only example in a London church.

In spite of the Gothic appearance of the post-fire church all its furnishings and fittings were originally Classical. As may be expected, the Victorians could not accept this and replaced most with Gothic Revival versions in 1877; fortunately the original pulpit was spared, as were the west doorcase and the font.

On the north wall of the **chancel** is an anonymous monument sculpted by *Bird*. It was commissioned by a lady to commemorate her late husband; however, she remarried before deciding on an epitaph and no inscription was ever added.

A rare example of a wooden Lord Mayor's sword rest, like the font dated 1682, faces north against the south aisle's third column from the east.

Beneath the church is a crypt which was discovered in 1835; it is not open.

ST MARY-AT-HILL *Wren 1676*

St Mary at Hill and Lovat Lane (626 4184)

Open Tuesday–Thursday 13.00–14.00.

Monument Station, Circle and District lines.

For once, Victorian décor and furnishings in a Wren parish church have been sympathetic to the point of genius, making this one of London's finest church interiors.

St Mary's is first recorded in 1177 as 'Sanctie Mariae Hupenhalle'. Aisles were added in the 15C and pews fitted for the congregation – a rare luxury at that time. Much of the fabric of the side walls and the tower, all of stone, survived the Great Fire and were re-used by Wren. However, he completely rebuilt the east and west walls, together with the interior. Wren's west front and the old tower were rebuilt by *George Gwilt* in 1780. The medieval side walls were repaired and rendered by *Savage* in 1828. Further major restoration and internal redecoration took place in 1849. St Mary's escaped bomb damage. According to Stow, Thomas à Becket was a parson at St Mary's.

The east front, with its projecting clock, facing St Mary at Hill (the street) is the only part of Wren's exterior to survive. It is faced with Portland stone but the plinth is of stucco.

•▶ *Follow the passage R, on the north side, to view the north façade.*

Immediately entered is the courtyard, previously the burial ground but, until the Reformation, part of the site of the town house of the abbots of Waltham. The abbot's permission was needed in the 15C to build the south aisle of the church, as his kitchen had to be demolished to make way for it.

Removal of some of the rendering of this façade in 1985 revealed that the medieval wall had not been completely demolished in 1826 as had previously been thought. The outline of a 15C window is apparent above the porch and it is planned to explore further in the hope of discovering more pre-fire details.

A tablet, L of the door, commemorates the closing of the burial ground in 1846.

◗ Return to the east façade and proceed southward along St Mary at Hill (the street).

The stone entrance to the south passage R incorporates a grim skull and crossbones in its pediment.

◗ Follow the passage to Lovat Lane.

Facing Lovat Lane is St Mary's brick tower and west façade, entirely the 1780 work of *Gwilt*. When the new tower was built it was decided, for the first time, to provide the church with a west entrance.

The Lovat Lane door is frequently closed; if so, return to the courtyard and enter the vestibule by the south-west door.

Immediately R is a 'Resurrection' relief, *c.*1600, which possibly once formed the tympanum of a gateway.

◗ Proceed to the nave.

The Greek Cross plan of St Mary's, in the Dutch style, is reminiscent of St Anne and St Agnes and St Martin-within-Ludgate but it possesses a shallow dome.

It is difficult to distinguish the original late-17C woodwork by *Cleer* from that of *William Gibbs Rogers*, added in 1849: a rare tribute to Victorian cabinetmaking.

Above the west door are the original Stuart arms.

On either side, at the west end, are the churchwardens' pews.

The congregation's box pews are original and the only examples to survive in the City.

Floral carving on the face of the west **gallery** is by *Rogers*.

Above this, the organ, made by *William Hill* in 1834, was rebuilt in 1971.

St Mary's possesses the City's largest collection of Lord Mayor's sword rests; five are at the west end and one beside the pulpit.

The interior was generally repaired and refitted by *James Savage* in 1828 but the painting of the shallow coffered dome and the ceiling vaults was changed to Adamsque style in 1849. Gilding was added in 1968 as part of general restoration.

Entirely the work of *Rogers* is the canopied pulpit and, facing it, the lectern.

The altar rail, altar and reredos (gilded 1968) are by *Cleer*.

As part of the 1968 restoration in the **sanctuary**, all the windows were overhauled, work which included the transfer of the 18C heraldic roundels to the east window from the large north and south windows.

Royal funeral hatchments displayed in the church are those of George IV, Queen Adelaide, the Duchess of Kent (Queen Victoria's mother) and Prince Albert.

In the south-west corner is the original marble font with its cover.

ST MARY-LE-BOW Wren 1683

Cheapside

Art exhibitions are held in the nave. Admission free.

Mansion House Station, Circle and District lines or St Paul's Station, Central line.

St Mary's, the 'Bow Bells' church and the most expensive of all those rebuilt by Wren, is reminiscent of St Bride's in that although it possesses a long history, a splendid steeple (regarded as Wren's finest), and a fascinating crypt (Norman) the disappointingly restored post-war interior is of little interest.

A Saxon church on the site burnt down and was rebuilt as St Mary New Church in 1087, an early London example of a stone building. The Norman crypt from this survives and its arches 'bows' gave the church its name. St Mary's has been prone to disaster. In 1091 its roof blew off and several passers-by were killed; the top of the tower collapsed in 1271 and more died; a goldsmith, Lawrence Duket, was hanged within the church in 1294; during a jousting tournament held outside St Mary's in 1331, and attended by Queen Philippa, a temporary wooden stand collapsed and many spectators died. With this record of bad luck, needless to say, the church was completely destroyed by the Great Fire and Wren's replacement gutted in the Second World War. Only the walls, tower and steeple survived the bombing. It was disappointingly restored by *Lawrence King* in 1964.

The **tower**, which Wren brought forward, is surmounted by a **steeple** which is judged his finest work and was certainly his costliest. Its design was inspired by the Basilica of Maxentius in Rome. After the Second World War it was found to be unsafe and taken down and rebuilt stone by stone. Unfortunately, the wooden spiral staircase within the tower was burnt beyond repair by fire bombs.

Work was completed in 1961 when the recast bells, shattered in the war, were installed. By tradition, a 'Cockney' is defined as anyone born within the sound of Bow bells. Allegedly, 'Cockney' like 'cock-eyed', derives from 'cokeney' meaning a cock's egg and implied that a person was misshapen or a simpleton. It is now, however, virtually a term of endearment. Bow bells are referred to in the 'Oranges and Lemons' nursery song and in the 15C they are said to have summoned Dick Whittington to return to the City from Highgate. From the 14C until 1847

Bow bells rang at 21.00 daily (originally for the curfew) and again at 05.45 to rouse sleeping Londoners.

Following the 14C collapse of the temporary stand at the jousting tournament, a permanent slid (balcony) was constructed on the north side of St Mary's tower. This feature was repeated by Wren and is linked to the tower's second stage by a vestibule.

The north and west doorways of the tower, with their carved cherubs' heads, are judged to be some of the finest Baroque examples in England.

•● *Enter the church.*

It will immediately be seen that most of the furnishings and fittings are Neo-Georgian.

All the galleries were removed in 1867.

From the west end descend to the **crypt**.

The crypt, from the church of 1087, is a rare central London example of Norman work. It is in the form of a subterranean church with its nave flanked by aisles. Allegedly, the crypt's many rounded arches, or bows, inspired not only the name of the church but also that of the Court of Arches (the Archbishop of Canterbury's Court) which once sat in the nave; St Mary's was in the possession of the see of Canterbury until 1847.

Wren rediscovered this crypt when work began on his new church. He rebuilt the vault of the nave with bricks and was probably responsible for blocking up the south aisle.

Although the columns and walls survived the bombing, new concrete vaults have been built in the nave (the Court of Arches) and in the reopened south aisle which has been a chapel since 1960.

The crypt's north aisle has been completely rebuilt and serves as a refectory.

ST MARY WOOLNOTH *Hawksmoor 1727*

Lombard Street

Bank Station, Central and Northern lines.

Due mainly to its unobstructed site, a rare example in the City, St Mary's presents an unusually imposing exterior. It is the only City church designed by Hawksmoor. Internally, apart from the familiar 19C removal of galleries and box pews, little has changed. The canopied altar is outstanding.

Whilst excavating for the foundations of the present church, traces of a Saxon timber structure were discovered. However, evidence of two even earlier religious buildings was also revealed. Both appear to have been pagan, the most ancient example possibly for nature worship, the other Roman and probably a Temple of Concord. The first recorded church, in 1191, was a Norman structure known as Wilnotmaricherche. This possibly referred to the nearby woolmarket; however it is known that a Wulnoth de Walebrok was living in the area in 1133 and he may have been an important benefactor whose name was adopted in gratitude. The complete dedication of the church, a rare one, is to St Mary Woolnoth of the Nativity. A newly built St Mary's was consecrated in 1445 by the Irish Bishop of Enochdune but its steeple was not added until 1485. Although badly damaged by the Great Fire, St Mary's structure was considered salvageable and repair work was completed by *Wren* in 1674. However, as this proved to be unsafe, it was demolished in 1716 and the present building immediately commissioned from Hawksmoor. It was one of the 'fifty new churches' provided for by the Act of 1711. The earlier St Mary's had been hemmed in by shops and houses; it was their removal which provided the architect with a site, rare in the City, from which most of his church would be clearly visible. St Mary's became a Guild church in 1952.

Hawksmoor's exterior, in English Baroque style, is dominated by two flat-topped **turrets**; these are supported by columns of the Corinthian Order which is used throughout the church.

Flanking the west façade are entrances to the Bank underground station. They are decorated with cherubs' heads, a frequently repeated motif throughout the church, and originally led to the burial crypt. The bones were removed to Ilford *c.*1900 and the crypt sold to the railway for conversion to the station's booking hall.

The west gates are original.

In the north wall are large recesses, a typical Hawksmoor theme.

The projecting clock on this façade is referred to by T. S. Eliot in 'The Waste Land'.

●● *Return to the west façade and enter the church.*

Hawksmoor amazingly achieves spaciousness from the small triangular site, with his favoured cube within a cube layout, derived from ancient Rome via Palladio and Inigo Jones.

Above the west door is the case of the *Schmidt* organ made in 1681. The organ originally stood in a west gallery which was removed by *Butterfield*, together with the north and south galleries, in 1876. He thought they were unsafe, but fixed their fronts to the walls to form an unusual frieze.

On the north wall is the memorial plaque to John Newton, d.1807, St Mary's most famous rector. Born in 1725, Newton was not ordained until the age of forty. He had been press-ganged into joining the Royal Navy and later, before his conversion to Christianity, became involved in the West African slave trade. Newton was appointed rector of this church in 1779 following sixteen years ministry at Olney where he wrote the words of the famous hymn 'Amazing Grace'. At St Mary's he inspired a parishioner, William Wilberforce, to work for the abolition of slavery. The tablet's epitaph was composed by Newton himself.

As part of his 1876 alteration, *Butterfield* removed the box pews and lowered the three-decker pulpit, although raising its canopy. The organ remains where he repositioned it but was rebuilt in 1913.

Polychrome floor tiles were added by *Butterfield* when he raised the floor level of the **chancel**.

Below the east fanlight are modern royal arms that were fitted in 1968.

The iron altar rail is original, as is the altar table with its baldachino (canopy), which is similar to that designed by *Bernini* for St Peter's in Rome.

The reredos is original but its lettering was repainted on new boards in 1968; the earlier boards survive beneath them.

Displayed in a glass case on the east wall, south side, are the helmet, gauntlet, spurs and arms of Sir Martin Bowes, d.1566, a Tudor ancestor of Queen Elizabeth the Queen Mother. He was a livery member of the Goldsmith's Company and became an alderman, sheriff (1540) and lord mayor (1545). Bowes bequeathed money for the upkeep of his tomb, that was eventually destroyed in the Great Fire, and the display of his banners, which can still be seen, renewed, at the south end of the west wall. Incorporated in his arms is the ancient lion's head of England which still forms part of the hallmark applied by the Goldsmith's Company to certify all items made of precious metal in England.

Of particular interest to those in the insurance business is the memorial tablet to Edward Lloyd, d.1713. It was his coffee house in Lombard Street that eventually became Lloyds, the world's largest insurance market.

ST MICHAEL CORNHILL *Wren 1672*

Cornhill

Bank Station, Central and Northern lines.

St Michael's is a prime example of the ruthless Victorian gothicizing of a Classical building. Its steeple, however, although also Gothic in style, is in fact early-18C work from Wren's office.

Unusually for a City church, St Michael's was first recorded in Saxon times when it was given to the Abbey of Evesham, *c.*1055. Its early medieval tower had a spire but this was not replaced when the tower was rebuilt in 1421. From here the curfew was rung until 1581. It is known that St Michael's already had congregation pews by 1475, one of the first City churches to provide them; men and women were segregated. Although the body of the church was destroyed by the Great Fire, its Gothic tower survived and was incorporated by Wren in his new Classical building. However, in 1715, the tower was deemed so unsafe and rebuilt. The Gothic style, once more adopted for it, was strangely prophetic of George Gilbert Scott's mid-19C work which was completely to alter the appearance of the interior. Since 1503, St Michael's has been the church of the Drapers' Company. Thomas Gray, the poet famed for his

'Elegy', was baptized here in 1716.

➥ Follow St Michael's Alley, R of the church, to view the south façade and tower.

In 1790, Wren's windows were reduced in size and made circular; *Scott* restored them to their original form but added 'Venetian' tracery.

Rebuilding of the **tower** began in 1715 but funds ran out and work ceased after two years. Eventually, its steeple was completed in 1722 with money obtained from the Fifty New Churches allocation. It is believed that *Hawksmoor* designed this, but he may have worked to original drawings by *Wren*. Some have also suggested that *William Dickenson*, an architect in Wren's office, had some responsibility for it. Pinnacles later replaced the original weathervanes.

Prior to the Reformation, the south churchyard was surrounded by a cloister with accommodation for the choir. In the centre stood a preaching cross erected in 1528 by Sir John Radstone, the Lord Mayor. According to Stow, this was similar to Paul's Cross which stood in the churchyard of St Paul's Cathedral.

➥ Return to the north **porch.**

This porch is entirely the work of *Scott.*

➥ Enter the **vestibule.**

Ahead, the font retains its original bowl of 1572 but the stem was made in 1860.

Against the west wall, behind the font, is a pelican which, in 1775, surmounted the reredos.

Several monuments to members of the Cowper family stand on the south side.

➥ Proceed to the **nave.**

Scott's gothicizing took place during two periods, 1858–60 and 1867–8. Fortunately, much of the wood carving was executed for him by the masterly *William Gibbs Rogers*, c.1860, although his work here never quite approached the quality that he achieved in St Mary-at-Hill.

Outstanding are the bench ends of the pews on both sides of the central alley, carved by *Rogers* with flowers and shields.

On the front pew, north side, is an 18C Lord Mayor's sword rest.

The eagle lectern is by *Rogers.*

At the east end of the north wall, in front of the organ, is the late-17C monument to John Vernon, d.1616. This replaced a pre-fire monument which had stood in the same position in the old church. A prayer is still said for Vernon during the Merchant Taylor Company's annual service on 23 December.

The organ, made by *Harris* in 1705, replaced an earlier instrument crafted by the same hand.

The pulpit is by *Rogers* but its unfortunate

canopy is modern.

Much of the reredos within the **sanctuary** is original and incorporates copies of Moses and Aaron paintings by *Streater*, Charles II's 'Sergeant Painter'.

ST MICHAEL PATERNOSTER ROYAL
Wren 1694

College Street

Cannon Street Station, Circle and District lines.

Fortunately, St Michael's many fine 17C furnishings were kept elsewhere for safety during the Second World War and have been returned to the rebuilt church. A modern window commemorates Dick Whittington, a benefactor of the earlier building, and his legendary cat.

St Michael's is first recorded in 1219 as St Michael of Paternosterchierch. In Paternoster Lane nearby, rosaries, also known as 'paternosters', were made. By 1361 the church had incorporated 'Riole' in its name, which has since been corrupted to Royal. This refers to La Riole near Bordeaux from where local vintners imported their wines. Wren completely rebuilt St Michael's after the Great Fire. Following damage by a flying bomb in 1944, restoration by *Eldir Davies* was eventually completed in 1968 to provide the headquarters of the Mission for Seamen. This is no longer a Guild Church but a chapel, responsible to the Bishop of London.

The **steeple**, added by *Wren* in 1713, was remodelled by *Butterfield* in 1866.

●➡ *Enter the church from College Street.*

The organ in the **west gallery** was made in 1749.

On the north side of the **nave**, attached to the front pew, is an 18C Lord Mayor's sword rest.

On the south side is a hat-rest for the Lord Mayor's attendants.

The pulpit is original but restored.

The chandelier was made in Birmingham in 1644 and is an early English example; it came from All Hallows-the-Great (demolished 1894).

Flanking the original reredos are carved figures of Moses and Aaron, also from All Hallows'.

Against the modern lectern, on the south side, is a figure of Charity, again from All Hallows'.

The three east windows, previously blocked, now contain modern stained glass.

Dick Whittington, four times Lord Mayor, lived in a house in College Hill, next to the pre-fire church which he had rebuilt incorporating a college. He was buried in the churchyard in 1423. The modern south-west window depicts him with his cat. The helpful cat legend is believed to originate from an early-17C engraving of Whittington which at first showed him with his hand on a skull. This was later altered to a small cat, as it fitted the same area and was considered more tasteful. Strangely, in spite of his services to the monarch, Whittington was never knighted.

ST NICHOLAS COLE ABBEY *Wren 1677*

Queen Victoria
Street

*Open Wednesday and
Friday 13.00–13.30.*

Cannon Street
Station, Circle and
District lines.

Owing to drastic external and internal
restoration, St Nicholas's is of less architectural
interest than most Wren churches. However,
many original furnishings survive, together with a
unique carved head from the pre-fire building.

St Nicholas's is first referred to in 1144 and again
in 1273, this time named St Nichi retro fishstrate,
i.e. behind Fish Street. London's fish market that
preceded Billingsgate then stood between the
church and the river. The later dedication of the
church, Cold Abbey and finally Cole Abbey, is
probably a corruption of Cold Harbour, i.e. a
lodging house providing shelter from the cold –
one may have stood nearby. Until Queen
Victoria Street was laid out in 1871, St Nicholas's
was approached from the north side of
Knightrider Street, a much narrower
thoroughfare. It is known that the steeple of the
medieval church was rebuilt and a south aisle
added in 1377. During the Great Plague, ninety-
six of the 125 parishioners died. The church was
completely rebuilt after the Great Fire and later
gutted by bombs. Restoration of a very drastic
nature was completed by *Arthur Bailey* in 1962.
St Nicholas's then became a Guild Church and is
now the headquarters of the London
Congregation of the Free Church of Scotland.

The top half of the **tower** has been rebuilt and
possesses a new spire. Wren's design was
trumpet-shaped and similar to St Edmund-the-
King's.

Its ship weathervane originally surmounted
St Michael Queenhythe (demolished 1876).

The windows of the south façade were
remodelled in the 19C.

◆● *Enter the church by the south door.*

Above the west door are the arms of Charles II.

The west screen retains some original carved
panels.

Stored elsewhere for safety during the Second
World War, but now returned, are the original
font cover, pulpit, outstanding chandelier and
altar rail.

Attached to the front pew on the south side is an
18C Lord Mayor's sword rest.

On the south wall, just before the door, is a small
cupboard; turn the key, which usually remains
inserted in the lock. Within, is 'the head in the
cupboard'. This is a carved stone head which had
decorated some part of the pre-fire church and
was later probably used as building material.

Above the south door are carved sections from
the original reredos.

ST OLAVE HART STREET *c.1450*

Hart Street

*Tower Hill Station,
Circle and District
lines.*

This is a rare example of a medieval City church
that escaped the Great Fire. In spite of bomb
damage, much of the interior and many of its
monuments survived.

The churchyard's macabre Dutch-style **entrance
arch** of 1658 is decorated with skulls and gained
for St Olave's Charles Dickens's appellation 'The
church of St Ghastly Grim' in his 'Uncommercial
Traveller'.

•● *Enter the churchyard on the south side.*

Owing to its dedication, St Olave is believed to
have had a Saxon foundation. It is recorded as
St Olave-towards-the-Tower in 1222 but an early-
12C reference to a St Olave's may also apply to
this church. Rebuilding took place in the mid-
13C and again *c.*1450. Like All Hallows-by-the-
Tower, St Olave's survived the Great Fire owing
to demolition of surrounding buildings by Sir
William Penn, father of the founder of
Pennsylvania. Badly damaged by bombs in 1941,
St Olave's was restored by *Ernest Glanfield* in
1954. At its re-opening service, the dedication
stone was laid by King Haakon of Norway and
the Bishop of London.

The brickwork of the top section of the **tower** was
added in 1732. Its turret and weathervane were
renewed in 1954.

Ahead, a plaque on the south wall of the church
commemorates the now blocked direct entrance
to the old Navy Pew which was at gallery level
and approached by an external covered wooden
staircase. The 17C Navy Office stood nearby in
Seething Lane.

•● *Enter from the churchyard by the door in the
modern porch.*

The Norwegian flag, at the west end,
commemorates King Haakon who worshipped
here whilst in exile during the Second World
War. St Olave, to whom the church is dedicated,
is the patron saint of Norway.

The two arcaded walls, with the columns of
Purbeck limestone, partly survived the bombing.
All the light-oak woodwork in the church is
modern.

•● *Proceed along the* **north aisle**.

On the north wall L is the monument to Sir
Andrew Riccard, d.1672. He was a chairman of
the East India Company.

Peter Cappone, d.1582, a Florentine merchant, is
commemorated on the south wall of the north
aisle.

The pulpit, allegedly by *Gibbons*, came from
St Benet Gracechurch Street (demolished 1867).

Four 18C Lord Mayor's sword rests stand in front
of the altar.

The carved altar rail is late-17C work.

On the **sanctuary** wall L is the monument to
Elizabeth Pepys, d.1669, wife of diarist Samuel,
by *Bushnell*. Pepys outlived his wife by over
thirty years and, in spite of detailed accounts in
the famous diaries of his appreciation of the
opposite sex, never remarried. They both lie
within the sanctuary but there are no tombstones.

Below is the monument to the Bayninge
brothers, both aldermen: Andrew, d.1610 and
Paul, d.1616.

There are two fragments from a large tomb chest
on the wall R of the altar. The figures represent
Sir John Radcliffe, d.1568, and below his wife,
Lady Ann, d.1583.

The east window was remodelled in 1822.

•● *Proceed R to the* **south aisle**.

In the south-east corner R, a 15C door leads to
the **vestry** built in 1662. Request permission to
view the interior which retains its contemporary
plaster ceiling decorated with a large angel.

The 17C painting above the overmantel is
believed to be by *De Witte*.

Above the vestry door, the monument to Sir
James Deane, d.1608, commemorates a wealthy
merchant adventurer.

In the centre of the south wall is the memorial to
the diarist Samuel Pepys, d.1703, by *A. W.
Blomfield*, 1884. The position of the bust marks
the old entrance to the Navy Pew of 1661 where
Pepys, who was Secretary to the Admiralty,
worshipped. It was demolished in 1853.

The **crypt** survives from the mid-13C church and
is entered from the west end of the south aisle
(the Baptistry). It has a groin-vaulted roof.

Within the crypt is an ancient well.

In the anteroom brasses from old monuments are
displayed.

ST PETER-UPON-CORNHILL Wren 1682

Cornhill

*Bank Station, Central
and Northern lines.*

St Peter's is, by tradition, London's oldest-
established church. Undamaged in the war and
unlike St Michael's, its neighbour, un-gothicized,
many 17C furnishings survive. Pride of place is
taken by the only example of a Wren screen to
remain in its original position in a City church
(that of St Mary Abchurch came from
elsewhere).

A plaque, recorded by Stow as already existing in
the church in the early 15C, states that St Peter's
was founded in AD179 during the reign of King
Lucius. There is no further evidence for this and
Lucius appears to be mythical; however
St Peter's is first recorded c.1040, a rare Saxon
reference to a London church. It stands on the
top of Cornhill, the highest point in the City and
owing to St Peter's undoubted age, its rector was
always given precedence in the medieval Whit
Monday procession of the City clergy to St Paul's
Cathedral. Probably for the same reason it was

specifically excluded from the Union of Benefices Act of 1860 which led to the demolition of many parish churches. A grammar school, one of four in the City, was founded at St Peter's c.1425. It occupied the ancient library until the Great Fire. After the fire St Peter's was rebuilt, apart from the lower section of its tower which had survived. There was no bomb damage. A corn market is recorded, again by Stow, as having been 'long held' in Cornhill.

St Peter's **east façade**, from Gracechurch Street, is its most impressive, although there is no entrance. Due to road widening, the church is 10ft shorter than its medieval predecessor.

Although rebuilt after the Great Fire, the base of St Peter's brick **tower** survived and has been re-used.

The weathervane surmounting the spire is in the form of a key, St Peter's emblem.

•● *Follow St Peter's Alley, immediately L of the east façade, to view the south side and the* **churchyard**.

The churchyard gate depicts St Peter with his keys.

It was in this churchyard that Lizzie Hexham suffered the unwanted courting of Bradley Headstone in *Our Mutual Friend* by Charles Dickens.

•● *Continue to Cornhill.*

Buildings clustering around the north side of the church occupy the old burial ground which was sold at the Reformation.

•● *Enter the* **vestibule**.

Ahead, on the wall R, is a 17C bread shelf.

Beneath is a German (?) 17C chest.

•● *Turn L and enter the* **nave**.

The organ, at the west end, is by *Schmidt* but much rebuilt. Part of its case is original.

The paving, glass and pews, except for the two high churchwarden's pews at the west end, are the work of *J. D. Wyatt*, 1872.

Much original woodwork remains, including the doorcases, part of the canopied pulpit (lowered) and the altar rail.

Most of the chancel screen was reputedly designed by Wren's daughter and is one of only two contemporary screens in a Wren church. Wren did not approve of them but here the rector insisted.

Within the **chancel**, the reredos is original and, unusually, incorporates a lamb of sacrifice's head and skin, possibly inspired by the nearby Leadenhall meat market.

Mosaics were added to the reredos in 1889.

On the chancel's south wall is an affecting monument by *Bartolozzi* to the seven

Woodmanson children, burnt to death in their house one evening in 1782 whilst their father was attending a ball at St James's Palace.

The font cover may pre-date the Great Fire. A cast-iron bracket for raising it survives.

Request to see the **vestry** at the west end of the church.

Within stands a Cromwellian altar table.

Fixed against a wall is the ancient brass plaque, re-engraved after the Great Fire, which describes the alleged foundation of the church in Roman times. According to this, St Peter's was the Metropolitan and chief church of the Kingdom for 400 years.

The keyboard of the organ played in the church by Mendelssohn in 1842 is displayed, together with the composer's signed note.

ST SEPULCHRE-WITHOUT-NEWGATE

Holborn Viaduct

*St Paul's Station,
Central line.*

St Sepulchre's is the largest parish church in the City and, although damaged by the Great Fire, much of its Gothic structure remains. Dame Nellie Melba and Sir Henry Wood are commemorated in its Musicians' Chapel and there are grim reminders of Newgate Prison.

A church has been recorded here since 1137, 'without Newgate', i.e. built outside the wall. It was first dedicated to St Edmund-King-and-Martyr but this was changed, probably during the crusades. In Jerusalem, the Church of the Holy Sepulchre stood outside the city's north-west gate in a similar way and thus probably inspired the new dedication; until recently St Sepulchre's was called the Church of the Holy Sepulchre. Rebuilding, under the direction of *Sir John Popham*, took place in the 15C. Most of this structure survived the Great Fire, however, the church had to be completely rebuilt internally. St Sepulchre's itself was undamaged by bombs but its vestry and Watch House of 1792 were lost. John Rogers, vicar of St Sepulchre's, became, in 1555, one of the first victims of Mary I to be burnt as a heretic.

Rebuilding of the upper part of the **tower**, including its battlement, took place in 1634, shortly before the Great Fire. This work was renewed in 1714 and again in 1878 when the pinnacles were enlarged as part of general remodelling of the top stage.

St Sepulchre's windows, which had been altered to a Classical format in 1790, were mostly restored to their Gothic appearance in 1878.

In the centre of the south aisle's parapet is a 17C sundial.

Much of the three-storey 15C **porch** was rebuilt and refaced externally in 1878.

•➡ *Enter the south porch.*

The 15C fan-vault of the porch is original.

Immediately L of the entrance to the nave is a font cover, *c.*1690, which was bravely rescued from Christ Church nearby by a postman whilst the building was ablaze following a bombing raid.

•● *Enter the* **nave**.

Some 17C pews remain on both sides of the entrance but most were removed at the same time as the galleries in 1878.

Following the Great Fire, the interior was restored and all the walls refaced; some believe by *Wren* but there is no evidence.

The coffered ceiling was formed in 1834.

In the south-west corner is a perspex model of the Church of the Holy Sepulchre in Jerusalem.

Beside this is one of the old bells of the church. St Sepulchre's bells, the 'Bells of Old Bailey', are featured in the 'Oranges and Lemons' nursery song. One of them tolled when prisoners were about to be executed at Newgate. Previously, when the gallows were at Tyburn, the condemned were taken there from Newgate Prison in an open cart (hence the expression 'in the cart' meaning trouble) and they were handed a nosegay as they passed St Sepulchre's.

•● *Proceed to the north chapel.*

This, formerly the Stephen Harding Chapel, became the **Musicians' Chapel** in 1955. The ashes of conductor Sir Henry Wood were interred here in 1940. He had been an assistant organist at the church and later gained fame as the founder of the Promenade Concerts. Sir Henry is commemorated in the central window.

The first window L commemorates the composer John Ireland.

Dame Nellie Melba's window, R of Henry Wood's, includes peaches in the lower corner R. These refer to 'Peach Melba', the dessert created for the Australian soprano by Escoffier at London's Savoy Hotel.

Below Melba's window is a 16C recess which probably served as an Easter Sepulchre.

The Festival of St Cecilia, patron saint of music (22 November), is celebrated in the church at an annual service attended by the Lord Mayor and the 'Bluecoat School' boys of Christ's Hospital which once stood in the City. The boys then march in procession to the Mansion House where they are given lunch by the Lord Mayor.

•● *Exit from the chapel L.*

High on the north wall is the doorway which originally gave access to the rood loft.

Below is the painting 'Marriage of the Virgin', a copy of the work by *Raphael*, 1504, which is in Milan.

Ahead, the organ case's face is part of the original made by *Harris* in 1671. Below is the monogram 'CR' of Charles II.

The south face of the case is Victorian but beneath are fixed some of the carved backs from the original galleries.

Originally, the organ stood in a west gallery but when this was removed in 1878, the instrument was relocated in the north chapel. It was moved to its present position in 1932. The organ itself has been entirely rebuilt.

Against the **north aisle**'s most easterly pillar, facing east, is a stone from the Church of the Holy Sepulchre in Jerusalem, presented in 1964.

Twin pulpits, unique in the City, serve as the lectern (slightly lower) and the pulpit. They were evidently acquired in 1854 but appear to be 18C work.

The iron altar rail and reredos were made c.1670.

•• *Proceed to the column in the* **south aisle** *that faces the pulpit.*

The hand-bell, displayed in a glass case on the column, was rung by St Sepulchre's clerk at midnight outside the condemned prisoner's cell in Newgate Prison to announce the day of execution. This was considered a charitable act which was paid for by the will of Robert Dowe and continued until early in the 19C.

On the other side of the same column is an early-18C Lord Mayor's sword rest.

•• *Proceed to the plaque at the rear of the most southerly choir stall.*

The plaque commemorates the burial in the church of Captain John Smith, later Governor Smith of Virginia. Captured by Cherokee Red Indians he was saved by the chief's daughter, Pocahontas, who successfully pleaded with her father for his life.

Opposite, on the south wall, is a 15C piscina.

The **south aisle** became a memorial chapel to the Royal Fusiliers Regiment in 1950.

Towards the centre of the south wall is a blocked arch; by tradition this once led directly to Newgate Prison.

The wall monument further west commemorates Edward Amis, d.1676.

The font and its cover were made in 1670.

At the west end of this aisle are the Hanoverian arms.

ST STEPHEN WALBROOK *Wren 1677*

Walbrook
*Open from
24 September 1987.*

*Bank Station, Central
and Northern lines.*

Probably Wren's most ambitious parish church, St Stephen's, with its dome, appears to have been, in part, a rehearsal for St Paul's Cathedral. This has recently become the church of Henry Moore's controversial 'cheeseboard' altar.

First mentioned c.1096, St Stephen's was then a small chapel on the west side of the Walbrook stream. A much larger church was built on the east side in 1439. Wren's post-fire church is a

slightly smaller building. In spite of having a dome, a steeple was added in 1717. Bomb damage was made good by *Godfrey Allan* in 1954 but structural problems became apparent and the church was closed in 1982. Generous public donations have helped to pay for its enormous restoration cost.

The design of the **steeple** is similar to that of St James Garlickhythe.

Until destroyed by the bombs, a small clerk's house, later converted to a shop, stood against the tower.

•• *Enter the church.*

Internally, St Stephen's has been judged Wren's parish church masterpiece; its plan is cruciform within a rectangle.

Eight of the sixteen columns support the **dome**, possibly the first dome to be built in England. It was rebuilt of wood and plaster after the Second World War.

Most furnishings survived the bombing as they were bricked up.

In the west **gallery** stands the organ. Wren designed a recess for one but no organ was fitted until 1765 when the present instrument and its case, with rococo decorations, were made.

On the north wall is a painting of the stoning of St Stephen by *Benjamin West*. West was the only American to become president of the Royal Academy.

In the **north aisle** is the monument to the great English Baroque architect and playright, John Vanbrugh. He was buried in the church in 1726. Its amusing epitaph 'Lie heavy on him Earth! For he laid many heavy loads on thee' was allegedly composed by fellow architect, Hawksmoor.

The altar rail, reredos, font and canopied pulpit are original.

Dominating the interior is the 'cheeseboard' altar made by Henry Moore in 1972. It is circular and weighs ten tons. The Court of Ecclesiastical Causes Reserved overruled, in 1987, the decision by the London Diocesan Consistory Court that the altar was incongruous.

Objectors feel that St Stephen's, a 17C masterpiece which retains practically all its original furnishings, is an unsuitable venue for such a dominating, uncompromisingly modern work.

In the crypt, the Samaritans organization was formed in 1953 and this remains their telephone headquarters.

ST VEDAST *Wren 1673*

Foster Lane

St Paul's Station, Central line.

Part of St Vedast's late-16C structure survived both the Great Fire and the Second World War. However, all the 17C fittings of the church, some outstanding, were lost. Fortunately, Wren period

replacements from other churches have been acquired.

Only three English churches are known to have been dedicated to St Vedast. Frequent anglicizing of the Saint's name, including Vaast, Vastes, Fastre, Fauster and Foster, took place in the Middle Ages and the thoroughfare which the church faces is now officially called Foster Lane. For a period, from the mid 14C, St Amandus seems to have been added to the dedication. St Vedast's, first recorded *c.*1170, was rebuilt towards the end of the 16C and extended eastward in 1614. Part of the structure was re-used by Wren after the Great Fire. Gutted internally in 1941 the structure survived and restoration of the church, by *Dykes Bower*, was completed in 1962. St Vedast's is the sole survivor of twelve parish churches that once stood in the area. Poet Robert Herrick was christened in the pre-fire church in 1591.

The lower part of the tower, the porch and, surprisingly, the west doors are pre-fire. Part of the 16C stone fabric can be seen at the south-west corner and at the south wall's east end.

St Vedast's delicately phased **steeple**, completed in 1712, is regarded as amongst Wren's finest. It is one of his few Baroque examples not to be embellished with urns.

•● *Enter from the west door and proceed through the narthex (ante chapel) to the* **nave**.

Unfortunately, the original plaster ceiling, which was outstanding, and fittings were all lost. However, other contemporary pieces have been obtained; their source is given.

The organ, at the west end, was made by *Harris* in 1731 but restored in 1960. Its 18C case came from St Bartholomew-by-the-Exchange (demolished 1841).

Centrally placed towards the west end is the 17C font with its cover from St Anne and St Agnes.

The altar rail is 18C.

Much of the reredos came from St Christopher-le-Stocks (demolished 1781).

North of the altar are the Stuart royal arms with modern heraldry over-painted.

The pulpit came from All Hallows Bread Street (demolished 1875). Some modern carving has been added.

Divided by a screen, the **south aisle** is now a chapel dedicated to St Mary and St Dunstan.

•● *Return towards the entrance to the church.*

The door R leads to **Fountain Court**, a small garden on the north side of the church.

On the south wall of the court is a section of Roman tessellated pavement, discovered nearby in 1886.

Originally, a colonnade with rooms above, in the

form of a cloister, led northward to the parish school. Although these buildings survived they have been mostly reconstructed.

TEMPLE CHURCH OF ST MARY

Church Court

Open 09.30–16.00 but closed throughout August and most of September.

Temple Station, Circle and District lines.

This is regarded as the finest surviving church in Europe to have been built by the Knights Templar. Its circular 12C nave, unique in London, possesses the City's only Romanesque portal.

The Knights Templar were a monastic military order, founded in 1118 to guard the Church of the Holy Sepulchre in Jerusalem and protect pilgrims visiting the Holy Land. Their first London base was in Holborn but they transferred here *c*.1160. Eventually the Templars became too powerful and were ruthlessly suppressed by Pope Clement in 1312. The Temple was acquired by the Knights Hospitaller of St John but as they were already accommodated at Clerkenwell the premises were leased to lawyers and the complex has formed a legal enclave ever since. At the Reformation, Henry VIII confiscated the property but allowed the lawyers to remain as leaseholders; the freehold was presented to them by James I in 1608. St Mary's serves the Societies of the Middle Temple and the Inner Temple, two of England's four Inns of Court, all of which are established in London and whose members are barristers or training to qualify. The round nave of the original church, built 1160–85, survives but its oblong chancel was rebuilt in 1240. Although the building escaped the Great Fire it was badly damaged by bombs in 1942; restoration was completed in 1958.

•• *Proceed to the south face of the circular* **nave**.

This is known as 'The Round'. Its shape emulates the Church of the Holy Sepulchre in Jerusalem and was often repeated by the Templars and the Knights of St John.

Originally attached to the south side of 'The Round' was St Anne's Chapel where it is believed the monastic knights received their secret initiation. Later, barren women made pilgrimages to this chapel to pray for a child. Following a fire, the ruins were demolished in 1826. A crypt survives but is not open.

•• *Proceed clockwise to the* **west porch**.

Although the nave was built in the Transitional style, when round-headed Romanesque merged with pointed Gothic, the latter style predominates. However, the west portal is a fine example of Romanesque (Norman) work and was sensitively restored in 1985. The porch itself has internal Gothic rib vaulting, much of which is original, but externally all was renewed in the 19C.

•• *Continue clockwise to the north façade.*

In the north-east corner of the yard is the tombstone of playright Oliver Goldsmith. His monument within the church was destroyed by bombs.

*● Return to the south side and continue eastward to view the **chancel**.*

The rectangular chancel 'The Oblong' was rebuilt in enlarged form in 1240 and is entirely Early English in style. It replaced the original chancel of 1185 and Henry II attended its reconsecration.

*● Enter the south porch, which leads directly to the **chancel**.*

The chancel's roof, Purbeck marble columns, stonework and woodwork (apart from the reredos) were completely renewed after the Second World War. This part of the church was not reopened until 1954.

● Turn immediately L.

The tomb chest of a recorder of London, Richard Martin, d.1615, stands at the west end of the chancel.

● Return eastward and proceed anti-clockwise.

At the east end of the south wall is a Purbeck marble effigy, believed to have come from the tomb of Bishop Silvester de Evedon of Carlisle, d.1256. The Bishop died at the Temple after falling from his horse during a visit. It is believed that he had been entertained too well!

Above L is the 13C double piscina; this type was mandatory for a short period as the pope forbade the draining away of the rinsings of the chalice.

The two chairs in the **sanctuary** were a gift from South African barristers.

Sir Christopher Wren, who married his first wife here in 1669, provided new furnishings for St Mary's c.1682. These included an organ screen, box pews, a pulpit and a reredos; however, during restoration by *Blore* in 1842, these were removed as the Victorians believed that their Classical design contrasted unhappily with the Gothic building. Only the reredos, by *Emmet*, 1682, for long exhibited in Barnard Castle, Durham, has been reinstated (in 1954).

The east windows, by *Carl Edwards*, 1958, contain what is judged to be some of London's best modern stained glass.

On the north side, destroyed by bombs, were the original *Schmidt* organ and the organ loft. Both were replaced, in enlarged form, in 1953.

The door R opens to a stairway which leads to a penitent's cell and the triforium passage. (Apply to the verger who will arrange entry whenever possible.)

Immediately L behind the door are two niches where food and drink would be left for the penitent.

*● Ascend the stairs to the **penitent's cell**.*

Walter le Bachelor, Grand Preceptor of Ireland, was the cell's best-known occupant.

*● Continue the ascent to the **triforium**.*

The floor of the triforium passage is paved with tiles, made in 1842, which were first laid on the floor of the church below.

➡ Descend the stairs.

At the west end of the north wall is the tomb of Edmund Plowden, d.1584. He was the treasurer responsible for building Middle Temple Hall which survives, little altered, nearby.

*➡ Proceed to the **nave**.*

This was restored and rededicated in 1958.

Internally, the Gothic style predominates in the nave but most of the detailing is the 1828 work of *Robert and Sydney Smirke*.

All the Purbeck marble columns were replaced in 1843.

The triforium passage above the aisles is an early English example of a blind arcade in the French style.

Although the nave's ceiling is of wood its ambulatory is stone vaulted.

Only the interlinking rounded arches of the blind arcade beneath the windows can be said to be a Romanesque feature within the church. Grotesque heads in its spandrels, 'heads that gape and grin' (Charles Lamb) are believed to represent souls in heaven and hell. They all appear to have been recarved during the *Smirkes'* restoration.

St Mary's famous stone effigies of knights, displayed on the floor, were badly damaged when the roof fell on them during an air raid. They were made in the 12C and 13C, the earliest being England's oldest known statues. They are not Knights Templar but probably knights who supported them. All have been restored; however, the most southerly example, known to be a member of the Ros family, escaped major damage.

The north-easterly figure, with a helmet, is believed to represent Geoffrey de Mandeville, described by a contemporary as 'a ruffian of the worst order'.

All the effigies have been moved several times and the whereabouts of the graves of those commemorated is unknown.

Ahead is the font, made in Norman style in 1842.

An inscription inside the building's west entrance commemorates the consecration of the church in 1185 by Heraclius, Patriach of the Church of the Holy Sepulchre in Jerusalem, in the presence, it is believed, of Henry II.

*➡ Return to the south porch and descend the steps R to the **undercroft**.*

This, the 12C chancel's undercroft, was discovered in 1950. It was probably at one time the knights' treasury but contained bones and coffins which were cleared. There is a piscina and a bench.

The City of Westminster

Many are surprised that the City of Westminster spreads so far from Westminster Abbey. This is because its boundaries roughly enclose the vast area of monastic land that was owned by the abbey until the Reformation.

Westminster incorporates practically all of London's West End and stretches eastward as far as the City of London's boundary.

Medieval buildings are few, as, apart from the area around the abbey, most of Westminster consisted of fields until the 18C. Its churches are generally open but where this is not so a telephone number is given.

The nearest Underground stations are indicated for each church and their positions shown on the map that follows.

All Saints Margaret Street
All Souls Langham Place
Church of the Assumption and
    St Gregory
Notre Dame de France
The Queen's Chapel of the
    Savoy
St Augustine Kilburn
St Clement Danes
St Cyprian Clarence Gate

St George Hanover Square
St James Piccadilly
St John Smith Square
St Margaret Westminster
St Martin-in-the-Fields
St Mary-le-Strand
St Mary Paddington
St Paul Covent Garden
St Peter Vere Street

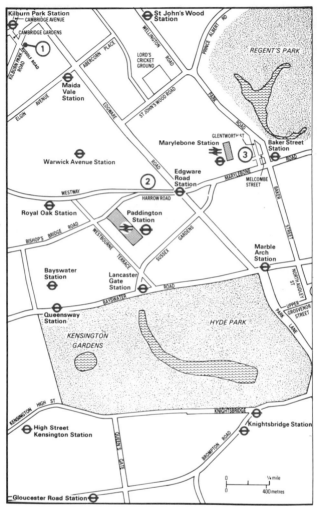

All Saints Margaret Street **7**
All Souls Langham Place **5**
Church of the Assumption and
  St Gregory **8**
Notre Dame de France **10**

The Queen's Chapel of the Savoy **6**
St Augustine Kilburn **15**
St Clement Danes **1**
St Cyprian Clarence Gate **17**
St George Hanover Square **3**

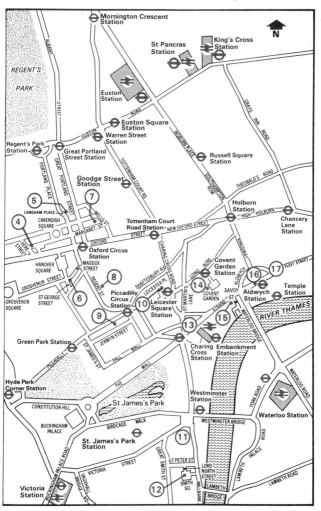

St James Piccadilly **9**
St John Smith Square **12**
St Margaret Westminster **11**
St Martin-in-the-Fields **13**

St Mary-le-Strand **16**
St Mary Paddington **2**
St Paul Covent Garden **14**
St Peter Vere Street **4**

ALL SAINTS MARGARET STREET
Butterfield 1859

Margaret Street

*Oxford Circus
Station, Central and
Victoria lines.*

Regarded as the epitome of High Victorian
Gothic, All Saints' interior is relentlessly
decorated with a plethora of materials which
create an overwhelming polychromatic effect that
has always been controversial.

All Saints', built as a 'model' church for Anglo-
Catholic worship under the auspices of the
Ecclesiological Society, replaced the Margaret
Chapel which had occupied the site. Although
structurally complete by 1852, varying
disagreements delayed its internal decoration and
consecration by seven years.

Externally, the 'Rhenish' **spire**, which is 2ft
higher than the towers of Westminster Abbey,
can only be appreciated from a distance. Its
original grey slates were replaced by the present
green variety in 1895.

☛ Enter the courtyard from Margaret St.

The church, and its surrounding buildings, which
are also by *Butterfield*, that form the courtyard
are built in rose brick with bands of vitrified
blue-black brick and stone. It was the first time
that a major church had been constructed in
brick, then considered an inferior material.
However, the high quality bricks that were
chosen cost more than stone. No doubt the
original external appearance was less forbidding
before more than a century of grime dulled the
colours.

A centrally placed, pinnacled buttress dominates
the façade. It is decorated with an Annunciation
sculpture, originally the only human figure
featured at All Saints'.

The windows and porch exterior are of stone.
Strangely, the porch is squeezed against the
adjoining building and one side of its surround
could not, therefore, be completed.

Immediately to the west stands the **vicarage**.

To the east is the **old choir school**. A young pupil,
Laurence Olivier, first performed Shakespeare at
All Saints'. The school was closed in 1968 and
converted to domestic use. However, the church
is still renowned for its outstanding choral music.

☛ Enter the building.

The visitor is immediately dazzled; no surface has
been allowed to remain undecorated. Stone,
marble, tiles, paintings, stained glass and gilding
combine to give an impression of petrified
restlessness. Butterfield wished to produce a
contemporary version of the Gothic style and
preferred motifs that were bold rather than
delicate. However, the total effect is more
Byzantine.

Columns of Aberdeen granite divide the aisles
from the nave. Their plinths are of black marble
and their capitals of alabaster, carved with stiff-
leaf decoration.

Immediately L, in the **baptistry**, stands the marble font presented by the Marquis of Sligo. It originally possessed an ornate cover of oak and brass but this was replaced by the present simple version in the late 19C.

The wooden roof of the baptistry retains its painting of a pelican in its piety, by *Butterfield*. Originally, the window incorporated stained glass by *Gerente* but this was destroyed in the Blitz. Cartouches of medieval glass were presented to the church and have been fitted as a replacement.

Against the north-east pier of the baptistry stands a replica of the large candlestick in the Certosa at Pavia, Italy.

Old Testament scenes are illustrated, below the **nave**'s west window, in painted tiles, executed in 1889.

Along the north wall of the **north aisle** runs a similar tile picture featuring the Nativity. This commemorates William Upton Richards, d.1873, the first vicar of the church; it was painted by *Alexander Gibbs* in 1873.

At the east end of the north aisle is the **Lady Chapel**. Its reredos and canopy are by *Comper* 1911. The patterned underside of the canopy had been whitewashed over but was restored in 1971 when the altar, pavement and steps were extended.

A 14C Italian 'Virgin and Child' painting hangs on the north side of the altar.

The **nave**, of three bays, is unusually short; its clerestory windows are punctuated by blind sections.

On the north side is the pulpit, an expensive piece, featuring multi-coloured inlaid marble.

Above this is the ivory crucifix presented by the Duke of Newcastle in 1909.

Butterfield insisted that the high altar should be visible to the congregation and a low wall of marble and alabaster rather than a screen therefore divides the chancel from the nave.

Its painted brass gate and the chancel's north and south iron screens are by *Potter*.

The vaulted two-bay **chancel**, lower than the nave, is faced with alabaster; the columns are of red serpentine. It was decorated by *William Dyce*, but all the visible paintings are the work of *Comper*. Restoration was completed in 1978.

Paintings on the north and south walls were added by *Comper* in 1909.

The **sanctuary** possesses two sedilias and a piscina.

Suspended above the altar is a pyx made by *Comper* in 1930 and presented by the Duke of Newcastle as a memorial to the choristers of All Saints' who had been killed in the First World War.

The reredos was made by *Dyce* but his original
paintings quickly deteriorated and were restored
by *Edwin Armitage* in 1864. Although these
remain they have been covered with replacement
paintings made by *Comper* in 1919.

At the east end of the **south aisle** is a screen which
fronts the area occupied by the organ. It is of
wood and was designed by *Lawrence King* in
1962. Leading figures in the Anglo-Catholic
movement are represented.

The decorated statue of the Virgin, carved by
Louis Grosse in Bruges, Belgium, was presented
in 1924.

ALL SOULS LANGHAM PLACE *Nash 1824*

Langham Place

*Oxford Circus
Station, Central and
Victoria lines.*

All Souls', an important part of his great Regent
Street scheme, is now the only church designed
by Nash to survive on the British mainland
(another exists on the Isle of Wight).

This is one of four early-19C Commissioners'
churches in Marylebone; the Commissioners paid
two-thirds of All Souls' cost.

Nash curved the portico and tower of the building
to provide satisfactory façades to both Portland
Place and Regent Street – a problem which arose
owing to the sharp bend in the road which was
necessitated by property acquisition difficulties.

A land-mine badly damaged the church in the
Second World War and almost half the **spire** has
been rebuilt. Nash's combination of a spire and a
Classical building earned him much ridicule when
the building was completed.

All Souls' was faced, unusually for Nash, with
Bath stone rather than stuccoed brick.

Between the capitals of the portico's columns are
angels made of Coade stone.

➡ Enter the church.

R of the entrance is a bust of Nash by *Behnes*,
1831.

Although the organ in the **west gallery** has been
rebuilt, its mahogany case, designed by Nash, is
original.

Restored after Second World War bombing, the
original **north and south galleries** have been
retained but the furnishings are ultra-modern.

To permit the post-war construction of a hall
beneath the church, the original floor level has
been raised 18in.

The altar painting 'Ecce Homo' by *Richard
Westall* was presented to the church by
George IV.

Request permission to view the **hall** below.

The site of All Souls' was swampy, necessitating
deep foundations. Nash's inverted arches formed
part of these and have been revealed since the
hall was created.

CHURCH OF THE ASSUMPTION AND ST GREGORY 'The Bavarian Chapel' *c.1785*

Warwick Street

Piccadilly Circus Station, Bakerloo and Piccadilly lines.

For a short time in the mid-19C this became the chapel of the Bavarian Embassy and is still known as 'The Bavarian Chapel'. The building is a unique survivor of the embassy chapels which were for long the only venues where British subjects could legally attend Catholic mass between 1588 and emancipation in 1829.

Its predecessor was built early in the 18C for the Portuguese Embassy in what were then the back gardens of Nos 23 and 24 Golden Square. This was destroyed in the Gordon Riots of 1780 and rebuilt. In 1847 the Bavarian Embassy acquired the present building. Bavaria joined the German federation in 1871.

➠ Enter by the first door L.

Most of the interior was remodelled in the 19C.

Above the main door R the motto of the Wittelsbach family, rulers of Bavaria, 'In Treu Fest' (steadfast in loyalty) remains.

NOTRE DAME DE FRANCE

Leicester Place

Leicester Square Station, Northern and Piccadilly lines.

The Chapel of the Blessed Sacrament, within this Roman Catholic church, was decorated by *Jean Cocteau*. Little else is of particular interest.

THE QUEEN'S CHAPEL OF THE SAVOY

Savoy Hill

Open Tuesday–Friday 11.30–15.30. Closed August and September.

Temple Station, Circle and District lines.

This, the chapel of the Royal Victorian Order, belongs to the Crown through its ownership of the Duchy of Lancaster. Some Tudor features survive.

The chapel, dedicated to St John the Baptist, occupies part of the site of the Savoy Palace built *c.1245* by Peter of Savoy who had been presented with the land by Henry III, his niece's husband. Later, the palace became John of Gaunt's residence but it was destroyed by Wat Tyler's rebels in 1381. Henry VII founded a hospital here for the Knights of St John early in the 16C and this chapel formed part of it. Suppressed at the Reformation, Mary I revived the hospital which later became in turn a barracks, a prison and a military hospital. Its function as a hospital ended in 1702 but its buildings, acquired by the Duchy of Lancaster in 1772, survived until the end of the 19C. All that remains is the chapel. In 1937 George VI provided this for the use of the Royal Victorian Order which had been formed in 1896 to honour those who gave 'signal service to the Crown'.

Rebuilding of the south front, with its bell tower, was completed by *R. Smirke*, *c.1820*, but the other walls survive from the original Tudor building, *c.1516*.

The **antechapel** and **vestibule** were added in 1958.

➠ Enter the modern extension and turn L to the chapel which is north/south orientated.

Internal reconstruction, following a fire, was completed by *S. Smirke* in 1864. Only the windows were damaged by the bombing.

The sixteen rear stalls belong to royal members of the Order.

There are 115 plaques of the Knight Commanders of the Order displayed within the chapel.

In the west wall's second window from the north are the arms, in stained glass, of the Cathedral of St John the Divine, New York; the chapel's plate was kept there for safety during the Second World War.

Washington Cathedral's arms are also featured.

Figures from old monuments have been used to decorate the corbels in the **chancel**.

On the chancel's west wall, at the north end, is the monument to Nicole Moray, d.1612.

Behind the altar is a small 14C Florentine painting.

Against the east wall is a Tudor piscina, long hidden by a monument and discovered after the 1864 fire.

Above the piscina is a carved Florentine head of Christ, *c.*1520.

A monument on the east wall commemorates Alice Steward, d.1513.

The west window, featuring musicians, commemorates Sir Richard D'Oyly Carte, producer of the Gilbert and Sullivan Savoy Operas.

•● *Exit to the antechapel. Turn L and proceed towards the* **vestry** *at the north end of the building.*

The vestry window ahead, facing the ante chapel, contains 13C and 14C stained glass, presented in 1954.

If convenient, visitors may be shown the sovereign's robing room in which a needlework panel 'The Garden of Eden', 1600, is displayed.

ST AUGUSTINE KILBURN *Pearson 1880*

Rudolf Road
(624 1637)

*Kilburn Park Station,
Bakerloo line.*

This is an outstanding example of High Victorian Gothic. St Augustine's size and soaring arches immediately impress even though the Gothic Revival detailing, as usual, falls somewhat flat.

Pearson adopted his favoured Early English Revival style for this long church, which has been judged one of the best of its date in England. The building was completed by 1878, designed for Anglo-Catholic worship, and stands on what had been swampy land.

Unfinished for twenty years, the **tower** was finally surmounted by a **spire** in 1898.

•● *Enter the north aisle from the north-west porch.*

Throughout, the nave and chancel are rib-vaulted in brick.

The feature of internal buttresses appears to be inspired by similar work at the church of St Cecile in Albi, France.

Also reminiscent of Albi are the vaulted, compartmental **galleries** which are almost as high as the nave.

The rood unusually includes a full complement of figures; in addition to Christ, The Virgin Mary and John the Evangelist are Longinus, Joseph of Arimathea, Mary Magdalene and Nicodemus.

A low **ambulatory** runs behind the sanctuary.

Important paintings, presented to the church by Lord Northcliffe and including works by *Lippi* and *Titian*, have, alas, been stolen.

ST CLEMENT DANES *Wren 1682*

Strand

Temple Station, Circle and District lines.

This is the only London church outside the City boundary to have been rebuilt by Wren (St James's Piccadilly was completely new). Most of the steeple was added later by *Gibbs*. The interior was almost completely rebuilt following Second World War bomb damage but some original fittings were saved. St Clement Danes is now the central church of the Royal Air Force.

Alfred the Great permitted Danes with English wives to settle around what is now Fleet Street in 886. They probably worshipped in a timber-framed church that was already standing and dedicated it to St Clement, the patron saint of Danish sailors. This building was replaced by a stone structure in 1022. In 1189 the Knights Templar acquired St Clement's but shortly after their dissolution in 1312 the church became the responsibility of the Bishop of Exeter, who lived opposite in Essex House where, however, he was soon to be murdered. Partial rebuilding took place in the 15C and again in 1640. Although St Clement's escaped the Great Fire, it had become dilapidated and the body of the church was completely rebuilt by Wren. The present St Clement's implies that it is the 'Oranges and Lemons' church of the nursery song as its bells play the tune on the hour every three hours 09.00–18.00. However, St Clement Eastcheap in the City also, and more believably, claims this distinction.

The masonry of the lower part of the **tower** is 15C, although completely encased by *Wren*. Everything from the clock level upwards was added by *Gibbs* in 1719. Surmounting the **steeple** is a weathervane in the form of a ship's anchor.

The **porch** is believed to have been retained from the 1640 building.

Doors on either side, now blocked, were once the only entrances to the galleries; which are now reached internally.

•➡ *Enter from the west porch and proceed through the vestibule to the* **nave**.

St Clement's was gutted by bombs in the Second World War but restored by *W. A. S. Lloyd* in

1955 to serve as the central church of the Royal Air Force – an incongruous choice in view of the maritime connections of its patron saint.

Slate badges throughout commemorate RAF squadrons.

At the west end, in the organ loft, is the instrument presented by the United States Air Force to replace the *Schmidt* organ destroyed in the Second World War.

Below the north gallery, on the west wall, is the American shrine. A book is displayed that lists the names of 19,000 members of the USA 8th and 9th Air Forces who died whilst serving in the UK; photostat copies beneath may be examined.

●● *Proceed eastward.*

The pulpit, allegedly by *Gibbons*, is original.

Beside this is a chair that commemorates Thelma Bader, d.1971. She was the first wife of Douglas Bader, the pilot who flew in the Battle of Britain after losing both legs. At the request of the RAF, no individual pilot is commemorated in the church but Douglas Bader's initial 'D' is embroidered alongside that of his wife 'T' on the chair's cushion. The ashes of Douglas Bader were brought to the church in 1982.

The aisle continues in front of the sanctuary forming an **ambulatory**, a rare feature in a parish church.

The two bishops' thrones in the **sanctuary** are embroidered with 15C Florentine silk.

The altar painting is by *Ruskin Spear*.

St Clement's is the only parish church by Wren to possess an apse. Its modern window is by *Carl Edwards*.

The lectern was presented by the Royal Australian Air Force.

●● *Return to the west end of the north aisle where the door, generally locked, leads to the* **north gallery**.

Ahead, on the first landing, is a reference to William Webb-Ellis who, as a schoolboy at Rugby, picked up the football thus creating the game of rugby; he was rector here from 1843–55.

Towards the east end of the north gallery, the plate R commemorates a famous 18C parishioner, Dr Samuel Johnson.

●● *Return to the nave, proceed to the vestibule and descend the stairs L to the* **crypt**.

Immediately L is an old church noticeboard.

The vaulted crypt survives from an earlier, possibly 15C, building. Services for small congregations are now held here but it was once a burial place.

Displayed on the west wall R are chains that protected coffins from theft by 18C body-snatchers who sold the bodies within for medical research.

●● *Exit R and cross to the north side of the road. Proceed eastward.*

From here it can be appreciated that St Clement's, unlike St Mary-le-Strand further west, was not originally designed for its island site. The north façade was obscured by other buildings and there is, therefore, no Baroque carving here as there is on the south façade.

Standing outside the east apse of the church is the monument to Dr Johnson, by *Fitzgerald*, 1910.

In front of Johnson's statue, a cast-iron plaque commemorates the sinking of a 191ft well nearby in 1807.

ST CYPRIAN CLARENCE GATE *Comper 1903*

Glentworth Street

Baker Street Station, Bakerloo, Circle, Jubilee and Metropolitan lines.

An uninteresting exterior is only the prelude to what is regarded as Sir Ninian Comper's masterpiece. Delicate Gothic motifs, profuse gilding, whitewashed walls and pre-Reformation features, including a rood screen, probably give the best impression of the interior of a medieval church to be obtained in London.

St Cyprian's, founded by Father Charles Gutch, a follower of the Oxford Movement, was built for Anglo-Catholic worship. It replaced a temporary chapel, adapted by *George Street* in 1866, from two adjoining houses which stood in nearby Park Street. The site was purchased from Lord Portman who accepted a good deal less than its market value.

Externally, St Cyprian's is one of London's plainest churches, lacking a tower, or indeed any outstanding feature. However, *Comper* had little alternative as funds were extremely limited.

As the site is adjacent to an old river bed, expensive concrete foundations, 18ft deep, were required to support the walls (and internal columns).

●● *Enter the church which is north/south orientated, and proceed to the south end.*

The **narthex** (antechapel) was created by the erection of the organ gallery above it in 1930; however, it had been part of the original plan.

Unfortunately, the organ possesses no decorative case, but some believe that its unusually fine tone is partly due to this lack.

Comper, a knowledgeable ecclesiologist, designed the building in the Perpendicular style of an important early-16C parish church; there is a clerestory and the aisles are high.

When consecrated, St Cyprian's possessed few decorative features; however Comper had already planned what might be added as funds became available, and he designed all the furnishings and fittings referred to.

The centrally placed font was erected in 1930. Its cover, added two years later, although decorative is hardly practical, as it is fixed and a colonette must be removed to allow space to baptize the infant: an operation requiring two pairs of hands!

On the west side is the pulpit, presented in 1914.

The north-west **chapel** was dedicated as the Chapel of the Holy Name in 1938.

Its screen was completed with figure paintings in 1926.

The wooden altar, not the work of Comper, came from the earlier chapel in Park Street, where it was used by Father Gutch.

Dividing the nave from the chancel is the rood screen and loft. These were completed on the nave side in 1924 and the chancel side in 1938.

Surmounting this is a tie-beam with its board above painted with Christ in Majesty – not, surprisingly, a Last Judgement scene as was usual above medieval chancel arches.

There are a triple sedilia, piscina and aumbry in the **sanctuary**.

The high altar, one of the largest in England, comprises a mensa (table top) made from one stone slab. Its linen coverings were designed by *Comper*.

High above is a canopy, decorated with a particularly youthful representation of Christ, unbearded, as is usual in Comper's work.

On the south-east side of the **nave** is the lectern, presented in 1906.

The east, **Lady Chapel** was partly restored in 1957. East of its altar is the brass memorial floor plaque to the founder, Charles Gutch, who died in 1896, just seven years before St Cyprian's was built. The plaque was transferred here from the Park Street chapel. Gutch had lived in the old clergy house, part of which had stood on the site of this chapel.

Between the second and third bays from the north, the wood-block floor in the **east aisle** was burned by an incendiary bomb which fell through the roof in 1940. The damage has been left as a memorial.

ST GEORGE HANOVER SQUARE *James 1724*

St George Street

Bond Street Station, Central and Jubilee lines or Green Park Station, Piccadilly and Victoria lines.

St George's, one of the West End's most impressive churches, is central London's only major work by John James.

It was built under the Fifty New Churches Act of 1711 and dedicated to honour George I. Important weddings in the church have included those of writers Shelley, 1814; George Eliot (Mary Evans Lewes), 1880; and John Buchan, 1907; and politicians Disraeli, 1839; Asquith, 1877; and a 'ranchman' destined to become President of the United States, Theodore Roosevelt, 1886. Handel, St George's most famous parishioner, had his own pew.

The **tower** is reminiscent of that of St James Garlickhythe by *Wren*.

St George's great portico, possibly influenced by St Paul's Cathedral, set a trend in parish church design, soon to be followed by St Martin-in-the-Fields and St George Bloomsbury.

On either side of the entrance are early 20C cast iron dogs by *A. Jones* (?) brought here in 1940 from a bombed shop.

●● Enter from the portico.

The interior of the church resembles St James Piccadilly.

At the west end is the original **organ gallery** fronted by the arms of George I. This was once flanked by galleries for charity school children.

The organ was made by *Gerard Smith*, nephew of the great Father Schmidt; part of its case is original.

The pulpit and altar rail in the **nave**, together with the reredos (incorporating the painting of 'The Last Supper' by *Kent*) in the **sanctuary** are original.

Also by *Kent* is the sanctuary chair.

Flemish stained glass, *c.*1525, in the east window was installed from an Antwerp convent in 1840.

In the **chapel**, at the east end of the north aisle, are two angels from a German altarpiece, *c.*1500.

ST JAMES PICCADILLY *Wren 1684*

Piccadilly

Piccadilly Circus Station, Bakerloo and Piccadilly lines.

Wren regarded this London church, the only one that he built on a completely new site, to be his most successful from a practical viewpoint. Authenticated carvings within by *Gibbons* survived the war. Brass rubbings may be made in the basement.

The church was built to serve the Jermyn estate which began with St James's Square *c.*1673 and marked the foundation of the 'West End'. Originally, St James's was entered from Jermyn Street, as Piccadilly had not then been laid out. Wren built little in central London outside the City itself; apart from this church, only St Clement Danes, part of Kensington Palace and probably the Tudor-style south range of St James's Palace, was his work. Much of St James's was destroyed in 1940. Restoration was completed by *Richardson* in 1954 and the new brickwork is apparent.

The first **spire** was added by Wren in 1699 but this was destroyed by the bombs and replaced by *Richardson* with a glass fibre version.

Externally, on the south wall, is a canopied pulpit added in 1902.

●● Enter the vestibule.

In the vestibule, R of the entrance to the nave, is the wall tablet (1929) commemorating the Van de Veldes, father and son, renowned 17C Dutch painters who specialized in naval scenes. Much of their work is displayed in the National Maritime Museum at Greenwich.

●► *Proceed to the* **nave**.

Outstanding furnishings by *Gibbons* were carved
in 1684. They are all authenticated and survived
the bombing as they had been stored for safety at
Hardwick Hall, Derbyshire.

Immediately L is the marble 'Adam and Eve'
font by *Gibbons* in which Pitt the Elder and
William Blake were baptized.

The organ by *Harris* came from the Whitehall
Banqueting House which served for a period as
the Chapel Royal; its case is by *Gibbons*.

The pulpit was made in 1862.

The reredos is, again, by *Gibbons*.

ST JOHN SMITH SQUARE *Archer 1728*

Smith Square

*Open for concerts
only.*

*Westminster Station,
Circle and District
lines.*

This is the only major work in central London by
Thomas Archer, regarded as England's most
Baroque architect. It now functions solely as a
concert hall.

St John's was the most expensive of the buildings
constructed under the Fifty New Churches Act of
1711. Fire in 1742 necessitated much internal
restoration, but the twelve structural Corinthian
columns were not renewed. Further alterations
took place in 1824. Everything internal was lost
in 1941 when incendiary bombs gutted the
church. Reconstruction as a concert hall was
completed in 1968.

●► *Proceed clockwise around the building to view
the exterior.*

St John's is a rare London example of whole-
hearted Baroque. The four corner **turrets** were
designed to equalize the weight of the building
which, it was feared, might sink in the marshy
ground. Reputedly, the church was described by
Queen Anne as an 'upturned foot stool'; she did
not live to see its completion but may have been
shown a drawing.

It will be observed that the north façade matches
the south, and the east façade the west.

ST MARGARET WESTMINSTER

St Margaret Street

*Westminster Station,
Circle and District
lines.*

This, the House of Commons church, possesses
in its east window London's most important
early-16C stained glass. Although structurally
Tudor, most detailing dates from the 18C and
19C.

It is known that Edward the Confessor founded
St Margaret's in the 11C within the precincts of
Westminster Abbey so that the monks should
suffer less disturbance to their services. First
records, however, date from the early 12C. A
new building was erected in the 14C, financed by
wool merchants and the parishioners. Geoffrey
Chaucer worshipped there. A new church was
completed in 1532 and this formed the core of the
present building. In 1539 builders came to take
stones from St Margaret's for the construction of
the Duke of Somerset's new mansion in the

Strand but the parishioners fought them off. The church was adopted by the House of Commons in 1614 when Puritans decided to worship here rather than in the adjacent abbey. On Palm Sunday that year the entire House assembled for corporate communion in St Margaret's. Important marriages within include those of Samuel Pepys, 1655, John Milton (his second), 1656, and Winston Churchill, 1908. The church was returned to the jurisdiction of the Dean and Chapter of Westminster Abbey by Act of Parliament in 1973.

● To view the exterior, proceed clockwise.

Owing to 18C and 19C remodelling, St Margaret's appears to be primarily a Gothic Revival work.

The east porch is the 19C work of *Pearson*.

All walls were encased in Portland stone and the three upper stages of the **tower** re-built by *James* in 1734.

Window tracery has been renewed in Tudor style.

The south-east **vestry** was built in 1778.

Below the west façade's window, north of the 19C west porch (*Pearson*) is a tablet commemorating the twenty-one Cromwellians disinterred from Westminster Abbey and buried in St Mary's churchyard at the Restoration.

● Enter the church by the west door or, if locked, return to St Margaret St and enter by the east door.

The large church seats one thousand worshippers.

● Proceed to the south-east corner.

The brass tablet beside the east door (push the button to illuminate it), commemorates Sir Walter Ralegh who was executed in Old Palace Yard, Westminster, by James I in 1618. His body is believed to have been buried beneath the altar. It is known that his severed head was interred at West Horsley, Surrey.

*● Proceed to the **chancel**.*

The most important feature of St Margaret's is its Flemish east window, commissioned by Ferdinand and Isabella of Spain in 1501. It is believed that this commemorates the marriage of their daughter, Catherine of Aragon, to Prince Arthur, eldest son of Henry VII and heir to the throne. Arthur died and Catherine eventually became the first wife of his younger brother, Henry VIII. The window was fitted in three different buildings before finally being installed here in 1758.

Below this, the reredos is formed by the centrepiece of a limewood tryptich, carved by *Siffrin Alten* in 1753. It depicts 'The Supper at Emmaus' as painted by *Titian*.

The chancel roof is 19C.

Only the nave's arcades and the tower arch are original Tudor work.

The south windows, with abstract designs, are by *John Piper*, 1967.

⬤ Continue ahead to the west door.

Above the door are the arms of Charles II.

The font, L of the door, was made by *Stone* in 1641.

The window, immediately R of the door, commemorates Milton and was made in 1888.

⬤ Proceed towards the east end of the north aisle.

St Margaret's possesses many monuments but few are of exceptional interest. Between the third and fourth windows from the west, one of the finest commemorates Cornelius Vandun, d.1577.

At the east end is the 19C organ.

In front of this stands the pulpit, also 19C.

⬤ Exit from the church.

William Caxton, England's first printer, is buried in the old churchyard but his grave is unmarked.

ST MARTIN-IN-THE-FIELDS *Gibbs 1726*

St Martin's Place

Open daily 07.30–21.30. Crypt open Sunday 20.00.

Charing Cross Station, Bakerloo, Jubilee and Northern lines.

This, the parish church of the sovereign, is the best loved work of the Scottish architect James Gibbs.

St Martin's was first recorded in 1222. It was then a chapel which probably served the monks from Westminster Abbey working in the nearby convent (now Covent) garden. Later, the building was called St Martin-near-the-Cross (i.e. Charing Cross). In the 16C St Margaret Westminster was still the parish church, where burials took place and those who died in the northern part of the parish, had to be taken there through the precincts of Whitehall Palace. The bodies of so many plague victims made this journey that Henry VIII gave St Martin's parish church status in 1542 in order to keep these contaminated corpses away from the royal presence. A new church was completed in 1544; here Charles II was baptized in 1630 and Nell Gwyn, his favourite mistress, was buried in the crypt (later transferred to the burial ground) in 1687; she was only thirty-eight. Early in the 18C it was decided that a new, grander building was required as St Martin's had become the parish church of the sovereign. An architectural competition was held in which John James and others took part. The adjudicating committee were taken by Gibbs to see his St Mary-le-Strand, then under construction nearby, they were impressed and he won the commission. Initially a round church was designed which suited the then partly concealed site, but this was rejected. Its plan was later adopted, however, for a church in Connecticut, USA. George I gave £1000 towards the cost of the new building and became its first churchwarden; no other sovereign has served in this office. John Constable, the painter, married here in 1816. Rector 'Dick' Shepperd kept the crypt of the church open during the First World War to provide accommodation for soldiers returning from France at Charing Cross Station. St Martin's has maintained this tradition of hospitality to itinerants and is known as 'the church of the ever-open door'. The building escaped serious bomb damage.

When the present church was built, it was surrounded by narrow streets, a clear view of its west façade only being revealed in 1824 when the formation of Trafalgar Square began with the eastward extension of Pall Mall.

The **tower** was rebuilt in 1824 as a replica. Its position, rising centrally behind the huge portico of what is virtually a Classical temple, has always been controversial, but this plan was soon adopted for many churches, particularly in the USA.

Unlike Gibbs's St Mary-le-Strand, St Martin's has few Baroque features.

As St Martin's is the parish church of the sovereign, the coat of arms of George I was carved on the pediment.

•● *Ascend the steps to the portico and enter the church.*

Gibbs supported the roof with monolithic columns punctuated by the galleries; Wren invariably preferred two tiers of columns.

The tunnel-vaulted ceiling was plastered by Gibbs's favourites, the Italians *Artari* and *Bugati*.

Originally, the only seating for the congregation was in the galleries. Box pews were first provided in 1799 but these were lowered, as usual, in 1858.

In the nave stands a prie dieu (prayer desk) which belonged to Edward VII and Queen Alexandra; it was presented to the father of rector 'Dick' Shepperd.

The pulpit was made in 1799.

•● *Proceed to the east end of the* **north aisle**.

On the north wall is a memorial to the prisoners of war who died horrifically whilst constructing the Burma–Siam railway for the Japanese in the Second World War. Two pieces of a sleeper from the track are displayed in a case; above is a commemorative plaque.

Against the aisle's east wall is a portrait of James Gibbs by *Soldi*, 1740.

Above this, the only monument to an individual permitted in the church commemorates a favoured servant of Queen Victoria; it was erected at the monarch's insistence.

•● *Proceed to the* **chancel**.

On the ceiling are the arms of George I.

Facing each other are, on the north wall, the Royal Box and, on the south wall, the Admiralty Box.

The choir stalls were made in 1799.

Contemporary with the church, the altar rail is the oldest known cast-iron example.

At the west end of the **south aisle** is the font of 1689 in which Cardinal Newman was baptized. It was probably made for the previous church.

On the aisle's west wall is the painting of 'St Martin and the Beggar' by *Francesco Solimena* (1657–1747).

The **crypt** is generally only open on Sunday evenings. Exhibited are a chest of 1597 and a whipping post made in 1751.

ST MARY-LE-STRAND *Gibbs 1717*

Strand

Temple Station, Circle and District lines.

St Mary-le-Strand has been judged London's best example of a small church in the Italian Baroque style.

The earliest records of St Mary's date from 1143 but the first building, sited nearer the river, was demolished in 1549 for the construction of Protector Somerset's palace. An early dedication was 'Church of the Innocents' and later, 'Church of the Nativity of our Lady and the Innocents of the Strand'. Following the demolition of this building the congregation worshipped in the nearby Chapel of the Savoy. Thomas à Becket was an early rector. The famous Strand Maypole is known to have been standing on the site of the present church by 1619 but this was removed during the Commonwealth. However, a new 134ft high maypole, erected in 1661, remained here until 1714. The first rank for the hackney carriage, predecessor of the taxi, was established beside it in 1634. St Mary's, commissioned in 1714, was the first church to be built under the Fifty New Churches Act. Although completed in 1717 it was not consecrated until 1723. Initially, Gibbs planned a short bell-tower for its west end instead of a steeple. In addition, possibly influenced by the old maypole, he designed a 250ft column to stand outside the west front. This would have been 80ft taller than Nelson's column in Trafalgar Square and the highest structure to be erected in Europe since Classical times. A massive statue of Queen Anne was made to surmount this by the Florentine Foggino, but just as it was ready for casting in 1714 the Queen died and both the projected column and its statue were abandoned. The fate of the statue, which was paid for, is unknown. St Mary's was Gibbs's first commission, and, unlike St Clement Danes further east, it was specifically designed from the outset for its 'island' site. To promote the Jacobite cause, Charles Edward Stuart, the Young Pretender, was secretly received into the church of England at St Mary's in 1750. It is believed that he lodged briefly at Essex House which then stood nearby on the south side of Strand.

•• *Enter from the west porch.*

It is not known how much of the interior is

Gibbs's work as his contract was terminated in 1715. He was a Scottish Roman Catholic which may have led to disagreements. There are surprisingly few decorative features apart from the coved, coffered ceiling; this is the work of English craftsmen, although the Italian style of *Fontana*, Surveyor to Pope Clement XI was adopted.

Gibbs omitted lower level windows to minimize distraction from traffic.

•● *Proceed eastward.*

Original furnishings include the altar rail, the font and the pulpit, possibly by *Gibbons*. The pulpit, however, lost its canopy in the 19C and was reduced in height; it was originally fixed to the wall.

Above the chancel arch are the arms of George I.

The two paintings in the **chancel**, above the original doorcases, are by the American *Mather Brown*, 1784.

The blue east windows are a recent, discordant, addition. Many hope that their days are numbered.

ST MARY PADDINGTON *J. Plaw 1791*

Paddington Green
(723 1968)

*Paddington Station,
Bakerloo, Circle,
District and
Metropolitan lines.*

This church is reminiscent of the work of *Dance the Elder*. It has been well restored – even possessing new box pews – and closely matches its original late-18C appearance. Mrs Siddons, the great actress, buried in the churchyard, is also commemorated within.

St Mary's, first recorded in 1220, was rebuilt in 1680 and the present structure is, therefore, the third on the site. William Hogarth, the artist, married in the second building in 1729.

•● *Approach the brick-built church from the south.*

Against the west face is a small semi-circular portico.

•● *Enter the* **nave** *from here.*

Above the west door are the arms of George III.

The original unusually shaped **gallery** remains.

Newly made box pews were restored to the church in 1973.

St Mary's, with its shallow dome, is designed with a Greek cross plan.

The slender iron altar rail is original.

Memorials of interest, all in the **sanctuary**, are as follows –

North wall west side: Frances E. Anst d.1796, by *Bacon* (lower part only).

North wall east side: Sarah Siddons, the great actress, d.1831.

South wall east side: Nollekens, the sculptor, d.1823, by *Behnes*.

South wall centre: General Charles Crosbie, d.1807, by *Bacon*.

Almost 100yds north of the church, in an enclosure R of the path, is the tomb of Sarah Siddons, d.1831.

West of St Mary's is the church hall. Its entrance commemorates a parishioner, Emma, Lady Hamilton, who lived on Paddington Green. She was the mistress of Nelson but died an alcoholic pauper at Calais, France, in 1815.

ST PAUL COVENT GARDEN *Inigo Jones 1638*

Covent Garden

Covent Garden Station, Piccadilly line.

Although mostly rebuilt, St Paul's, England's first Classical church, retains much of the external appearance of Inigo Jones's 'handsomest barn in England'. Many British actors and actresses are commemorated within.

At the Reformation, the Russell family acquired Westminster Abbey's convent garden. It was not until almost one hundred years later, however, that the development of what is now Covent Garden began. Francis Russell, fourth Duke of Bedford, obtained special permission from Charles I, who had banned further building in the capital, to construct a piazza in the Italian style. Its focal point was to be a chapel-at-ease to St Martin-in-the-Fields. The Duke was anxious that not too much money should be spent on this and allegedly, Jones, who had designed the piazza, promised him a simple barn, but 'the handsomest barn in England'. St Paul's was finished in 1633, only the second London church to be built since the Reformation (St Katherine Cree, in the City, basically still a Gothic building, had been completed two years earlier); however consecration did not take place until 1638. Allegedly, the proportions of the building followed those of the Temple of Solomon in Jerusalem. St Paul's became a parish church in 1645. The building was renovated by *T. Hardwick* in 1788 but in 1793 it was gutted by fire, and major restoration was required. Only the walls, portico and a south-east chapel survived; the church was rebuilt by *Hardwick* and re-consecrated in 1798. W. S. Gilbert, the librettist of the Savoy Operas, was christened here in 1837.

➡ *Proceed to the* **portico**.

Jones had planned that the main entrance should be from the east end, beneath a stone portico facing the piazza, but Archbishop Laud insisted that the high altar should stand in its usual east position, thus making entry from there impossible. The east portico was kept but the door is false. It is basically the work of Jones although probably restored by *Hardwick*. Originally the portico appears to have been flanked by two wings and the roof supported cupolas.

The portico at first stood on a plinth which was approached by steps, but the pavement of Covent Garden has since been raised. In 1662 Samuel

Pepys records in his diary an early Punch and Judy performance outside the portico. Later it was used as an election hustings. It was here that Professor Higgins met Eliza Doolittle in Bernard Shaw's *Pygmalion*, later adapted as the musical, *My Fair Lady*.

●● *Proceed to the north side of Covent Garden. L is King St. First L a passage leads to St Paul's churchyard. If its gate is locked proceed to Bedford St first L and enter Inigo Place first L.*

The brickwork is Victorian and replaced Hardwick's stone walls; Inigo Jones's had been of stuccoed brick.

●● *Enter the church from the west door and proceed through the screen.*

The carved wreath L was presented by St Paul's Cathedral. It is the work of *Grinling Gibbons* and commemorates his burial in the church in 1721.

The painter J. M. W. Turner was born nearby in Maiden Lane and baptized within the original building in 1775. His parents had married at St Paul's in 1773 and the plaque at the west end of the north wall was erected by Turner in 1832 to commemorate their burial here.

St Paul's is the headquarters of the Actors' Church Union and many well known members of the theatrical profession are commemorated by wall plaques.

The pulpit was made up from sections of an early-19C pulpit and lectern.

Two monuments by *Flaxman* face each other in the **chancel**: on the north wall Edward Hall, d.1798; on the south wall, John Bellamy, d.1794.

On a niche in the south wall, at its east end, is a silver casket containing the ashes of the actress Ellen Terry.

Between the two most easterly windows in the south wall is a tablet commemorating actor Charles Macklin who evidently died aged 107.

ST PETER VERE STREET *Gibbs 1724*

Vere Street

Open Monday–Friday, generally afternoons only.

Bond Street Station, Central and Jubilee lines.

The interior of this, the second of Gibbs's three London churches has been described as a St Martin-in-the-Fields in miniature.

St Peter's was built as a private chapel for Edward Harley, third Earl of Oxford. It was first known as the Mary-le-bone Chapel and later the Oxford Chapel. Following restoration in 1832 the church was dedicated to St Peter. It is now administered by the London Institute for Contemporary Christianity.

●● *Enter from Vere Street.*

Unfortunately, the aisles have been partitioned to provide offices.

Good plasterwork survives, particularly in the ceiling; it is the work of Gibbs's favourites, the Italians *Artari* and *Bugati*.

The 19C stained glass windows were designed by *Burne-Jones*.

On either side of the **sanctuary** are the Harley family's private boxes.

London north of the Thames
(except the Cities of London and Westminster)

Most of the parish churches north of the Thames are medieval and originally served small villages which, since the nineteenth century, have expanded and merged to form London boroughs.

Very few of these churches are open on a regular basis and it will almost always be necessary to make arrangements in advance. Telephone numbers, usually of the rectories or vicarages, are given and callers will be advised how to visit the churches.

Details of public transport from inner London and from other churches of interest nearby are given for all except the most central locations which are served by several Underground stations and are easily found. (BR) indicates a British Rail station – occasionally a station is served by both systems.

Barking, St Margaret
Bloomsbury, St George
Chelsea, All Saints
Chelsea, Holy Trinity
Chelsea, St Luke
Clerkenwell, St James
Clerkenwell, Priory Church of St John
Cranford, St Dunstan
East Bedfont, St Mary-the-Virgin
East Ham, St Mary Magdalene
Enfield, St Andrew
Hackney, St John-at-Hackney
Harefield, St Mary-the-Virgin
Harlington, St Peter and St Paul
Harmondsworth, St Mary
Harrow, St Mary
Hayes, St Mary-the-Virgin
Hendon, St Mary
Hillingdon, St John-the-Baptist
Holborn, St Etheldreda
Holborn, St Giles-in-the-Fields
Hornchurch, St Andrew
Ickenham, St Giles
Kensington, St Cuthbert
Laleham, All Saints
Limehouse, St Anne

Little Stanmore, St Laurence Whitchurch
Littleton, St Mary Magdalene
Marylebone, Holy Trinity
Marylebone, St Marylebone
Northolt, St Mary
Perivale, St Mary-the-Virgin
Pinner, St John-the-Baptist
Rainham, St Helen and St Giles
St Pancras, St Pancras
St Pancras, St Pancras Old Church
Shoreditch, St Leonard
South Kensington, Brompton Oratory
Spitalfields, Christ Church
Stanwell, St Mary-the-Virgin
Stepney, St Dunstan and All Saints
Stoke Newington, St Mary Old Church
Twickenham, All Hallows
Twickenham, St Mary-the-Virgin
Uxbridge, St Margaret
Wapping, St George-in-the-East
Wennington, St Mary and St Peter
West Ham, All Saints

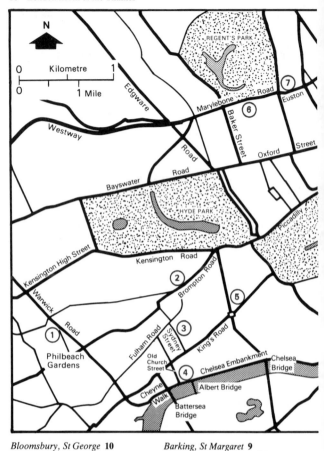

Bloomsbury, *St George* **10**
Chelsea, *All Saints* **4**
Chelsea, *Holy Trinity* **5**
Chelsea, *St Luke* **3**
Clerkenwell, *St James* **14**
Clerkenwell, *Priory Church of St John* **12**
Holborn, *St Etheldreda* **13**
Holborn, *St Giles-in-the-Fields* **8**
Kensington, *St Cuthbert* **1**
Marylebone, *Holy Trinity* **7**
Marylebone, *St Marylebone* **6**
St Pancras, *St Pancras* **9**
St Pancras, *St Pancras Old Church* **11**
Shoreditch, *St Leonard* **15**
South Kensington, *Brompton Oratory* **2**
Spitalfields, *Christ Church* **16**

Barking, *St Margaret* **9**
East Ham, *St Mary Magdalene* **8**
Enfield, *St Andrew* **1**
Hackney, *St John-at-Hackney* **4**
Hornchurch, *St Andrew* **11**
Limehouse, *St Anne* **6**
Rainham, *St Helen and St Giles* **10**
Stepney, *St Dunstan and All Saints* **5**
Stoke Newington, *St Mary Old Church* **2**
Wapping, *St George-in-the-East* **3**
Wennington, *St Mary and St Peter* **12**
West Ham, *All Saints* **7**

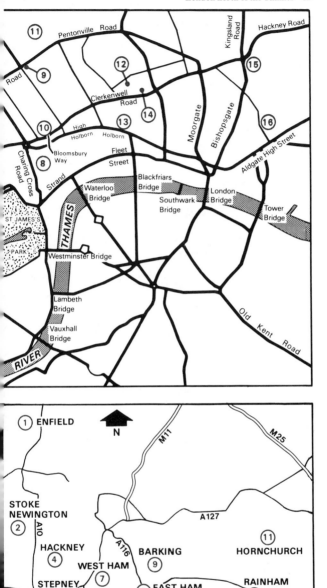

(11) Pentonville Road
Kingsland Road
Hackney Road
(9) Road
(12)
(15)
Clerkenwell Road
(14)
Moorgate
Bishopsgate
(16)
(10) High Holborn Holborn
(13)
Aldgate High Street
(8) Bloomsbury Way
Fleet Street
Charing Cross Road
Strand
Blackfriars Bridge
Waterloo Bridge
London Bridge
Southwark Bridge
Tower Bridge
THAMES
ST JAMES'S PARK
Westminster Bridge
Lambeth Bridge
Old Kent Road
Vauxhall Bridge
RIVER

(1) ENFIELD
N
M11
M25

STOKE NEWINGTON
(2)
A10
A127
HACKNEY
(4)
A116
BARKING
(9)
(11) HORNCHURCH
WEST HAM
(7)
STEPNEY
(8) EAST HAM
RAINHAM
WAPPING
(5) (6)
(10)
(3) LIMEHOUSE
(12)
WENNINGTON

KILOMETRES
0   3
0 MILES 2

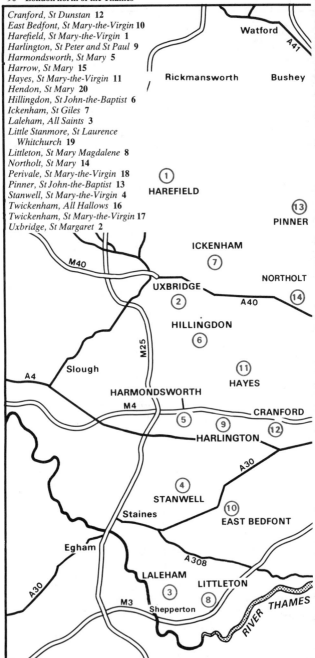

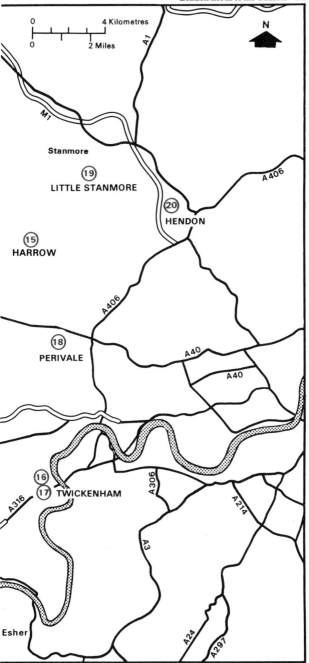

BARKING   ST MARGARET

London Road

*Open Thursday and
Friday 09.30–12.00.*

**From Central
London:** *Barking
Station.
Exit R from Barking
Station and continue
ahead following East
Street to London
Road; the church lies
ahead.*
**From East Ham,
St Mary Magdalene:**
*Bus 101 or S1 to East
Ham Station;
Underground to
Barking Station;
proceed as above.*
**From Hornchurch,
St Andrew:**
*Upminster Bridge
Station to Barking
Station; proceed as
above.*

*All stations are on the
District and
Metropolitan lines.*

Barking's parish church retains its 13C chancel;
most of the remainder is late medieval.

St Margaret's was built within the precincts of
Barking Abbey, *c.*1216. It has always served the
parish and remained entirely separate from the
massive abbey church which was demolished at
the Reformation; this is why it escaped
destruction. The original chancel survives, but
most of the present building was constructed in
the 15C and 16C. Unusually, St Margaret's
possesses two north aisles. Captain Cook the
explorer married in this church.

Externally, St Margaret's offers a picturesque
scene. Its churchyard is approached through the
arch of the Curfew, or Fire Bell Tower, the only
structure remaining from the abbey; this is
described later.

Stone foundations of more abbey buildings were
found, north of the church, during excavations in
1910.

•● *Continue ahead to the tower of the church.*

The **tower** with its north stair turret, was built of
Reigate stone in the late 15C. Until 1894 the bells
were rung at 08.00 and 17.00 during the winter
months to guide travellers across the marshes in
the twilight.

Its doorway is modern.

•● *Proceed clockwise around the church.*

Stretching behind the stair turret is the **inner
north aisle**.

Attached to this is the gabled west end of the
outer north aisle which was added between 1501
and the mid 16C. Work began at the centre,
continued to this end, and was then completed
eastward.

The early-16C **north porch** has two blocked
arches and its outer spandrels are decorated with
the Tudor rose.

Before the eastern part of the aisle's wall was
built, the abbey was demolished and some of its
Norman stonework re-used here.

•● *Continue past the north-east door, now the
usual entrance, and proceed to the chancel.*

The **chancel** survives from the church of *c.*1216.
Lancet windows remain in the north and south
walls but its east window is early 16C.

South of the chancel is the 15C **vestry**.

The eastern section of the **south aisle**'s wall is
early 15C.

Brick buttresses have been added to support the
central section of the wall which began to lean
outwards; much of this part of the wall is early
13C.

Past the last buttress, the western section of wall
is late 15C.

● *Continue to the north-east doorway and enter the church. Turn R and proceed westward along the* **outer north aisle**.

The arcade's octagonal piers are 16C.

The roof, which resembles a wooden boat, was probably built by local shipwrights.

At floor level, just past the porch, are the top sections of two windows (one partly hidden by a heater), indicating that the floor level here has been greatly raised.

Against the wall is the tomb of William Pownsett, d.1553.

West of this, a two-light window from the old abbey has been built into the wall.

Towards the most westerly window is the monument to Dr John Bamber, d.1753; the bust is believed to be by *Roubiliac*. It is protected by the original railings.

In the north-west corner, a monument commemorates Bamber's son-in-law, Crisp Gascoigne, who became, in 1753, the first Lord Mayor of London to reside at the Mansion House. The well known television presenter and author, Bamber Gascoigne, is a descendant.

● *Proceed to the* **inner north aisle**.

Much of this aisle's arcade is early-13C work but its most westerly bay was rebuilt in the 15C with a higher arch.

The medieval timber roof was revealed in 1929 with the removal of the plaster; some repair and replacement was necessary.

● *Proceed to the area at the base of the* **tower**.

Above the west door is a platform which is enclosed by the rail that once protected the high altar.

The royal arms are Hanoverian.

A shrine from Barking Abbey has been inserted within the tower's north-east pier. Standing in this is a glass case containing part of the shaft of a 7C Saxon cross.

The nave's roof had also been plastered but when this was removed in 1931 its woodwork was found to be in good condition.

The **south aisle**'s piers were renewed in the late 15C.

● *Proceed to the west end of the* **south aisle**, *now the baptistry.*

The font, made c.1635, was removed in 1872 and its bowl and stem eventually became detached; they were reunited and returned to the church in 1928.

On the north wall is the monument to Sir Orlando Humphreys, d.1737; its rail is original.

The south arcade's most westerly bay, like the north arcade's, was entirely rebuilt in the 15C and, similarly, its arch is higher.

At the east end of the aisle's south wall, facing the pulpit, is a small recessed double arch. This was discovered in 1929, together with part of a newel staircase. Both are believed to have once formed part of the access to the rood loft.

A plaster ceiling at this end of the aisle was removed in 1929 to reveal the timber roof.

The aisle continues, to form the Chapel of Youth, created when the organ was removed in 1929.

Figures on the altar screen include prison reformer Elizabeth Fry who is buried nearby in the Quaker cemetery and explorer Captain Cook who was married at St Margaret's in 1762.

●● *Proceed to the east end of the* **nave**.

St Margaret's once had a crossing and transepts which is why both the most easterly bays of the nave's arcades are wider.

The pulpit is 18C.

Above the chancel arch is a beam which retains traces of medieval painting.

The chancel's screen was made in 1891.

The vaulted roof of the **chancel** was plastered in 1772.

Both its arcades were renewed in the 15C.

On the north wall of the **sanctuary** is the monument to Francis Fuller, d.1636, possibly by *Stone*.

Below this, an incised stone slab commemorates Martinus, d.1328, the first recorded vicar of the church.

The recess with a brick moulding was once an Easter Sepulchre.

On the east wall, north of the altar, is an aumbry.

The piscina with its Norman shaft, on the south wall, was discovered in 1929.

Next to this, Sir Charles Montague, d.1626, is depicted on his monument as a cavalier in a battle tent.

The south lancet window, overlooking the altar, retains some medieval decoration.

Two Jacobean chairs stand in the sanctuary.

North of the chancel is the organ, originally sited in a gallery at the west end of the church. Its case was made in 1772.

West of the organ, a triple arch is built into the wall facing the inner north aisle; this probably came from Barking Abbey after its demolition in 1541.

●● *Proceed to the* **outer north-east chapel**.

The circular, Norman piers on the south side are also believed to have come from Barking Abbey.

On the north wall, beneath the window, a 12C marble slab commemorates Mauritius, Bishop of London, 1085–1108 and Alfgiva, Abbess of Barking.

The window above was reconstructed from the original stonework, found nearby in 1928. It had previously been filled with the monument which has been re-sited west of it.

This monument commemorates Captain John Bennett, d.1706, and is decorated with outstanding carvings of nautical items.

A small, framed list of abbesses of Barking, R of Bennett's monument, includes Mary Becket (1173–5). She was a sister of Thomas à Becket, Archbishop of Canterbury, and no doubt her appointment by Henry II was due to the King's remorse following the archbishop's murder in his cathedral.

▰● Request permission to view the **Curfew Tower** *and exit from the church with guide.*

Barking Abbey was founded as a Benedictine nunnery c.666 by St Erkenwald whose sister, St Ethelburga, became its first abbess. The abbey's 12C church was demolished along with the other monastic buildings in 1541. Only this, the Curfew (or Fire Bell) Tower, one of its three gateways, was reprieved. It was built in 1370 but reconstructed in 1460.

Before the tower of the parish church was built in the late 15C, a bell was rung from a small turret in this tower to summon parishioners to services. There is no record of either a curfew or a fire bell having been installed, in spite of the tower's name.

▰● Ascend the stone newel staircase to the first floor.

This floor is dedicated as the **Chapel of the Holy Rood**. The mid-12C(?) stone rood is believed to have once stood outside the abbey walls as it appears to be weather-worn.

There are two blocked windows in the room.

Modern shields feature the arms of Barking Abbey, the Archbishop of Canterbury, the Bishop of Chelmsford and the old Borough of Barking.

BLOOMSBURY   ST GEORGE
Hawksmoor 1731

Bloomsbury Way

Tottenham Court Road Station, Central and Northern lines or Holborn Station, Central and Piccadilly lines.

St George's is Hawksmoor's only London church west of the City.

It was one of the six built by Hawksmoor under the Fifty New Churches Act of 1711.

The obelisk-shaped **spire** is based on Pliny's description of the tomb of Mausolus. Originally, lions and unicorns decorated its base but these were removed in 1871. Surmounting the spire is a statue of the unpopular George I representing St George; this led to some ridicule.

Reproductions of the spire as it originally appeared form the two lamp standards flanking the steps.

The **portico** is modelled on that of the Pantheon, Rome.

●● Before entering the church, pass through the gate in the west corner and proceed along the passage adjacent to St George's. R Little Russell Street.

The **north façade** is designed in Renaissance style.

●● Return to the south façade and enter the church.

The high altar has been relocated at the north end.

Internally, Hawksmoor's favoured cubic proportions are adopted.

In the west chapel, screened by a curtain, is the monument to Charles Grant, d.1823, by *Manning*.

●● Proceed to the north end of the church.

Some furnishings were acquired from St John Red Lion Street, destroyed in the Blitz.

Originally the high altar was placed conventionally at the east end; however, this was moved in 1781 to its present position in what had been the north baptistry.

The exceptionally large size of this baptistry was probably due to its intended use for total immersion. The rearrangement is not immediately apparent to many because of the symmetrical plan of the interior.

It is believed that the reredos came from the private chapel of nearby Montague House, demolished for the construction of the British Museum.

The **east apse**, where the altar had been, was blocked in and a new gallery, later removed, constructed across it to increase St George's seating capacity.

The ceiling relief in this apse and the gilded flower in the ceiling of the nave are both by *Isaac Mansfield*.

CHELSEA   ALL SAINTS (CHELSEA OLD CHURCH)

Old Church Street

Open Tuesday–Friday 11.00–13.00 and 14.00–17.00, Saturday 11.00–13.00

Sloane Square Station, Circle and District lines. Exit ahead King's Road. Bus 11, 19, 22 or 49 westbound to Old Church St.

Most of the church was destroyed by bombs and the nave and tower have been completely rebuilt. However, sections of the walls of the 13C chancel and the 14C Lawrence Chapel, together with practically all of the 14C More Chapel, were saved and it was also possible to restore most of the outstanding monuments.

The first recorded church in Chelsea was built here in the 13C. Chapels flanking the chancel were added in the 14C and the nave and tower rebuilt c.1670. A cupola surmounting the tower was removed in 1870. Structurally, only sections at the east end survived the bombing, complete rebuilding of the tower and nave being required.

All the post-war restoration work was by *W. H. Godfrey*. There is a tradition that Henry VIII secretly married Jane Seymour here in 1536, immediately after Anne Boleyn had been beheaded. All Saint's was Chelsea's parish church until 1820 when St Luke's was built.

Enter the **porch**.

On the north wall, in the corner, is the Ashburnham Bell, presented to the church in 1679 by the Hon. William Ashburnham as a thanks offering to God for his escape from drowning.

Continue to the **nave**.

At the west end of the church the organ loft displays the arms of Elizabeth II.

The font L was made in 1673, but its cover is a reproduction.

Proceed to the north wall of the nave.

Stained glass in the west window is 17C Flemish.

The monument to Lady Jane Cheyne, 1699, in the niche in the wall just before the chancel, was carved by *P. Bernini*, a relative of the great Italian sculptor and architect Lorenzo Bernini. The figure is by *Raggi*.

The 17C Jervoise memorial R is in the form of a Roman arch.

Proceed ahead to the **Lawrence Chapel**.

Stained glass L, in the north window, which was revealed by the bomb damage, is 16C German or Flemish.

Facing this window, the monument to Sarah Colville, d.1631, depicts her shrouded figure.

Against the east wall the Stanley monument, 1632, with its realistically carved children's busts, provides an early example of Renaissance sculpture in this country.

Above this R, the small monument to Thomas Lawrence, made in 1593, includes an alabaster group of the goldsmith's family.

Proceed to the **sanctuary**.

The altar rail is 17C.

Curtains behind the altar were part of the hangings made for the coronation of Elizabeth II at Westminster Abbey in 1952.

On the north wall, L of the door, is the monument to Thomas Hungerford, d.1581, and his wife.

Behind the altar, in the east wall, is a medieval niche which may have served as an aumbry.

On the south wall is part of another larger niche the purpose of which is uncertain.

Against the south wall, R of the altar, is Sir Thomas More's monument, made in 1532. His two wives are buried in the tomb. More wrote the epitaph himself, intending to lie beneath it, but his headless body was almost certainly buried in the Chapel of St Peter ad Vincula within the Tower of London, following his execution on Tower Green in 1535. More's head, which was kept by his daughter, Margaret Roper, at her home in Eltham, is buried at St Dunstan, Canterbury.

The pulpit has been remade but incorporates much carving from the original of *c*.1690.

●● *Proceed to the* **More Chapel** *at the east end of the south aisle*.

This chapel almost entirely escaped Second World War bomb damage. Although built in 1325, it was remodelled in 1528 for More, who worshipped here.

The columns that support the arch from the chancel have Renaissance capitals made in the French style. They were part of the 1528 remodelling and represent some of England's earliest Renaissance work. It has been alleged that *Holbein* designed them.

In the south-east corner L is the tomb of Jane Guildford, d.1555. She was Duchess of Northumberland, and the mother-in-law of Lady Jane Grey.

A wall tablet commemorates the American-born writer Henry James. He became a British citizen and died at Chelsea in 1916.

The timber ceiling at the west end had been plastered over and was rediscovered after the bombing.

●● *Proceed westward along the south wall of the* **nave**.

The huge wall monument, possibly by *Nicholas Janssen*, commemorates Gregory, Lord Dacre, d.1594.

The west window on the south wall incorporates 17C Flemish stained glass.

In front of this window are chained 17C and early 18C volumes, the only examples in a London church; they were presented by Sir Hans Sloane.

The window on the west wall incorporates a 17C German stained glass cartouche.

●● *Exit and proceed L to the south-east corner of the* **churchyard**.

The large memorial by *Wilton* commemorates Sir Hans Sloane, d.1753 aged 93. He was president of the Royal Society and his name has been adopted by several Chelsea thoroughfares.

CHELSEA   HOLY TRINITY *Sedding 1888*

Sloane Street

Sloane Square Station, Circle and District lines. Exit R Sloane Square. Second R Sloane St.

The harmonious style, both externally and internally, was influenced by the Pre-Raphaelites.

Stained glass for the east window was made by *William Morris* to a design suggested by *Burne-Jones*.

CHELSEA   ST LUKE   *Savage 1820*

Sydney Street

Open Monday–
Saturday 12.00–
14.00.

Sloane Square
Station, Circle and
District lines. Exit
ahead King's Road.
Bus 11, 19, 22 or 49
westbound to Sydney
Street.

St Luke's was London's first church to be built in
the Gothic Revival style. The unusually large size
of both the church and its surrounding burial
ground gives the impression of a provincial
cathedral within its close. St Luke's was built as
Chelsea's new parish church because All Saints
had become too small. Charles Dickens married
here in 1836. Charles Kingsley, author of
Westward Ho! and *The Water Babies* was curate
at St Luke's in the mid-19C; his father had been
an early rector. Acoustically, the building is
outstanding and concerts are frequently
performed.

The walls of the church, supported by flying
buttresses, are panelled with Bath stone, a rarity
in London, where pollution has been unkind to
this relatively soft material.

•➡ Enter the church.

The **nave**, at 60ft, is higher than that of any other
parish church in London. Above the arcades run
a triforium and a clerestory.

At the west end is the old organ which retains
much of its original casing by *Nicholls*, 1824.
Displayed on this are the arms of George IV.
John Ireland, the composer, was an organist at
the church and played the instrument.

Below the organ loft are two sets of six stalls
made in 1824 for wardens and guardians. Their
modern canopies are of glass fibre.

Congregation box pews were removed in the late
19C and the chancel floor raised.

The pulpit was made in 1893 but the lectern is
modern.

Following bomb damage, the east window was
replaced.

The east end of the south aisle was adapted to
provide the **Punjab Chapel** in 1951 and objects
from a British Army church in India are
displayed.

The font, L of the exit, was made for St Luke's in
1826.

CLERKENWELL   ST JAMES   *Carr 1792*

Hayward's Place
(253 1568)

Farringdon Station,
Circle and
Metropolitan lines.
Exit R Farringdon
Rd. First R
Clerkenwell Rd.
Second L Clerkenwell
Green leads to
Aylesbury St. First L
Hayward's Place.

This elegant church has recently been restored
externally. An unusual curved gallery gives
added character.

The **steeple** is surmounted by an obelisk and is
similar to that of St Martin-in-the-Fields. It was
rebuilt as a replica in 1849.

•➡ Enter the vestibule from the south door.

Elegant stairs at the east and west ends lead to
the galleries.

The 18C(?) chandelier is in the Chinese style.

On the north wall is the monument to Thomas
Cross, d.1712, and his wife, Dorothy.

Ahead R, above the entrance to the nave, is the Hanoverian coat of arms.

The interior of the **nave** was mostly restored by *A. Blomfield* in 1882.

Unusually, the west end of the church is curved and this is emphasized by the **gallery** which curves with it.

The simple pulpit is original.

On the west wall of the **north aisle** is the monument to Elizabeth, Dowager Countess of Exeter, d.1653.

CLERKENWELL
PRIORY CHURCH OF ST JOHN

St John's Square
(253 6444)

*Open Tuesday,
Friday and Saturday,
11.00 and 14.30 as
part of the St John's
gatehouse guided tour
(telephone first).*

*Farringdon Station,
Circle and
Metropolitan lines.
Exit L Farringdon
Road. First L
Cowcross St. Second
L Peters Lane. First
L St John's Lane
leads to St John's
Square.*

The present church was built in 1956; however its original crypt, partly Norman and partly Early English, has survived.

The nave of the original 12C church was circular, like those of the Knights Templar, but it was destroyed by Wat Tyler's rebels in 1381. The **crypt** is from this building.

An outstanding 16C alabaster effigy of a Spanish knight lies at the east end of the crypt.

CRANFORD   ST DUNSTAN

Cranford Park
(897 8836)

**From Central
London:** *Paddington
Station (BR) to
Southall Station
(BR). Bus 195* from
Southall Station to
The Crane, North
Hyde Road. First L
Roseville Rd.
Continue ahead to the
footpath which leads
to Cranford Park; the
church lies ahead.*
**From Hayes,
St Mary:** *Bus 195 also
to The Crane,
proceed as above.*
**From Perivale,
St Mary:** *Return to
Perivale Lane L. First
L Argyle Rd; Bus 297
to Ealing Broadway.
Bus 207 to High St,*

Although so close to the M4 motorway, St Dunstan's, standing in the north-east corner of Cranford Park, has one of the prettiest settings of any church in the London area. In spite of its small size there are some excellent monuments within.

The church probably had a Saxon foundation but is first recorded in Domesday. It became the property of the Knights Templar and later, following their dissolution in 1312, was acquired by the Knights of St John who retained the church until the Reformation. St Dunstan's was rebuilt in the 15C and the chancel and most of the tower of this building survives. A fire in 1710 destroyed the nave and the upper part of the tower; these were rebuilt in 1716.

The flint and ragstone stages of the **tower** are 15C work but the 18C belfry is of brick.

Immediately to the north is the **vestry**, added in 1895.

•● *Proceed clockwise around the church.*

The **nave** was rebuilt entirely of brick following the fire.

Southall. Bus 195 to The Crane; proceed as above.

*The 195 service is infrequent and a taxi would be preferable.

Unfortunately the 15C **chancel** has been rendered with pebbledash.

On its north wall is an original door, re-opened in 1937, but once again blocked, because of vandalism.

The east window was remodelled in 1896 and placed off-centre.

Outside the east wall are the impressive carved arms of the Berkeley family.

The chancel's south window is original 15C work.

Surprisingly, there is also a blocked lancet window which appears to be mid-13C. Possibly this had been re-used, or perhaps part of the fabric of the wall pre-dates the 15C.

•● *Enter the church from the west door.*

The marble font is early 18C.

At the west end is the organ and choir **gallery**; it was built in 1936, replacing an earlier gallery that had been removed in 1895.

On the wall above is the funeral hatchment of the Earl of Berkeley.

The roof of the church was renewed in 1895.

Suspended from this are two leather banners, Crimean War trophies of the Berkeleys.

Most furnishings, including the pews, pulpit and lectern, were made in 1938.

Against the north wall of the **nave** is the monument to William Smythe, d.1720.

The north wall of the **chancel** is dominated by the monument to Sir Roger Aston, d.1613. It is the work of the King's master mason, *William Cure*. Aston served James I as Barber and Gentleman of the Bedchamber and Keeper of the King's Great Wardrobe. Life-size alabaster figures of Aston's two wives, four daughters and infant son are incorporated in the monument which was restored and relocated two feet further west in 1936. To accommodate the new position it was necessary to raise the height of the north wall at this point.

On the east wall of the **sanctuary** is the monument to Dr Thomas Fuller, d.1661, Chaplain to Charles I and Charles II. He was rector at St Dunstan's from 1658 until his death.

The sanctuary's black and white marble floor is 16C work.

Above the altar is a restored baldachino.

Fragments of a 15C fresco survive on the east wall at upper level.

On the south wall is the outstanding monument to Lady Elizabeth Berkeley, d.1635. This was made by **Nicholas Stone** in Rome, possibly in the studio of *Bernini*.

The nave's second large monument, on the south wall, commemorates Pelsant Reeves, d.1727 and his family. Much of its moving inscription was composed by Reeves, in appreciation of his late wife.

•➤ *Exit from the church.*

North of St Dunstan's are stables, all that remains of Cranford House, the manor house of Cranford St John, which was demolished in 1945.

EAST BEDFONT   ST MARY-THE-VIRGIN

The Green
(750 0088)

*Open daily
09.00–17.00.*

**From Central
London:** *Hounslow
West Station,
Piccadilly line. Cross
the road and take bus
203 to The Green,
Bedfont.*
**From Harlington,
St Peter and St Paul:**
*Bus 90B to Hatton
Cross and cross the
Great South West
Road. Bus 203;
proceed as above.*
**From Laleham, All
Saints:** *Bus 218 to
Staines. Bus 203;
proceed as above.*

St Mary's retains much early Norman work, including a doorway and chancel arch. Its two mid-13C wall paintings are amongst the finest in the country.

The church, founded in Saxon times, was rebuilt c.1150. This was shorter than the present structure and had, at its west end, a wooden bell-turret and spire. Extensions in the 19C almost doubled the size of the church but, of the ancient building, only the bell-turret and the nave's west and north walls were lost.

Apart from the brick extension on the north side, the church is built of ragstone.

Protruding from the south wall of the nave are the **tower** and **porch**; these, like the west end of the nave, were built as extensions in 1865.

•➤ *Proceed anti-clockwise around the church.*'

The south wall of the **nave** is early-Norman.

Immediately past the porch is a round-headed window, c.1150.

Next to this, the three-light cinquefoil window is 15C.

Projecting from the wall is an early-16C brick turret which once accommodated the stairs to the road loft.

Most of the south wall of the **chancel** is also early Norman.

The first two windows are 14C, the second being less restored.

These are followed by the chancel's doorway, formed in 1865.

East of this is the 15C extension to the chancel.

Its south and east windows are original, although the latter has been restored.

The north chancel wall begins with the 15C extension and is followed by Norman work, including an original window of c.1150.

North of this is the 19C vestry with, behind it to the west, the large north transept, added in 1829.

Further north is the brick meeting hall of 1954.

•➤ *Return to and enter the **south porch**.*

The original Norman doorway is a rare survival in the London area.

•➤ *Enter the **nave** and turn L.*

Against the south wall is a wooden Crucifixion

scene. It is Flemish, probably 16C, and belonged to the Empress Eugénie, consort of Napoleon III of France. The 19C westward extension to the nave follows.

Both north windows are modern.

● Return eastward.

It has been said that the long, narrow and aisleless interior resembles a typical parish church in northern England.

The 15C roof was rebuilt in 1964.

Sadly, the 19C pews were removed at the same time and replaced by the present incongruous chairs.

Although restored, the original chancel arch is a rare Norman example in the London area.

In the corner, north of the chancel arch, is a double recess, decorated with mid-13C Last Judgement and Crucifixion wall paintings. Their quality and condition are unsurpassed in England. The work, almost certainly lime-washed over at the Reformation, was rediscovered during the alterations of 1865.

● Enter the chancel.

On the north wall is a cartouche, believed to be the only surviving part of a monument to a 17C parishioner, John Hawes.

The Norman window in the north wall contains the only ancient stained glass in the church; it is 15C work and depicts flowers.

On the south wall, above the altar rail, is a small cavity fitted with a modern door. Within is carved stonework that probably formed part of the original piscina which would have stood in this position before the chancel was extended.

Against the southern section of the chancel's west wall is the monument of most interest in St Mary's; a wooden panel, painted with the arms of Thomas Weldish, d.1640.

EAST HAM   ST MARY MAGDALENE

High Street South
(470 0011)

From Central London: *East Ham Station. Bus 101 or S1 to Norman Rd.*
From Barking, St Margaret: *Barking Station to East Ham Station; proceed as above.*
From West Ham, All Saints: *Bus S1 to Norman Rd. Both stations are on the District and Metropolitan lines. The church is*

Standing in England's largest churchyard, now a nature reserve, St Mary's is one of the finest examples of a complete Norman church in the London area. Original Romanesque features include three windows, a well-preserved portal and an apse which retains its unique unrestored timber roof, *c.*1130.

The body of the church was constructed *c.*1130.

The **west porch**, now serving as a vestry, was built in the 19C.

● Proceed clockwise around the church.

The **tower** was added early in the 13C but rebuilt in the 16C. It is of stone with brick castellations.

The brick buttresses of the tower are 16C.

The round-headed first window on the north side of the **nave** is typically Norman.

approached from Norman Road and lies within the Passmore Edwards Nature Reserve.

Two larger windows that follow replaced Norman originals in 1845.

At the east end of the north wall of the **chancel** is the doorway to what was a hermit's cell.

The east apse is a rare Norman example to survive; most chancels were extended and squared off in the 13C. Its buttresses were constructed to support an internal vault.

On the south side of the chancel is a three-light 17C window.

The **nave**'s most easterly south window is 19C and replaced a 14C example which had itself replaced a Norman predecessor.

East of the restored south porch is the third Norman window.

The most westerly window is, again, a 19C replacement.

•● *The church must generally be viewed with a guide from the Passmore Edwards Museum and will probably be entered from the south porch. Turn L.*

Between the nave and the tower is the outstanding Norman **portal**. For a short time its west side faced the elements but the construction of the tower in the 13C, and its 16C replacement, has helped to preserve the mouldings.

Internal buttresses to the tower, in both west corners, were built in the 16C.

•● *Return eastward along the **nave**.*

Fixed to the pews on both sides of the nave's central alley are churchwardens' prickers, dated 1805. Parishioners lulled to sleep by the long sermons were awakened by a sharp jab.

The font, east of the south door, comprises a bowl of 1639 on a late-17C stem.

A blocked section of a Norman window survives, adjacent to the nave's third window from the west on the south side.

Against the south wall, at the east end, is the alabaster monument to William Heigham, d.1620, and his wife; this originally stood in the apse.

Behind the lectern is a blocked door with, below, a holy water stoup.

•● *Cross to the north wall of the **chancel**.*

Next to the pulpit is the staircase that once led to the rood loft.

Most of the chancel's north wall is blind-arcaded with a typical Norman interlaced design. This was repeated on the south wall opposite until mainly destroyed by the insertion of the 17C window.

The monument to Giles Breame, d.1621, is fixed to the north wall at upper level.

Below this is part of the early-16C opening to a hermit's cell.

Fixed to the arch of the apse is a Flemish painting of the Virgin, probably 16C.

Above the arch to the apse are traces of a medieval wall painting.

Fixed by wooden pegs, the unrestored Norman roof timbers, discovered in 1931, are a unique survival in England.

Evidence suggests that there was originally a stone vault which presumably collapsed at some time.

A large, early-17C alabaster monument commemorates Edmund Nevill, Lord Mortimer, and his family. Nevill claimed a right to the earldom of Northumberland, hence the coronet on his wife's head, but this was disputed.

Immediately south of the east window is a pilaster which would have supported the stone vault. Evidently there is another example on the north side, now hidden by the Nevill tomb.

On the south wall is a 13C double piscina.

This is followed by a 13C priest's door.

●● *Exit from the church.*

East Ham's churchyard of 9½ acres is reputedly the largest in England. It is now a nature reserve managed by the Passmore Edwards Museum.

ENFIELD ST ANDREW

Market Place

When closed telephone the caretaker (363 7491)

From Central London: *Moorgate Station East (BR) to Enfield Chase Station (BR). Exit R Windmill Hill. Ahead, Church St leads to Market Place.*

Enfield's parish church is basically late-medieval with a south aisle rebuilt early in the 19C. Some 13C work survives in the chancel and there are examples of ancient glass. Monuments include the outstanding Tiptoft brass.

St Andrew's was first recorded in 1136 and some Norman foundations survive. A church probably stood here in Saxon times. St Andrew's was completely rebuilt in Early English style in the 13C and almost completely rebuilt again in the 14C.

Immediately ahead, the 14C **south aisle** of the church was rebuilt of brick in 1824. It had been much lower than the late-15C north aisle and was heightened to match this and to accommodate a gallery.

●● *Turn L and proceed clockwise around the church.*

The **tower** is late 14C with most windows renewed.

Adjoining the tower L is the west wall of the **north aisle**. A modern doorway has been inserted in its wall.

●● *Proceed to the north side.*

The north aisle was rebuilt and probably heightened in the late 15C.

The clerestory of the **nave** wall behind may have been added at the same time but the windows were not glazed until 1522.

Between the first two windows of the aisle's north wall are traces of an earlier doorway, now blocked.

The tower's lower window on this side is an original 14C example; all others are relatively modern.

The **east turret** was built to accommodate a staircase which led to the rood screen loft.

Immediately past the turret, the north aisle of the **chancel** was rebuilt in 1530 to link with and match the recently rebuilt north aisle of the nave.

The **north porch** and **choir vestry** attached to it were added in 1867.

Forming the oldest external wall of the church is the central section of the **chancel's east wall**. It is 13C and, together with the chancel's south wall, was retained during the 14C rebuilding. Its present window was formed in 1873.

•● *Proceed to the south porch and enter the church.*

Both arcades are 14C.

•● *Turn L and proceed R to the corner of the* **nave**.

Carved alternately between the clerestory windows are 16C rosettes and wings, the emblems of Sir Thomas Lovell, minister of Henry VII and Henry VIII. Lovell, a benefactor of the church, provided the original glass for the clerestory windows.

•● *Proceed to the north wall of the* **north aisle**.

Above the entrance to the north chapel is a door which originally gave access from the outer staircase turret to the rood screen loft.

The doorway to the north chapel is believed to date from the rebuilding of 1531 and if so is the oldest still in use in the church.

Visitors may be shown the **north chapel** if convenient. Here, a chantry was founded at Enfield by Agnes Myddleton in 1471 for her parents, four husbands and herself. This was rebuilt in 1531, but the chantry was abolished, like all others, in 1547. It is now used as a vestry and is generally closed.

•● *Exit and continue eastward.*

The wall monument commemorates Robert Delcrowe, d.1586.

The monument to Martha Palmere by *Stone*, 1617, is on the north wall of the **sanctuary**.

In the north-east corner of the sanctuary stands the monument to Sir Nicholas Raynton, d.1646, and his family. Raynton was a Lord Mayor of London and built Forty Hall, which survives north of Enfield, and stands on the site of Henry VIII's Elsynge Hall which was demolished for it.

On the east wall is a breadshelf *c.*1640.

The altar tomb of Lady Jacosa Tiptoft, d.1446, on the south wall, is the most important monument in

St Andrew's. Its brass is outstanding and well-preserved. The canopy was added *c*.1530, probably to commemorate her grandchildren, Edmund and Isabel. Their father was Sir Thomas Lovell.

The 13C south wall of the chancel is contemporary with the east wall. It was originally an outer wall and its lancet window survives, although now unglazed. Traces of the sockets for the iron glazing bars can be seen.

The sedilia has recently been rebuilt.

All woodwork in the sanctuary is 19C.

•● *Proceed to the* **nave**.

The pulpit is 19C.

The chancel arch, enlarged in 1777, incorporates much 14C stonework. Around the arch, the Crucifixion scene was painted in 1923 as a First World War memorial.

Traces of a blocked doorway to the rood screen loft remain by the north side of the arch, below St George.

•● *Enter the* **Memorial Chapel** *in the south aisle of the chancel.*

A chantry chapel, dedicated to St James, was founded here by Baldwyn de Radington in 1398.

Ancient door jambs, recently discovered built into the 19C south wall of the south aisle, immediately R of the screen, probably formed part of the late-14C outer doorway to the chapel.

The blocked recess below the lancet window in the north wall, may have been a 'squint', from where the high altar could be observed. Its angle, however, has led many to dispute this.

L of the screen is the font.

Immediately R of the 'squint' is the Italian marble monument to Thomas Stringer, d.1706, by *Guelfi*, 1731.

Three 14C angel roof corbels survive on the north wall of the south aisle.

Two adjacent early-17C monuments in the south-east corner commemorate Francis Evington, d.1614, and Henry Middlemore, Groom of the Privy Chambers to Elizabeth I.

•● *Proceed westward along the* **south aisle** of the nave.

The third window from the east in the south aisle incorporates the oldest stained glass in the church. Arms of Thomas Roos, with T. R. and 1530, commemorate the first Earl of Rutland.

Below this, additional fragments of 16C stained glass, depicting 'eight nuns', are the remains of a window commemorating Sir Thomas Lovell.

The organ in the **west gallery** was built in 1753. Its

HACKNEY ST JOHN-AT-HACKNEY
Spiller 1797

Lower Clapton Road
(985 5374)

**From Central
London:** *Bethnal
Green Station,
Central line. Exit R
and cross Cambridge
Heath Road. Bus 106
or 253 to Dalston
Lane R Lower
Clapton Rd.*
**From Shoreditch, St
Leonard:** *Cross
Hackney Road, bus
35 or 55 to Dalston
Lane; proceed as
above.*
**From Stoke
Newington, St Mary:**
*Bus 73 to Stoke
Newington Common.
Bus 106 to Lower
Clapton Rd.*

This monumental, late-18C parish church was
damaged by fire in 1955 but its important Tudor
monuments, transferred from the earlier
building, have survived.

Seen to the south-west of St John's is the 16C
tower of St Augustine-of-Hippo, all that is left of
Hackney's original 13C parish church.

St John's **north porch** and **tower** which also,
unusually, faces north, were added in 1813.

The tower's Portland stone **spire** is of an eccentric
design.

Built in yellow London stock bricks, the body of
the church achieves a monumental quality
because of its great size; the wide eaves even
recall Hawksmoor.

➥ *It is probable that the church will be entered
from the south-east door. Turn L and proceed
towards the west end.*

St John's follows an unusual Greek cross plan.

The fire in 1955 destroyed much of the interior
and the roof was completely rebuilt.

The west **gallery** curves around both corners.

Pews in this gallery are the only original examples
in the church.

Below the gallery stands the late-18C marble
font.

Most furnishings and fittings were replaced in the
1880s. Surviving the 1955 fire is the huge pulpit.

Italian 17C candlesticks and a crucifix stand on
the altar within the **sanctuary**.

Behind is the 19C reredos which also survived the
fire.

Also in the sanctuary, on the south side, are the
sedilia and rector's stall which were made from
the remains of the carved 19C choir stalls.

Originally, the east window was flanked by two
others but these are now blocked.

➥ *Proceed to the **north-west lobby**.*

The reconstructed tomb chest of Lucy, Lady
Latimer, d.1583, bears an outstanding alabaster
effigy.

➥ *Continue to the **Urswick Chapel**, east of the
north porch.*

The tomb chest, with brass effigy of Christopher
Urswick, d.1522, rector of the earlier parish
church from 1502 until his death, was transferred
here from St Augustine's where it had served as
an Easter Sepulchre; it has recently been
redecorated. Urswick was Dean of St George's
Chapel, Windsor Castle; he gave generously
towards the cost of that building and is
commemorated there by the magnificent chapel
that he appropriated for his own chantry.

Recessed above Urswick's tomb is the bust commemorating David Doulbeu, Bishop of Bangor, d.1633.

Against the north wall stands the monument to Henry Bannister, d.1628; kneeling figures of his wife and children are featured.

The chapel's 18C altar, with its rail, was originally the high altar of the church.

●● *Exit from St John's and proceed to the north-west corner of the old churchyard, now gardens.*

Beneath a tiled roof is a portable whipping post/ducking stool of 1630.

HAREFIELD   ST MARY-THE-VIRGIN

Church Hill
(420 3221)

From Central London: *Uxbridge Station, Piccadilly line or Northwood Station, Metropolitan line. Bus 347 or 348 from either station to Church Hill, Harefield.*
From Uxbridge, St Margaret: *Bus 347 or 348; proceed as above.*

Incomparable! St Mary's medieval parish church is famed throughout the country for its monuments of outstanding artistic value. Great craftsmen whose works are represented include *Gibbons, Colt, Rysbrack* and *Bacon*.

First recorded in the Domesday Book, St Mary's was probably founded in Saxon times as a wooden building. This appears to have been rebuilt of stone in the 12C. Its chancel, as usual, was extended and a north chapel built in the 13C. The nave was mostly reconstructed and a south chapel added in the 14C. The tower was built, and the north aisle rebuilt early in the 16C. A south aisle was formed in the 19C by extending the south chapel westward. The Knights of St John had jurisdiction over the church from the 12C until the Reformation, but it was not until 1898 that St Mary's acquired parish church status.

Immediately ahead is the west front of the **tower**, built of flint early in the 16C. Its brick refacing and castellation is 17C work.

●● *Proceed clockwise around the church.*

The **north porch** was added in 1841.

Immediately east of this is a wall plaque commemorating Robert Mossendew, d.1744. He was employed by the Ashby family, apparently as a gamekeeper, and the tribute to him, composed by William Ashby, is surprisingly fulsome from a master to a servant.

The **north aisle** was built early in the 16C.

Rendering of the north wall of the church was a later addition.

A blocked lancet window in its north wall betrays the **chancel's** 13C origin.

Its east window was formed in 1768.

In the chancel's south wall is a blocked Perpendicular window.

When built, the 14C **south chapel** consisted of two bays faced with flint/limestone chequer work; this was extended westward by another two bays to form a south aisle in 1841.

A blocked 14C priest's door survives.

Attached to the south wall are remains of a mass dial, dated 1765.

Whilst the west wall of the **south aisle** is of brick, the adjoining west wall of the **nave** is of flint at lower level with brick above. Part of this extremely thick wall is believed to include 12C fabric and is therefore the oldest part of St Mary's.

●● *Continue to the north porch and enter the church.*

Most internal architectural features, including the arcades, are 14C.

Neo-Gothic style 18C box pews stand below the north-west gallery; there are similar examples at the east end of the nave.

Fronting the **gallery** are carved royal arms.

The ceiling of the **nave** is barrel-vaulted.

Funeral hatchments are displayed on the north and west walls of the nave (also on the north wall of the south aisle).

Restored figure-head corbels decorate the ends of the south arcade and the south windows.

The two east bays of the **south aisle** were built in the 14C to form the Brackenbury Chapel, in honour of the family that owned the manor at the time, but no monuments to them have been identified. In 1951 this became the **Australian Memorial Chapel** in honour of the 111 Australian soldiers who died at Harefield's temporary hospital during the First World War. They are buried in the churchyard.

The chapel's west wall was demolished when the south aisle was created in the 19C.

Early members of the Newdegate family, Lords of the Manor from the early 16C, were buried in a vault beneath and their monuments dominate both this chapel and the chancel. In the 17C their name was, for the first time, spelt Newdigate and from then on this form predominated, although not exclusively.

Below the second window from the east is a tomb chest, *c.*1500, with an unidentified occupant, possibly a Brackenbury.

Between the two most easterly windows is the oldest monument in the church, a small brass to Edith Newdegate, d.1444.

In the south-east corner is the brightly decorated monument to Sir John Newdegate, d.1610, by *William White.*

On the east wall is the tomb chest of John Newdegate, d.1528, and his wife Amphilisia, d.1544. Its brass illustrates their seventeen children.

Below this is a much restored 14C piscina with figure-corbels.

In the north-east corner is a marble monument to Sir Richard Newdigate, d.1678, by *William*

Stanton. He was Chief Justice during the Commonwealth but lost his position for refusing to find royalists guilty of high treason.

•● *Exit from the chapel.*

The 18C pulpit, a complete three-decker, is a rare survivor in London but, unfortunately, it has no canopy. The lowest section, a pew for the parish clerk, was not wide enough for him to kneel; this now serves as the lectern. Attached is the vicar's pew.

•● *Ascend the steps to the raised* **chancel**.

Major restoration of the chancel took place in 1768 when the arch from the nave was enlarged and the barrel-vault roof decorated with plaster Neo-Gothic panels. Beneath the floor is the family vault of the Newdigates.

On the south wall are examples of funeral armour: helms and gauntlets from the 15C to the 17C.

In three niches are urns with Classical figures commemorating female relatives of Sir Roger Newdigate. These are, from east to west: Sophia, his first wife, d.1774; Elizabeth, his mother, d.1765; Hester, his second wife, d.1800, by *Bacon junior*.

In a recess stands the tomb-chest of John Newdegate, d.1545, and his wife, Anne. The brass features them and their eight sons and five daughters. Although a space is left, the date of Anne's death is not recorded.

In the south-east corner is St Mary's most famous monument: the four-poster tomb of Alice Spencer, Countess of Derby, d.1637, almost certainly by *Maximilian Colt*. Kneeling figures in this highly decorative work represent her three daughters. The manor of Harefield had been purchased by the Countess in 1601 and remained in her family until 1675 when it became once more the property of the Newdigates' after an interlude of ninety years.

Standing outside the small sanctuary are two sumptuously carved chairs; these, together with the low altar rail and the reredos within the **sanctuary**, were presented to the church in 1840. They are all late-17C Flemish work and came, allegedly, from a monastery.

The carved angels on the reredos, that look up to the Commandment Boards of frosted glass, are believed to be 16C.

North of the altar, on the east wall, is the monument to Sir Richard Newdigate, d.1710 and his wife, Mary, d.1692. Mary's effigy is by *Gibbons*.

On the chancel's north wall are important monuments to three Newdigates. From east to west these are: Sarah, d.1695; Richard, d.1727, surmounted by a bust by *Rysbrack*; Edward, d.1734, probably also by *Rysbrack*.

Between Richard and Edward, at lower level is the 'Tree of Life' plaque, commemorating Charles Parker, d.1795, by *Bacon junior*.

●● *Return to the nave and ascend the steps R to the north Breakspear Chapel.*

The screen enclosing the chapel on its south and west sides, was made *c*.1500 but has been much restored.

The Breakspear family were known to have lived in Harefield in the 14C but none are commemorated in this chapel although it still bears their name. By tradition, they were descended from the only English pope, Nicholas Breakspear, who was elected Pope Adrian IV in 1154.

Set in the floor are two outstanding 16C palimpsests (re-used brasses) of members of the Ashby family and this is, in practice, their chapel. The Ashbys were local landowners from the mid-15C and possibly connected with the Breakspears by marriage.

Casts of the reverse sides of the palimpsests are mounted on the west section of the screen.

The earliest Ashby commemorated is George Ashby and his wife Margaret. Both died in 1474 and their brass is on the north wall.

Within the chapel are two chests and a brass chandelier presented in 1743.

Against the north wall, stands the late-17C parish chest with the usual three locks. On its face are carved the names of the churchwardens and the date 1691.

Above this is the outstanding alabaster monument commemorating Sir Robert Ashby, d.1617, and his wife. Below are their five sons and R the kneeling figure of their eldest son, Sir Francis, d.1623.

In the chapel's east window is a roundel of 16C glass which features the Ashby rebus of an ash tree and the letters 'BY'. Other roundels in the window are believed to be 16C Flemish work.

On the south wall is the monument to a curate of St Mary's, John Pritchett, d.1680 who is buried in the chapel. He became the incumbent of St Andrew Undershaft in the City of London but was dismissed by the Puritans because of his Royalist sympathies. At the Restoration, he regained his position at St Andrew's and became Bishop of Gloucester in 1672.

●● *Exit from the chapel.*

Against the **nave**'s north arcade, between the two most easterly arches, is a bust and a plaque commemorating William Ashby, d.1760, probably the work of *Sir Robert Taylor*. The family's punning rebus is again featured.

The font, beside the north door, appears to be mid-16C but its cover is mid-17C.

HARLINGTON   ST PETER AND ST PAUL

Harlington High
Street
(759 9569)

**From Central
London:** *Paddington
Station (BR) to Hayes
and Harlington
Station (BR). Bus
90B, 98 or 140 to the
White Hart,
Harlington High
Street.*
**From East Bedfont,
St Mary:** *Bus 203 to
Hatton Cross. Bus
90B; proceed as
above.*
**From Hayes,
St Mary:** *Cross
Church Rd. Bus 90B
or 98; proceed as
above.*

Harlington's ancient parish church retains many
Romanesque and Decorated Gothic features.
Outstanding is its south doorway, one of the
finest Norman examples in England.

St Peter and St Paul appears to have been
founded in the Saxon period, as Domesday
reports that the church then standing occupied
the site of an earlier structure. No evidence of the
11C building survives and it was probably of
wood. Complete rebuilding, using stone, took
place in the 12C and the chancel was again rebuilt
in the mid 14C.

•➡ *Approach the west face of the* **tower**.

The tower was added in the late 15C and its
doorway, window above and smaller belfry
windows are original.

•➡ *Proceed clockwise around the church.*

The tower's north-east turret is surmounted by an
18C cupola and weathervane.

Although added in 1880, the **north aisle**
incorporates some features from the original
north wall of the nave which were sensitively
re-used.

Its west wall is lit by a 15C window.

In the north wall of the aisle is a blocked
medieval doorway.

This is followed by a 12C round-headed window,
much restored.

The **chancel** was rebuilt and enlarged with,
unusually, a higher roof than the nave's, *c.*1340.

It retains original Decorated style windows on
the north and south sides.

The east window replaced a 17C example in 1895.

On the south side are two further 14C windows.

The south wall of the 12C **nave** retains its original
fabric.

East of the south porch is a 15C window.

The **porch** was built in the 16C but has been
reconstructed and its low level brickwork is
modern.

West of the porch is a 12C window.

•➡ *Enter the porch.*

The south doorway is one of London's finest
Norman examples. It is in excellent condition and
displays, in addition to the usual dogtooth
pattern, an unusual frieze of cats' heads.

•➡ *Enter the nave and turn L.*

Beneath the tower, in the **baptistry**, is the
Purbeck marble font, *c.*1190, presumably made
for the church.

A gallery was erected at the west end of the nave
in 1842 but this was removed, together with

box pews, during the restoration of 1880. It was mainly due to the loss of seating in the gallery that the north aisle was built.

At the same time, the 14C(?) trussed-rafter roof of the **nave** was revealed by the removal of plaster and the present arch to the chancel built.

Displayed on the central window-sills of the **north aisle** are two holy water stoups.

In this aisle's east wall is an early-16C doorway which now leads to the vicar's vestry.

The north-west window of the church was blocked by an organ between 1880 and 1962.

Against the north wall of the **chancel** is a recess with an elaborate early-16C canopy that once formed an Easter Sepulchre.

Within a recess in the north wall of the sanctuary is the tomb chest of Henrietta Fane (date unknown).

Against the same wall is the recumbent figure of Jane, Countess of Salis, d.1856, by *R. C. Lucas*.

Opposite, against the south wall, is a similar monument to her husband, Jerome de Salis, d.1836, also by *R. C. Lucas*.

In the apex of the east window are fragments of 17C glass from its predecessor.

Brass effigies on the chancel's south wall were brought here from the Easter Sepulchre opposite. They represent Gregory and Anne Lovell and were made in 1545. It is believed that this is the Gregory Lovell who was a member of the jury that tried Sir Thomas More.

On the south wall of the **nave**, beside the pulpit, is a mid-14C carved bracket which, in the 18C, was used to hold the hourglass that timed sermons. It may originally have supported a candle.

East of the south door is the monument to Sir John Bennett, Lord Ossulstone, d.1686, and his two wives; their busts are judged exceptional.

HARMONDSWORTH   ST MARY

High Street
(759 1652)

From Central London: *Paddington Station (BR) to West Drayton Station (BR) Bus 223 to Hatch Lane (north end). Follow the High St to the church.*
Alternatively: *Heathrow Central Station, Piccadilly line. Bus 223; proceed as above.*
From Uxbridge, St Margaret: *Bus*

This Gordian knot of a church is, basically, a rare example of the brief Transitional period, when Romanesque and Gothic merged. Many original features survive, including an outstanding Norman doorway. Also of great interest is St Mary's unusually large set of medieval pews. An attractive rural setting adds much to its charm.

Even for an ancient parish church, the evolution of St Mary's is complex. First recorded in 1087, earthworks, discovered west of the present building, may be connected with a Saxon predecessor. On the existing site, St Mary's has known five major building periods and evidence of each one survives. In the 11C, a tower and, in line with it, an aisleless nave and probably a small apsidal chancel were built on part of the site. In

223; proceed as above.
From Harlington, St Peter and St Paul:
Bus 140 to Heathrow. Bus 223; proceed as above.

the 12C, north and south aisles were added. Between the late 12C and early 13C the church was enlarged and relocated slightly further north in the following way. The external south wall was demolished, the south arcade was replaced by a new external south wall, the north arcade was retained to serve as the south arcade, the external north wall was adapted to become the north arcade, a new external north wall was built and a larger chancel was added to the re-formed nave. Towards the end of the 14C, a chapel was built on the north side of the chancel and the north aisle and chancel were extended eastward to link with it.

In the 14C, St Mary's was the property of Holy Trinity Abbey in Rouen, France; however, Edward III confiscated the estate in 1340. It was granted to William of Wykeham, Bishop of Winchester, by Richard II in 1389 as an endowment to his recently founded Winchester College.

Surmounting the **tower**, which was rebuilt in the 15C, is an early-18C cupola. The lower part of the tower evidently retains some masonry from the 11C building but it is entirely faced with brick and thus contrasts with the flint body of the church.

•● *Proceed anti-clockwise around the church.*

Adjoining the tower is the **south porch**, mostly restored in the 19C.

The Norman **south doorway** is an elaborate example but the lack of symmetry in its design indicates that it has been re-used, presumably from the earlier building. It possibly formed the original tower's west entrance portal.

The oak door is 19C.

On the wall of the **south aisle**, R of the doorway, is a sundial, believed to be Saxon.

Windows in this late-12C wall were altered, probably from lancets, *c*.1400, and although restored, retain their Perpendicular form.

It has been suggested that the window decorations on the south wall of the **chancel** may depict Henry VII.

St Mary's large east window dates from the chancel's extension, *c*.1400.

The two windows of the late-14C **north chapel** also received their tracery, *c*.1500.

Lancet windows survive in the early 13C wall of the **north aisle**.

The west window of the **nave** was rebuilt in the 19C.

•● *Enter the church and proceed to the west end of the* **north aisle**.

The arcaded wall of the north aisle was built in the 12C, originally as the solid external north wall of the church. Its 12C piers and arches, inserted early in the 13C, came from the original south arcade which had stood on the site of the present south wall.

The combination of pointed arches and rounded piers are the hallmark of the Transitional period. Capitals and bases of the piers were altered, before their re-erection, to fit the current style, which is why they now appear different from their counterparts in the south aisle.

The eastern section of the north arcade was erected *c.*1400 when the aisle was extended to provide a small chantry chapel.

A clumsy, Early English join with Perpendicular is exhibited in the north-east arch of the arcade.

St Mary's set of low congregation pews, *c.*1500 is most rare, and those in the north aisle are of particular interest. Some of the other pews, however, were made to match in the 19C.

In the **north chapel**, partly obscured by the organ, is a hammerbeam roof, erected when the chapel was remodelled in the 16C.

Remains of an early-16C piscina survive in the south wall.

When built in the late 14C, the chapel could only be entered from outside the church, but the wall that it shared with the chancel was opened up *c.*1400.

●→ *Proceed to the* **nave**.

The nave's tie-beam roof was probably built by *William of Wykeham* in the late 14C.

The **chancel** was extended eastward and its arch removed, *c.*1500.

Its roof was rebuilt and heightened in the 19C.

Floor tiles were laid in 1919.

On the south wall are a piscina and a sedilia, *c.*1500.

The arcaded south wall of the **nave** probably retains some late-11C stonework as it originally formed the outer south wall of the Norman church. Pointed arches and rounded piers were inserted when it was converted in the 12C.

The bases of the piers on this side have been refaced with cement and their original design is uncertain.

As is often the case with extended churches, the **south aisle** is narrower than its northern counterpart.

In the south wall, just before the doorway, is the restored top section of a 15C holy water stoup.

The base of the tower houses the **baptistry**.

On the north wall, at upper level, are traces of a 12C arch.

The font has a 12C Purbeck marble bowl but its base is modern.

HARROW ST MARY

Church Hill

Closed Monday.
Apply in writing to
make brass rubbings.

From Central
London: *Harrow-on-*
the-Hill Station,
Metropolitan line
(Amersham,
Chesham or Watford
direction). At the
barrier turn L and
descend the steps.
Ahead Station
Approach. L
Lowlands Rd. Follow
the footpath uphill
through the green R.
At the end turn L and
follow the path to the
terrace.
From Pinner,
St John: *Return to*
Pinner Station,
Underground to
Harrow-on-the-Hill
Station; proceed as
above.

Although the 19C flint facing to the body of the church gives St Mary's a Victorian appearance, it is basically a medieval structure and part of its tower was built in the late 11C. John Lyon, who refounded Harrow School in 1572, is commemorated by a brass and a monument. It has been suggested the famous school had its origins in the small 14C room above the south porch of the church.

Harrow belonged to the Archbishops of Canterbury from 825 until the estate was seized by Henry VIII in 1545. Much of it was then granted to Sir Edward North. The name Harrow is believed to derive from the Saxon word *hergae* meaning a temple or shrine. However, there is no record of a church on the site in Saxon times. Earliest information available refers to the church consecrated by St Anselm in 1094.

The lower stages of the **tower** are all that survive from the 11C building.

The upper stage, together with the spire, was added in the mid 15C.

The tower's west portal, south window and north windows (seen later) are Romanesque.

Above the west portal is a small lancet window.

South of the tower, an upright black stone commemorates Thomas Port. Its inscription refers to his death in 1838 after being struck by a train.

●● *Proceed anti-clockwise following the south side of the church.*

The **nave** was rebuilt c.1235. It was heightened in the mid 15C when the clerestory was added in Perpendicular style. At the same time the aisle windows were remodelled.

Battlements were added and the body of the church refaced in flint by *George Gilbert Scott* in 1849.

●● *Continue towards the south porch.*

A floor was added in the 14C, thus dividing internally the high late-12C **south porch** to provide an upper level **parvise** (priest's room or chapel). At the same time the porch was also remodelled externally and gargoyles were added.

The outer doorway of the porch has been renewed.

●● *Continue eastward.*

It is believed that the **south transept** was erected, like the north transept, when the nave was rebuilt in the 13C.

Although the **chancel** was built in the late 12C, only its south wall survives from this period as *Gilbert Scott* rebuilt the remainder in 1849 when he restored the church.

The lancet windows on this wall had been blocked but were opened up and restored in 1893.

Figure-corbels and gargoyles, probably 14C, decorate much of the exterior of St Mary's.

Continue anti-clockwise to the north side of the chancel.

The chancel's **north chapel** and the **north porch** were added by *Gilbert Scott* in 1849.

A north **vestry** was built in 1908.

The **north transept**, like the south, is believed to be late 13C.

Two further Romanesque windows survive on this side of the tower.

Although stonework is now exposed at the tower's lower level, it is believed that this part of the church has always been rendered.

Enter the church from the south porch.

The tie-beam roof was constructed in the mid 15C when the nave was heightened for the new clerestory.

Its twelve wall posts, carved to represent the apostles, are supported by grotesque head-corbels.

Immediately L, the **south aisle** wall has been stripped of rendering to reveal its 13C stonework.

Steps L of the door lead to the **parvise** which may be viewed, with an attendant, if convenient.

When conversion took place in the 14C, probably to provide a chantry chapel, two round-headed windows were blocked and the present 14C window added. The outline of the east window is clear.

On the east wall, a carved niche probably supported a statue of the Virgin.

Traces of 14C decoration survive.

*Return to the **south aisle** L.*

The early-13C Purbeck marble font, discarded in 1800, was retrieved from a local garden in 1846.

*Proceed to the **tower**.*

From the tower it can be seen that some columns in the nave are set at angles, indicating settlement. As their capitals are horizontal, work may have been halted until the settlement ended.

In the tower's Romanesque south window L, modern stained glass depicts John Lyon, the founder of the present Harrow School.

Stained glass in the tower's Romanesque north window, also modern, depicts Archbishop Lanfranc.

*Proceed eastward following the **north aisle**.*

L of the north door is the monument to Lord North by *Hopper* 1831.

The late-12C north door was originally the external door of the south porch. It was presumably transferred here in the 14C following the remodelling of the porch.

The most easterly arch of the north aisle arcade is incomplete; the reason for this is a mystery.

Figure corbels supporting the **north transept** arch from the crossing have been dated 1236. This may, therefore, be the approximate completion date of the present nave and transepts.

● Proceed to the north transept's west pier.

On the south side is the brass commemorating John Lyon, d.1592, and his wife. It was taken from the original floor slab and fixed here in 1880.

Above is Lyon's monument by *Flaxman* 1813.

On the east wall of the north transept are alabaster fragments from the tomb of William Gerard, d.1609, and his sister.

*● Proceed to the **nave**.*

In front of the lectern is the white floor slab made in 1880 to mark the burial place of John Lyon.

The pulpit, *c.*1675, was acquired in 1708. Its tester is of a later date.

On the north wall of the **chancel**, L of the aisle, is the monument to James Edwards, d.1816. He was a bookseller and it is recorded that his coffin was made, at Edward's request, from his library shelves.

The reredos is by *Webb c.*1908.

Glass in the east window was designed by *Comper*, also *c.*1908.

Some of the splays (angled sides) of the lancet windows on the south wall of the chancel retain original, late-13C decorations. Chevrons are believed to be *c.*1400. The stained glass was made in 1893 when the windows were unblocked.

The **south transept's aisle** is believed to be late 12C. If so, this would indicate that the earlier nave also had transepts.

To the L of the transept's east window are traces of an earlier window, possibly a double lancet.

On the west wall is the monument to Joseph Drury by *Westmacott*, 1835.

Just before the south door is a chest, *c.*1200.

HAYES   ST MARY-THE-VIRGIN

Church Green (off Church Road)
(573 2470)

From Central London: *Paddington Station (BR) to Hayes and Harlington Station (BR). Cross the road. Bus 90B, 98 or 195 to Church Road (north end).*
From Cranford, St Dunstan: *Bus 195; proceed as above.*
From Harlington,

St Mary's, described by the late Sir John Betjeman as 'one of the gems of Middlesex', possesses a huge wall painting of St Christopher and a 'lich-gate', both dating from the early 16C. Its chancel retains 13C features.

A Saxon church on the site is first recorded in 830 when the Manor of Hayes was bequeathed to Canterbury Cathedral; Canterbury maintained close ties with St Mary's until the Reformation. The church was presumably rebuilt of stone during the Norman period but there are no records or Romanesque elements surviving. As usual, the chancel was rebuilt and enlarged in the 13C, the tower and north aisle were added in the 15C and the south aisle, with its porch, in the 16C.

St Peter and St Paul:
Bus 90B or 98;
proceed as above.
From Hillingdon,
St John (or Uxbridge,
St Margaret): *Bus 207*
to Church Road,
Hayes. Cross
Uxbridge Road;
Church Road runs
southward R.

St Mary's is approached through its picturesque early-16C **gate**. This is known generally as a 'lich-gate' although technically it is a tapsell gate, as the central section originally swung; a lich-gate has a fixed bench in the centre. Tapsell gates are extremely rare and probably not more than half a dozen exist in England.

●● *Approach the west face of the* **tower**.

The flint and ragstone tower is 15C but its battlement is modern.

The tower's west door and window above have been restored.

Oak panelling from the parish church of Stratford-upon-Avon was installed in the west porch in 1893.

●● *Proceed anti-clockwise around the church.*

The flint **south aisle** and its much restored **porch** were added early in the 16C.

At the east end of the south aisle is a blocked priest's door.

The most easterly window in the 13C **chancel's** flint south wall is 14C.

The large Perpendicular window in the chancel's east wall probably replaced triple lancets in the 15C.

Original lancets, however, survive in the chancel's north wall.

The ragstone and flint north wall of the 15C **north aisle** retains partly restored, original windows.

Its door has been entirely restored.

In the west wall of the north aisle is an early-15C window.

The north-west **vestry** was added by *George Gilbert Scott* in 1873 as part of his restoration work.

●● *Enter the church from the north door.*

Although the north aisle is 15C and the south aisle is 16C the piers of both are octagonal.

At the west end of the **north aisle** is the outstanding stone font, *c.*1200; its 19C wooden cover is probably the work of *Scott*.

In the north aisle are unrestored figure-corbels; an exceptional foliated head is at the west end.

The aisle's tie-beam roof is original.

The west screen, between the base of the tower and the choir stalls, was made up from existing woodwork in the church which probably once formed chapel screens.

Bosses in the early-16C waggon roof of the **nave** feature the arms of England and Aragon, Spain; the latter in deference to Henry VIII's consort, Katherine of Aragon.

During the 19C restoration, tie-beams were removed from the roof causing the walls to splay; metal ties were hastily added.

The 16C **south aisle** also possesses a tie-beam roof.

At the east end of the south wall is the tomb chest of Thomas Higate, d.1576, and his wife, Elizabeth; its brass illustrates their nine children.

The 15C waggon roof of the **chancel** partly extends over the nave.

An armoured demi-figure, on the south wall of the **sanctuary**, commemorates Edward Fenner, d.1615.

Also on the south wall are the original sedilia and piscina.

On the east wall is an aumbry.

In the floor of the sanctuary a very early brass commemorates Robert Lellu, d.*c*.1370.

Against the north wall of the sanctuary is the recumbent figure of Sir Edward Fenner, d.1612; he was a barrister and the father of Edward, commemorated oppposite.

●● *Proceed to the east end of the north aisle.*

This became the **Lady Chapel** when the organ was relocated after the Second World War.

Its east window commemorates the coronation of Elizabeth II.

There are traces of medieval wall painting.

The tomb chest of Sir Walter Grene, d.1456, commemorates a Lord of the Manor of Hayes.

In the centre of the wall of the **north aisle** is the pride of St Mary's, a large wall painting of St Christopher, probably executed *c*.1500. It was customary to paint this saint facing the main door so that he could easily be seen by passers-by as well as worshippers. This was because many believed that if they saw his effigy they were protected that day from unforeseen death.

An important event in the history of Hayes parish church has been strangely ignored by all other guide books – on 16 March 1963 it witnessed the marriage of the author of this book.

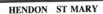

HENDON   ST MARY

Church End
(203 4673)

From Central London: *Hendon Central, Northern line. Exit R Watford Way. Second R the Boroughs leads to Church End.*
From Kilburn, St Augustine: *Bus 32 to Broadway. Cross the road. Bus 183 to Church End, Hendon.*
From Little Stanmore, St Lawrence: *Bus 186 to Church End, Hendon.*

Hendon's parish church is a combination of 13C and 20C buildings, virtually two churches in one. It is a place of pilgrimage for those who have connections with Singapore, as Sir Stamford Raffles, founder of the country, is buried here.

St Mary's existed in the mid-12C but was rebuilt in the 13C and its north aisle, together with the original nave and chancel, survive. The west tower was added in the 15C and the north chapel in the 16C. However, in 1915, the original south aisle was demolished and its place taken by a new nave with its own chancel and south aisle, all designed by *Temple Moore*. The north section of the church is, therefore, of greater historic interest.

●● *Approach the west **tower**.*

The 15C tower's clock is 18C.

●● *Proceed clockwise around the church.*

Although the north aisle and the old chancel are
13C no original features remain externally.

In the east wall of the old **chancel** is a 15C window.

•➡ *Continue to the **south aisle**.*

At the west end of the south wall, built *c*.1915, a
14C window from the original south aisle's east
end has been re-used.

•➡ *Enter the south aisle from the south porch and
turn L.*

In the north corner of the **new nave's** west wall is
a buttress with traces of Norman carving; this
marks the line of the original south wall.

In the **baptistry**, at the base of the tower, is the
Norman font, *c*.1150.

The **old nave** retains its tie-beam roof.

On the north wall, before the entrance to the north
chapel, are remains of the painted arms of James I.

At the west end of the north wall of the **north
chapel** is the monument to Sir William
Rawlinson, d.1703.

Towards the east end is a Baroque monument to
Edward Fowler, Lord Bishop of Gloucester,
d.1714.

In the south bay is the black, Flemish marble
tomb chest of Sir Jeremy Whichcot, d.1677.

On the north side, beside the arch of the **old
chancel**, is the blocked entrance to the rood loft.

The old chancel's arch was renewed in 1827.

Traces of a 13C arcade survive on both sides of
the original **sanctuary.**

The 15C east window pierces an original 13C
arch, part of which is now exposed.

In the south wall is a 16C window jamb.

Below is part of the medieval piscina.

Against the south pier of the old chancel's arch is
the tomb of Sir Charles Colmore, d.1795, by
Flaxman.

A tablet on this pier commemorates Sir Stamford
Raffles, d.1826.

•➡ *Proceed to the **chancel** of the new church.*

Raffles, the founder of Singapore (and London
Zoo), is buried in St Mary's and his burial stone is
in the floor of the new chancel, by the north pier.

The hangings and posts of the high altar in the
new sanctuary were designed by *Comper*.

HILLINGDON   ST JOHN-THE-BAPTIST

Uxbridge Road
(0895 33932)

**From Central
London (or Uxbridge,
St Margaret):**
Uxbridge Station,

St John's was extended eastward in the 19C but
its medieval nave and aisles survive. The mid-13C
chancel arch, with grotesque corbels, is one of
London's finest Early English examples. A 17C
monument, which unusually combines kneeling
and standing figures, is of great historic interest.

Piccadilly line. Bus 207 to the Red Lion, Hillingdon. Cross Uxbridge Rd to the church.
From Hayes, St Mary: *Follow Church Rd L to Uxbridge Rd. Bus 207 to the Red Lion, Hillingdon; proceed as above.*

Although referred to in Domesday, there is no trace of the church that preceded the mid-13C building and it may, therefore, have been of wood. The 13C nave remains, but not its chancel. Aisles were added in the 14C and these also survive, although much restored externally. A medieval tower existed but no details of its construction are known; it was replaced in 1629. At the east end, the nave was extended and a new chancel and transepts were built by *George Gilbert Scott* in 1848. The north vestries were added in 1964.

The knapped flintwork of St John's exterior largely disguises the many periods in which the building evolved.

•● *Approach the west* **tower**.

Surmounting the castellated tower, rebuilt in 1629 and dated at the top of its west face, is a late-17C(?) cupola.

The original stone jambs of the west door were discovered and restored in 1901.

All windows in the 14C **north aisle** were rebuilt in 1848.

•● *Proceed anti-clockwise to the west wall of the* **south aisle**.

Although, like its north counterpart, this aisle was built in the 14C, it is of slightly earlier date.

The west doorway is the only external medieval feature in the body of the church to survive. At one time this was protected by a 17C porch and formed the main entrance, but the porch was demolished in the early 19C.

•● *Continue to the south wall, enter the* **south aisle** *and turn L.*

The octagonal columns of the 14C arcade have been partly restored.

Although the king-post roof is original, the panelled ceiling is more recent work.

At upper level, from the position of the nave's west gallery which was removed *c.*1908, rises an oak staircase made in 1629.

Against the south aisle's north pier, at the west end, is the Lestrange brass, one of the most famous in London. It illustrates Lord John L'Estrange of Knocking and his wife, Jaquetta. Jaquetta was the sister of Edward IV's consort, Elizabeth Woodville, mother of the 'Princes in the Tower'. The brass, which was originally fixed to the top of the Lestranges' tomb chest (now lost), was commissioned by their daughter, Joanna, in 1509.

At the west end of the **nave**, against its south wall, is the monument to Thomas Lane d.1795, by *Bacon*.

The nave's king-post roof was constructed in 1848 and dormer windows were added to increase the light in 1901.

Oak pews in the church date from the 19C restoration.

The **north aisle**'s 15C timber roof is supported by stone corbels, carved as busts.

Octagonal columns of the 14C north arcade have been partly restored.

At the west end, the font is 19C.

As part of the modifications by *Scott* the **nave** was extended eastward, swallowing up the small mid-13C chancel, and a new chancel and transepts were built.

Fortunately, the original chancel arch was kept, although repositioned in 1848 and again in 1902. This was made *c*.1260 and is one of London's finest Early English examples. Its shafts are carved with stiff leaf capitals, that on the north side being unrestored.

Corbels supporting the arch are carved with small monsters and grinning heads sticking out their tongues.

The 19C waggon roof of the **chancel** was painted in 1953, based on the 14C decoration of the church at Palgrave, Norfolk.

On the north wall of the **sanctuary**, repositioned of course, is the tomb chest of Henry Paget, Earl of Uxbridge, d.1743, by *Cheere* (?).

Facing this, on the south wall, is the unusual monument to Sir Edward Carr, d.1675, and his wife, Jane. It includes an extremely late example of kneeling figures, the Carrs, but an early example of two standing figures, their daughters, who appear to be about to walk away from the tomb chest.

HOLBORN ST ETHELDREDA *c.1300*

Ely Place

Chancery Lane Station, Central line

St Etheldreda's was built as a private chapel to Ely House, the late-13C London residence of the Bishops of Ely. The building is a rare London example of the Decorated style and its window tracery is exceptional.

John of Gaunt moved to Ely House when his Savoy Palace was destroyed by Wat Tyler's rebels in 1381 and died there in 1399. Christopher Hatton, a favourite of Elizabeth I, acquired much of the estate in the 16C when the house and its famous gardens were divided by order of the Queen, between him and the Bishop. Two of Shakespeare's plays refer to Ely House. John of Gaunt makes his famous 'This sceptred isle' speech here in *Richard II*, and in *Richard III* the Duke of Gloucester requests strawberries from the gardens. The house became the Spanish Embassy in the 17C but was demolished in 1772. All that remains is St Etheldreda Church, built as the Bishops' chapel. It is Britain's oldest existing Catholic church and reverted to the faith in 1879. Roman masonry has been found in the fabric and, traditionally, a 3C church stood nearby.

The east gable is dominated by the intricate,

early Decorated window tracery. Originally, there were pinnacles on either side.

●● *Enter the church through the porch of the adjoining house L. (Ring the bell if the door is closed.)*

The corridor was once an open cloister. Here, by tradition, Henry VIII was introduced to Thomas Cranmer whom he later appointed Archbishop of Canterbury.

●● *At the end of the corridor descend the steps R to the* **undercroft**.

The windows have been renewed but all the east end L are blocked 13C examples. All the piers were renewed in the 19C.

●● *Ascend the steps and turn R. Ascend further steps to the upper church.*

On the wall L is the Stuart coat of arms.

●● *Enter through the door R to the upper church.*

The church was much restored by *George Gilbert Scott* in 1874 and again, following the Second World War. Its early Decorated window tracery has been judged some of the finest in existence. The stained glass is modern.

HOLBORN   ST GILES-IN-THE-FIELDS
Flitcroft 1733

St Giles High Street

Tottenham Court Road Station, Central and Northern lines or Holborn Station, Central and Piccadilly lines.

This is the most important work in London by Flitcroft, the Palladian Revival disciple of Lord Burlington.

St Giles's was established in 1101 as the chapel of a monastic leper hospital founded by Queen Matilda, consort of Henry I. It is dedicated to the patron saint of outcasts. A village soon grew up around the hospital and by 1200 its chapel was also being used by the villagers. Following the Reformation, the chapel became the parish church. St Giles's was rebuilt in 1630, but London's Great Plague broke out nearby in November 1664 and so many were buried in its churchyard that the building was structurally damaged,. The present church was commissioned under the Fifty New Churches Act of 1711 and Flitcroft won the architectural competition against Gibbs and Hawksmoor. Prisoners on their way from Newgate to Tyburn for execution were charitably offered a soporific drink from the 'St Giles Bowl' as they passed by. The bodies of many were soon returned to the churchyard for burial. Sir John Oldcastle, allegedly the prototype of Shakespeare's Falstaff, was burnt to death at the stake nearby in 1417. Famous men buried in St Giles's churchyard include Oliver Plunket, the Bishop of Armagh who was murdered in 1661, painter Godfrey Kneller, 1723, and architect Sir John Soane, 1823. Actor David Garrick married in the church in 1749.

The **tower** rises immediately above the west front, as at St Martin-in-the-Fields, but here there is no portico. 'Flitcroft', the architect's name, is prominently carved below the pediment.

Facing the west door is the 'Resurrection Arch' made in 1800, and so-called because it originally incorporated a wooden 'Day of Judgement' lunette made for the tympanum of St Giles's lich-gate in 1687; this was replaced with a facsimile in 1986. The arch stood in St Giles High Street on the north side of the church until 1865.

•● *Enter the* **north porch**.

On the wall L, the monument to Flaxman, d.1826, was erected by the Royal Academy in 1930. It is a cast of one of his own works.

•● *Continue ahead to the* **rotunda**.

Flitcroft's original model of St Giles's is displayed.

The iron ecclesiastical chest in the **south porch**, made in 1630, is believed to be continental.

It is probable that the original 'Day of Judgement' lunette will eventually be displayed above the doorcase. The design is based on Michelangelo's painting in the Sistine Chapel, Rome.

On the north wall of this porch is the tomb slab of Richard Pendrell, d.1671, brought here from the churchyard in 1922. Pendrell helped the future Charles II escape from the Puritans during the Civil War by hiding him in an oak tree and later in his home.

The mosaic on the west wall by *Watts* was brought here from St Giles's School in 1947.

•● *Proceed to the* **nave**.

St Giles's interior, although modified in the 19C, is little changed and evokes that of St Martin-in-the-Fields.

The largest of the four brass chandeliers is believed to have been made in 1680; the others are 18C.

The west **gallery** bears the arms of George III.

Its organ with its case, made in 1734 by *Schmidt*, have been restored.

At the west end of the **north aisle**, the monument to George Chapman, d.1634, was reputedly designed by the poet's friend *Inigo Jones*. Chapman translated Homer into English.

The white pulpit, at the east end of the aisle, came from the West Street Chapel. It was originally the top section of a three-decker pulpit from which both John and Charles Wesley preached 1743–91.

The pulpit in the nave was made for the previous church in 1676.

In the **sanctuary**, on either side of the original reredos, are paintings of Moses and Aaron by *Francisco Vieira the Younger,* court painter to the King of Portugal.

At the west end of the south aisle is a rare Greek-style font made in 1810, probably by *Soane*, who was a parishioner. Its cover was made in 1952.

HORNCHURCH ST ANDREW

High Street

Open Monday–
Friday 09.30–12.00
and 14.00–16.00.
(04024 41571)

From Central
London: *Upminster*
Bridge Station . Exit L
and proceed to High
St.
From Barking,
St Margaret: *Barking*
Station to Upminster
Bridge Station;
proceed as above.
Both stations are on
the District line.

St Andrew's, with its needle spire, is a fine
example of the Perpendicular style. Surmounting
the east wall is the famous horned bull's head that
gave Hornchurch its name.

By tradition, a Saxon church existed here, but
St Mary's is first recorded in 1163. This building is
believed to have occupied the site of the present
north aisle but no trace remains. Complete
rebuilding took place in the mid-13C to provide an
aisled nave and a chancel. The tower was added
c.1400 shortly after William of Wykeham had
acquired the church. St Andrew's stood on land
that had been owned by the Priory of Havering
until confiscated by Richard II, and Wykeham
purchased the estate from the Crown as an
endowment for New College which he had
founded at Oxford. St Andrew's was, therefore, a
'Peculiar' and outside the jurisdiction of the
bishops; as recently as 1683 an archdeacon was
refused entry. New College still appoints
St Andrew's chaplains but not its incumbent, as
the church is now part of the Chelmsford Diocese.
Both aisles were rebuilt c.1500.

St Andrew's is approached through a lich-gate
built c.1918.

The **tower**, like most of the church, is constructed
of flint and ragstone. It is believed to have been
built c.1400 by *William of Wykeham* as it
resembles the tower of his New College, Oxford.

On the top of its west face, the south-west turret is
embellished by the figure of a bishop, probably
Wykeham, who was Bishop of Winchester.

The needle spire of St Andrew's once served as a
navigational aid to Thames shipping and Trinity
House subscribed towards its upkeep.

It appears that although the west doorway has
been renewed, its ancient door is original.

All windows throughout the church are in the
Perpendicular style.

•► *Proceed clockwise.*

The north doorway and its door are original to the
rebuilding of the **north aisle** c.1500.

Incorporated in the north aisle's wall, as an
unusual building material, are black bottles.

Perpendicular clerestory windows were added to
the nave, probably when the aisles were rebuilt.

No 13C details remain on the **chancel's** exterior.

Surmounting the apex of its east wall's gable is
St Andrew's famous horned bull's head that gave
Hornchurch its name. A horned church was first
referred to in 1222 but not until 1610 was it
recorded that horns (of lead) were fixed to the east
wall of the church. The bull's head was repaired in
1824, when its horns were found to be made of
copper, indicating that the head of 1610 had been
replaced. Its significance is unknown but there
may be a heraldic or even a pagan origin.

The east window was reconstructed after bomb damage.

Unlike the rest of the church, the **south aisle**, rebuilt *c*.1500, is constructed of brick.

Fixed to the south wall's second bay from the east is the top of the original west doorway.

•➡ Enter the south aisle via the new parish hall attached to its south side. The south door was newly formed in 1970 when the modern extension was added. Turn L.

The roof of the **south aisle** retains some original 15C timber.

At the west end of the south wall is the monument to Thomas Withering, d.1651. He was Charles I's Postmaster General, the first to occupy that post. The smaller of the two skeletons on the monument represents his son, who died, aged five.

The base of the **tower** is entered through its unsympathetic oak screen of 1934.

In the north-west corner is an ancient stone coffin lid, the oldest monument in the church. It is believed to have come from the tomb of a prior of the monastery which once stood at nearby Havering.

•➡ Return to the nave.

The circular piers of both arcades were probably erected in 1243 as part of the original construction of the aisles following a grant made to the church by the Abbey of St Nicholas and St Bernard in Montjoux, its owners since 1158. Henry II had given the estate to the monastery, which is still renowned for its use of dogs (St Bernards) in rescue work.

The nave's original 15C roof was discovered in 1957 when a plaster ceiling was removed. Its head bosses have been repainted.

At the west end of the **north aisle**, against the wall, is the alabaster monument to Francis Rame, d.1517, his wife, eleven sons and one daughter.

•➡ Continue to the north chapel.

In the 16C, William Ayloffe created north and south chancel chapels. All that survives is the north aisle's restored screen, now partly hidden. Carved on its east face are the Ayloffe arms.

Octagonal piers in the north (and south) chapel are probably early-16C work.

Against the north chapel's north wall is the alabaster monument to Richard Blakestone, d.1638, and his wife.

St Andrew's only remaining medieval glass has been assembled in the chapel's east window. The crucifixion scene is 15C work but the head of Christ was replaced at some time with that of the Virgin Mary.

•➡ Proceed to the chancel arch.

The 15C head above the arch is an early depiction of a Negro.

On the **chancel's** north wall is the tomb chest of William Ayloffe, d.1517.

Against the **sanctuary's** north wall is the monument to Richard Spencer, d.1784, by *Flaxman*.

In the south wall of the sanctuary are a piscina and a three seat sedilia with a squint behind its most westerly seat. All are 13C but have been heavily restored since their discovery in 1871.

At the east end of the **south aisle**, against the wall, is the monument to Sir Francis Prujean, d.1666; traces of its original decoration survive.

ICKENHAM   ST GILES

Swakeleys Road
(0895 632803)

**From Central
London:** *Ickenham
Station. Exit L.
Second R Long Lane
leads to the church.*
**From Uxbridge,
St Margaret:**
*Ickenham Station;
proceed as above.
Both stations are on
the Piccadilly line.*

Ickenham's 14C church is renowned for its medieval timber roofs. An unusual 17C burial chapel and three outstanding 16C brasses are also of interest.

St Giles's was first recorded in 1335 but that church was rebuilt in the late 14C, with the nave preceding the chancel. The present bell turret was built in the 15C. A north aisle was added to the nave in 1580. In 1958 the nave was extended westward by two bays.

The timber-framed south **porch** was built *c.*1500; it was restored in 1962 and the low level brickwork is entirely modern.

Although originally open, the porch is now enclosed by the 16C(?) south door of the church which has been brought forward.

West of the porch against the south wall of the **nave** is a buttress; the two bays west of this were built when the nave was extended in 1958.

The remainder of the south wall is late-14C work and probably of flint but now rendered.

The window immediately west of the porch was remodelled in the 19C.

The 15C timber **bell turret**, possibly built as a replacement for an earlier version, originally marked the west end of the church.

●● *Proceed anti-clockwise around the church.*

East of the porch is an original 14C window.

The **chancel's** south and east windows are also original.

Rendering was removed from the chancel's east wall in 1962 to reveal the flintwork and wooden beam.

In the 16C east wall of the **north aisle** is a reset late-14C window, presumably from the original north wall of the church.

The north aisle's wall is of Tudor brick, *c.*1580.

Both windows are original.

●● *Return to the south door and enter the porch.*

It may, however, be necessary to enter from the north-east door; if so, proceed to the south wall and view the interior of the porch.

On the east wall of the **south porch** are remains of a holy water stoup.

Most of the timbers of the nave's outstanding 15C king-post roof are original.

The north arcade was rebuilt in the 19C.

At the west end of the north aisle is the **vicar's vestry**, built *c.*1650 as a burial chapel dedicated to St John; it was restored in 1960. Coffins lay in the niches but were removed and reburied in the churchyard in 1914.

The 14C vestry door was reset from elsewhere.

Above this, on the east face of the wall, is the memorial to John George Clarke, d.1820, by *Banks*.

In the west wall of the **north aisle**, R of the door, is a blocked window, probably 14C.

On the north side of this wall is a monument to the Reverend Thomas Clarke, d.1796 by *Banks*.

Monuments on the north wall commemorate other members of the Clarke family, owners of the famous Carolean mansion, Swakeleys, that survives nearby (now converted to offices).

In the north-west corner is the late-17C wooden font with a richly carved base; its cover is probably 18C.

Low down, on the left splay of the reset 14C window in the aisle's east wall is some graffiti, mostly late 16C.

Also on the east wall is a brass, *c.*1545, which possibly depicts a member of the Say family; this is one of St Giles' three outstanding brasses.

The chancel arch is 19C.

The tie-beam roof of the **chancel** is late 14C.

On the north wall of the **sanctuary** is the brass of Edmonde Shordiche, d.1584, his wife and three children.

Opposite, on the sanctuary's south wall, is the brass of William Say, d.1582, with effigies of his wife and sixteen children. Say was responsible for adding the north aisle to the church.

Set in this wall is a late-14C piscina.

On the sill of the chancel's south window is the outstanding shrouded figure of an infant, Robert Clayton Knight, d.1665, a few hours old. This was found in 1921, buried in the churchyard and its original position in the church is unknown.

On the south wall of the nave, behind the pulpit, is another late-14C piscina. Its position may indicate that the high altar stood against the nave's east wall before the chancel was built.

Inserted in the nave's south-east window are fragments of 14C stained glass.

KENSINGTON ST CUTHBERT *Gough 1887*

Philbeach Gardens
(370 3263)

*Earls Court Station,
District and
Piccadilly lines.
Leave by the
Warwick Rd exit.
Turn R. First L
Philbeach Gardens.
Proceed to the north
end and follow the
short passage L to the
church.*

St Cuthbert's, designed for Anglo-Catholic
worship, is renowned for its highly decorative
interior. Although pre-Reformation in content,
with a rood and wall paintings, the Arts and
Crafts style, hinting at the coming Art-Nouveau,
predominates.

•→ *Enter the* **nave** *by the north-west door.*

Throughout the church are copies of Italian
Renaissance paintings.

Most of the furnishings and fittings were designed
for St Cuthbert's by *W. Bainbridge Reynolds*,
*c.*1887 in the Arts and Crafts style.

Stations of the cross are painted on the nave's
north and south walls by *Vinck*.

The sounding board of the pulpit, by *Reynolds*,
was added in 1907 to the design of *J. Harold
Gibbons*.

Entirely by *Reynolds* are the lectern, altar rail,
sedilia, piscina and screens.

The rood was erected on its loft in 1893, the
figure of Christ being a copy of that in Granada
Cathedral, Spain.

Choir stalls in the **chancel** possess misericords
which are copies of existing designs from various
sources.

The chancel's massive reredos, incorporating
forty statues of saints, was designed by the
Reverend Ernest Geldart.

Relics of St Cuthbert – pieces of his stole and
chasable – are placed on the high altar on the
saint's feast days, 20 March and 4 September.

In the south-east **Lady Chapel** is a reredos
designed by *Harold Gibbons*.

The chapel's altar rail by *Reynolds* was copied
from a screen in St Anselm's Chapel, Canterbury
Cathedral.

At the west end of St Cuthbert's is the clock by
Reynolds.

In the circular west **baptistry**, the font is carved
with the sacraments, based on paintings by
Müller in Dusseldorf.

LALEHAM ALL SAINTS

The Broadway
(0784 57330)

**From Central
London:** *Waterloo
Station (BR) to
Staines Station(BR)
or Shepperton Station
(BR). Bus 218, 466 or
469 to The
Broadway, Laleham.*
**From East Bedfont,
St Mary:** *Bus 203 to*

Although Laleham's church, apart from its 16C
Lucan Chapel, is basically 18C and 19C, fine late-
Norman arcades are retained within.

A Norman church was built here in the late 12C
but only its west wall, arcades and remnants of a
doorway remain. During the Tudor period,
probably *c.*1500, the nave's south wall was
demolished and the south arcade bricked up to
become the new south wall; the nave was reduced
in length by the removal of its most easterly bay
and a new chancel was built. Shortly afterwards,
a north (Lucan) chapel was added to the chancel.

Staines; proceed as above.
From Littleton, St Mary Magdalene: *Bus 218, 466 or 469; proceed as above.*

The chancel was again rebuilt and a tower added to the church in the 18C. North and south walls of the nave's aisles were rebuilt in the 19C.

The **tower** was built early in the 18C (a brick is dated 1732) to an idiosyncratic design. Its turret is recent work.

The clock was presented in 1842.

Proceed clockwise around the church.

Windows of the **north aisle**, which was rebuilt in 1828, were remodelled in Gothic style in the late 19C.

Originally, the nave stretched one bay further east until it was shortened when a new chancel was built in the 16C.

Tudor diaper brickwork forms the **north chapel's** north and east walls.

The 18C east and south walls of the **chancel** were possibly built *c*.1732.

The wall of the **south aisle** follows the line of the Norman south arcade which was filled in to become an external wall in the Tudor period. It was rebuilt, like the north wall, in 1828 but the Norman arcade was again incorporated.

Pass the modern south porch and continue to the north door, normally the entrance to the church. Enter the north aisle and proceed to its west wall.

Both arcades are late 12C, some pillars being inscribed with ancient grafitti.

On the **north aisle's** west wall the painting of Christ saving Peter from drowning is by *G. H. Harlow*, *c*.1815.

Against the same wall is a medieval stone mensa (altar table) which, after the Reformation, had served as a gravestone.

The west wall of the **nave** is late 12C.

*Return eastward following the **north aisle**.*

On the north wall is a funeral hatchment that belonged to a member of the Lucan family; the earls once lived nearby in Laleham House, now Laleham Abbey. A recent Lord Lucan gained notoriety by suddenly disappearing following a murder at his residence. He has never been found.

Below is a brass tablet commemorating Dr Thomas Arnold, headmaster of Rugby School, who began his teaching career at Laleham.

The red brick arches at the east end are Tudor.

The chandelier in the **chancel** is a copy of those at Westminster Abbey which were made in the 18C.

On the south wall of the **sanctuary** is the monument to Henrietta Hartwell, d.1818, by *Chantrey*.

East of the chancel's south door is the monument to George Perrott, d.1780, by *W. Tyler*.

Retained within the 19C south wall of the **nave** is the 12C Norman arcade.

Carved stones from a Norman doorway have also been reset in this wall.

In the churchyard, east of the building, is the grave of Field-Marshal Lord Lucan who was renowned for giving the order for the disastrous charge of the Light Brigade in the Crimean War.

LIMEHOUSE ST ANNE *Hawksmoor 1724*

Commercial Road

Open for Sunday services only at 10.30 and 18.30.

From Central London: *Fenchurch Street Station (BR) to Stepney East Station (BR). Proceed eastward along Commercial Rd.* **From Stepney, St Dunstan:** *Continue southward along Stepney High St to Belgrave St. Second L Commercial Rd, proceed eastward.*

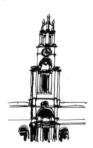

St Anne's was the first of Hawksmoor's three East End churches to be built. Most of the interior has been renewed.

The church was consecrated in 1730, six years after completion; the delay was possibly due to the inability of the poor parish to pay an incumbent's stipend, but this is surmise.

Hawksmoor designed the tower in his usual idiosyncratic manner. Its clock is the highest in a London church.

The interior, with its Greek cross plan, was influenced by Wren's St Anne and St Agnes but the nave is slightly longer.

The roof and most fittings, including the font and pulpit, were renewed by *John Morris* and *P. C. Hardwick* in 1857 following a major fire. Further restoration was carried out by *A. Blomfield* in 1891, and again after Second World War damage.

In the churchyard is an unusual pyramid, the origin of which is unknown.

LITTLE STANMORE
ST LAURENCE WHITCHURCH *James 1715*

Whitchurch Lane (952 0019)

Open Saturday and Sunday 14.00 to dusk.

From Central London: *Canons Park Station, Jubilee line. Exit L Whitchurch Lane and continue ahead. The church lies L.*

Conceived in the Italian Baroque style, with painted walls and ceiling throughout, by the first Lord Chandos, St Laurence was described by Sir John Betjeman as possessing 'one of the most splendid Georgian interiors in England'. Believed to have been employed in its recently restored decoration were *Laguerre, Verrio, Sleter, Bellucci* and *Brunetti*. There is outstanding carving by *Gibbons* and the organ keyboard, played by Handel, is displayed.

Although little certain is known of its early history, records, and the dedication, indicate that St Laurence's probably had a Saxon foundation.

From Hendon,
St Mary: *Bus 186 to*
Whitchurch Lane;
proceed as above.

The body of the present church is believed to be the third on the site. In medieval times, St Laurence's was owned by the Priory of St Bartholomew; it was probably entirely rebuilt in the late 15C but only the tower of this church has survived. Following the death of his first wife in 1712, John Bridges, first Duke of Chandos and Earl of Caernarvon, purchased her family's Tudor mansion, Canons, which stood near to the church. This he rebuilt to provide what Daniel Defoe described as 'a most magnificent palace' (now demolished). Shortly afterwards he rebuilt the nave and chancel of St Laurence. Between 1973 and 1975 the church was closed for urgent restoration work, particularly on the north wall, and many of the paintings were cleaned. In 1980, experts from Tübingen in Germany, a centre of Baroque building, began the restoration of the paintings in the church and their work was completed within five years.

On the west face of the late-15C **tower** are a door and circular window, both formed in the 18C. The door was built as a private entrance for the Duke; the window now lights a first floor vestry which was constructed recently.

Fabric in the lower section of the tower appears to be early medieval.

•► *Proceed anti-clockwise around the church.*

The neat brickwork and round-headed windows are typical of the style of the architect, *James*.

On the north side, the protruding section was added in two stages after the main building was completed. The most easterly bay, presumably by *James*, is now the ante-room to the mausoleum, built initially to house the Duke's monument.

The next two bays, in lighter coloured brickwork, were designed by *Gibbs* in 1735, when the Duke decided to build a larger mausoleum following the death of his second wife.

•► *Enter the church from the south-west door.*
Continue ahead and ascend the stairs L to the west
gallery.

The funeral hatchments displayed on the walls of the staircase are 19C.

From the gallery it is immediately apparent that an attempt has been made to imitate the Italian Baroque style.

The east end is virtually a stage beneath its proscenium arch; the walls are decorated with *trompe-l'oeil* paintings of statues and all the ceiling areas are painted with biblical scenes.

Within the gallery it is almost certain that the central box was private to the Duke and his family; there are remains of a fireplace, now concealed by panelling, which appears to have provided the only heating in the church.

By tradition, the Duke's bodyguard occupied the small north box and his more important servants,

the south box. This layout gives the impression of
a private chapel but the church has always served
the entire parish and the Duke's own chapel,
within his house, Canons, was built in 1720.

The oak woodwork of the gallery is original and
its golden colour, like that in the rest of the
church, was restored in 1975 by the removal of
dark 19C varnish.

Above the ducal box, the Transfiguration scene is
based on the work by *Raphael* in the Vatican.
This is almost certainly by the Venetian *Antonio
Bellucci* but disconcertingly little documentation
of the paintings within the church exists and the
attributions to many of the artists is no more than
expert conjecture.

•● *Descend the stairs to the* **nave**.

In the north-west corner is the marble Italian font
presented by the Duke in 1716. The box pews are
original; those on the north side were occupied
by males, some of whom carved their initials on
them, whilst the south boxes, where there are no
carvings, were reserved for females.

North and south walls are decorated with grisaille
(grey monochrome) *trompe-l'oeil* paintings of
statues representing Faith, Hope, Charity and
the Evangelists. Those on the north side, *c*.1736,
are attributed to *Francesco Sleter*, possibly
assisted by *Brunetti*, but similar work on the
south side is by an unknown hand.

The nave's ceiling is believed to be entirely the
work of *Louis Laguerre*. It is painted in sepia
tones and features Christ's miracles. Surprisingly,
the scenes run chronologically from east to west,
beginning with the north-east panel; this is
followed by the south-east panel and the north–
south procedure continues. Miracles depicted
are: Turning water into wine, Gadarene swine,
Feeding the five thousand, Pool of Bethesda,
Walking on the water, Healing the blind man,
Raising of Lazarus and Doubting Thomas.

The 18C Dutch-style chandeliers are modern and
were installed in 1984.

Original to the church are the 18C pulpit, altar
rail and chancel pavement.

Within the **chancel** the altar and choir stalls were
made *c*.1900.

The ceiling is painted with the Adoration of
Jehovah by *Laguerre*, judged the most truly
Baroque work in the church.

Flanking the altar are paintings of the Nativity
and the Descent from the Cross, both attributed
to *Bellucci*.

The gilded panels above them, and possibly the
four Corinthian columns, were carved by
Gibbons.

Grisaille paintings of St Peter and St Paul
decorate the north and south sections of the east
wall.

●● *Ascend the steps on the north-east side and proceed behind the altar to the* **retrochoir**.

The organ case was carved by *Gibbons*. Before the enlargement of the instrument, this stood further east, allowing room in front for musicians.

Gerard Smith, nephew of the famous Father Schmidt, originally made the organ but it has since been rebuilt.

A detached console was installed (in front of the north pews) in 1913 and the original keyboard, with the white and black keys reversed, was replaced in its original position. It is known that Handel played on this whilst he was under the patronage of the Duke between 1717 and 1721. However, he was the composer in residence at Canons, not the church organist.

Flanking the organ are paintings of Moses receiving the Ten Commandments and the Sermon on the Mount, both possibly by *Verrio*.

The *trompe-l'oeil* sky above was painted by an unknown artist; it is lit by a concealed window.

●● *Proceed to the north* **antechamber**.

This was completed later than the body of the church, presumably by *James*, to house the Duke's monument; however, his second Duchess, Lydia, died in 1735 and the Duke decided that a larger mausoleum would be needed.

Funeral hatchments displayed are those of the second and third dukes and the two wives of the latter; two are duplicates.

The ceiling, which had long disintegrated, was completely reconstructed in 1985 based on existing photographs.

On the west side, wrought-iron gates were installed in 1735 when the wall was opened up.

●● *Continue to the* **mausoleum**.

The mausoleum was built by *Gibbs* in 1735. It is painted with *trompe-l'oeil* work by *Gaetano Brunetti*.

Against the west wall is the monument to the first Lord Chandos, d.1744, and his first two wives, Mary and Cassandra. This was designed *c.*1717 by *Gibbons* who appears to have been assisted in its carving by *Andrew Carpenter* (alias *Andries Carpentier*) and *Jan Van Nost*.

At the south wall's east end is the monument to Mary, the first wife of the second Duke, d.1738, by *Cheere*.

This is followed by the monument to Margaret, first wife of the third Duke, d.1760. Forty-one members of the Brydges family lie in the vault below the mausoleum.

●● *Return to the west end of the church*.

Beneath the tower is the **Lady Chapel**, created in 1966.

LITTLETON ST MARY MAGDALENE

Squires Bridge Road
(093 28 62249)

**From Central
London:** *Waterloo
Station (BR) to
Shepperton Station
(BR). Bus 218, 461 or
469.*
**From Laleham, All
Saints:** *Bus 218, 466
or 469.*

*Bus 218 entails a half
mile walk from
Laleham Rd along
Squires Bridge Rd to
the church. Buses 466
and 469 pass the
church but are
Greenline services
and less frequent.*

A 12C Transitional period south arcade, together
with a 13C Early English period north arcade and
late-12C chancel survive at Littleton. The church
possesses an outstanding set of medieval pews.

It is recorded that St Mary's was consecrated in
1135 but there were probably wooden Saxon
predecessors of this building. In the late 12C, the
chancel was extended and a south aisle built.
Early in the 13C a north aisle was added. It is
known that St Mary's was served by priests from
the Benedictine Abbey of St Peter, at nearby
Chertsey, between 1135 and 1308.

The late-16C **tower** retains its original west door
with window above.

An upper stage for a bell chamber was added in
the 17C.

•● *Proceed clockwise around the church.*

The body of the church is basically of flint and
ragstone but there is some brickwork.

Although the **north aisle's** external wall is early
13C, windows were remodelled *c* .1600.

The aisle's east wall is of chequered brick.

The nave's brick clerestory was probably formed
in the 17C.

Extensions north of the chancel were made in the
18C.

The **chancel's** north wall retains two original late-
12C lancet windows; the outline of a third,
blocked example, survives above the door.

Traces of two Early English windows also remain
in the east wall; there was originally a third.

The chancel's east and south walls are of
ragstone.

Lancet windows in the wall of the **south aisle** are
modern copies of those on the north side.

Detailing on the wall dates from its refacing in
the 19C.

The south **porch** is probably 17C.

•● *Enter the **south aisle** from the south door.*

The late-12C south arcade in the Transitional
style has bulkier columns than its slightly later
north counterpart and its central pillar is
rounded.

In the south-west corner is an early-16C
muniments (church records) chest.

The floors of both aisles and the nave are paved
with Tudor tiles.

At the west end of the **nave** is St Mary's ancient
font which may date from the original Norman
building.

St Mary's is fortunate in possessing a complete
set of congregation pews, dated 1420, even

though many have been restored.

The nave's roof was rebuilt in the 17C.

Internally, the clerestory is of brick.

The central pier of the early-13C **north arcade**, unlike that on the south side, is octagonal.

Eight funeral hatchments decorate the church; they belong to members of the Wood family, local squires from 1660 to 1898.

The chancel's rood screen, allegedly from Westminster Abbey, was made c.1500 but has been heavily restored.

Hanging from the roof are twenty colours of the Grenadier Guards.

The choir stalls and panelling within the **chancel** are early 15C but much restored. It is believed that they came from Winchester Cathedral.

The aumbries and the altar rail are late-16C and probably Flemish.

On the south wall of the **sanctuary** is a late-12C double piscina.

The high window behind the early-18C pulpit is originally believed to have lit the stairs to the rood loft.

In the wall at the east end of the **south aisle** is a late-12C piscina with a medieval aumbry immediately to its west.

MARYLEBONE   HOLY TRINITY   *Soane 1828*

Marylebone Road

Great Portland Street Station, Circle and Metropolitan lines or Regents Park Station, Bakerloo line.

A rare survivor of the work of Sir John Soane. Internally, there are no furnishings and fittings of interest as the church was adapted to become the headquarters of SPCK bookshops in 1956.

In 1821 Parliament allocated £1 million for the new 'Waterloo' churches and Holy Trinity was built from this fund. Lord Roberts and Florence Nightingale both worshipped here.

Holy Trinity was built of Bath stone and the parishioners were requested to pay for the 'purely decorative' urns and columns on the west façade.

The external pulpit, north of the west door, was added as part of a memorial to Canon William Cadman, rector 1859–91.

Enter the building.

Originally, the east end of the church was flat but the present apse was added by *Somers Clarke* in 1878. Much of the rest of the interior was remodelled at that time.

MARYLEBONE   ST MARYLEBONE
T. Hardwick 1817

Marylebone Road

Baker Street Station, Bakerloo, Circle, Jubilee and Metropolitan lines.

St Marylebone was begun as a simple building but completed in its present form to harmonize with the grand new Regent's Park scheme of Nash. It was here that the poets Robert Browning and Elizabeth Barrett married in secret.

This is the fourth parish church of what is now called St Marylebone and there have been three different sites. The first was built *c*.1200 and dedicated to St John. A new church was completed *c*.1400, almost one mile further north, on the banks of the Tyburn. It was dedicated to St Mary-le-Burn (the stream) which became corrupted to St Marylebone and gave its name to the parish. In that church two famous playrights were married; Sir Francis Bacon in 1606 and Richard Brinsley Sheridan in 1733. Rebuilding took place on the same site in 1740 and Lord Byron was baptized there in 1788. When the present church was built, again further north, the old St Marylebone was demoted to chapel-at-ease status but not finally demolished until 1949. Its churchyard now provides a garden of rest in Marylebone High Street. The architect Gibbs, sculptor Rysbrack and preacher Charles Wesley are buried there. Originally, the parish church was to be built elsewhere. However, when half completed, St Mary's contributory importance to Nash's grand Regent's Park scheme became apparent and it was decided to upgrade it to parish church status. A steeple was then added and the portico greatly enlarged, thus forming a suitable end of vista from the park. Only the windows of the church were damaged in the Second World War.

•● *Enter from the north door beneath the portico.*

The high altar is sited, unusually, at the south end.

When built, there were double galleries on the east and west walls; only the **north gallery** survives. On its front are the royal arms.

The church once possessed many private pews, curtained and with fireplaces; two survive at the south end.

Originally, the ceiling of the church was coved.

In the **chapel**, at the south end of the east aisle, is a painting of the Holy Family by *West* which originally formed the reredos.

•● *Proceed to the* **chancel**.

A cross on the ceiling denotes the point below which the high altar originally stood. It was moved further south in 1885 when the apse was added to the church; much amendment to the south end then took place.

•● *Proceed towards the exit and request to see the* **Browning Room**.

The poets Robert Browning and Elizabeth Barrett were married clandestinely at St Marylebone in 1841 in order to escape the wrath of Elizabeth's despotic father. The 'Browning Room', R of the exit, contains souvenirs of the poets.

An 18C bread shelf is also displayed.

NORTHOLT   ST MARY

Ealing Road

From Central London: *Northolt Station, Central line. Exit R Mandeville Rd. First L (the L fork) Ealing Rd. The church lies on a slight hill L.*
From Perivale, St Mary: *Return to Perivale Station, Central line. Underground to Northolt Station; proceed as above.*

Perched on its hill top site, St Mary's, although small, presents one of London's most picturesque church exteriors. Its early-14C nave retains outstanding, if rather faded tracery. Within is an attractive timber gallery and an exceptional late-14C font. There are three good brasses.

Domesday refers to a priest at Northolt, indicating a Saxon foundation. Almost certainly the church would have been wooden and no Norman additions in stone appear to have been implemented. Rebuilding in stone rubble took place *c.*1300. This structure consisted of the present nave with a shallow apse which served as the chancel. Apparently there were not sufficient funds to build a long chancel as was usual at that time. However, a chancel was eventually built early in the 16C and this survives.

Externally, the church has been rendered.

•● *Proceed to the west end of the* **nave** *(L of the south porch).*

The nave's three most westerly windows possess exceptional tracery; they are original and, although basically Early English, incorporate naturalistic carved foliage and mouldings, more typical of the Decorated period. Unfortunately, they are built of soft Reigate sandstone which has weathered badly and detail is better observed internally. Repair work in cement has contributed to their decline and the windows are now protected by rather unsightly sheets of plastic. It is to be hoped that funds will become available for sympathetic restoration in a more durable material.

The buttress immediately L of the south-west window was added in 1714 but, like most of the others, has been restored.

One of several original buttresses (all small) stands adjacent to this.

•● *Proceed to the west wall.*

Both large buttresses, of brick, were added in 1718 as the church appeared to be leaning westward.

The **bell tower** is believed to be early 16C but has undergone frequent restoration.

•● *Proceed to the north wall of the* **nave***, passing two further windows which match that previously seen.*

In this wall is the blocked door that originally gave private access from the moated manor house.

The nave's most easterly windows on this and the south side are now believed to be contemporary with the others even though their style is rather later.

Apparently the north wall of the nave was extended eastward between 1500 and 1540 to form the north wall of the **chancel**. Tudor brickwork was used but this was rendered in 1940; traces may be seen internally.

Originally, there were additional windows on to the chancel but these have been blocked. The windows in the north and east walls are original but the latter was rebuilt following bomb damage.

South of the chancel is the **vestry**, added in 1951.

The south **porch** was built in 1943.

➡ *Enter the church.*

Some of the original stonework has been revealed around the south door.

The early-16C king-post roof was built throughout the church when the chancel was added.

At the west end is a timber **gallery**, built in 1730 'for the singers and servant men'.

Above this is the ceiling of the lower stage of the **bell turret**; its beams are original.

Immediately north of the window, in the west wall of the **nave**, beside the foliated carving, is a grotesque head. A matching head on the south side has disappeared.

In the north wall are traces of the blocked door.

Beside this are late-17C Stuart arms which originally stood above the chancel entrance. Beneath hangs the benefactions board.

Owing to its lack of monuments or furnishings, St Mary's bare **chancel** is a disappointment. The altar has been brought forward.

Against the north wall of the **original sanctuary** is a section of the churchwardens' pews.

In the centre of the floor (lift the protective mat) is a 16C brass, set in a Purbeck marble slab, commemorating Susan and John Gyfford and their children. Evidently the brass is a palimpsest (re-used) as there are further, earlier brasses on the reverse side (not visible).

Against the south wall, in the east corner, is the brass of Isaiah Bures, d.1610; it has been set in marble.

Further west, now leading to the vestry, is the 16C priest's door.

In the south section of the east wall of the **nave** is a blocked window; its counterpart on the north side was lost, together with the east apse, when the chancel was added.

Originally, this part of the nave was the Chapel of St Stephen and its piscina survives on the south wall.

Below the protective mat is St Mary's oldest brass; it commemorates Henry Powdell, d.1452.

On the south wall of the nave is a triptych, the 'Adoration of the Magi'. Little is known of the painting's origins but it is probably a copy of an

18C Dutch or Flemish work.

Before the south door is St Mary's exceptional 14C font. This was originally decorated and traces of red and black paint survive.

Its oak cover was made in 1624.

Above the south door is a board in the style of a funeral hatchment, installed in 1945. This commemorates the execution of a former rector of Northolt, Archbishop Laud, in 1645. The Latin inscription reads 'I desire to depart and to be with Christ', allegedly Laud's last words spoken on the scaffold.

Beside the door is a badly restored holy water stoup.

PERIVALE   ST MARY-THE-VIRGIN

Perivale Lane
(997 1948)

When arranging to view, ensure that there is no confusion between this and the modern parish church of Perivale which is also dedicated to St Mary but located elsewhere.

From Central London: *Perivale Station, Central line. Exit L Horsenden Lane. Cross Western Avenue by pedestrian bridge and Perivale Lane. A footpath ahead leads to Pitshanger Park. The church lies L within the park.*
From Cranford, St Dunstan: *Bus 195 to High St, Southall. Bus 207 to Ealing Broadway. Bus 297 to Argyle Road, Perivale. R Perivale Lane. First R follow the footpath to the church.*

This tiny church nestles picturesquely between trees which completely shield it from the adjacent Western Avenue. Late-medieval detailing disguises what is mainly a Norman structure.

St Mary's was built c.1135 and its chancel rebuilt, probably early in the 14C. It was not until 1951, when an ancient will was discovered referring to 'St Mary of Little Greenford', that the dedication was established. Previously it had been referred to on some maps as the church of St James. Major restoration took place c.1870 and in 1964.

The **tower** was weatherboarded in the 16C.

•● *Proceed anti-clockwise around the church.*

Walls of the body of the church were constructed from flint and stone rubble which have been cement-rendered, and dressings of Reigate stone.

No 12C details survive in the **nave**, the windows being remodelled in the 15C.

The modern **porch** had a 17C predecessor.

It is probable that the **chancel** was rebuilt in the 14C.

The small low window in its south wall, east of the buttress, may have been a leper window.

The east and north windows of the **chancel** were formed in 1964.

•● *Enter the church from the south porch.*

The nave's king-post roof is 15C.

At the west end, the **gallery** is also 15C.

Beneath this, against the west wall is the list of rectors.

The 13C west doorway which now leads to the vestry was originally the main entrance to the church. Within this doorway, on the vestry side, are fragments of a holy water stoup.

Stained glass in the most westerly north window of the **nave** commemorates Henry Condell, a parishioner who became the first mayor of Melbourne, Australia.

Set in the nave's pavement, before the chancel's

steps, are five 16C brasses. These commemorate Henry Mylett, d.1500, his two wives and fifteen children.

The chancel arch was built in 1870; it had no predecessor, the former division between nave and chancel being made by the rood beam which was sited further east. A modern rood is now suspended from the arch.

Against the centre of the **chancel's** north wall is the monument to Ellen Nicholas, d.1815, by *Westmacott*.

Surviving medieval glass from St Mary's has been reassembled in the modern window at the east end of the chancel's north wall.

Against the chancel's south wall is the oldest monument in the church; this commemorates Joane Shelbury d.1623.

Beside the doorway of the **south aisle** is the late-15C octagonal font; its cover is dated 1665.

PINNER   ST JOHN-THE-BAPTIST

Church Lane

From Central London: *Pinner Station, Metropolitan line (Amersham, Chesham or Watford direction). Exit from the station ahead. R Marsh Rd. First R High St. Second R Church Lane.*
From Harrow, St Mary: *Harrow-on-the-Hill Station, Metropolitan line to Pinner Station; proceed as above.*

Apart from its Victorian south aisle, Pinner's church is a 15C building which has re-used much of the fabric of its 13C predecessor. Carved panels from the early-17C choir stalls decorate the south aisle.

The present church, consecrated in 1321, replaced a small 13C chapel that had stood on the site.

Its **tower**, added in the 15C, received new battlements as part of the 1978 restoration.

●▬ Proceed clockwise around the church.

The west wall of the **south aisle** (and north aisle), with its lancet windows, is all that survives of the original massive west wall. The rest was demolished in the 15C, when an opening was made to provide a link with the new tower.

The south **porch** was rebuilt in the 15C.

Dormer windows were added to the **nave's** roof by *Pearson* in 1880.

Walls of the **south transept** are believed to incorporate fabric from the 13C chapel.

The **chancel's south aisle** was added in 1859. Its triple lancet window is a replica of the original window of the chancel's south wall that had to be demolished when the aisle was built.

●▬ Return to the south porch and enter the church.

The roof was part of the major restoration by *Pearson* in 1880. It was redecorated in 1958.

The floor was relaid in 1958.

*●▬ Proceed to the **north aisle**.*

Internally, both windows in the north aisle are 14C (they have been rebuilt externally).

In front of this aisle's blocked north door is a 15C

octagonal font, much restored. Its modern cover
is by *Spooner*.

Like the south transept, the **north transept**'s walls
are believed to retain fabric from the 13C chapel.
Its staircase and doorway were built in 1954.

The pulpit, L of the arch, was designed by
*Pearson c.*1880.

The Jacobean altar rail was recently brought
forward.

It is believed that the north wall of the **chancel**
incorporates, at its east end, some 13C material.

The east window was formed in the 15C.

A black 17C marble tablet commemorates John
Dey, vicar of the church.

The 16C altar, usually covered, came from
St George Hanover Square, Mayfair.

•➡ *Proceed to the* **Lady Chapel** *at the east end of
the south aisle.*

The chancel's south wall was demolished in 1859
when the south aisle was constructed to
accommodate members of the Royal Commercial
Travellers' School. It was replaced by the present
arcade.

The aisle was heightened and extended eastward
in 1880 to house an organ that was finally
dismantled in 1967. It was dedicated as a Lady
Chapel in 1936.

Fixed to the wall on both sides of the south door
are carved and decorated panels from the early
17C choir stalls which were replaced in 1937.

At the west end of the south wall is the
monument to Sir Christopher Clitherow, d.1685.
The skull at the base has no jaw bone, indicating
that he was the last male member of the family.

The east arch of the **south transept** was formed in
1859 to provide a link with the chancel's new
south aisle.

RAINHAM　ST HELEN AND ST GILES

The Broadway
(04027 52752)

**From Central
London (or Barking,
St Margaret):**
*Barking Station,
District and
Metropolitan lines.
From Barking Station
(BR) train to
Rainham Station
(BR). Exit L and
proceed to The
Broadway.*
From Wennington:
*Bus 375 or 723. Both
are London Country
Buses and the service*

This is, without doubt, the finest completely
Norman church in the London area. Although of
late-12C date, practically all is Romanesque and
there are few signs of the imminent pointed
Gothic style. Particularly outstanding are the
chancel arch, the unique clerestory and the
chancel's east wall, with its unusual disposition of
five, round-headed windows.

Rainham's church, built *c.*1170, is recorded in
Domesday, but Saxon finds in the area indicate
the probability of an earlier structure. Its double
dedication to St Helen and St Giles is extremely
unusual. Richard de Lucy, a son-in-law of Henry
II, was responsible for the building. He also
founded Lesnes Abbey, eventually serving there
as a monk and, on his death, the King, in
deference to him, presented the manor of
Rainham to the abbey and this stayed in its

is irregular.
Telephone 688 7261
for details.

possession until the Reformation. The church then passed, briefly, to the Knights of St John, but they too were soon suppressed and it then became privately owned. Apart from the rebuilding of the chancel's north wall in the 14C and the upper part of the tower in the 16C, little significant maintenance was carried out and by the late 19C Helen's was in a bad condition, with the south wall on the point of collapse. However, restoration by *Geldart* began in 1897 and was executed in a surprisingly sensitive manner for the period.

The two lower stages of the **tower** are Norman with their 12C windows restored. An upper (bell chamber) stage was added in the 13C but this was rebuilt in the 16C and surmounted by a brick battlement which, however, was replaced by a parapet in 1959.

Positioned outside the tower's west wall are three 13C coffin lids.

•• *Proceed clockwise to view the exterior of the church.*

In the west wall of the **north aisle** is an original, round-headed window.

The north doorway is 12C but brickwork denotes renovations, *c*.1600. Its ancient door retains part of a decorative late-12C(?) hinge.

Another small original window is followed by a larger 14C example.

Above, the shape of the nave's clerestory window is unique. The 18C stonework is believed to reproduce the enlarged 13C design.

In the aisle's east wall is a restored late-15C(?) window.

The north wall of the **chancel** was rebuilt in the 14C. Its blocked doorway once led to a vestry.

The north window has been rebuilt.

Prior to the restoration of 1897, all the windows in the chancel's east wall had been blocked; the lower three were then completely rebuilt re-using, externally, some old stonework in their splays. However, we do not know what evidence the 19C restorers had for determining their size and position. It would appear that existing traces of Norman originals were rather limited, owing to the construction of a new window in this wall in late medieval times.

Above, flanking the circular window (of unknown date), are two 12C windows which, although restored, retain their original splays.

Apart from the restored areas around the windows, the remainder of this wall is 12C.

All three lancet windows in the chancel's south wall have been reconstructed but some splays are original.

The remainder of this wall is 12C.

Its small Norman doorway was the priest's

private entrance; most decoration is original and judged outstanding.

In the **south aisle**'s 12C west wall is a restored 14C(?) window.

Apart from the 16C buttresses and restoration around the windows, the south wall is 12C.

Its most easterly window is completely modern.

This is followed by a 12C window which is original, but almost completely restored.

The south **porch** was rebuilt in 1897, its predecessor having become dilapidated.

●● *Continue to the north door and enter the* **north aisle**.

Both arcades consist of round-headed arches supported by massive square piers with their moulded corner shaftings indicative of late-Norman work. Although by 1170 the Transitional period had arrived, there is no example at Rainham of early pointed arches.

Only on the north side of the north arcade are moulded shafts omitted, possibly an indication of the ancient belief that the north side of the church was less sacred.

On the most easterly pier, facing the pulpit, is a good example of 13C medieval wall painting.

The roof of the **nave** was rebuilt in 1897.

The clerestory windows appear to be a combination of 12C and 13C work.

The pulpit, lectern and pews are all late 19C.

In the north-east corner of the nave are two 13C arches, cut into earlier, larger arches. An altar probably stood in one of the niches, as the most southerly arch incorporates a squint.

The outstanding 12C chancel arch incorporates a three-dimensional zig-zag design. Its original round-headed shape has been slightly modified due to the later widening.

Below is a cut down, late-15C screen.

The **chancel** is unusually large for its 12C date.

Its king-post roof is late 14C.

The choir stalls, organ and altar are 19C but the front of the latter was made of oak from the 15C pews.

On the north side, the chair incorporates a carved lion and poppy head from the old pews.

In the east wall are traces of a medieval window.

At the west end of the chancel's south wall, the west splay of the priest's doorway was designed so that the door could be opened wide.

●● *Proceed to the south-east corner of the* **nave**.

At upper level, R of the chancel arch, is the doorway to the rood loft from the top of the stairs.

•● *Proceed to the north-east corner of the* **south aisle**.

Immediately L is the entrance to the rood loft staircase, once blocked but rediscovered in the 19C. Inscribed within this entrance and protected by perspex, is a medieval graffito of a sailing vessel.

Below the aisle's east window is a 16C parish chest, covered with leather and provided with iron straps.

Against a recess in the south wall, at the east end, is a late-12C piscina on a pedestal.

The roof of the south aisle incorporates timbers from the old nave's roof.

At the west end of the **nave**, facing the entrance to the tower, is the font. Its circular 12C bowl rests on a 15C stem.

The arch to the tower is 12C.

Above the arch, partly preserved by an earlier gallery, is the most significant example of 14C decoration in the church.

ST PANCRAS   ST PANCRAS
W. and H. W. Inwood 1822

Euston Road

Closed Monday afternoon and Tuesday.

Euston Square Station, Circle and Metropolitan lines or King's Cross and St Pancras Station, Circle, Metropolitan, Northern, Piccadilly and Victoria lines.

This is probably the most thoroughly 'Grecian' building in London.

Designed by *Henry Inwood* and his son *William* who visited Greece after the commission had been gained to make studies of the ancient ruins, St Pancras was London's first Greek Revival church; it is built of brick but faced with Portland stone.

Both **east wings** feature copies of the caryatids from the Erechtheum in Athens. Unfortunately the ladies were made too tall and the removal of their middle sections gives them a dumpy appearance.

The design of the **tower** of St Pancras was inspired by the Tower of the Winds, Athens, and its portico, like the east wings, was influenced by the Erechtheum.

•● *Enter the church from the portico.*

The **chancel** was formed in 1889. Its scagliola (plaster imitating marble) columns were copied from the Temple of Minerva in Greece.

Further remodelling of the church took place in 1914 when the present high altar was made.

The original altar may still be seen in the **Chapel of the Blessed Sacrament**, at the east end of the south aisle.

ST PANCRAS   ST PANCRAS OLD CHURCH

Pancras Road
(387 7301)

King's Cross and St Pancras Station, Circle, Metropolitan, Northern, Piccadilly and Victoria lines. Exit R Euston Rd.

Now over-shadowed by the less than picturesque rear of St Pancras Station, it is difficult to accept that this church was known, until the 18C, as St Pancras in the Fyldes! Some genuine Norman traces survive amongst the Romanesque pastiche created in the 19C. The prize possession of the church is its rare 6C Saxon altar top.

By tradition, a church dedicated to St Pancras was

*Second R Midland Rd
leads to Pancras Rd.*

first built on the site *c*.314. Evidence of a Roman encampment nearby survived up to the 17C and some Roman tiles have been re-used in the fabric of the present structure, which is basically Norman. A tower was added, or rebuilt, in the 13C which later, probably in the 16C, was given a picturesque ogee roof. In 1822 the new parish church of St Pancras was built in Euston Road and the ancient building became a chapel-at-ease, gradually falling derelict. Restoration was unfortunately entrusted to *Roumieu* and *Gough* who in 1848 produced the present Romanesque Revival work.

The west front, which is entirely 19C, stands 30ft west of the earlier building, an extension that was achieved by demolishing the 13C west tower. As 'compensation' *Roumieu* and *Gough* built a **south tower** in the Flemish style on the site of the south porch. Fortunately, its top section was soon removed and replaced by the present, less dominating, timber-framed structure.

Externally, the only original Norman feature to survive is the **chancel**'s rather faded south doorway, now blocked.

•● *Enter the church from the west door and proceed through the parish room.*

The **nave**'s ancient roof timbers had been covered with 19C plaster and were revealed in 1925.

In the north-west corner is the font with its cover made *c*.1700.

Part of the north wall, after the second window, has been exposed to reveal a doorjamb and a blocked doorway – both Norman, together with a mid-14C window splay.

Roman tiles have been re-used in the wall, indicating the presence nearby of a Roman settlement.

Further east is displayed the top of a medieval tomb chest, relocated from the sanctuary. Its brasses have long disappeared but by tradition they represented members of the Gray family that gave its name to the legal society of Gray's Inn.

Against the **chancel**'s north wall an elaborate 17C cartouche commemorates John Offley, his wife and five children.

St Pancras's most interesting possession is the 6C mensa of the high altar inscribed with five consecration crosses; only one similar example is known to exist. This was first recorded at St Pancras in 1251 but lost during the Civil War. It was rediscovered, together with some valuable Elizabethan plate, in the foundations of the west tower during its 19C demolition. Evidently all had been hidden from Cromwell's troops, fifty of whom lodged in the church in 1642.

Beneath the east window is the reredos designed by *A. Blomfield* in 1888.

A tablet on the south side of the east wall commemorates the painter Samuel Cooper, a specialist in miniatures, d.1672, and his wife.

The late-13C piscina and 15C sedilia on the south wall have been almost completely restored.

Also on the chancel's south wall is the monument to William Platt, d.1637, and his wife, Mary, d.1687.

A monument in the style of *Nicholas Stone*, in the south-east corner of the nave, commemorates Philadelphia Woollaston, d.1616.

📌 *Exit from the church.*

In the **churchyard**, the poet Shelley first saw Mary Godwin whom he immediately fell in love with. She was visiting the grave of her mother, Mary Wollstonecraft, the pioneer of women's education.

At the east end of the churchyard is the monument to Elizabeth Soane, d.1815. It was designed by her husband, the architect, Sir John Soane, d.1837 who also lies here together with their son.

Buried nearby is J. C. Bach, the composer and a member of the famed musical family; he was born in Germany.

SHOREDITCH ST LEONARD
Dance the Elder 1740

Shoreditch High Street
(739 2063)

Open Monday–Friday 12.00–14.00.

From Central London: *Liverpool Street Station, Central, Circle and Metropolitan lines. Exit R Bishopsgate. Bus 5, 6, 22, 22A, 35, 47, 48, 78, 149, 243A, 263A to Shoreditch church.*
From Hackney, St John: *From Mare St bus 35 or 55 to Shoreditch church.*

St Leonard's is one of three London churches designed by Dance the Elder, best known as the architect of The Mansion House. Apart from the usual Victorian removal of galleries and the lowering of the pulpit, little of this severely Classical but stately building has been altered. Its famous steeple remains an important East London landmark.

The first reference to the parish church of Shoreditch was made *c*.1145 when it was granted to the Priory of Holy Trinity at Aldgate; however, by tradition, there had been a Saxon foundation. Much rebuilding took place and by 1483 the medieval St Leonard's unusually possessed four aisles. In 1716 part of the tower collapsed and although the need for a new building had become obvious approval for this was not given until 1735. A strike by English builders protesting about the low pay rates accepted by Irish labour working on the new church led to anti-Irish demonstrations; however, St Leonard's was completed within five years and became, in 1817, London's first church to be gas lit.

The west front is of Portland stone, with the remainder of brick.

The **tower** follows the precedent set by *Gibbs* at St Martin-in-the-Fields, rising immediately behind the portico. Its 192ft high **steeple**, in spite of modern buildings, remains a landmark in Shoreditch.

The **north aisle** was rebuilt after the Second World War.

📌 *Enter the church.*

It is immediately apparent that the interior is

strongly influenced by the work of *Wren*.

Above the west doorway are the arms of George II.

The organ, in the west **gallery**, was made in 1756 and retains its original mahogany case.

On the front of the gallery is the clock which possesses an exceptionally fine carved surround attributed to *Chippendale*.

When built, the church also possessed north and south galleries but these were removed in 1857.

In the west corner of the **north aisle** is the font, made for the church from a solid block of marble in 1740. Further east, against the north wall, is a bread cupboard, unusually designed as a Doric temple. Its twin is fixed to the south wall, opposite.

James Burbage built the first English playhouse in 1576; it stood near the church and was called simply, The Theatre. The London Shakespeare League commemorated this by erecting a large monument against the north wall in 1903. Several Elizabethan players are referred to, including Gabriel Spencer who was mortally wounded by playwright Ben Johnson in a duel in 1598.

On the north and south walls of the **sanctuary**, boards record benefactors of the parish from 1585 to 1791.

The present east window's glass serves as a memorial to those who died in the Second World War. It replaced outstanding early-17C Flemish stained glass depicting 'The Last Supper' which had formed the east window of the previous church and been re-used. Unfortunately, this was not removed for safety in the Second World War and a bomb, which fell nearby, shattered it.

The altar was made for the church in 1740.

At the east end of the **south aisle** against the wall is the most dramatic monument in the church. This commemorates Elizabeth Benson: 'in the 90th year the threads of her life were not spun to the full but snapped 17 December 1710'. The sculptor was *Bird* and he depicts the tree of life being snapped by two aggressive skeletons.

Further east, a simple plaque commemorates a parishioner, Dr James Parkinson, d.1824, who identified the disease that bears his name.

The pulpit, which retains its canopy, was made for the church in 1740. It was reduced in height from a three-decker in 1857 at the same time as the north and south galleries were removed.

•● *Exit and proceed to the north side of the* **churchyard**.

Exhibited is the parish stocks/whipping post, protected by a roof which, until recently, was thatched.

To the north-west of the church is 118½ High Street, built in 1735 as the Clerk's House. It is believed to be the oldest private residence to survive in Shoreditch.

SOUTH KENSINGTON
BROMPTON ORATORY *Gribble 1878*

Brompton Road

*Knightsbridge Station
or South Kensington
Station, both
Piccadilly line.*

Apart from Westminster and Southwark
Cathedrals this is London's most important
Roman Catholic church.

Famed for its church music, the official name is
the Church of the Oratory of St Philip Neri and
The Immaculate Heart of Mary.

The church was built in Italian Baroque style with
a **dome** by *Sherrin* above the crossing.

•● *Enter the church and proceed along the* **nave**.

The statues of the Apostles between the pilasters
by *Mazzuoli*, 1685, came from Siena Cathedral,
Italy.

In the south transept's **Lady Chapel** is an altar
from Brescia, Italy, made in 1693.

SPITALFIELDS   CHRIST CHURCH
Hawksmoor 1727

Commercial Street
(247 7202)

*Open occasionally for
concerts, otherwise
apply at the crypt
door L.*

**From Central
London:** *Liverpool
Street Station (BR),
Central, Circle and
Metropolitan lines.
Leave the station by
the Bishopsgate exit.
L Bishopsgate.
Fourth R Brushfield
St. Continue ahead to
Commercial St.*
**From Shoreditch,
St Leonard:** *Return
by bus to Liverpool
Street Station;
proceed as above.*

Christ Church, the largest of Hawksmoor's three
East End churches, has for many years been
undergoing extensive restoration and its
furnishings have not yet (1987) been replaced.
One is, therefore, visiting an empty, but
impressive, shell. It was built under the Fifty New
Churches Act of 1711. The body of the church is
reminiscent of the same architect's St Alfege at
Greenwich.

Rebuilding of the **spire** in 1822 led to the
disappearance of many of its decorative
appendages. Other alterations to the church were
made following damage by lightning in 1841.

The windows, altered in 1866, have recently been
restored to their original appearance.

•● *Enter the church.*

It is intended that Christ Church will eventually
match its original internal appearance with the
restoration of north and south galleries and box
pews.

The church retains its original font and lectern,
together with a pulpit converted from the 18C
reader's desk. These will be relocated in the
church when building work is completed.
Unfortunately, the reredos disappeared many
years ago and its design is unknown.

Although Christ Church is unfurnished,
Hawksmoor's skilful handling of special elements
is, as usual, immediately apparent.

The flat, coffered ceiling of 1729 has been
restored.

On the north wall of the chancel is the monument
to Sir Robert Ladbroke, Lord Mayor of London,
by *Flaxman*.

Facing this, on the south wall, is the Edmund
Peck monument by *Dunn*, 1737.

STANWELL ST MARY-THE-VIRGIN

High Street
(07842 52044)

**From Central
London:** *Hounslow
West Station,
Piccadilly line. Cross
the road. Bus 203 to
High St, Stanwell.*
**From East Bedfont,
St Mary:** *Bus 203;
proceed as above.*

St Mary's has been built over many periods, but
the surviving detailing is basically late medieval.
The chancel is decorated with an exceptional
flamboyant arcade and its original rare pillar
piscina survives. The large Jacobean monument
to Lord Knyvett and his wife is an outstanding
work by the great sculptor *Nicholas Stone.*

Stanwell's church probably had a Saxon
foundation as the parish is referred to in
Domesday. Part of the nave's fabric is believed to
survive from the Norman rebuilding in the 12C.
The present chancel and the aisles were added in
the 13C but the north aisle was virtually rebuilt in
1863.

Apparently, the **tower** was built in three periods:
the lower stage is 13C, the second 14C and the
upper, with spire, late 14C to early 15C. It is of
flint combined with Kentish ragstone
chequerwork.

Digits on the clock face are placed in a cross
formation and the date, 1678, is displayed.

The weathervane surmounting the spire
incorporates the arms of the Windsor family,
Lords of the Manor until the 16C (unconnected
with the royal house of Windsor).

•● *Proceed clockwise.*

The **north aisle** was rebuilt externally in 1863.

Above, the nave's clerestory windows were
formed **c**.1500.

Most of the **chancel** is 13C but its west end has
been rebuilt in brick.

Between the early-14C north windows stands the
Victorian **vestry**.

The chancel's east window is also 14C but later.

On the south side, the chancel's windows are
again early 14C and match those on the north
side.

Unfortunately, the south wall of the chancel has
been rendered with pebbledash.

The **south aisle**, from internal evidence, seems to
have been created in the 13C but apparently
rebuilding of its south wall took place *c*.1380.

Its east window, however, is early 14C.

Like the tower, the south aisle and nave are built
of flint and Kentish ragstone.

•● *Enter the church from the north porch and
proceed eastward.*

Both arcades are 13C, with circular and
octagonal piers alternating.

Fixed against the wall of the **north aisle** are
boards displaying the Lord's Prayer, the Ten
Commandments and the Creed; they originally
formed part of the reredos.

The 15C king-post roof of the **nave** is supported

by figure-corbels of various designs.

Also probably 15C is the **chancel's** trussed-rafter roof.

Both the north and south walls of the chancel are decorated with a sumptuous blind arcade, possibly added in the early 15C by the monks from nearby Chertsey Abbey.

On the north side, this arcade is interrupted by the outstanding monument to Thomas, Lord Knyvett, d.1622, and his wife, by *Stone*. As Justice of the Peace for Westminster, Knyvett was involved in prosecuting Guy Fawkes and other members of the Gunpowder Plot. He was a confidant of James I and Lady Knyvett, brought up the King's daughters. The school, founded at Stanwell by Knyvett, still stands nearby – at the junction of High Street and Bedfont Road.

On the **sanctuary's** south wall is a rare pillar piscina, discovered buried in the wall in 1948. It is probably contemporary with the chancel, i.e. 13C, but some have suggested a date of 1115.

Next to this is a 14C(?) two-seat sedilia with ogee arches.

•• *Proceed to the* **south aisle**.

The original 14C roof of the aisle has been replaced, but the figure-corbels that supported it are displayed on both walls of the aisle.

At the east end is a 14C piscina.

Above is a small aumbry.

Between the aisle's most easterly windows is a copy of 'The Madonna del Cardelino' by *Raphael*; the original is in the Uffizi in Florence.

Standing on the window-sills are sections of a Norman holy water stoup and fragments of an Easter Sepulchre which, until the 19C, stood on the sanctuary's north wall and formed the tomb of Lord Windsor, d.1486.

•• *Proceed to the west end of the north aisle*.

On the west wall, R of the door, are the old charity boards.

Against the back of the organ is a copy of the painting 'The Madonna of the Rosary' by *Murillo*.

STEPNEY   ST DUNSTAN AND ALL SAINTS

Stepney High Street
(790 9961)

From Central London: *Stepney Green Station, Metropolitan line. Exit and cross Mile End Road. Ahead White Horse Lane leads to Stepney High St.*
From Limehouse,

This is East London's most completely medieval church. Most detailing is 15C but within are features dating back to Saxon times.

It is believed that a small wooden church occupied the site until the late 10C when it was rebuilt of stone by Dunstan, Bishop of London. Initially, this church was dedicated only to All the Saints, but on Dunstan's canonization in 1029 his name was added. Rebuilding took place in the 13C and the chancel's structure survives from this period. The huge parish of Stepney covered all of Middlesex, east of the City, until the 14C when

St Anne: *Bus westward along Commercial Rd to Stepney East Station. Cross the road. Second R Belgrave St leads to Stepney High St.*

the first of sixty-six new parishes were created in the area. Unless this subdivision had happened, St Dunstan's would undoubtedly have been rebuilt in a greatly enlarged form in the 18C. The aisled nave and tower were rebuilt in the 15C and it is the Perpendicular style of this period that therefore predominates. St Dunstan's parish once included Ratcliffe which, in medieval times, was London's port; the association between its church and mariners, therefore, became strong and many lie in its churchyard. Often referred to as the 'Church of the High Seas', births, marriages and deaths at sea were registered at St Dunstan's until fairly recently. It is recorded that John Wesley preached here in 1785.

Externally, most of the building was refaced with Kentish ragstone in 1872.

In 1945 a flying bomb exploded in the churchyard and the resulting damage necessitated reconstruction of the upper part of the 15C **tower**.

The tower's west doorway was rebuilt in the 19C.

•● *Proceed clockwise around the church.*

Most detailing survives from the 15C but flint additions to the structure, and all the porches, are late 19C.

Some gargoyles survive but are much faded.

Although the fabric of the **chancel** is 13C its east window was rebuilt in the 19C.

On the south side there are traces of more gargoyles but the feature of greatest interest is the projecting **tower** that accommodated the stairs to the rood loft.

•● *Enter the church, generally from the south porch.*

The arcades on both sides are 15C.

Immediately L, against the wall of the **south aisle**, is the monument to Dame Rebecca Berry, d.1606.

Trusses of the aisle's 15C roof are supported by damaged figure-corbels.

The **nave**'s 15C roof also survives; its carved bosses have been gilded.

Above the west entrance are the arms of Queen Victoria.

Supporting the most westerly arch of the **north aisle** is a 15C figure-corbel, partly concealed by the organ.

Behind the organ, on the north wall, is the early 17C memorial to Joseph Somes who, the epitaph relates, 'died of an unexpected internal malady'.

The font, in the north aisle, has been much remodelled, but its bowl probably has Saxon origins.

A 13C coffin lid is displayed at the east end of the aisle.

*◆● Proceed to the centre of the **nave**.*

In the 15C the chancel was set back two bays and the arch removed. Its position is indicated by the cavity at upper level in the north wall where the rood screen, which stood beneath the arch, was originally fixed.

The roof structure also changes, where the arch stood.

Its first beam is decorated with 15C figure bosses but, unfortunately, most of the **chancel**'s 15C roof was destroyed by a fire in 1901.

Above the chancel's north door is a 14C(?) Annunciation carving which for many years stood outside the church.

On the north wall is a Jacobean monument to Robert Clarke, d.1610, and his daughter Frances, d.1620.

Below this is a squint which was discovered in 1899. It originally provided a view of the high altar but this has since been brought forward.

Further east, in a recess in the **sanctuary**, is the canopied tomb chest of Sir Henry Colet, d.1510. He was Lord Mayor of London in 1486 and 1495 and his tomb once provided an Easter Sepulchre.

On the east wall, behind the altar, is a stone 10C Saxon rood. Although it stood outside St Dunstan's until 1899, the figures of Christ, the Virgin Mary and St John may still be deciphered.

The mid-13C triple sedilia, in the south wall, retains carved foliage on its central arch and is the chancel's only original feature to survive.

Above the door is a memorial erected in 1621 to Sir Thomas Spert, d.1541. He had been Henry VIII's Comptroller of the Navy and founded Trinity House.

On the south wall is the entrance to the rood loft stairs.

West of this is displayed the stone from Carthage, with its grim inscription by Thomas Hughes, dated 1663. It appears to have been brought to England as a souvenir of a visit to the ancient site in Tunisia.

STOKE NEWINGTON
ST MARY OLD CHURCH

Stoke Newington
Church Street
(254 6072)

**From Central
London:** *Bus 73
(from Hyde Park
Corner, Marble
Arch, etc.)
northbound to Stoke
Newington church.*
**From Hackney,
St John:** *Bus 106 to
Stoke Newington*

Situated beside Clissold Park, Stoke Newington's original parish church presents a surprisingly picturesque scene in this otherwise built-up area. St Mary's is a rare example of a post-Reformation Tudor church and its original brick south arcade is outstanding.

The usually meticulous Domesday Book in its reference to Stoke Newington – Anglo-Saxon for 'the new town in the woods' – makes no reference to a parish church and it is therefore probable that the foundaton was Norman. A rector, Thomas de London, chaplain to Edward III, is recorded in 1313. The church became ruinous

Common. Bus 73 to Stoke Newington church.

and was entirely rebuilt *c*.1560; nothing survives of the earlier building. Complete renovation by *Sir Charles Barry* took place in the 19C.

The clock on the **tower** was presented in 1723 but its minute hand was not added until 1808.

The timber **spire**, first erected by *Barry* in 1829, was renewed as a replica in 1928.

•➡ *Proceed to the north wall.*

In 1716, an outer north aisle was added to extend the capacity of St Mary's. This was demolished by a bomb in the Second World War and not replaced. All the north side's exterior now dates from the rebuilding in the 1950s; the inner north aisle had been extended westward by *Barry* in 1829 to line up with the tower.

•➡ *Proceed anti-clockwise to the south wall, as the east façade cannot be passed.*

Inscribed above the south-west door are the words 'Ab Alto' (from above). It may be the lower part of the Saxon sundial that was removed in the 18C when the tower's clock was installed.

Brick and stone surrounds to the 16C windows in the **south aisle** are original but the tracery is *c*.1808.

The outer south **porch** possesses a late-16C plaster vault.

Above the south-east door are the arms of William Patten, together with his initials and motto 'Prospice' (Look to the future). Patten was rector of St Mary's 1550–71.

•➡ *Enter the church and proceed westward.*

Outstanding is the **south aisle**'s arcade. This is a rare example, within a church, of late Tudor brickwork. It was only revealed *c*.1930 when 19C plaster was removed.

The inner south porch is connected in an unusual way with the later south aisle wall by short cross walls.

Blank recesses in the south aisle's west and south walls are another mysterious feature.

In the 19C *Barry* built a north and **west** gallery but, following the destruction and non-replacement of the outer north aisle, the latter is much curtailed, and the organ has been moved from it.

Box pews are Victorian and none of the church furnishings pre-date the 19C.

At the east end of the **north aisle** is the monument to Joseph Hurlock, d.1793 and his wife, by *Banks*.

The organ was rebuilt in 1928 and now occupies the north side of the **chancel**.

Against the chancel's south wall is St Mary's finest monument. It commemorates a Lord of the Manor, John Dudley, d.1580, and his wife, Elizabeth, d.1602.

The massive Gothic Revival pulpit, which partly obscures the Dudley tomb from the nave, was part of the 19C restoration.

 Exit from the church.

Immediately opposite is the 19C church of St Mary which took over the parochial function of the old church. It was built, in Early English Gothic Revival style, by *George Gilbert Scott* and consecrated in 1858.

TWICKENHAM ALL HALLOWS

Chertsey Road
(892 1322)

From Central London: *Waterloo Station (BR) to Twickenham Station (BR). Exit R Whitton Rd. Fourth R Erncroft Way leads to Chertsey Rd.*
From Twickenham, St Mary: *Exit L Church St. First R London Rd leads to Whitton Rd, proceed as above.*

Although the body of the building is of little architectural interest, All Hallows' incorporates the rebuilt tower of Wren's All Hallows Lombard Street, in the City of London and most of that church's outstanding 17C furnishings.

An All Hallows had stood in Lombard Street in the City of London since the Saxon period. It was rebuilt, for the third time, by *Wren* following the Great Fire. Eventually, owing to soil subsidence, the structure became dangerous and was demolished in 1938. Its Portland stone tower, however, was carefully taken down and re-erected here at Twickenham as part of a new church, designed by *Robert Atkinson* in 1940.

The body of Twickenham's All Hallows' is a simple brick structure consisting of a nave/chancel linked to the old tower by a narthex (ante-chapel).

The east entrance to the **tower** is surmounted by Death and Father Time.

 Enter the church.

The 18C chandelier was made by *John Townsend*, Master of the Pewterer's Company.

Against the north wall is a 17C wooden gate which originally stood in Lombard Street at the end of an alley leading to the old City church. As it was in danger of disintegrating, the gate was moved into the church in 1865. It is carved with the death emblem.

On the west wall is the monument to the founder of the Royal College of Surgeons, Edward Tyson, d.1708. His bust was carved by *Edward Stanton.*

 Proceed through the modern narthex where several old monuments from All Hallows' are displayed.

At the west end of the **nave**, from All Hallows', are the doorcases flanked by church warden's pews and, above, the organ case. All these are 17C but the organ **gallery** is modern.

The white marble font came from St Benet Gracechurch Street, another demolished City church. Although not the original, its 17C cover was made to fit.

The pews in the church are 18C.

Two Lord Mayor's sword rests, made in 1800 and 1831 respectively, are displayed.

The canopied pulpit is a copy of that of St Mary Abchurch, in the City.

Suspended near the pulpit is a chandelier that was designed by *Comper* in this century for St John's, Red Lion Square, Holborn, another London church that has been demolished.

Against the south wall, behind the lectern, are 16C bread shelves.

The Wren period altar rail is from All Hallows'.

Decorating the 17C reredos are panels painted in 1880.

TWICKENHAM   ST MARY-THE-VIRGIN

Church Street
(892 2318)

Open infrequently apart from services.

From Central London: *Waterloo Station (BR) to Twickenham Station (BR). Exit L London Rd. Continue to the King St/York St junction. Second L Church St.*
From All Hallows, Twickenham: *Proceed to Whitton Rd L. Continue to London Rd; proceed as above.*

St Mary's combines a medieval tower of ragstone with an 18C brick nave and chancel. Excellent 17C monuments (from the earlier building) and 18C monuments include one to Alexander Pope, the poet. The riverside village situation is most picturesque.

The earliest record of a church on the site is in 1332. St Mary's was rebuilt of Kentish ragstone towards the end of the 14C but its nave collapsed in 1713. This was rebuilt in brick by *James*, but the ancient tower was retained.

Externally, the fine quality of the brickwork is apparent.

•➡ *Enter from the north door.*

Renovations in 1860 removed the box pews but the galleries, although altered, were retained.

The ceilings of the nave and the sanctuary have recently been redesigned by *Richardson*.

The **north aisle**'s east window commemorates the painter Sir Godfrey Kneller who is buried in the church. His monument, intended for St Mary's, is in Westminster Abbey.

Although the pulpit was made in 1714 its tester is modern.

In front of the chancel step L, a brass floor plate commemorates the burial in the church of the poet Alexander Pope, d.1744. The plate was presented by three American scholars. Pope lived nearby at Pope's Villa in Cross Deep, since demolished.

He lies beneath the adjoining stone inscribed with a 'P'.

The altar rail and reredos are original.

In the **sanctuary** is the monument to Sir W. Humble, d.1680, and his son, by *Bird*(?). This was brought from the earlier church.

On the east wall of the **south aisle**, beneath the gallery, a monument, also from the earlier church, commemorates Francis Poulton, d.1642, and his wife.

•➡ *Return to the west end of the church.*

Beneath the **tower** are two 17C monuments: Sir Joseph Ashe, from the studio of *Gibbons*; and

General Lord Berkeley of Stratton.

*●▶ Proceed L to the door in the south-west corner. A further door L leads to the **south gallery**. Unfortunately, this will be locked unless there is an attendant present.*

The monument to George and Anne Gostling is by *Bacon the Younger*, 1800.

Nathaniel Piggott, d.1737, is commemorated by a monument designed by *Scheemakers*.

●▶ Proceed to the door in the north-west corner. A further door R leads to the north gallery – again probably locked.

The monument to Admiral Sir Chaloner Ogle is by *Rysbrack*, 1751.

Alexander Pope is commemorated by a memorial commissioned by his friend Bishop Warburton in 1761.

At the east end, a further memorial to Alexander Pope commemorates, not the poet, but his father and mother, by *Bird*.

Below this is a memorial to author Richard Owen Cambridge, d.1802.

UXBRIDGE ST MARGARET

Windsor Street,
Uxbridge
(0895 39055)

*Open Monday–
Friday 11.00–14.00.
(Rebuilding during
1987–8 may entail the
occasional closing of
the church. When this
work has been
completed
St Margaret's will
probably remain open
later.)*

**From Central
London:** *Uxbridge
Station, Piccadilly
line. Exit and cross the
road to the Market
House; the church
stands behind.*
**From Harefield,
St Mary:** *Bus 347 or
348 to Uxbridge
Station; proceed as
above.*
**From Hillingdon,
St John:** *Bus 207 to
Uxbridge Station;
proceed as above.*

St Margaret's is a 13C building, much altered and extended in the mid-15C. Some features survive from both periods, including the timber roof and arcades. In the sanctuary is the macabre Bennet monument. The church is in the process of being reorientated (1987).

A church at Uxbridge is first recorded in 1200 but nothing appears to have survived from this building. It may have had a Saxon foundation although there is no reference to Uxbridge in Domesday. Complete rebuilding of the body of the church took place c.1240. Nothing is known of a tower at this period, but it is possible that some of the fabric of an earlier structure was re-used when this was built (or rebuilt) c.1360. In the mid-15C the chancel was extended eastward, a north chantry chapel added to it and the south aisle rebuilt in a greatly enlarged form.

The entire church was refaced with flint in the 19C.

Although the upper part of the **tower** was rebuilt c.1820 the lower stage, with its unusual feature of a north portal, survives from c.1360. Originally, doors were not provided to this external entrance, only to the doorway within.

A cupola surmounted the 19C section of the tower and this feature was re-created in 1986.

●▶ Proceed clockwise around the church.

The windows east and west of the north door predate the mid-15C extensions.

Forming a **north chapel** to the chancel is the Shyrington chantry, built c.1450, almost certainly at the same time as the chancel itself was extended eastward.

The **south aisle** is considerably larger than the nave and chancel. It replaced a much smaller aisle, c.1450, to provide a chapel for the Guild of St Mary and St Margaret, founded at Uxbridge in 1448.

Apart from the two most westerly windows in the south wall, which are original, the south aisle's windows were all enlarged in the 19C.

Its west wall's window, formed in 1886, replaced a small, 13C example that had survived because part of the earlier south aisle's west wall in which it stood had been re-used.

Although the fabric of the **nave**'s west wall is 13C, its window was rebuilt in the 19C.

The west corner of the **north aisle** was flattened out c.1820 to facilitate road widening. In this section is a re-set 13C window that had previously been positioned centrally in the aisle's west wall.

•● *Enter the porch from the north door in the tower.*

Ahead, the doorway to the church appears to be weatherworn, probably indicating that it served as an external entrance before the tower was built.

•● *Enter the original* **nave**.

Both arcades are late medieval.

The higher roof indicates the eastward extension of the chancel in 1450.

The nave's chandelier was presented in 1735.

It is planned to reorientate the church by the end of 1988. Several alterations in connection with this will take place.

The high altar will once again stand at the west end of the south aisle, a position which it had long occupied prior to the reorganization of 1872.

It is hoped that a new lantern in the roof can be constructed at the east end of the original nave to increase natural light.

The late-15C font, with its cover, c.1850, may be brought from the north aisle to stand beneath the new lantern.

The original chancel's screen was designed by *W. L. Eves* in 1920 to serve as a First World War memorial; it is to be repositioned.

Many ancient furnishings were unfortunately lost during 19C alterations.

The east chandelier was made in 1695; St Margaret's is one of only twelve churches in the country to possess a 17C example; it may be relocated.

Against the old sanctuary's north wall is St Margaret's most important monument, the tomb chest of Lady Leonora Bennet, d.1638. In the front of its base a recess is carved to depict a charnel house behind bars which are gripped by a skeletal hand.

The original **south aisle**, which is to become the new nave and sanctuary, retains its 15C hammerbeam roof supported by corbels, some of which are carved with heads.

Surviving from the 17C reredos are the paintings of Moses and Aaron; the remainder was replaced by the present alabaster and stone reredos designed and made locally in 1885. The location of these paintings is dependent on the reorientation.

West of the north door, at upper level, is a small blocked doorway which originally led to the belfry stairs. It was presumably approached via steps or a gallery, no trace of which remains.

•● *Exit from the church.*

The Market House which screens St Margaret's north façade, was not built until 1788.

WAPPING ST GEORGE-IN-THE-EAST
Hawksmoor 1726

Cannon Street Road

From Central London: *Shadwell Station, East London line. Exit R Cable St. L Cannon St Rd.*
From St Anne, Limehouse: *Take any eastbound bus along Commercial Rd to Cannon St Rd.*

The church was bombed in the Second World War and only the exterior has been restored to its original appearance. It has been proposed that St George's should be converted to provide a Church of England museum during the 1990s.

The **tower** is judged to be Hawksmoor's most distinctive.

Internally the church is modern and dates from the 1964 restoration by *Bailey*.

WENNINGTON ST MARY AND ST PETER

Wennington Road (04027 52752)

From Central London: *Barking Station, District and Metropolitan lines. Proceed from Barking Station (BR) to Rainham Station (BR). Exit and cross the road. Bus 375 or 723 to Wennington church. Both are London Country buses and services are irregular. Telephone 688 7261 for times and precise details of bus stop locations. A taxi from Rainham is preferable.*
From Rainham, St Helen: *Proceed from Rainham church as above.*

This is basically a 13C church with a 14C tower and north aisle. Features from eight centuries of development survive, together with a re-used Norman doorway which probably came from an earlier church on the site. The Jacobean pulpit is exceptional.

Little is known of the early history of the church. Its chancel, nave and south arcade are 13C but the Norman doorway points to an earlier building. The north aisle was added in the 14C and this was soon followed by the tower which is built entirely of Kentish ragstone.

•● *Proceed anti-clockwise around the church.*

The south doorway of the **tower** was formed *c.*1500.

A completely new south wall was built in 1886 thus creating a south aisle once more. Its 13C predecessor had been demolished, possibly in the 17C, and the south arcade was then filled to form the outer wall.

The south window of the **chancel** is 14C but its tracery is modern.

In the south wall is a re-used Norman doorway, not in its original position; this was presumably retained from an earlier building on the site.

The chancel's east window also retains original 14C splays but, again, its tracery is modern.

A 13C lancet window survives in the chancel's north wall.

The 14C **north aisle** retains its original door splays but the remainder, and all three windows, are modern.

Complete rebuilding of the north **porch** took place *c*.1900.

The wooden north door is 14C.

Enter the **north aisle**.

A central octagonal pier supports the two-bay 14C arcade.

Facing the entrance is the 13C Purbeck marble font; its cover is Jacobean.

Standing in the aisle is a 13C hutch-type oak chest with the usual three locks as specified by Thomas Cromwell in the 16C.

At the east end, above an old piscina canopy in the south wall, is the memorial to a 17C rector, Henry Bust, d.1625, and his son, d.1626.

The early-17C pulpit has some fine Jacobean carving; its wooden base was removed at some time and replaced by the present stone support. A footstool was made from the old section.

Adjacent to the pulpit, and projecting from a pier, is a 17C wrought-iron hourglass stand.

The chancel arch is 15C.

A beam in the **chancel**'s 14C king-post roof is decorated with fleurs-de-lis.

The two **sanctuary** chairs are late 17C.

In the sanctuary's south wall is a 13C piscina.

Diapering decorates the re-used Norman doorway to the **south aisle**.

The 13C south arcade, with its circular pier was unblocked in 1886 when the new external south wall was built.

At the west end of the **nave**, looking into the tower, is the 13C lancet window. It appears that this preceded the building of a tower at Wennington as its west side is rebated for an external shutter.

The 14C west doorway from the nave was built when the tower was completed.

WEST HAM   ALL SAINTS

Church Street
(519 0955)

*Open Friday
08.30–11.45.*

**From Central
London:** *Plaistow
Station, District and*

Although part of the core of 19C dockland, West Ham possesses an ancient parish church which has miraculously escaped rebuilding. It retains a partially blocked clerestory and wall fabric from the Norman period. However most external detailing is late medieval. Within, are a 15C tie-beam roof, 13C arcades and some extravagant 17C monuments.

Metropolitan lines.
Exit L. Take any
westbound bus to
Church St (West
Ham).
From East Ham,
St Mary Magdalene:
Bus S1 to West Ham
church.

All Saints', founded in Saxon times, was rebuilt
c.1180. East and west extensions were made and
north and south aisles added to the nave c.1250.
The west tower was built and the nave extended
eastward c.1400. Aisles were added to both sides
of the chancel in the 16C.

The early-15C **tower** was completely restored in
1978. Its bell was made in 1857 as a prototype for
Big Ben.

•● *Proceed clockwise around the church.*

Partly blocked Romanesque clerestory windows
in the north wall of the **nave** indicate the length of
the Norman building.

The original stonework of the 13C **north aisle**
survives; at its east end the brick tower housed
the stairs to the rood loft.

In the early years of the Reformation, most
church plate was confiscated by the sovereign but
All Saints' sold theirs just in time and built the
chancel's north aisle of Tudor brick with the
proceeds. It was completed c.1550.

The east window of the **chancel** was rebuilt in the
19C.

It is believed that work on the **chancel's south
aisle** was begun towards the end of the 15C and
this therefore predates its northern counterpart.
Tudor brickwork survives.

The 13C **south aisle** was completely refaced in
yellow bricks in the 19C.

Again, on this side, the partly blocked Norman
clerestory survives in the **nave**.

The medieval 'Long Porch' was reconstructed in
the 19C. A two-light, late medieval window, L of
its entrance, has been re-used from Stratford
Langthorne Abbey which owned All Saints' until
the Reformation.

•● *Enter the* **south aisle** *and turn L.*

Above the south-west vestry door, a lion and
unicorn flank the painted monogram of William
IV.

Both the nave's arcades were created in the mid-
13C by piercing the Norman walls; they are
identical and possess circular piers.

The tie-beam roof was built throughout the nave
and chancel c.1500.

All Saints' possesses three fonts; its Victorian
example stands in the centre, at the west end of
the **nave**.

A west organ gallery was removed in the 19C and
the arch to the base of the **tower** was thereby
reopened.

Inserted in the north wall of the tower in 1903
was the stone decorated with skulls, which also
came from Langthorne Abbey.

In the **north aisle**, at the west end, is a medieval
font.

At the east end is another font, inscribed with the names of three churchwardens and the date 1707.

Fixed to the chancel arch beam are the arms of George II.

Proceed to the **chancel's north aisle**.

The piers of both the chancel's 16C aisles are octagonal.

With the removal of the west gallery in the 19C the organ was re-sited here.

The tie-beam roof of the chancel, *c*.1500, continues that of the nave.

Against the north side of the east wall of the **sanctuary** is the monument to Thomas Foot, Lord Mayor of London, d.1688, and his wife, Elizabeth. There is no family connection with Michael Foot, the ex-leader of the Labour Party.

On the same wall, in a pedimented niche to the south, is the monument to James Cooper, d.1724, and his wife.

George Gilbert Scott was responsible for the late-19C restoration of the church and the reredos was made to his design.

Against the south wall of the sanctuary are monuments to John Faldo, d.1613, and Francis Faldo, d.1632.

The chancel's south aisle was partitioned to form the **St Thomas Chapel** in 1966. Its name was chosen to commemorate an adjacent parish that had recently been integrated with West Ham.

Lettering, painted in the 16C, was discovered above the chapel's north arch in 1977 and this has been preserved by the Passmore Edwards Museum.

Against the chapel's north wall is the monument to William Fawcett, d.1631, his wife and her second husband.

A monument on the west wall by *Edward Stanton* commemorates several of the Buckeridge children who died between 1698 and 1710.

Exit from the church.

A school once stood in the churchyard where, in 1723, girls were given public education for the first time in England.

London south of the Thames

Fewer London parish churches of interest exist south of the Thames, mainly because the cities of London and Westminster were situated on the north bank and only one bridge crossed the river until 1750.

As on the north side, most of those selected are medieval and again it will usually be necessary to make visiting arrangements in advance.

Public transport information is given in the same style as that for north London churches.

Addington, St Mary
Barnes, St Mary
Battersea, St Mary
Beddington, St Mary
Bermondsey, St Mary
  Magdalen
Bexley, St Mary-the-Virgin
Carshalton, All Saints
Charlton, St Luke
Cheam, St Dunstan (Lumley
  Chapel)
Chislehurst, St Nicholas
Coulsdon, St John-the-
  Evangelist
Crayford, St Paulinus
Deptford, St Paul
Greenwich, St Alfege

Kew, St Anne
Kingston, All Saints
Merton, St Mary-the-Virgin
Morden, St Lawrence
Orpington, All Saints
Petersham, St Peter
Plumstead, St Nicholas
Putney, St Mary
Richmond, St Mary
  Magdalene
Rotherhithe, St Mary
Southwark, St George-the-
  Martyr
Southwark, St Peter
Tooting Graveney, All Saints
Wimbledon, St Mary-the-
  Virgin

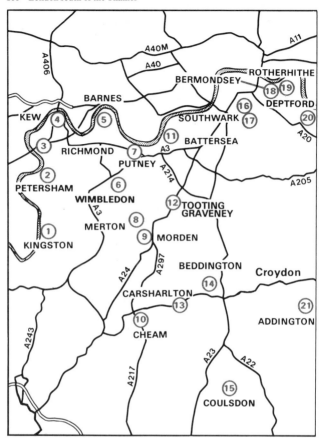

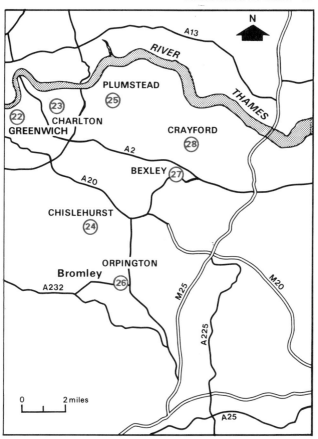

Kew, St Anne **4**
Kingston, All Saints **1**
Merton, St Mary-the-Virgin **8**
Morden, St Lawrence **9**
Orpington, All Saints **26**
Petersham, St Peter **2**
Plumstead, St Nicholas **25**

Putney, St Mary **7**
Richmond, St Mary Magdalene **3**
Rotherhithe, St Mary **19**
Southwark, St George-the-Martyr **16**
Southwark, St Peter **17**
Tooting Graveney, All Saints **12**
Wimbledon, St Mary-the-Virgin **6**

ADDINGTON   ST MARY

Addington Village
Road
(0689 42167)

*Open mornings
except Thursday.*

**From Central
London:** *Victoria
Station (BR) to East
Croydon Station
(BR). Bus 130 or
130B to Lodge Lane,
Addington. Ahead
Addington Village
Rd. The church lies in
the park L.*
**From Beddington,
St Mary:** *Bus 403 to
East Croydon
Station; proceed as
above.*

Apart from its attractive rural setting, St Mary's
is renowned for its Norman chancel and triple
round-headed window – a great rarity in the
London area. Five 19C archbishops of
Canterbury, who resided at Addington Palace
nearby are commemorated in the church.

St Mary's was built in 1080 and the chancel of this
building survives. A south aisle was added in
1210 but there was no north aisle until the present
structure was built in 1876 when, also, the tower
was rebuilt on its Norman foundations. The
church was refaced in flint by *Blore* in 1850.

Although built in the early 13C, detailing in the
south aisle is entirely Victorian.

The south **porch** was rebuilt in 1843.

•➔ Proceed anti-clockwise around the church.

Fortunately, the **chancel** retains its set of Norman
round-headed windows.

Below the south wall's westerly example is a later
leper window rebated on both sides, presumably
for shutters.

The window further east has been blocked
internally.

In the east wall, the upper window was blocked
from the 13C until 1897 when it was re-opened.

Below is the stepped triplet, added in 1140, a rare
example in the London area.

In the north wall of the chancel is another
original window.

The north-east **vestry** was added for Archbishop
Sutton in 1808 and below this is his family vault.

The remainder of the north side of St Mary's is
entirely late 19C work.

*•➔ Return to the south porch and enter the **south
aisle***.

The alternating circular and octagonal piers of
the south arcade were built, when the aisle was
added, in 1210; their bases have been obscured
by the subsequent raising of the floor level.

On the south-west window-sill the Elizabethan
figure of an unknown lady is part of a monument;
the torso of her husband lies outside the vestry
but the remainder has disappeared.

The base of the tower was converted to a
baptistry in 1912 when the present Arts and
Crafts alabaster font was made.

A gallery was removed from the west end of the
nave in 1876.

The arcade of the **north aisle** marks the position
of the external north wall prior to the aisle's
addition in 1876.

Between 1805 and 1897 Addington Palace, which
stood nearby, was an out-of-town residence of
the archbishops of Canterbury following their

disposal of Croydon Palace in 1780. Because of this, many monuments commemorate 19C archbishops, two of whom lie in the church and three in the churchyard. Unfortunately, none are judged to be of great artistic value.

The chancel arch was rebuilt in 1876.

Decoration was added to the **chancel**'s walls in 1897 to commemorate Archbishop Benson; one speculates if he would have been flattered.

On the north wall is the large composite monument to three generations of the Leigh family, lords of the manor from 1447 to 1737. The top section commemorating L John Leigh, d.1503 and his wife, Isabel, and R their son, Nicholas, with his wife, Anne, was made for Nicholas before his death in 1540. The bottom half, commemorating Sir Oliph Leigh, the son of Nicholas and Anne, and his wife, Jane, was added c.1612.

In the **sanctuary** stands the bishop's chair, presented in 1897.

By tradition, a lamp has burned in the sanctuary since the Middle Ages to represent the close connection between St Mary's and St Mary Overie, at Southwark, now Southwark Cathedral. The present lamp was given in 1947.

In the centre of the south wall of the chancel is the exceptional monument by *Wilton* to a lady born in Boston, USA: Grizzel Trecothic, d.1769.

In a niche on the south wall, R of the leper window, is an urn commemorating a Lord Mayor of London, Barlow Trecothic, d.1775. Locally, this is called facetiously the 'Addington pickle jar'.

BARNES   ST MARY

Church Road

Open Monday–
Friday 10.30–12.30.

From Central
London: *Waterloo*
Station (BR) to
Barnes Bridge Station
(BR). From the
platform descend the
steps and turn R. R
The Terrace. First R
High St. Second L
Church Rd.
From Putney,
St Mary: *Proceed*
northward along
Putney High St to
Putney Station (BR);
train direct to Barnes
Bridge Station.
NB: Barnes Bridge
Station is closed on
Sunday and the

Although St Mary's was badly damaged by fire in 1978, with the loss of many important monuments, practically all of its ancient sections have been salvaged and incorporated in the rebuilt church. Restoration work, in fact, revealed some of the best examples of late-12C internal decoration that can be seen in the London area.

A chapel, built c.1100, was doubled in size c.1190, a date only recently established. The tradition that this building was consecrated on its completion by Stephen Langton when he returned to London from the Magna Carta ceremony in 1215, therefore, seems to be unjustified. Most of the north side of St Mary's was rebuilt and enlarged between 1777 and 1905; practically all this work was destroyed by the fire of 1978 and rebuilding, by *Cullinan* in 1984, provided what is virtually a new church.

Surviving from the late-12C are the south and east walls of the original chancel, now the **Langton Chapel**. This follows the second buttress; both buttresses were erected c.1480.

approach must then be made from Barnes Station (BR), the previous stop.

In the east wall of the chapel are three late-12C lancet windows, blocked in 1777 but rediscovered and restored in 1852.

Most work north of this point is by *Cullinan* 1984.

The stone section of the clergy **vestry**, which protrudes eastward, immediately north of the Langton Chapel, survives from the extension of 1905.

•● *Return westward, passing the south porch.*

Immediately west of the porch is a further short section of the late-12C wall which was extended westward in the 13C to the point where the tower now stands.

The **tower** was added *c.*1480. Its clock and sundial were made in 1792.

•● *Return eastward to the south entrance.*

This entrance was formed *c.*1480 and the original Norman doorway, slightly further east, was then blocked.

The present porch was built in 1777.

At the same time the buttress R was erected at the point where the old doorway had stood.

•● *Enter the church.*

Following the recent rebuilding, the high altar was re-sited to the north.

•● *Turn L.*

The modern font was made of stones from the ruined part of the church.

On the south wall of the **old nave**, R of the window, is an example of the double line-block pattern with rosettes executed in the 13C(?) and discovered after the fire.

On the west wall are fragments of early 17C Black Letter script.

•● *Return eastward, passing the entrance door, and follow the south wall.*

Within the filled early-12C doorway are traces of late-12C single line-block pattern decoration together with a more elaborate pattern.

Until it was destroyed in the fire, the Hoare family monument, the most imposing in the church, had stood in front of the blocked doorway. Banker Sir Richard Hoare, d.1787, was the owner of Barn Elms, a late-17C residence which had replaced an earlier mansion owned by Elizabeth I's Secretary of State, Sir Francis Walsingham. The house stood near the river but was demolished in 1954.

Just before the chancel arch is a curved recess, remains of the stairway to the rood screen loft.

The walls of the old chancel, now the **Langton Chapel**, are decorated with 14C angel bosses which came from the earlier roof. They bear the Downshire arms.

Between the last two east windows is the

memorial to Rector John Squier, d.1662.

Fragments of a 14C frieze survive above the east wall's lancet windows.

On the north wall of the chapel, below the first window from the east, is the brass of the Wylde sisters, 1508. It was previously set in the chancel floor.

●● *Proceed northward.*

The old part of the church is linked by a short nave to the **new sanctuary** with its **transepts**.

All this work is new, but some small windows, and the large window (1852) above the altar, were saved from the fire and re-used.

By 1777, the north wall of the medieval church had disappeared completely owing to extensions, and there was further major rebuilding on this side in 1852 and 1906. Very little of the medieval St Mary's structure was, therefore, lost in the fire.

BATTERSEA ST MARY *Joseph Dixon 1776*

Battersea Church Road
(228 9648)

From Central London: *Bus 19 (Piccadilly Circus, Sloane Square, etc.), 39, 45, 49 to Battersea Church Rd (second stop after Battersea Bridge has been crossed).*
From Chelsea, All Saints: *Follow Cheyne Walk westward. First L Battersea Bridge. Second R Battersea Church Rd.*

Battersea's late-Georgian church which overlooks the river has suffered little from 'improvements'. Its galleries survive and against their walls are displayed several fine monuments. The vestry, from where J. M. W. Turner painted his Battersea sunsets, may be visited and his chair in the sanctuary inspected. Rare 17C stained glass in the east window is attributed to *Van Linge.*

First recorded in 1157, it is believed that Battersea's parish church was founded in the 9C. Rebuilding took place on several occasions.

●● *Enter the churchyard through its exceptional iron gates.*

The present church of brick, with stone quoins and trims, was completed by *Dixon* in 1776 and little had changed externally. Nothing structurally exists from earlier buildings.

●● *Enter the south porch, proceed to the* **south aisle** *and turn left.*

Against the south wall is the monument to a merchant, James Bull, d.1713. Local tradition claims that he was the prototype of England's figurehead, 'John Bull'.

The west **vestry**, flanked by two doors, is little altered from the early 19C when the great painter J. M. W. Turner, frequently sat there to paint his Battersea sunsets.

On the north side of the **nave**'s west wall are beadles' wands, presented to St Mary's in 1737.

Two modern windows in the **north aisle**, by *John Hayward*, commemorate Turner and William Blake, the artist and poet, who married Catherine Boucher in this church in 1782.

In the north-east corner of the aisle is the font, made for the church, but with a later cover.

The central pews were originally box-type but altered as part of reorganization by *A. Blomfield* in 1878.

Similarly cut down was the pulpit, once a three-decker.

Flanking the chancel arch are the royal arms of: L, Elizabeth I and R, George IV.

The chair at the south end of the **sanctuary** is believed to have been used by Turner whilst painting in St Mary's vestry; it now serves as the bishop's chair.

Stained glass in the east window was made *c*.1631 and came from the earlier St Mary's. It is attributed to *Van Linge* and commemorates Battersea's St John family. Their coats of arms and portraits of their illustrious Tudor ancestors Margaret Beauchamp, Henry VII and Elizabeth I are incorporated.

The circular flanking windows of a lamb and a dove were painted by *John Pearson* in 1796.

St Mary's incongruously modern chandelier was made in 1962.

The **south aisle** windows by *Hayward* commemorate William Curtis the botanist, d.1799, and Benedict Arnold, d.1801, who fought in the American War of Independence; he is buried in the crypt.

Unusually, the galleries were not removed in the 19C restoration, probably because the most important monuments can only be reached from them.

•● Ascend, with an attendant, to the **north gallery.**

At the west end is an early example of a Classical style monument. It commemorates Sir Oliver St John, Viscount Grandison, d.1630, and is by *Stone.*

Further east is the monument to politician and philosopher Henry St John, Viscount Bolingbroke, d.1751, by *Roubiliac.* He married Mary, Clara des Champs de Marcilly, the niece of Madame de Maintenon who secretly became the second wife of Louis XIV of France.

Against the east wall is the monument to Sir John Fleet, a Lord Mayor of London, d.1712.

•● Return to the nave and ascend to the **south gallery.**

At the west end is a Coade stone monument to John Camden, d.1792, and his daughter, Elizabeth Neild.

A 17C 'James Bond' is commemorated at the east end. Edward Wynter, d.1686, according to the relief killed a tiger and fought off sixty mounted Moors single-handed. He, of course, was on foot!

BEDDINGTON ST MARY

Church Road
(647 1973)

**From Central
London:** *Victoria
Station (BR) to
Carshalton Station
(BR). Exit L to High
St (see Carshalton,
All Saints). Bus 403,
408, 716, 726
eastbound to Church
Rd, Beddington.*
**From Carshalton, All
Saint:** *Proceed as
above from
Carshalton High St.*

Most of this church was built in the late 14C and
early 15C. However, St Mary's greatest
architectural attraction is the chancel's south
chapel, added in 1520 for Sir Richard Carew, and
retaining most of its original Tudor features.
Outstanding furnishings include the early-15C
stalls with their carved misericords, a Norman
font, and a Jacobean font cover and pulpit.

St Mary's is recorded in Domesday, but that
church, probably of wood, was rebuilt in the late
12C. Part of the fabric of the chancel's piers and
the outer north aisle's east and west piers are all
that remain of this Norman building and none of
this is visible. Most of the church was rebuilt
between the late 14C and mid 15C following a
bequest, in 1391, by Nicholas Carew, Lord of the
Manor. The Carew Chapel was added, south of
the chancel, in 1520. In 1869 major external and
internal restoration took place and the tower was
virtually rebuilt; also added at this time were the
outer north aisle and the north-west vestry. Most
of St Mary's was refaced with flint in 1915.

The church is approached through a **lich-gate**,
built *c.*1868.

Much of the structure of the **tower** is early 15C
but major restoration took place early in the 19C
and again when the clock was added in 1869, the
date displayed on the weathervane.

The **south aisle** and its **porch** were also completed
early in the 15C.

Dormer windows were added to the roof of the
nave in 1915.

The tracery in the west window of the 16C **south-
east chapel** is original.

The **chancel** was probably completed in the late
14C but its east window is modern.

•● *Return to the south porch and enter the church
(it is not possible to pass the mostly 19C north
façade).*

The south and inner north arcades were built in
the late 14C with octagonal piers, but the north
arcade was heavily restored in 1869.

An unusual design feature of the piers is their
central grooving.

At the west end of the **inner north aisle** is the
Purbeck marble font, *c.*1190, which now
possesses a Jacobean cover.

The **vestry** was added north of the west tower in
1869 when the outer aisle was built. The 19C
piers of the **outer north aisle** mark the position of
the original north wall.

Against the west wall of this aisle is St Mary's
earlier reredos, a copy of a medieval German
altarpiece, which was presented to mark the 19C
restoration.

The window at the east end of the **inner north
aisle** retains its original early-15C tracery.

The **nave**'s roof was rebuilt in 1869.

The **chancel**'s arch and roof were rebuilt and a screen and decoration added by *Joseph Clarke* in 1869. While this work was in progress, a 14C mural was discovered above the chancel arch.

The organ was moved to its present position north of the chancel in 1852 following the demolition of St Mary's galleries. Its carved **loft**, regarded as exceptional work by *William Morris*, was erected to accommodate the present organ when it was made in 1869.

Outstanding are the chancel's nine choir stalls with carved misericords, made *c.*1410; two stand on the north side, seven on the south. It has been suggested that they were provided for the 'four fit chaplains' whom Nicholas Carew, in his will of 1391, arranged to pray for his soul; however, it seems more likely that they came from nearby Merton Abbey's church, following its dissolution in the 16C.

There are several good brasses in the chancel floor; the earliest commemorates Philippa Carew, d.1414.

The altar rail was made in 1713.

On the **sanctuary**'s south wall are a piscina and a sedilia, constructed *c.*1869; they do not appear to have been replacements.

South of the chancel, separated by the original Perpendicular screen, is the **Carew Chapel**, added by Sir Richard Carew shortly before his death in 1520.

The tomb of Sir Richard stands in a canopied recess in the centre of the south wall.

East of this is the alabaster monument to Sir Francis Carew, d.1611, commissioned by his niece, Elizabeth Throckmorton, wife of Sir Walter Ralegh.

More recent members of the Carew family lie beneath the chapel and are commemorated by less imposing monuments.

Although Jacobean, the pulpit's decoration incorporates Tudor-style linenfold panelling. It is possibly contemporary with the font cover and may have been presented by Sir Francis Carew.

Exit from the church.

To the east, the churchyard is separated from the ancient Manor House by a 17C brick wall. The house was sold following the death and bankruptcy of Charles Hallowell Carew in 1872. It is now a school but retains the Tudor hall with its hammerbeam roof.

BERMONDSEY   ST MARY MAGDALEN

Bermondsey Street
(407 5273)

*On Friday mornings
the famous*

St Mary's, rebuilt in 1680, was remodelled externally in the 19C but retains part of its 15C tower. Remarkably, its three original galleries survive within. An outstanding altar is ascribed to the great Huguenot ironsmith, Jean Tijou.

Bermondsey 'flea' market is held beside the church.

From Central London: *Bus 42, 78 (from Tower Bridge) to the Bricklayers Arms, Bermondsey.*
From Rotherhithe, St Mary: *Bus 188 westwards along Jamaica Rd to the Bricklayers Arms, Bermondsey.*

Bermondsey's parish church is first recorded, as a chapel, in 1296. It was built within the grounds of the Cluniac Bermondsey Priory which was founded in the 11C and upgraded to abbey status in 1399. The abbey, which stood south of the church, was dissolved in 1537 but part of it survived physically until the 19C as outbuildings of Bermondsey House. St Mary's, probably rebuilt in the 15C, was extended and altered in the 17C, but by 1680 its structure had become unsafe and rebuilding was put in hand. Retained was part of the 15C tower and, possibly, some of the north wall's fabric. The architect of the new building was *Charles Stanton* but most external features now date from the 19C remodelling.

Originally, the **west front** consisted of a portico which extended over the pavement into Bermondsey Street. Above this, a long, narrow chamber served as a schoolroom. Both were dismantled in 1829 because the church had begun to lean northward following the demolition of the rectory which had apparently buttressed the north wall. This façade was then remodelled by *George Porter* in a fanciful style, more reminiscent of Strawberry Hill's 18C Neo-Gothic then the more serious Gothic Revival which was then gaining popularity. At the same time, the exterior of the church was stuccoed.

The medieval **tower** had been extended by two storeys, surmounted by a small dome and a lantern, but these additions were also removed in 1829 as an additional safety measure. Sections of the fabric of the tower's three lower stages were examined in 1972 and pronounced to be of 15C stonework.

The existence of what appears to be a genuine 14C Decorated style window on its west face is, therefore, a mystery. If it were contemporary with the stonework, it would be Perpendicular in style and has either been re-used, or designed as a pastiche at a more recent date.

•● *Proceed anti-clockwise to the* **south transept**.

Originally the transept was built with an entrance portal but this was bricked up in 1795 so that a pew could be formed within for children from the new deaf and dumb school which stood nearby.

The **chancel** was extended eastward by one bay in 1885 to accommodate choir stalls. Its east window then replaced a three-light example.

•● *Enter the church, probably from the modern north-east vestry. Turn L and follow the* **north aisle**.

Internally, St Mary's evokes an enlarged Wren City church and has certain similiarities with his St Martin-within-Ludgate.

Both arcades incorporate Tuscan columns and the aisles are paved with bricks.

Against the north wall are funeral hatchments of the Gaitskell family; most of them are 18C. They evidently have no connections with Hugh

Gaitskell, a recent leader of the Labour Party.

At the north-west end stands the font; its bowl is late 17C but the stem was made in 1808.

The **north gallery** is original to the church but part of the **west gallery** was destroyed by fire in 1971 and has mostly been rebuilt.

Also damaged in the fire was the organ case made in 1750; the organ within was replaced in 1853.

The **south gallery** was added in 1795 when the south door was blocked. Beneath it, the arch has been enclosed to form a choir vestry.

At the west end of the church, south of the central arch, is the churchwardens' box pew, with its original desk.

At the east end of the **south aisle** is a wrought-iron altar, originally made for another church within the parish, St Olave, Tooley Street, which was closed in 1918. It is ascribed to the great French ironsmith *Jean Tijou*. This altar was first moved to St John, Southwark where it was damaged by a bomb in 1940 and thereby lost its marble top.

In the **nave** the pews and the lectern were made as part of major alterations in 1883.

At the same time, the original, late-17C three-decker pulpit was reduced in height and its canopy removed.

St Mary's possesses two outstanding chandeliers, inscribed respectively 1698 and 1703.

The church is paved with black and white marble.

Several monuments in the **chancel** commemorate further members of the Gaitskell family.

Against the north wall is the monument to Josiah Watson, founder of one of the country's first deaf and dumb schools, in nearby Grange Road.

The late-17C reredos is original.

BEXLEY   ST MARY-THE-VIRGIN

Bexley High Street
(0322 523457)

From Central London: *Charing Cross Station (BR) to Bexley Station (BR). Exit R and continue ahead.*
From Crayford, St Paulinus: *Crayford Station (BR) to Bexley Station (BR); proceed as above.*

St Mary's is renowned for its unusual 'candle snuffer' steeple. In spite of heavy Victorian restoration, most of its medieval structure survives embellished with Early English lancet windows and doorways. Within are displayed the unique 'hunting horn' brass and a colourful, late-16C monument to the Champneis family.

Domesday records a church at Bexley which was probably Saxon. St Mary's was granted, *c.*1130, to the Holy Trinity Priory at Aldgate but passed to the Crown at the Reformation. The church was rebuilt *c.*1200, apparently in the new Early English style. Its chancel was extended and a large north aisle, equal in size to the nave and original chancel combined, was added in the 13C. This aisle was extended eastward in the early 14C to form a chapel. Major restoration of the church by *Basil Champneys* took place in 1883. The grandparents of Queen Elizabeth the Queen Mother were married here in 1853.

The **tower**, *c*.1200, is original and retains two lancet windows on its west face and one on its south face.

Also on the south face is the outline of a doorway, blocked in 1883.

Much restoration of the tower took place early in the 19C when its 'candle snuffer' spire was virtually rebuilt externally; however part of its timber structure still appears to be medieval.

☞ *Proceed clockwise around the church.*

All the buttresses were built during the 19C.

In the **north aisle**'s west wall, a small circular window, at upper level, was blocked in 1883.

The aisle's fabric is 13C but, like the remainder of the church, it was refaced with flint in 1883.

The north porch, built in 1883, was converted to form a parish office in 1971.

East of the porch is a lancet window.

Originally, the aisle ended just before the most easterly buttress on its north wall, but early in the 14C it was extended eastward to provide a **chapel**.

This chapel's north window is original, although like all the medieval windows in the church, the tracery was completely restored in 1883.

The window in the chapel's east wall is late 19C.

An original lancet survives in the **chancel**'s north wall at its west end.

Both the north and east walls of the chancel were entirely rebuilt in 1883.

Five dials, probably used for indicating the times of mass, remain in the chancel's south wall; their gnomons (pointers) have gone, but holes indicate where they were fitted.

One lancet survives in the chancel's south wall.

The south wall of the church west of this was built *c*.1200.

A lancet window survives at the east end of the **nave**.

The south porch replaced a mid-18C structure which had a vestry above, in 1883.

During the alterations the original Early English south doorway was discovered.

☞ *Enter the **nave** from the south porch.*

It is immediately apparent that the interior consists of a nave and a north aisle of equal size.

A Victorian plaster ceiling was removed in 1956 to reveal the medieval timbers.

Two 18C galleries were demolished in 1883.

In the south-west corner of the **nave** is the font, with its bowl dated 1684 resting on a medieval stem. The cover was presented in 1883.

Against the nave's west wall, south of the door, is

a bench dated 1809.

The 13C arcade of the **north aisle** was heavily restored in 1883. It occupies the position of the original north wall, the foundations of which survive.

Three 18C funeral hatchments are displayed on the west wall of this aisle.

The doorway to the parish office within the north porch is, like its southern counterpart, Early English.

The north wall was extended eastward in 1443 to create the chantry chapel of John Brenchley. It is now the **Lady Chapel**. Against this wall is the famous 'hunting horn' brass, believed to commemorate Henry Castilayn, d.1407. Parts of it, including the inscription, disappeared long ago.

East of this, is the large monument to a Lord Mayor of London, Sir John Champneis, d.1590. Also commemorated are three ladies: Sir John's second wife, Meriel, and the two wives of his son, Justinian. Its decoration dates from restoration in 1971. The 19C restorer of the church, Basil Champneys, was a descendant.

The arch between this chapel and the chancel was created in the 14C when the extension took place.

●● *Proceed to the centre of the* **nave.**

Prior to *c.*1500, the chancel and nave had been separated by a stone arch which was then removed and replaced by a timber rood screen. The present 19C screen occupies the same position.

Against the south wall is the turret built in 1883 to replace the original which had accommodated stairs leading to the rood loft.

Most of St Mary's furnishings were replaced by *Champneys* in 1883 including the pews, screens and pulpit.

Medieval tiles which originally paved the Lady Chapel and chancel were discovered in the 19C; copies were made by *William Morris* and now pave the **sanctuary**.

In the south wall of the sanctuary are a piscina and a triple sedilia, probably 15C but heavily restored in 1883.

CARSHALTON   ALL SAINTS

High Street
(647 2366)

From Central London: *Victoria Station (BR) to Charshalton Station (BR). Exit L and continue ahead.*
From Beddington, St Mary: *Bus 403,*

All Saints' combines a very early Early English church with a huge late-19C extension by *A.* and *R. Blomfield*. Within, are traces of Saxon work in the tower and an outstanding arcade, *c.*1200, with carved capitals. However, it is the extensive 20C decorative work of *Sir Ninian Comper* which, to many, is the greatest attraction of All Saints'. The rural appearance of Carshalton's village is a pleasant surprise to many, considering its suburban situation.

408, 716, 726
westbound to
Carshalton High St.

It is believed that All Saints', recorded in
Domesday, was founded in the late 8C and the
present east tower, built *c*.850, retains Saxon
work. A Romanesque north aisle was added in
the mid-12C. The chancel was lengthened and a
south aisle added, all in Early English style,
c.1200. Comprehensive Gothic Revival
extensions by *Arthur*, and later, *Reginald
Blomfield* took place between 1893 and 1914 and
altered the appearance of the north and west
parts of the church. Although the Norman north
aisle was lost, the ancient tower, nave, south aisle
and chancel were fortunately retained. As the
extensions included a new nave and chancel the
old nave became the south aisle and the old south
aisle an outer south aisle; the earlier chancel is
now the Lady Chapel. Unification of the old and
the new was greatly facilitated by the outstanding
decorative work of *Ninian Comper* between
c.1921 and 1948.

•● *Proceed eastward, passing the 19C extension,
to the old projecting chancel. Externally,
comprehension is facilitated by considering the
earlier parts of the building as if they retained their
original functions and they are therefore described
in that way.*

The early-13C **chancel** of Reigate stone appears
to have been extended by one bay in the 15C, but
this section may simply have been rebuilt.

Its east window is contemporary with this work.

In the south wall, both Perpendicular style
windows were formed in the 19C.

Between them are traces of two original lancets,
now blocked.

The lower 30ft of the **tower** retains Saxon
stonework, probably indicating that the structure
was built partly to act as a defence against Danish
invaders. Its position at the east end of the church
is unusual and has led to speculation that the
sanctuary was once accommodated in its lower
stage.

The upper part was remodelled in 1830 when
castellation was removed and the spire replaced a
small central turret surmounted by a cupola.
Unsympathetic restoration took place in 1937.

The south **porch** is a 19C addition.

Externally, the **south aisle** combines flint and
ragstone with later brick repair work.

Buttresses, added in the 13C, were rebuilt of
Portland stone in the 18C.

The windows at the east end were inserted early
in the 18C when the height of this part of the aisle
was raised.

The remainder of the aisle was also heightened in
1723 and its two ranges of windows were inserted
then.

At the west end are traces of a blocked 15C
window in which the early Georgian window was
inserted.

The blank west wall of the aisle was once lit by a window.

Originally, the **nave**'s west wall was a direct continuation of this; it had a door and a large window above.

The western extension of the church, including the half-octagonal **baptistry**, was begun in 1913 by *Reginald Blomfield*, nephew of *Arthur Blomfield* who had begun the new work at All Saints', *c.*1893 but died in 1899. The date '1913' is inscribed on the south side of the extension.

•● *Enter the church from the 19C north porch.*

Both 19C arcades imitate the Early English style of the early-13C arcade of the outer south aisle.

The 19C arcade of the **inner south aisle** replaced mid-12C arches and Norman piers. Capitals of the latter were saved and may eventually be displayed within the church.

The modern nave's **west gallery** was designed and its organ case decorated by *Comper* 1931–8.

In the west **baptistry**, the font is believed to have been designed by *Bodley*, *c.*1900; its cover was remodelled by *Comper* in 1947.

Against the west wall is a stone, inscribed in medieval times with a consecration cross.

Fortunately, the south arcade of *c.*1200, now the arcade of the **outer south aisle**, was retained. It is an early example of the Early English style. Unusually, although each of the four capitals of the octagonal columns are carved with leaves their designs differ.

Against the aisle's west wall is the monument to Sir John Fellowes, d.1724.

An 18C gallery was removed from the south wall in 1815 and the ceiling constructed at that time.

At upper level, towards the west end of the south wall, are traces of a blocked 15C window.

The monument to an early Governor of the Bank of England, Sir William Scawen, d.1722, and his wife, stands at the aisle's east end; its original protective railing has been moved to the east tower.

Beside this monument, part of the **tower**'s Saxon fabric has been revealed.

The west arch of the tower was widened in the 13C; it may have replaced a narrow chancel arch if the theory that the sanctuary stood within the tower is correct.

The present ceiling to the base of the tower is 15C.

There would not have been an east tower arch until the chancel of *c.*1200 was built.

At its apex the west side of this arch is carved with foliage.

Separating the tower from the old chancel, now the Lady Chapel, is the railing, *c.*1722, which was brought here from the Scawen monument in the 1940s.

The king-post roof of the **Lady Chapel** is probably early 15C.

At upper level, in the south wall, are two blocked lancet windows.

The altar rail is early 18C.

On the north wall, at the east end, is the tomb chest of Nicholas Gaynesford, d.1497, and his wife, Margaret, which may have served as an Easter Sepulchre. Traces of its original decoration survive. Originally kneeling figures of their daughters were included but these were stolen long ago.

Above are rare example of brasses which retain some of their original enamelling.

The early 18C reredos was decorated by *Comper* in 1936.

In the south wall is a rare double piscina. It was made early in the 13C but stands in the area which is believed to be a 15C extension; if so, it has obviously been moved slightly eastward.

West of the south wall's east window is the monument to Henry Herringman, d.1703, by *Kidwell*.

●● *Return through the tower and proceed to the east end of the* **modern nave**.

On the north side, the 18C pulpit is a cut-down three-decker; its canopy and stairs were added by *Comper* in 1946.

The screen to the chancel, like the font, is believed to have been designed by *Bodley*, c.1914. This was heightened, decorated and a balustrade added, all by *Comper* in 1933. Paintings of the saints were added later by *Comper* and completed in 1941. A plaque records this wartime work 'added during the Battle of Britain 1940 so that in the worst times the best things might be done'.

Above the screen, the rood was designed by *Comper* in 1938.

At the apex of the arch is the figure of Christ in Majesty by *Comper* 1947.

The curved steps to the chancel were added by *Comper* in 1948.

On the north side of the east wall of the **sanctuary** is the first work by *Comper* at Carshalton, the aumbry made in 1921.

The triptych reredos, also attributed to *Bodley*, c.1900, was decorated by *Comper* in 1932.

In the 19C arch, between the sanctuary and the Lady Chapel, stands the iron grille designed by *Comper* in 1933.

CHARLTON   ST LUKE *c.1630*

Charlton Church
Lane

**From Central
London:** *Charing
Cross Station (BR) to
Charlton Station
(BR). Exit from the
station. R Charlton
Church Lane. Ascend
the hill to The Village
L (there is no bus
service). Enter St
Luke's churchyard.*
**From Greenwich,
St Alfege:** *Proceed
southward along
Greenwich High Rd
to Greenwich Station
(BR). Train direct to
Charlton Station
(BR); proceed as
above.*
**From Plumstead,
St Nicholas:** *Cross the
road. Bus 177, 180,
269A to Charlton
Station; proceed as
above.*

St Luke's, constructed entirely of brick, is a rare
London example of a church built in the reign of
Charles I. Although still basically Gothic, some
Renaissance features are apparent.

The manor of Charlton, named from a settlement
of churls (free husbandmen), was given to Bishop
Odo by William the Conqueror, his half-brother,
in the 11C. Soon, however, it passed to the Priory
of Bermondsey. Charlton is mentioned in the
Domesday Book and a Saxon church probably
stood on the present site, although St Luke was
first recorded in 1077. The present church was
built with a legacy by Sir Adam Newton, who had
purchased the manor from the Crown. Some of
the fabric of the earlier walls was incorporated.

Above the first window of the **south aisle** is a
sundial, a 1934 replica of the mid-17C original.

It is known that an earlier mid-15C legacy had led
to some rebuilding of the **chancel**, and its existing
south window may be a re-used survivor of this
work. The chancel was extended in 1840.

The **north aisle** was added to the nave in 1639.

At the north-east corner of the church are
vestries built in 1956.

The Dutch-style gabled **porch** is the only typically
Carolean feature of the church. Its door is
original.

•● *Enter the church from the south porch and
turn L.*

The base of the **tower** serves as the baptistry. Its
font is 17C.

Fixed to the roof, immediately above, is the
sounding board of the 17C pulpit.

On the north wall of the tower is the large
monument commemorating Grace, Viscountess
of Ardmagh, d.1700.

The rounded arches of the **north aisle**'s arcade
represent the most obvious Renaissance feature
of St Luke's.

Against the west wall of the aisle is the
monument to Spencer Perceval. The bust is the
work of *Chantrey*. Perceval, who is buried in the
church, was the only British prime minister to be
assassinated – in the House of Commons Lobby
in 1812.

The north aisle's window includes 17C heraldic
stained glass featuring the coats of arms of
notable local families, including the Wilsons and
Longhorns, owners of Charlton House.

A **chapel** was created in the north aisle in 1927.
Its altar came from the chapel at Charlton House
which had been consecrated and dedicated to St
James in 1616.

The pulpit was made for the rebuilt church
*c.*1630. It bears the arms of Sir David
Cunningham.

On the south wall of the **south aisle**, just west of the chancel, is the monument to the Surveyor General of Ordnance to George I, Brigadier Michael Richards, d.1721 by *Guelfi*(?).

Past the door on the south wall is the wall plaque commemorating Edward Wilkinson, *d.*1567. He had been Master Cook to Elizabeth I and prior to this, Yeoman of the Mouth to Henry VIII, Anne Boleyn and Edward VI.

Near the entrance is the monument to Sir Adam and Lady Newton by *Stone*. Sir Adam, d.1629, was not only the benefactor who made possible the building of the present church, but also the builder of the nearby Jacobean mansion, Charlton House, a unique, virtually unaltered survivor in the London area.

•➡ Exit from the church.

In the **churchyard** is a flagpole from which the British Ensign is flown twice annually, on St George's and St Luke's Days. The privilege was granted to the church to commemorate when, in the early 18C, the flag was flown from the top of the tower as a navigational aid to Thames shipping.

CHEAM   ST DUNSTAN (LUMLEY CHAPEL)

Church Road
(642 0810 or
644 9110)

From Central London: *Victoria Station (BR) to Cheam Station (BR). Exit to Station Way R. Cross High St and follow The Broadway ahead to the church.*
From Carshalton, All Saints: *Bus 403, 408, 716, 726 westwards to High St, Cheam; proceed as above.*

The Saxon-built, Lumley Chapel houses three of England's finest late-Tudor/Jacobean monuments.

St Dunstan's parish church consisting of a Saxon chancel and an 18C nave was replaced by *Pownall* in 1864, but the ancient chancel was retained to form the Lumley Chapel. This lies to the south of the later building and is not linked with it.

•➡ Proceed to the north wall of the chapel.

On this wall are sections of two blocked Romanesque windows and in the north-east corner a low blocked window.

•➡ Continue clockwise around the church.

In the east wall, the Perpendicular window has been renewed.

On the south wall is a corbel followed by a restored 13C arch which is blocked with brick and flints; an octagonal pier with its capital survives. This arch once gave access to five chantry chapels.

The west wall and its entrance door were built in 1864.

•➡ Enter the chapel.

Immediately R is the tomb chest, completed in 1590, of Jane, Lady Lumley, d.1577.

Interiors of the Elizabethan Nonsuch Palace, that stood nearby, are valuably depicted in the background. The monument is of alabaster with gold leaf decoration. This and the two other Lumley monuments occupy their original positions in the old chancel; other monuments were brought here from the nave when it was demolished in the 19C. Lady Jane's monument partly obscures the blocked arch.

Against the west end of the north wall is the alabaster tomb chest, made in 1592, of Elizabeth, Lady Lumley, d.1617.

East of this is the Fromonde palimpsest (re-used brass), judged one of the finest in the London area.

The tomb of Lord John Lumley, d.1609, combines Jacobean strapwork at its base with a more Classical style above. Its Latin plaque is a duplicate of that at Chester-le-Street.

A ribbed tunnel-vault roof to the chapel is concealed by tie-beams which were constructed in 1592 and plastered with a fruit pattern frieze.

CHISLEHURST   ST NICHOLAS

Church Lane
(467 0196)

From Central London: *Charing Cross Station (BR) to Chislehurst Station (BR). First L Summer Hill. Third R Watts Lane. Fourth L Church Lane.*
From Orpington, All Saints: *Bus 61 to Church Lane, Chislehurst.*

Basically, St Nicholas is a mid-15C church which had its chancel rebuilt and a south aisle added in the 19C. The lofty spire has been a well known local landmark for centuries. Outstanding internally are the Tudor screens to the chancel and north chapel and the mid-15C arcade.

St Nicholas is first recorded in 1089, but during restoration in 1957 what appears to be a blocked Saxon window was discovered, thus pointing to an early foundation. The church was rebuilt c.1460 and much of this building survives. A south aisle, porch and vestry were added and the chancel rebuilt by *Ferry* in 1849. The lich-gate, built in 1866, was moved to its present position in 1890.

Although the external wall of the **south aisle** and its **porch** were built in 1849, the 15C south doorway and the windows from the earlier south wall of the nave were kept and incorporated.

•● Proceed anti-clockwise around the church.

The **chancel**, rebuilt in 1849, was extended eastward by one bay in 1896 and its east window formed.

•● Pass the north-east, inner vestry, added in 1849, and the north, outer vestry, added in 1896.

Both the **north aisle** and the **tower** were built c.1460 and most of their rough flint cladding is medieval work.

The tower's clock, installed in 1867, replaced an earlier specimen, presented in 1786 by an influential parishioner, Richard Barwell, in exchange for permission to divert a public footpath to Perry Street that ran through the grounds of his mansion, Homewood.

A fire in 1857 necessitated the rebuilding, one year later, of the shingled **spire** which was heightened by 5ft.

Discovery of a blocked Saxon window in the **nave**'s west wall, above the west window, indicates that some of the fabric of the earliest

church at Chislehurst was incorporated in the 15C nave.

●● *Proceed to the south* **porch**.

Both the south doorway and its wooden door were retained from the 15C south wall when this was demolished.

Also re-inserted was the holy water stoup R.

●● *Enter the church – generally from the south door.*

Within the church, the inner porch, together with the arms of George V, was presented in 1936.

The arcade of the **south aisle** marks the position of the 15C outer wall and was erected when this was demolished in 1849.

●● *Proceed to the west end of the* **nave**.

Chislehurst was once in the diocese of Canterbury and the board, L of the west door, lists every archbishop.

On the other side of the door is the rectors' board, commencing with the incumbent of 1260; earlier details are not known.

In front of the **tower**'s south-east pier stands the restored Norman font.

The arcade of the **north aisle** is mid-15C.

In the north-west corner of this aisle is the monument to Lord Thomas Bertie, d.1749. At its base is an outstanding relief of a naval battle, possibly by *Cheere*.

The oak screen to the **north chapel** is mostly 15C but the vine-patterned cornice and lower panels were made in 1927.

This chapel, formed in the mid-15C, is called the Scadbury Chapel as it commemorates the Walsinghams who owned the nearby manor of Scadbury.

In its north-east corner is the tomb chest of Sir Edward Walsingham, d.1549; the inscriptions at the back were added in 1581.

Above this is what appears to be a 12C corbel, but carved so crudely that many do not believe it to be genuine Norman work.

On the south wall, at east and west ends respectively, are the Lancastrian and Yorkist badges. 'H6 1422' and 'E4 1461' refer to the reigns of Henry VI and Edward IV. These are believed to be the early-17C work of a local antiquary, William Camden.

●● *Proceed to the east end of the* **nave**.

The pulpit R was presented in 1936; its canopy was added in 1953.

The chancel's 15C oak screen originally stood beneath the rood loft.

When the **chancel** was rebuilt in 1849 an arch to the nave was created for the first time.

The west bay of the **sanctuary**'s north wall is the only 15C section of the chancel to be retained. Within its recess, a demi-brass commemorates Alan Porter, the rector who presided over the 15C rebuilding of St Nicholas's.

Standing against the east wall is the alabaster reredos, made in 1896.

At the south wall's east end, within the **Lady Chapel**, is the large monument to William Selwyn, d.1817, made by *Chantry* in 1823.

Further west, but east of the door, a large cartouche commemorates Sir Philip Warwick, d.1682.

COULSDON   ST JOHN-THE-EVANGELIST

Cannon Hill
(71 52152)

From Central London: *Victoria Station (BR) to Coulsdon South Station (BR). Exit R. Follow the first path R to Chaldown Way. Cross the road. Bus 190, 411 to the Tudor Rose. Cross Coulsdon Rd to the church.*
From Coulsdon, All Saints: *Bus 127, 127A southbound to Brighton Rd, Purley. Bus 409, 411A, 419 to the Tudor Rose; proceed as above.*

Only the south wall of the 13C church was lost when a new nave and chancel were added in 1958. Outstanding is the original chancel with its arcading and combined piscina/sedilia, which is regarded as one of the finest in the country.

St John's, recorded in Domesday, had been founded in Saxon times. It was rebuilt in 1260 on the old foundations. The tower was constructed and the arcades of both aisles rebuilt in the 15C. A new church was added to the south in 1958, which incorporated the old south aisle, thus necessitating the demolition of the original south wall.

●▶ *Proceed to the south entrance of the modern building.*

The new church was built by *J. Sebastian Comper* (the son of Sir Ninian Comper) in 1958. At the south end of the **west aisle** is the medieval south doorway of St John's, which was saved and re-used when the original south wall was demolished; it once had a porch.

●▶ *Proceed clockwise.*

St John's is built of Reigate stone combined with flint and later brick repair work.

The old **south aisle**'s 13C end walls were retained.

An original lancet window survives in its west wall.

The outer **porch** of the 15C tower is modern. Within, against its east wall, stands an ancient coffin lid.

On the **tower**'s north side are two medieval windows that light the stairwell.

A 13C lancet window also survives in the west wall of the **north aisle**.

The north walls of the church are 13C, although rendering has been added to the aisle's wall and the windows have been altered.

On the south side of the **chancel** is the 13C priests doorway, discovered in 1929.

●▶ *Enter the modern building and proceed northward. NB The high altar of the new building stands at its south end.*

Within the entrance arch to the old church are traces of red, medieval paintwork.

Both arcades of the **nave** were rebuilt in the 15C with octagonal piers.

Inscribed, at upper level on the west side of the south arcade's central pier, is a consecration cross.

The **north aisle** has been partitioned to provide a choir's vestry.

Against its west wall is the unusual monument to Grace Rowed, d.1631. She is depicted standing on a skull, presumably overcoming death (?).

The **chancel** is decorated with an outstanding blind arcade on both its side walls. At the west end, the shafts are so short that they virtually become corbels.

On the south wall, in one exceptional composition, are a piscina and a sedilia.

CRAYFORD   ST PAULINUS

Church Hill
(0322 522078)

Open Monday–
Saturday 09.00–16.00

From Central
London: *Charing*
Cross Station (BR) to
Crayford Station
(BR). Exit L. First L
Crayford High St.
Fourth L Church
Hill.
From Plumstead,
St Nicholas: *Bus 96 to*
London Rd,
Crayford. First L
Crayford High St.
Third L Church Hill.
From Bexley,
St Mary: *Bexley*
Station (BR) to
Crayford Station
(BR), proceed as
above.

This is one of only three English churches that possess twin naves which are served equally by a centrally placed chancel. Romanesque, Early English and Perpendicular features survive at St Paulinus, which has almost entirely escaped post-medieval alterations.

The church of 1100, whose predecessor was referred to in Domesday, is believed to have had a Saxon foundation. Between 1190 and the 15C, St Paulinus developed in a most complex way. It appears that the present north nave occupies the entire area of the aisleless Norman nave and chancel except that the chancel was slightly narrower. A south aisle and a south chancel chapel were added in 1190, but early in the 14C it was decided that a much larger church was needed. The nave was extended eastward to incorporate the chancel and the south chapel; the south aisle's outer wall was moved further south thus forming a twin nave, and a completely new chancel was built to the east serving both naves equally. Work began on the tower late in the 14C and further additions to the church in the 15C included a north vestry, south porch and south and north chapels to the chancel. All this work survives, the only structural alterations being the south extensions of the south chapel and the addition of north-east vestries. Originally, Crayford lay within the Deanery of Shoreham which was a Peculiar of the Archbishop of Canterbury i.e. directly responsible to him.

St Paulinus is built of Kentish ragstone combined with flint.

It is known, from a legacy, that the **tower** was under construction by 1406 and a commencement in the late 14C seems likely. It does not appear to have had a predecessor.

The clock was presented in 1862.

☛ *Proceed clockwise around the church.*

The west wall of the **north nave** survives from the Norman church of c.1100.

Immediately below its window are traces of the lower courses of a blocked Norman doorway.

All windows in the church were replaced in the 15C and most renewed in 1862.

The first three bays of the north wall also formed the original nave's north wall.

In the north-west corner the original unaltered quoins survive.

At upper level are blocks of black tufa, a chalk deposit used by the Normans as a building material.

Four blocked, round-headed windows occupy their original positions; they represent enlargements made to the earlier windows in the late 12C.

The north doorway was built in Early English style, also in the late 12C. As this was the Transitional period, the builders retained Romanesque windows but preferred the new pointed Gothic style for the doors; the door itself is modern.

Beside the third window from the west are traces of the stairs that led to the rood loft.

The wall of the nave's most easterly bay was built early in the 14C when the nave was extended to incorporate the old chancel.

Between the north nave and the early-15C vestry (only visible from the east side) is the lean-to **chapel** that was added later in the 15C to fill the gap.

Protruding northward from the old vestry are 19C extensions.

•● *Continue around these to the east walls of the 15C north* **vestry***; proceed to the chancel.*

Built in the early 14C, the **chancel** aligns centrally with the arcade that divides the two naves immediately west of it.

The chancel's castellated **south chapel** is a 15C addition that was extended southward, c.1865, to house the organ (later moved).

Material from the south wall of 1190, including the windows, was re-used in the 14C when this was moved southward to its present position thus forming the **south nave**. Three of the windows remain blocked but one was opened up in the late 19C; it is not certain that they correspond exactly with their original positions.

As on the north wall, the present larger windows were formed in the 15C but rebuilt in the 19C.

•● *Enter the* **south nave** *and proceed clockwise.*

The tie-beam roof of the church was constructed in 1630.

Immediately L is the 15C font which was restored in 1971.

The screen to the tower was made in 1935.

Dividing the two naves is the arcade which probably follows the position of the earlier building's south wall. It was first built in 1190 but reconstructed in the 15C.

Between the west wall of the north nave and the first column is the early 16C parish chest.

Surviving in this nave's north-east corner is the partly hidden entrance to the rood loft stairs.

Traces of a blocked triple window, c.1200, remain in the east wall.

The arch to the chapel was heightened c.1862.

This **north chapel**, founded as his chantry by John Marshall in the late 15C, now accommodates the organ.

Against the chapel's east wall is the alabaster monument to William Draper, d.1650, and his wife, Mary, d.1652, by *Thomas Stanton* (?). As well as depicting their son and daughter, the monument includes a stillborn child, a most unusual commemoration.

In the **north nave** stands the Carolean pulpit, c.1630. In spite of its date there are, suprisingly, no indications of Classical motifs.

It is probable that the Perpendicular chancel arch was rebuilt in the 15C when the arcade was reconstructed.

Against the south wall of the **sanctuary** are the remains of the 14C piscina and sedilia.

It is believed that the south wall of the **chancel** aligns with the position of the external wall of the late 12C south aisle that was moved back in the 14C.

The arch from the **south nave** to the chancel's south chapel was heightened in the 19C.

In this chapel, now the **Lady Chapel**, is the 18C monument to Dame Elizabeth Shovel. Her husband, Sir Cloudesley Shovel, was a shoemaker's apprentice who ran away to sea and eventually became Admiral of the Fleet. Shipwrecked off the Scilly Isles, he managed to swim ashore but was found exhausted by a local woman who coveted his ring and murdered him.

DEPTFORD   ST PAUL   *Archer 1713–c.1724*

High Street
(692 1419)

Open daily on application to the gardener.

From Central London: *Charing Cross Station (BR) to Deptford Station (BR). Exit R High St. Cross the road.*

Thomas Archer is regarded as the most Baroque of English architects and here at Deptford this large church approaches the vitality combined with monumentality achieved by *Hawksmoor* at his best. Probably no other church in London is so reminiscent of Rome in style as St Paul's. Except for the cut-down pulpit and organ case, the original furnishings have gone but all three galleries and the exceptional plaster ceiling remain.

Built under the Fifty New Churches Act of 1711, this is one of only two London churches designed

**From Rotherhithe,
St Mary:** *From
Jamaica Rd bus 47,
47A, 188 eastbound
to Deptford High St.*
**From Plumstead,
St Nicholas:** *Any
westbound bus (or
walk) to Plumstead
Station (BR). Train
to Deptford Station
(BR); proceed as
above.*

by Archer. St John, Smith Square, the other, was
gutted during the war and its building is now used
as a concert hall. The newly-formed parish of
Deptford was poor and could not afford to pay
for a rector therefore, although virtually
completed by 1724, consecration was not possible
and the building remained unused. Eventually,
Parliament agreed to pay the rector's stipend and
St Paul's was consecrated in 1730, almost six
years after it was ready. The site chosen had been
a market garden owned by the famous gardener
Henry Wise and later his brother Richard, who
sold it to the Commission for the New Churches
in 1713; construction began almost immediately.
Work appears to have proceeded in a haphazard
way and was greatly hindered by repeated
flooding. Archer had visited Rome before he
designed St Paul's and similarities between this
building and the church of S. Maria della Pace,
built there by *Pietro da Cortona* in 1667, have
been noted, in particular the design of the
portico.

The church is built entirely of Portland stone.

An 'inclination towards central planning' was
stipulated by the Commission and this is
emphasized externally by dominating central
features of each façade.

The **tower** is circular and protrudes from the west
end. Apart from this, its design is not dissimilar
from that of St Mary-le-Bow in the City, which is
judged to be Wren's finest.

Surmounting the spire are a copper vase and
weathervane decorated with gold leaf.

Apparently, the domed **portico** with its great
Doric columns which took ten years to build was
an afterthought by Archer and necessitated a
complete re-design of the west front.

All the walls of the church have pilasters, a
common feature of Baroque churches in Rome.

•● *Proceed clockwise around the building.*

On the **north façade**, a Palladian style double
staircase gives access to the door, now
permanently closed.

The large pediment is a motif that was popular
with English Baroque architects.

On the east façade, the semi-circular **apse**
continues the emphasis on centralization. Its
Venetian window and pediment curve with it in a
very Baroque way.

The design of the **south façade** duplicates its
north counterpart.

•● *Enter the church from the portico and proceed
through the unlit lobby beneath the tower.*

A Greek cross plan has been created, with the
corners being filled by staircases. However, the
English tradition of an east-west axis is not
entirely lost as the chancel tapers towards its
apse.

With short north and south aisles, the square within a square pattern is reminiscent of *Hawksmoor*, except that the monolithic Corinthian columns around the church are placed in a Baroque curve at the east end, rare at that time in England.

The gilded wooden capitals were carved by *Joseph Wade* and *Richard Chiceley*.

These craftsmen were also responsible for the roses in the coffered ceiling, which was plastered by *James Hands* and *James Ellis*.

Fortunately, all three galleries remain, but the box pews were removed in 1850.

The **west gallery** was enlarged by 5ft in 1748 and an organ installed. This was built by *Richard Bridge* whose work was greatly admired by the composer Handel. It has since been restored but the case is original.

On the gallery's face, above the clock, are the arms of Queen Anne; these incorporate her personal motto 'Semper Eadem' (always the same), rather than the usual 'Dieu et Mon Droit'. Supporting this gallery are short Corinthian columns.

In the centre of the **nave**, facing the west door, is the unsuitable Romanesque Revival font, presented by Rochester Cathedral in 1897. It replaced the elegant original, by *Archer*, which had inappropriately been given away to a missionary.

The stairways on the west corners lead to the north and south galleries.

In the west window of the north wall is a stained glass saint, regarded as unusually fine mid-18C work.

The pulpit is the remaining section of a three-decker that was initially designed by *Archer* but simplified by *John James* in 1721. This was cut down in 1850; its iron stairs are original.

Stairways in the east corners appear to have led to private pews, now demolished.

The iron chancel gates are original.

On the north side of the **sanctuary** is the 18C monument to Vice-Admiral James Sayer and his family, by *Nollekens*.

Matthew Ffinch, d.1745, and his brother Benjamin are commemorated on the south wall. Benjamin presented the church with its organ as a tribute to Matthew.

The original reredos, like the pulpit, had been designed by *Archer* and *James*, but was disposed of *c*.1850.

On the upper level of the apse the painting includes some cherubs with moustaches, presumably representing acquaintances of the artist, *Henry Turner*.

It was usual in Classical churches for all the

windows to be filled with clear glass. St Paul's was no exception until, in 1813, stained glass was presented for its Venetian east window. This work has since been replaced but unfortunately by more unsuitable stained glass.

The **crypt** of the church, with its pillars and vault of brick, was the work of a local builder, *Thomas Lucas*. It originally provided a burial crypt but all the coffins were removed in 1964 when the area was adapted to provide a social club. It is not generally open.

GREENWICH   ST ALFEGE *Hawksmoor 1714*

Greenwich Church Street
(858 6828)

Generally open by appointment only apart from services.

From Central London: *Charing Cross Station (BR) to Greenwich Station (BR). Alternatively, Greenwich may be reached by river boat. Boats leave Charing Cross Pier (opposite Embankment Station, Bakerloo, Northern, Circle and District lines) from 10.00 and from Westminster Pier (south of Westminster Station, Circle and District lines) from 10.30. Calls are made at the Festival Pier and the Tower Pier. Check the time of the last boat if returning by river.*
From Charlton, St Luke: *Return northward along Charlton Church Lane to Charlton Station (BR). Train direct to Greenwich Station (BR) and proceed as above.*

St Alfege's is regarded as one of Hawksmoor's finest churches; however, little survives internally from his time.

A 12C church is the first to be recorded here. The roof of the St Alfege that preceded the present building collapsed during a storm in 1710. In that church, Henry VIII had been baptised and Thomas Tallis, the Tudor organist and composer, buried. The rebuilt body of St Alfege's was the first to be paid for with money allocated under the Fifty New Churches Act of 1711. Initially, the medieval west **tower** was retained but eventually it was encased by *James* in 1730.

His steeple was completely rebuilt in 1813 as a replica.

At the east end, the original railings are punctuated by stone piers, surmounted by urns decorated with cherubs, now rather faded.

•● *Proceed to the west end and enter the church.*

St Alfege's was gutted by bombs in the Second World War and much was lost.

Little of the original monochrome painting by *Thornhill* in the **apse** survived apart from that on the pilasters. The remainder has been repainted.

The wrought ironwork is original.

The pulpit is a reproduction.

Undoubtedly the great loss was the woodwork by *Gibbons*. However, the carved supports of the Royal Pew in the **south aisle** survived the conflagration.

Wolfe of Quebec is buried in the crypt.

KEW   ST ANNE *1714*

Kew Green

Open afternoons in Summer.

From Central London: *Kew*

St Anne's 18C structure has been much altered. Two great English painters, Gainsborough and Zoffany, lie in its small churchyard.

The church originated as a simple chapel and replaced an early Tudor structure. Its nave was lengthened, and the north aisle added, by *J. J.*

Gardens Station, District line. Pass beneath the railway line by subway and exit from the station. Ahead Station Parade. First R Station Approach leads to Kew Gardens Rd. Second R Kew Road leads to Kew Green L. Alternatively, boat from Westminster Pier, Easter–September. NB the earliest arrival time is 12.00. From the landing stage proceed ahead to Kew Green. Continue to the south-west side.
From Richmond, St Mary Magdalene: *Return to George St and take bus 65 to Kew Green.*

Kirby, a friend of the painter Gainsborough, in 1768.

The **south aisle** and the **west façade**, altered by *Wyatville* in 1838, were added in 1805.

The east end of the church, including the cupola, was rebuilt by *Stock* in 1884.

Extending eastward from this is the **mausoleum** built for the Duke and Duchess of Cambridge by *Ferrey* in 1851.

•▶ *Enter from the west portico.*

The west **gallery** was added to accommodate George III's large family in 1805.

At the east end of the **south aisle** is the only impressive monument in the church, to Dorothy, Lady Dowager Capell, d.1721.

•▶ *Exit L.*

Buried in the **churchyard** are two famous painters. Gainsborough's tomb is L of the south porch and surrounded by railings.

Zoffany's tomb lies east of the church.

KINGSTON   ALL SAINTS

Clarence Street

From Central London: *Waterloo Station (BR) to Kingston Station (BR). Leave the station by the exit ahead R. Cross Wood St and proceed ahead to Fife Rd. R Clarence St. Cross Clarence St to All Saints.*
From Petersham, St Peter: *Take bus 65 southward to Kingston Station; proceed as above.*

The Victorian flint cladding of All Saints disguises a splendid medieval church, a fact easily appreciated immediately the interior is entered. It is likely that many of the Saxon kings were crowned in an earlier chapel attached to the church.

A Saxon and in turn a Norman church stood on the site of the present All Saints'. Little certain is known about them. King Egbert of Wessex held his Great Council of 828 at Kingston and the Saxon church may have been its venue. It has even been surmised that Egbert built the church expressly for this event. The same building included a chapel that probably housed the coronation ceremonies of seven Saxon kings which are known to have taken place at Kingston, beginning with Edward the Elder, son of Alfred the Great, in 902 and ending with Ethelred II 'The Unready' in 978. Nothing survives of this building, and it was probably destroyed by the Danes during their raids in 1009. Gilbert, the Norman Sheriff of Surrey, built a larger church c.1130 and presented it to the priory that he had recently founded nearby at Merton. Part of its fabric survives, encased in the present walls, and some Norman stonework is visible internally. Unfortunately, the last known example of 12C detailing at All Saints', a Romanesque portal discovered at the west end in the 19C, was, although photographed, almost immediately destroyed.

The present **chancel** dates from the mid-15C when it was rebuilt and enlarged by the addition of north and south chapels.

Tracery in the east window is 19C.

Perpendicular tracery in the chancel's north window is original 15C work and survived only because the Victorians had blocked it.

Flint cladding of the entire body of the church was added in 1866.

The stone-built north **vestry** was added in the mid-15C.

Both **transepts** were probably rebuilt in the late 14C but enlarged in the 19C.

The **nave** was rebuilt, this time with aisles, c.1370.

The aisle windows were altered and clerestory windows added by *Brandon* in 1866.

All the buildings clinging to the north side of the nave are 19C additions.

A tall wooden spire which had been added to All Saints' **tower**, probably in the 13C, was struck by lightning in 1445. The tower, with a new spire, was completely rebuilt in 1515, but storm damage in 1703 necessitated the reconstruction of its upper section. This time, the architect *Yeomans* used brick rather than stone and omitted a spire.

The tower's 18C alterations were completely refaced in 1973 but its 16C lower section of stone survives.

•● Enter the church from the west porch.

The **nave** roof was rebuilt c.1855.

Old tombstones in the churchyard were used to form the new floor in 1973.

Rebuilding of the nave commenced c.1370 but probably took several years to complete as the north aisle's pillars are more slender than the south aisle's. They are also positioned differently, aligning with the outside of the tower's north piers, whereas the south pillars align with the centres of the tower's south piers. For this reason the centre of the nave does not coincide with the centre of the crossing.

*•● Turn L and proceed to the **north aisle**.*

The roofs of both aisles were rebuilt in 1721. Above the north door is the monument to Philip Meadows by *Flaxman* 1795.

*•● Continue ahead to the **crossing**.*

Although the four piers that support the tower are believed to be Norman, they are encased in 13C stonework, the oldest visible structural element within the church.

The east and west crossing arches were heightened by *Pearson* in 1883 and the roof of the crossing was raised, part of several steps taken to improve visibility for the congregation – a three-decker pulpit was lowered, box pews removed and galleries dismantled.

The sanctuary, with its high altar, was relocated to its present position in the crossing in 1979.

•● *Turn L and enter the* **north transept**.

This transept now serves as an extension to the vestry.

Behind the door ahead R, which leads to the tower staircase, is a 13C piscina, indicating that this transept was once a chapel.

Stone casing of the staircase wall is 13C work.

Two original lancet windows are visible at upper level.

•● *Proceed ahead to the* **Holy Trinity Chapel**.

The fraternity of the Holy Trinity was formed at Kingston in 1477 by Robert Bardsey. It evolved from the Shipmen's Guild, important to the town in medieval times, as Kingston was then a major river port.

The recessed tomb in the north wall L is probably that of the chapel's leading benefactor, Robert Mylam, d.1498.

Immediately R of this tomb is the lower section of a 13C arch, indicating that an earlier room preceded the 15C vicar's vestry which now lies on the other side of it.

The colours which hang here, and elsewhere in the church, are those of the East Surrey Regiment, which adopted this as their memorial chapel. The Regiment no longer exists as such.

A 15C tomb lies R of the altar.

R of this is a piscina of the same period.

•● *Pass through the modern screen to the* **chancel**.

Immediately R, the 18C beadle's pew has recently been restored. Carvings surmounting the two front panels are possibly remnants of the church's medieval rood screen.

When the sanctuary was relocated in 1979 the chancel became the retrochoir. Its 15C wagon roof was decorated by *Comper* in 1949.

Immediately L, in the chancel's north wall, is the 14C doorway to the vicar's vestry.

Above the arch to the vestry are monuments to M. Snelling, d.1633; these incorporate some Carolean strapwork.

A similar monument commemorates Francis Wilkinson, d.1681.

•● *Proceed southward and continue through the arch to the Baptistry in* **St James's Chapel** *(the chancel's south aisle)*.

This was built as a chantry chapel in 1459 and retains part of its original wagon roof.

The three pillars of the arcade were constructed when the chapel was lengthened in 1549.

Two mid-15C brasses on the stone table, L of the font, came from the tomb of Robert and Joanna Skerne. Joanna was an illegitimate daughter of Edward III; her mother was Alice Perrers.

The font is dated 1669 but its stem is of later date.

Displayed on a wooden pedestal, next to the penultimate arcade column, is the stone shaft of a Saxon cross. Its sides are carved with an interlaced pattern, much faded; this once stood in the churchyard.

In the south-east corner R is the tomb of Sir Anthony Benn, d.1618, by *Janssen*. He was a Recorder of London and is dressed in his legal gown. There is no relationship with the 20C Rt Hon. Anthony Wedgwood Benn, MP.

A 15C niche R probably accommodated the Easter Sepulchre.

Above this is the monument to Anthony Fane, d.1643.

The monument to Richard Lant, d.1682, is on the south wall, L of the arch to the south transept.

•● *Proceed to the* **south chapel.**

This is known as the 'Vicar's Burial Ground' as many of All Saints' vicars have been interred beneath its floor.

The 14C east window originally formed the west window of St Mary's Chapel which was once linked with the church. St Mary's Chapel, built in Saxon times, served as a Lady Chapel to the church and the coronation ceremonies may have taken place there. It was demolished following a major structural collapse in 1729 when a sexton was killed.

Two monuments commemorate separate Henry Davidsons, one, d.1781, by *Reghert* and the other, d.1827, by *Ternouth.*

•● *Proceed to the crossing's south-east pier.*

A late-15C memorial brass to Katherine Hertcombe is attached to the east side of this pier. The effigy of her husband, John, has been lost.

On the same pier's north side, a 17C brass records the death, in infancy, of all ten children of Edward Staunton, vicar of Kingston, 'ten children in one grave a dreadful sight'.

•● *Proceed to the* **south transept.**

On the west side of this pillar is a restored painting of a bishop, *c.*1400, believed to represent St Blaise. This is all that remains of the many brightly coloured paintings that once decorated the church. St Blaise, martyred in the 4C, was allegedly tortured with iron combs used for gathering wool. The figure is depicted holding one and the saint was, therefore, adopted as the patron saint of woollen drapers; they had a large guild in Kingston in medieval times.

Within the transept, on the south side of the tower's south-west pier, is a statue of Louisa Theodosia, Countess of Liverpool, and the wife of the early 19C prime minister, Lord Liverpool. It is the work of *Sir Francis Chantry* and one of his few free-standing figures.

▪● Proceed westward along the south aisle.

The most easterly column, seen first, is of noticeably greater diameter than the others and the only one to have no base.

On the south wall, between the two most westerly windows, a small stone commemorates John Heyton, d.1584. He was Sergeant of the Larder to Mary I and Elizabeth I.

At the west end of this aisle, on the south wall, is a monument to Elizabeth Bate, d.1607.

Norman stones, with axe marks, survive where the final south aisle column joins the west wall of the church. They were probably salvaged from the Norman building and re-used.

▪● Exit from the church L.

In the southern section of the churchyard, brass plates and stones mark the position of St Mary's Chapel. Its foundations were excavated in 1926.

MERTON   ST MARY-THE-VIRGIN

Church Lane
(542 1760)

The church is open daily.

From Central London: *South Wimbledon Station, Northern line. Exit R. Bus 152 westbound to Mostyn Rd, Merton. Follow Mostyn Rd. Second L Church Park leads to Church Lane.*
From Morden, St Lawrence: *Bus 80 northbound to Morden Road Station. Follow Dorset Rd L (before the station). Second L Melrose Rd leads to Church Lane.*
From Tooting Graveney, All Saints: *Tooting Bec Station, Northern line to South Wimbledon Station, proceed as above.*

St Mary's possesses in its nave, and particularly in its chancel, outstanding examples of medieval timber roofs. It is virtually a museum of English architecture as features survive in the Romanesque and all three Gothic styles. Although both aisles are 19C additions, the delicately carved early-15C north porch and, behind it, a rare Norman oak door were re-used.

Referred to in Domesday, Merton's church was rebuilt *c*.1115 by Gilbert the Norman two years before he founded the Augustinian Merton Priory which stood nearby until the Reformation. The church, dedicated to the Virgin, consisted of an aisleless nave with a small apsidal chancel and most of the fabric of this building survives. Rebuilding of the chancel took place in the 13C; both aisles were added in the 19C.

The west end of the **nave** that protrudes from its later aisle, was built *c*.1115 but, as with the rest of the church, the flint cladding is 19C work.

Its west doorway, built in the 14C, retains traces of two figures, possibly representing Edward III the reigning monarch at the time and his consort, Philippa of Hainault.

A small **spire**, first added in 1547, was replaced in the 18C by the present structure.

The small, north-west window is Norman.

▪● Proceed clockwise around the church.

When the **north aisle** was built in 1866 the timber north **porch** of *c*.1400 was refitted against it; the carved figure at its apex and the tracery appear to be original.

Behind the porch is a Norman doorway which has also been re-used. Sadly, this was completely recarved in a crude fashion when it was installed in the new wall in 1866.

The oak door itself is another matter; it was made

in 1121 and retains original decorative ironwork.

Dormer windows, installed in 1929, replaced medieval predecessors.

An organ chamber built in the 19C at the east end of this aisle necessitated the demolition of the west end of the **chancel**'s north wall but the c.1340 window, with its original iron bars was re-used.

In this wall the first window passed is 15C, followed by two original 13C lancets.

The east window, c.1400, was repositioned at a higher level, probably in the late medieval period when the chancel floor was raised to accommodate a coffin below. Although the floor was restored to its original position in 1935 the window was not.

In the chancel's south wall the first, 15C window is followed by a 13C lancet. Another lancet existed before this but is blocked.

The **south aisle** was added in 1856, ten years before its north counterpart.

•➡ *Enter the* **vestibule** *from the west porch.*

On the vestibule's south wall is a copy of a painting of Christ falling with his cross. The original by *Van Dyck* hangs in St Paul's church, Antwerp.

The arch to the **nave** was formed in 1897.

Both arcades were inserted in the Norman walls in the 19C when aisles were added for the first time; box pews were then replaced and a west gallery demolished.

The roof of the nave is restored 13C work although the tie-beams may date from the Norman building. It was discovered in 1929 when a plaster ceiling was removed.

Attached to the north inner wall of the nave, facing south, are two funeral hatchments. In addition, those of Lord Nelson and Sir William Hamilton were presented to the church by Lady Hamilton and will again be displayed in 1987 after restoration.

In the first bay of the **north aisle**'s outer wall is the restored Norman doorway; this side is plain.

At the aisle's east end, partly hidden by the organ, a small rose window incorporates some 14C stained glass; of particular interest are the arms of Merton Abbey and of Edward III.

Against the aisle's east wall is the Smith memorial by *R. J. Wyatt* inscribed 'Rome 1832'. The model for the figure was the sculptor's sister, Caroline. It was presented by Elizabeth, a member of the Smith family, who married Captain Cook, the explorer, and retired to Merton after his death.

The exceptional roof of the **chancel** was built of chestnut, c.1400. It is referred to as a 'boat roof' and is supported by hammerbeams which are, unusually, concealed by timber coving.

Both side walls are lined with blind arcades, a recurring feature in local medieval churches.

The reredos was made by *Ewan Christian* in 1889.

Against the south wall is the alabaster monument to Sir Gregory Lovell, d.1597, and his two wives. His nine children are also depicted below. Sir Gregory was the treasurer of Elizabeth I's household and lived in a house built on the site of the dissolved Merton Priory.

This monument conceals a lancet window in the south wall.

The 13C priest's door in the south wall of the chancel now leads to the vestries.

The south aisle's **east chapel** was created by *Colin Shrewing* in 1956 and dedicated to St Augustine.

On the south wall of the **nave**, facing north, are three more funeral hatchments. The most easterly bears the arms of Rear-Admiral Isaac Smith, who sailed with Captain Cook, and was reputedly the first European to set foot on Australian soil. Cook's widow stayed with Smith, her cousin, when she moved to Merton.

Four stained glass windows in the nave's south wall commemorate John Innes; they were designed by *Burne Jones* and made by *William Morris* at Merton in 1907. However, they are a late example of the famous partnership's work and not regarded as exceptional.

Beside the west door are the arms of Charles I, made in 1625.

●● *Exit from the church.*

Ahead, an extravagantly carved **archway**, *c.*1175, leads to the vicarage. This, the most important survivor from the buildings of Merton Priory, is believed to have formed the entrance to its guest house. At the priory's demolition it was retained and incorporated in a house under construction nearby. This house in its turn was demolished in 1914 but once more the arch was saved. It was erected on its present site in 1935 (see the plaque).

MORDEN ST LAWRENCE *1636*

London Road
(648 3920)

From Central London: *Waterloo Station (BR) to Morden South Station (BR) or from Wimbledon South Station (BR), District line. Exit R. Bus 80, 93, 293 to the London Rd/Epsom Rd junction. Cross the*

St Lawrence was rebuilt in 1636 during the troubled reign of Charles I when few churches in England were constructed. It is a late example of the Gothic style and completely ignores the English Renaissance, as well as the Classical buildings of Inigo Jones which had been recently completed.

It is not clear whether the church, first recorded in 1205, is dedicated to St Lawrence of Canterbury or St Lawrence of Rome. The former would suggest a foundation by the Saxons as dedications were frequently made to their own saints. In 1301, St Lawrence was appropriated by

road to the church.
From Merton,
St Mary: *From*
Church Lane R
Melrose Rd. Second
R Dorset Rd.
Continue ahead to
Morden Rd. Bus 80
to the London Rd/
Epsom Rd junction;
proceed as above.

Westminster Abbey, but in 1338 it became the property of Edward III and later, the lords of the manor. Almost nothing is known of the building history of the church, but early in the 17C it had become dilapidated and fund-raising for its replacement began. Much of the ancient fabric was probably retained, encased by external brickwork and internal plaster. Extensive new vestry offices were linked with the tower's north wall in 1984.

The brickwork of the **tower** is darker than that used for the body of the church.

Restoration in 1887 included the addition of stone quoins and replacement of the window tracery.

It is known that the tower's predecessor was also castellated, possessing in addition a short spire.

⚫ *Proceed anti-clockwise to avoid a detour around the long north-west extension.*

The **south porch**, like the tower, was built of darker brick.

A porch had been fixed, in a similar position, to the earlier church.

Flemish bond (black mortar), experimented with on the south wall, was apparently considered unsatisfactory and abandoned.

Windows in the body of the church are designed in the 15C style and may have simply copied what existed before the rebuilding.

The priest's door in the **chancel**'s south wall may have been re-used.

Tracery in the east window was altered in 1828.

Protruding at the north-east end of the church is the **vestry**, built in 1805.

Its construction entailed filling the lower half of the north wall's most easterly window.

⚫ *Enter the east porch of the modern extension. Turn L and proceed to the area at the base of the tower.*

The **west gallery** of 1792, from which the organ was removed in 1979, conceals an arch between the tower and the nave that may have been re-used from the earlier building. No aisles were added as part of the 17C rebuilding, nor was any separation between nave and chancel created, probably indicating a lack of finance.

The barrel vault is plastered and supported by a king-post roof.

This is decorated with thirteen funeral hatchments.

Against the north wall of the **nave** is the monument to Peter Leheup, d.1777.

Just before the pulpit stands the monument to Richard Garth, d.1787, by *Westmacott*.

The canopied pulpit, originally a three-decker, was presented by a parishioner, Elizabeth

Gardiner, and inscribed 'EG 1720'.

The altar rail was also made in 1720.

Stained glass in the east window of the **chancel** depicts Moses and Aaron; it is mostly Flemish 17C work, in the style of *Van Linge*, although partly renewed in 1828.

On the south wall of the **nave** hang the royal arms of Queen Anne.

ORPINGTON ALL SAINTS

Church Hill
(0689 24624)

From Central London: *Charing Cross Station (BR) to Orpington Station (BR). Exit R. Station Rd leads to High St. Second R Church Hill.*
From Chislehurst, St Nicholas: *Bus 61 to High St Orpington; proceed as above.*

The small medieval church now serves as an ante-chapel to a new building but only its south wall has been lost and most of the structure is early 13C. A great rarity is its Saxon sundial with Runic words, one of only three to have been discovered in south-east England. A carved Transitional style doorway survives behind the 14C north porch.

All Saints', formerly dedicated to St Nicholas, was first referred to in 1032 and later recorded in Domesday. Apparently, before the restoration of 1871, Saxon work was still visible in the south-east corner of the nave. Although this has now gone, some Saxon fabric may remain and part of a Saxon sundial has been recovered. Partial rebuilding took place *c.*1200 in the Transitional style, and from this period the unusually placed north-east tower and west doorway survive. The chancel was rebuilt possibly in the 13C but probably later. A north porch was added in the late 14C and a north chapel in the 15C. The new church was added to the south by *Geddes Hyslop* in 1958 and linked with the old building, which now serves as its antechapel.

All Saints' old church is mostly faced with flint but some medieval Merstham stonework survives.

•• *Proceed to the* **west porch** *of the old church.*

The porch was built in the mid-14C for the rector, Nicholas de Ystele, d.1370, who requested that he should be buried within. His tomb chest stands against the north wall covered by a Decorated style canopy which appears to have formed an Easter Sepulchre.

The extravagant doorway, *c.*1200, in the Transitional style, was restored in 1874.

Its medieval holy water stoup R was added later.

The west window of the **nave** was formed *c.*1500.

In the gable is a circular window inserted in 1874.

•• *Proceed clockwise to the* **north wall**.

Both the nave's windows are early 14C although restored.

Between them is a blocked doorway, *c.*1400.

The north-east **tower** was remodelled *c.*1200 but possibly retains some Saxon fabric. In the 18C it possessed three stages surmounted by a battlement and a short spire.

The upper stage, badly damaged by a storm in 1771, was rebuilt in timber but destroyed by lightning in 1809. No replacement was made, which is why the tower is now lower than the nave's roof.

External refacing of the tower took place in the late 18C.

In its north wall is a lancet window, *c.*1200.

A similar lancet in the east wall is blocked.

Attached to the east side of the tower is the **Rufford Chapel**, added as a chantry in the 15C. Its Perpendicular window has been restored.

Extending northward from the chancel is the **vestry** which, although probably contemporary with it, was heavily restored in 1874.

There are traces of a blocked door on its west wall.

On its east wall is a lancet window.

The east window of the **chancel**, in the style of three 13C lancets, was formed in 1874.

On the south wall also, the chancel's windows were all probably rebuilt in 1874 but they may match predecessors.

A 15C priest's door survives in the chancel's south wall.

•➡ *Turn L and continue past the east wall of the modern nave to its porch. Enter the building, turn R and continue ahead to the* **old nave**.

The three arches were formed in 1957 when the ancient south wall of the nave was removed. At no period had aisles been provided for the old church.

The narrowness of the nave indicates a Saxon plan.

Against the west pillar, facing north, is part of a Saxon sundial, discovered in 1957 when the south wall was demolished. It had been used in the 14C as the frame of a window, and is strong evidence that All Saints' existed, built of stone, in Saxon times. Originally the sundial, which is mounted upside down, would have been fixed to the outside of a south-facing wall. Around the circumference is part of an Anglo-Saxon Runic inscription. When completed, this proclaims that anyone who wishes to establish the time must know how to do it, i.e. make seasonal adjustments. The gnomon (pointer) has gone, but around it are OR.....UM, parts of a Latin word, probably oralogium (clock).

A west gallery that accommodated the organ and choir was removed in the 19C.

•➡ *Proceed to the* **north transept** *which is formed by the base of the tower.*

The arch from the nave is 13C.

At one time this area formed a chapel, possibly a chantry, but has served as the baptistry since 1958.

The base of the 13C font has been restored; its cover is 15C.

The groin-vaulted roof is 13C.

In the north-east corner, the 13C piscina indicates that an altar once stood here, presumably against the east wall.

When the adjoining Rufford Chapel was built to the east in the 15C a lancet window on the east wall was blocked and the present doorway formed.

The **Rufford Chapel** is in the Perpendicular style and its vault is cross-ribbed. It now accommodates the organ.

Flanking the door to the vestry in its east wall are the Rufford arms carved in stone. However, it is not known which member of the family created this chantry chapel.

The arch to the chancel is 15C.

•➡ Return through the baptistry to the east end of the old nave.

The early-13C chancel arch is in the Early English style.

Its screen was made by *W. D. Caröe* in 1916.

Fixed to the north wall of the old nave, between the Rufford Chapel and the vestry, is the brass of Thomas Wilkynson, d.1511, rector of All Saints.

The north-east door to the vestry is 13C.

Against the north wall of the **old sanctuary** are Grecian-style tablets commemorating William Gee, d.1815, and Richard Gee, d.1817; both are by *Chantrey*.

On the north and south walls are aumbries and, on the south wall a sedilia, all 13C work but restored in 1874.

There is no trace of the piscina.

Above the priest's door, in the **old chancel**'s south wall, is a further Grecian-style tablet by *Chantrey*; this commemorates Richard Carew, d.1816.

In the south wall of the **old nave**, slightly west of the pulpit, was a blocked 15C doorway, which once led to the rood loft stairs; this has been re-used in the new church.

*•➡ Proceed to the **new sanctuary** at the south end of the church.*

Here, inserted in the west wall, is the blocked 15C doorway referred to above.

Inserted in the south pillar of the new **west aisle**, facing the altar, is a 15C carved bracket or corbel. This had been embedded in the old south wall and was discovered during its demolition in 1957.

The reredos in the new sanctuary was designed by *Hyslop* and its panels painted by *Brian Thomas* in 1958.

PETERSHAM ST PETER

Petersham Road (off)

*If the church is locked
the key may be
obtained from the
adjacent Church
House.*

**From Central
London:** *Richmond
Station (BR), District
line. Exit from the
station and take bus
65 or 71 southward to
the Petersham Gate of
Richmond Park
(request stop). From
the bus stop cross the
road, turn L and
continue southward
passing the Dysart
Arms. First R the lane
leads to the church.*
**From Kingston, All
Saints:** *Return to
Kingston Station and
take bus 65 from
Richmond to The
Dysart Arms,
Petersham; proceed
as above.*

Although small, St Peter's, with its box pews and
galleries, is a rare example of an English village
church that retains its early 19C internal
appearance.

The original Saxon church was rebuilt. *c.*1266
and part of its chancel survives. George
Vancouver, discoverer of Canada's Vancouver
Island, is commemorated in the church and
buried in the churchyard. The parents of Queen
Elizabeth The Queen Mother, the Earl and
Countess of Strathmore, were married at St
Peter's in 1881.

The lower part of the **tower** was built in 1505 and
the upper part in the 17C. Surmounting this is a
lantern, added in 1790.

Immediately L of the tower is the **north transept**,
built in the 17C, but with its upper part *c.*1790.

Much rebuilding took place following Second
World War bomb damage.

• Proceed clockwise to the chancel that
protrudes on the east side.

The north wall of the **chancel** is 13C and retains
the only lancet window (blocked) in the church.

The **south transept** was also built in the 17C but
mostly rebuilt in 1840 when it was enlarged.

Some 17C brickwork remains at the base of the
south transept's east wall.

Alongside the south wall, towards the east end of
the churchyard, is the tomb of Captain George
Vancouver.

• Continue to the west porch, built in 1840, and
enter the church.

Displayed immediately R is a beadle's uniform.

The short **nave**, rebuilt in 1805, is virtually the
crossing of the church and does not extend west
of the tower.

Immediately ahead is the font, dated 1740.

The west music **gallery**, above the entrance, was
built in 1838. Other galleries were erected in
1840.

A beadle's staff is displayed L of the entrance.

North of this is the wall plaque that
commemorates George Vancouver, 1798.

The box pews are late 18C and rare surviving
examples.

The pulpit, against the east wall of the north
transept, was made in 1796.

Above the chancel arch are the arms of George
III, acquired in 1810.

Against the north wall of the **sanctuary** is the
monument to George Cole, d.1624, and his wife
and grandson.

Below the altar, in the Dysart vault, lies the

Duchess of Lauderdale, 17C owner of nearby Ham House.

The reading desk, R of the chancel, is believed to be part of a late-18C three-decker pulpit.

PLUMSTEAD ST NICHOLAS

High Street
(854 0461)

From Central London: *Charing Cross Station (BR) to Plumstead Station (BR). Exit L to Plumstead High St (the railway bridge). Take any eastbound bus (or walk) to Plumstead church.*
From Crayford, St Nicholas: *Bus 96 to Plumstead church.*
From Charlton, St Luke: *Return to Woolwich Rd. Cross the road. Bus 177, 180, 269A to Plumstead church.*

The 12C nave and a section of the 13C south transept were incorporated in the new church when it was built in 1907. Some Norman detailing survives but the tower and the nave's arcade are 15C.

Plumstead Manor was given to England's premier Benedictine monastery, St Augustine's Abbey, Canterbury, by King Edgar in 960 and it is likely that a simple wooden structure, housing an altar, would have been erected shortly after this. However, the first church at Plumstead was recorded in the 12C, when the nave of the present St Nicholas was built. It possibly incorporated a shallow apsidal chancel. The chancel was enlarged and transepts added c.1230 but, as most parishioners were drowned in the great Thames flood of 1236, expansion of the church became unnecessary. Because of this, it appears likely that the work was never completed although much is open to conjecture. In the 15C, a north aisle was added, and in the 17C the tower was built into this at its west end. The north wall of the aisle was rebuilt in 1818. An explosion at the nearby Woolwich Arsenal in 1907 seriously damaged the church. Restoration and enlargement took place which included an outer north aisle, a new chancel and a south chapel; the capacity of St Nicholas's was thereby trebled. Following these additions, the original nave became the south aisle. A V2 rocket fell nearby in 1945 and, although the damage was repaired, the south chapel and most of the south transept were not rebuilt.

The brick west **tower** was erected in 1664; there appears to have been no predecessor.

Its flagstaff acted for many years as a navigational aid to ships on the Thames. The present pole replaced the original which was blown down during a storm in the mid-19C. It was 'loaned' by the War Department in 1884.

•● *Proceed anti-clockwise around the church.*

In the 12C west wall of the **old nave** is a blocked 15C door.

South of this is an original blocked round-headed window.

Two further examples, unblocked, are in the nave's ragstone south wall.

The porch is modern.

The tracery of both of the larger windows was designed in 1868.

Between these windows is a blocked 14C doorway.

The **south transept** with its modern south window

was rendered following repair work to the bomb damage.

South of the transept's present south wall are foundation stones that indicate its length prior to the Second World War.

East of the transept and preserved *in situ* is a section of a doorway from the 13C chancel, discovered in 1907. This indicates that the chancel was once slightly wider than the nave.

All the remaining exterior is 20C work.

*•● Enter the **old nave** from the south porch. Turn R.*

At the east end of the south wall, within the blocked door, is a painting of the 'Virgin and Child', possibly by *D. Towner*; it was presented in 1821.

The 15C arcade was preserved when the **north aisle** was rebuilt in 1818.

Brackets are fixed to the spandrels of the arches. Masons' black lettering marks, made in the 15C, survive on the bracket which projects from the second pillar from the west.

North of the arcade is the extension of 1908.

On the east wall of the **south transept** is a recess that was once pierced by a squint. Two bays of this wall originally had a blind arcade in which stood altars with lancet windows above.

PUTNEY   ST MARY

Putney Bridge (South side)
(788 4575)

*Open Monday–Saturday
10.00–12.00*

From Central London: *Putney Bridge Station, District line. Exit L and cross the bridge. Immediately L is the church.*
From Barnes, St Mary: *Barnes Bridge Station (BR) to Putney Station (BR). Exit R Putney High St and continue to the bridge. Immediately R is the church.*

Bishop West's early-16C chapel is one of the finest chantries to be built in a London village church; its fan-vaulted ceiling and panelling are exceptional. The 15C tower and arcades of the church also survive, although heavily restored.

Between the 11C and the Reformation, the Manor of Putney was the property of the archbishops of Canterbury and St Mary's was then a chapel-at-ease to Wimbledon. Much rebuilding took place in the 15C and the chantry chapel of Bishop West was added in the 16C. The outer walls of the nave's aisles were rebuilt, in brick, by *Lapidge* as part of extensive restoration in 1837. Gutted by fire in 1973, the church was restored and re-orientated by *Ronald Sims* in 1982. Oliver Cromwell's Putney Debates took place at St Mary's in 1647.

Rebuilt of brick in the 15C, the **tower** was inaccurately restored in 1837.

The exterior of the **porch** appears to be entirely 19C work but the ceiling is partly original.

Benefactors of the 19C rebuilding, and details of income from parish land, are detailed on boards against the wall.

•● Enter the church through the modern extension on the south-west side and turn immediately L.

The **sanctuary** has been re-sited, on the north side of the building.

Although much restored, the **nave**'s
Perpendicular arcades retain some medieval
work. Angels' busts decorating the piers have
been gilded.

When built, the **West Chapel** stood south of the
chancel but was taken down in sections and re-
erected on the north side by *Lapidge*, c.1837.
Bishop West of Ely was born at Putney, which is
why he commissioned this lavish chantry chapel
for what was then an insignificant village church.

Fan vaults of the chapel and its bays incorporate
the arms of the bishop.

Panelled arches open R to the **Cromwell Room**.
In this room, then the sanctuary, Oliver
Cromwell and his followers held the first
recorded public discussions of democratic
principles in England. They took place on 28
October and 9 November 1647, with the altar
providing the debating table; it is recorded that
hats were not removed by those present. The
plaque commemorating the debates was
presented by the Cromwell Association in 1982
and fixed to the south wall of the church.

RICHMOND   ST MARY MAGDALENE

Paradise Road

**From Central
London:** *Richmond
Station, District line
and (BR) from
Waterloo Station
(BR). Exit from the
station L, The
Quadrant leads to
George St. First L
Church Walk.*
**From Petersham,
St Peter:** *Return to
Petersham Road and
take bus 65
northward to George
St; proceed as above.*

St Mary Magdalene is renowned for its
outstanding monuments.

This, the parish church of Richmond, is first
recorded in 1211. The early church probably
stood on the present site but not trace of that
building remains. St Mary's was rebuilt in 1487
and its tower survives.

When completed c.1507, the **tower** is believed to
have had only two stages; the third was probably
added in 1624. It was entirely refaced with flint
and stone in 1904.

The clock was added in 1812 but its dial is older
(date unknown).

•➡ *Proceed to the west entrance.*

Both brick buildings, incorporating porches on
either side of the entrance, were added in 1864;
stairs once led from them to the north and south
galleries.

The entrance doorway is original.

•➡ *Turn L and proceed clockwise around the
church.*

A north aisle was added in 1699 but this
disappeared when the **nave** was entirely rebuilt in
1750.

The present central window was formed in 1864.
It replaced a north porch, which had been the
main entrance. The brick cornice was added at
the same time.

Against the wall is the obelisk commemorating
Sir Mathew Decker by *Scheemakers*, 1759.

•➡ *Continue clockwise passing the* **vestry,
chancel** *and* **south chapels.**

This eastern section was built by *Bodley* in 1904 when the small Tudor chancel was demolished.

➡ *Continue to the south façade of the* **nave**.

An aisle was added to this side of the nave in 1617. Like the later aisle, on the north side, it also disappeared when the nave was rebuilt in 1750. Unlike the north façade, there was no porch, instead there was a pediment above the central windows.

➡ *Enter the* **nave** *from the west door in the tower*.

The arch leading from the entrance porch to the nave is Tudor. No other part of the interior structure of the church pre-dates the rebuilding of 1750.

The roof was constructed by *A. W. Blomfield* in 1866.

Above the entrance are the royal arms.

➡ *Turn L.*

On the west wall above the door is the monument to *John Bentley*, d.1660, and his family, by *Burman* (?). It has been damaged and rearranged.

Below R is the monument to Shakespearian actor Edmund Kean by *Loft*. This originally stood outside the church which is the reason for its dilapidated condition.

Towards the east end of the **north aisle**, between the last two windows, is the monument to Robert Delafosse, d.1819, by *Flaxman*.

In the corner, before the organ, is the brass commemorating Robert Cotton, d.1591 (?). He was employed in the royal household of Mary I and Elizabeth I. It is the oldest monument in the church.

Above is the monument to Simon Bardolph, d.1654. He is believed to have been a friend of Shakespeare's and it is said that No 1 Richmond Green was his residence. The bard, who almost certainly performed in his own plays at Richmond Palace, may have stayed there. Shakespeare used the name Bardolph for characters in *Henry IV* parts 1 and 2 and *The Merry Wives of Windsor*.

The organ by *Knight*, 1769, has been much rebuilt. It was transferred to its present position in the **vestry** from the west gallery in 1907. There were three galleries in the 18C; all have been removed.

The pulpit, L of the sanctuary, is believed to be late 17C.

➡ *Proceed to the* **south aisle**.

The font has an 18C bowl, but its stem is modern.

Between the second and third windows from the east is the monument to the Hon. Barbara Lowther, d.1805, by *Flaxman*.

●➡ *Continue to the south-west corner.*

A floor plaque marks the burial place, in the vault below, of Edmund Kean.

The monument to Major George Bean by *Bacon the Younger* commemorates an officer who was killed at the Battle of Waterloo in 1815.

Just before the exit L is the monument to Viscount Brounckner, d.1687, whom Pepys described as 'a pestilent rogue, an atheist that would have sold his king and country for 6d [3p] almost.'

ROTHERHITHE ST MARY *James 1715*

St Marychurch Street (231 2465)

From Central London: *Rotherhithe Station, East London line. Proceed ahead to Marychurch St.* **From Bermondsey, St Mary Magdalen:** *Bus 188 eastbound to the Rotherhithe Tunnel entrance stop. First L Paradise St leads to Bradd St. R Rotherhithe St. St Mary's lies R.*

St Mary's neat, 18C exterior helps its immediate surroundings to retain some feeling of a riverside village. Within, much original dark woodwork survives. Of particular interest to American visitors is the plaque commemorating a 17C parishioner, Christopher Jones, Master of the *Mayflower.*

Rotherhithe's parish church is first recorded in 1280. This building was replaced by the present structure in the 18C, but only in 1984 was its architect identified with certainty as John James. Work began in 1714 and St Mary's was consecrated in 1715; however the body of the church was still incomplete by 1737 and its tower had yet to be added.

The **tower** was built by *Dowbiggin* in 1747, James having died the previous year. There was a medieval predecessor and the present structure probably incorporates some of its fabric.

The **spire** was rebuilt in 1861.

As with all James's parish churches in London, the building is of brick with Portland stone dressings.

●➡ *Enter the church.*

The **west gallery,** approached by its original stairs, and the organ case were built in 1764.

Flanking the west door of the **nave** are the benefactions and donations to the poor boards.

Galleries, built originally against both side walls, were removed during restoration by *Butterfield* in 1876.

All the seating is original.

Three brass candelabras, the central example in the Dutch style, were made for the church c.1715.

Above the **north aisle**'s east door are the arms of Queen Victoria.

A gilded brass on the north wall commemorates Peter Hills, d.1614.

Against the same wall is the monument to Captain Anthony Wood, d.1625.

Below this monument is a modern plaque, made in 1965 to mark the 250th anniversary of the consecration of St Mary's. This commemorates Christopher Jones, d.1622, Master of the *Mayflower*.

The pulpit is the top section of the original three-decker, cut down in 1876. Beside this stands the mobile font of gilded wood.

Sections of the lectern are 18C.

The altar rail and the **chancel**'s panelling are original.

Panels of the 18C reredos were painted in the late 19C.

At the east end of the **south aisle**'s south wall a rococo cartouche commemorates Joseph Wade, d.1743, the King's Carver at Deptford dockyard.

SOUTHWARK   ST GEORGE-THE-MARTYR
Price 1736

Borough High Street (407 2796)

Open Monday, Wednesday and Friday 12.00–14.00

From Central London: *Borough Station, Northern line. Exit and cross Borough High St to the church.*
From Southwark, St Peter: *Bus 35, 40, 184 northbound to Borough Station; proceed as above.*

St George's elegant exterior is reminiscent of *Wren*'s St James's Piccadilly. Internally the three galleries and many original furnishings survive. The Te Deum ceiling by *Champneys* is outstanding late 19C work.

Although not mentioned in Domesday, St George's may have existed in Saxon times, as William the Conqueror had entirely demolished Southwark *en route* to London. The Norman church was first recorded in 1122, when it was presented to Bermondsey Abbey, but this was replaced in the late 14C. By the early 18C complete rebuilding of the medieval structure became necessary owing to deterioration, in spite of two restorations in the 17C, and the present church was consecrated in 1736; Price, the architect, did not live to see its completion. Problems soon developed with the new building and essential repairs, including a new floor and ceiling, were already required by 1807. At this time, architect *William Hedges* made alterations to the interior. St George's was damaged in the blitz and a fire in 1979 necessitated further major restoration. This was the only London church dedicated to St George until the accession of George I in 1714 led to its sycophantic adoption by several new parishes. For long, Borough High Street had marked the commencement of the only route from London to the Continent and travellers prayed here for a safe journey. Charles Dickens's heroine Little Dorrit spent a night in St George's vestry when she was locked out of the Marshalsea. As a boy, Dickens had lived nearby and knew the church well. Nahum Tate, who wrote the words for the carol 'While shepherds watched their flocks by night' was buried in this church.

St George's is built of brick with a porch, steeple and dressings of Portland stone.

◀● *Enter the church.*

Immediately ahead, the font is believed to resemble its Tudor predecessor.

The moulded and painted ceiling of the **nave** was

the work of *Basil Champneys*, 1897; originally it was flat. Most of this was remade in 1951 during restoration of war damage by *T. Ford*.

Both side galleries were lowered in 1842; the boxes are modern.

The **west gallery** houses the 17C organ retained from the earlier church.

Fixed to its parapet are the carved arms of Charles II which were brought here from St Michael Wood Street.

Formerly, two small additional galleries above accommodated charity school children. Against the west wall of the nave, south of the gallery, a rare lead cistern of 1738 serves as an alms box.

In the south-west corner is the 'Dorrit' vestry.

The box pews survive; they were all the height of those at the back until lowered in the 19C.

Originally, the pulpit was a three-decker, allegedly the highest in London, but it was cut down, probably in 1842.

The iron altar rail is original.

SOUTHWARK ST PETER *Soane 1825*

Liverpool Grove
(703 3139)

From Central London: *Borough Station, Northern line. Exit and cross Borough High St. Bus 35, 40, 184 to Liverpool Grove (off the south end of Walworth Rd).*
From Southwark, St George: *Proceed as above from Borough Station.*

This delicate Grecian-style building is a rare surviving work of Sir John Soane and appears to have been designed as a model for Holy Trinity, Marylebone Road which he completed three years later. Much of the detailing is in the architect's idiosyncratic style.

Alterations were made to the east end by *Ewan Christian* in 1888 and restoration, following Second World War bomb damage, was completed by *T. Ford* in 1953.

Four monolithic Ionic columns dominate the **west façade**.

➥ *Enter the church.*

A **vestibule** has been formed at the tower's base.

Galleries survive on three walls.

Standing in the north-west corner of the **nave** is the eagle lectern, one of several fittings that came from All Saints, Surrey Square.

The reredos in the **sanctuary** was designed by Soane.

In the south-west corner of the nave is the font. This was made in 1839, two years after Soane's death, but it is in his style and may have been based on one of the architect's designs. It was restored in 1982.

TOOTING GRAVENEY   ALL SAINTS
Temple Moore 1906

Brudenell Road
(672 3706)

From Central London: *Tooting Bec*

The late Sir John Betjeman described this large Gothic Revival church as 'a masterpiece that should really have been the cathedral for South London'. Probably of greatest interest to most visitors in the collection of Renaissance

Station, Northern line. Exit R Tooting • Rd. Fifth L Brudenell Rd. The church lies ↖ ahead R.

furnishings acquired from the Continent by the first vicar, Canon John Stephens.

The parish and its church were established by a huge bequest from Lady Augusta Brudenell-Bruce in memory of her husband, Lord Charles. Canon John Stephens, one of the trustees, selected Tooting Graveney, because a large new housing estate for the area had been approved. Temple Moore, with whom Stephens had worked before, was appointed architect and he designed the building in his usual, late-14C Gothic Revival style. Ample funds permitted a long typically Gothic nave resulting in what is apparently the largest church in South London. Stephens, who was to become the first vicar of All Saints', was an avid collector of Renaissance church furnishings and insisted on installing a high, Baroque reredos. Temple Moore was equally adamant that the furnishings should harmonize with his Gothic building and in particular that the east chapel should be seen from the west entrance, necessitating a low, Gothic reredos. The autocratic Stephens would not agree and the architect resigned in protest. Much of the interior and most of the new furnishings were, therefore, the work of his successor, *Walter Tapper*. Because of its exceptional acoustics All Saints' has become a popular venue for recording music.

In spite of a castellated north-west tower and east chapel, the yellow London stock brick exterior is basically plain.

•● *Enter the church, generally from the north-east porch.*

In addition to its great length, the double-aisled **nave** is exceptionally high and possesses a clerestory.

Above the central arch of the west door, a tablet commemorates Canon Stephens, d.1925. In the north-west corner is the font designed by *Tapper* who adopted the colour green and gilding on several furnishings to harmonize with the Baroque reredos already acquired by Stephens.

It is possible that the pulpit, assigned to *Tapper*, was designed by *Temple Moore*.

The chancel is flanked by single aisles that continue around it to form an ambulatory.

Within the **chancel** are the Renaissance furnishings acquired from Italy by Stephens, which caused the friction between him and Temple Moore. The walnut choir stalls, preacher's chair (north side of the sanctuary), reredos and credence tablet (south of and just behind the high altar) came from a suppressed monastery in Bologna; they are late Renaissance work in the Baroque style.

Enclosing the sanctuary is a 14C(?) wrought iron grille acquired from a church above Lake Como.

Set within the reredos is a copy of the Crucifixion by *Velazquez* (the original painting is in the Prado, Madrid). It is the work of *Raoul Maria*, a pupil of the Spanish master.

Florentine candle standards flank the altar.

The early-16C reredos in the east **Chapel of the Blessed Sacrament** was made in northern France but its gilded leather frontal is German.

Above, the carved Crucifixion scene is believed to be 14C.

On the south side of the **nave** is the copy of an 18C Italian lectern which Stephens had acquired earlier. The original remains at his first church in Blankney, Lincolnshire.

The organ case, in the south-east corner, is by *Tapper*.

Above the **outer south aisle**'s west door is the memorial to Lord Charles Brudenell-Bruce, d.1897, the husband of the founder of the church, by *Tapper*.

WIMBLEDON   ST MARY-THE-VIRGIN

St Mary's Road

From Central London: *Wimbledon Station, District line, or (BR) from Waterloo Station (BR). Exit R Wimbledon Hill Rd which becomes High St. Ninth R Church Rd.*
Alternatively, from the station cross Wimbledon Hill Rd and take bus 80 or 93 northward to Church Road.
From Barnes, St Mary: *Return to Barnes High St. First L Station Rd, pass Barnes Station and ascend the steps L. R Rocks Lane. R Upper Richmond Rd. Take bus 37 eastbound to Putney Hill (request stop). From the bus stop continue ahead. First R Putney Hill. Cross the road and take bus 80 or 93 to Wimbledon High St (the stop after the Rose and Crown). Return westward. First R Church Rd.*

Although the bulk of the church is mid 19C, St Mary's medieval chancel and 17C Cecil Chapel remain.

It is probable that a small Saxon building occupied the same site, as a church in the area is mentioned in the Domesday Book. No trace of this building exists, however, as complete rebuilding took place, probably in the late 13C. The nave was again rebuilt in the 18C.

St Mary's was refaced with flint and its tower constructed by *George Gilbert Scott* in 1843.

•● *Proceed to the south wall of the* **nave**.

Originally, the nave had only been slightly longer than the chancel, but it was rebuilt, in extended form, in 1786. A westward extension was added in 1843 by *Gilbert Scott* who also added its clerestory, fitted new Gothic Revival windows and built the **south porch**.

•● *Proceed eastward along the path, following the south wall.*

Vestries, added in 1920 and 1955, now obscure the south wall of the Cecil Chapel at the east end of the church.

The fabric of the walls of this chapel and the adjoining chancel is original.

The chancel's east window was restored in Bath stone, probably in 1860.

Brickwork flanking the chancel is all that can be seen of the 18C **nave**.

•● *Enter the church from the west porch.*

Immediately L. within the **porch**, is the monument to James Perry, d.1821, a proprietor of the *Morning Chronicle*.

•● *Continue eastward to the* **chancel**.

No furnishings in St Mary's pre-date the mid 19C.

The late-13C(?) chancel is the most ancient part

of the church. Its floor tiling and seating date from the restoration of 1860.

At this time the old rafters were exposed and decorated.

There are traces of a blocked doorway in the north wall.

In the north wall, at low level, is the oldest memorial in St Mary's, an Elizabethan tablet *c.*1540 commemorating Philip, d.1462, and Margaret Lewston.

•● Proceed through the arch R to the **Cecil Chapel**.

The Cecil Chapel was added to the church *c.*1628 by Sir Edward Cecil, Lord Wimbledon, as a family mausoleum. This could not originally be approached directly from the church but had its own external entrance.

An arch was formed in the north wall, linking it with the chancel, probably in 1860. Its west wall was demolished in 1920 to provide a link with the newly built Warrior Chapel.

The large window in the south wall possesses the most important stained glass in the church. In its light L are the 16C arms of Lord Wimbledon's father, Sir Thomas Cecil, Earl of Essex. This was one of three cartouches that made up an earlier east window of the chancel.

The knight on the 15C section R carries a shield bearing the arms of St George. This is part of an earlier window from the north side of the chancel.

Four small windows at upper level survive in the chapel. There were originally six, representing the two wives and four daughters of Lord Wimbledon. The other two were removed to the Warrior Chapel from the west wall when this was demolished.

The altar tomb of Lord Wimbledon, d.1628, stands in the centre of the chapel.

Suspended from the ceiling is a viscount's coronet.

•● Proceed westward through the modern oak screen to the **Warrior Chapel**.

This chapel was built in 1920 as a First World War memorial and replaced the vestry of 1860.

Its north wall originally formed the external south wall of the chancel and here, at low level, is an early-14C leper window, discovered in 1920. This was not originally quite so low; the floor has since been raised 21 ins.

Opposite, in the south wall, are the two small 17C windows removed from the west wall of the Cecil Chapel.

Church buildings and their contents

Terms used in this book that may not be generally understood are described. In addition, the historical development of certain features is explained.

Abbey A monastic community, presided over by an abbess (for nuns) or an abbot (for monks). Following Henry VIII's rift with the pope, all were closed down (Dissolution of the Monasteries) and their possessions appropriated by the Crown. The smaller establishments were dissolved in 1536 and the larger in 1539. With the exception of Westminster Abbey, the buildings were either sold or left in ruins. Some abbey churches were purchased locally to serve as the parish church.

Aisle Aisles are areas that run parallel to the nave in most churches, usually on the north and south sides. They are generally narrower and lower than the nave from which they are separated by arcades. Occasionally, the chancel and transepts may also be aisled; double aisles have sometimes been built in churches, usually as a means of extension.

Altar Table at which Holy Communion/mass is celebrated. Earliest churches only provided shelter for the altar, not the congregation. A church may possess additional altars, situated in chapels, generally against an east wall. The high altar (most important) is usually placed at the east end of the building, i.e., in the direction of Jerusalem, the rising sun, and from where it was believed that Christ would return. When sited elsewhere, its position is still referred to as liturgical east. From 1076 until the celebration of the mass was outlawed in England at the Reformation, the mensa (altar top) was made from one slab of stone. The altar top symbolizes Christ's body and stone mensas were inscribed with five crosses representing the stigmata (wounds of Christ). Frequently the altar's stone base was hollowed to contain relics. In 1550, stone altars were made illegal by Edward VI at the prompting of Bishop Ridley who believed that they were inspired by Jewish sacrificial tables. Altars of stone were fixed to the floor, but their replacement, 'The Lord's Board', had to be of wood and movable. Now known as communion tables, these were often brought forward to the centre of the chancel, or even the nave. Elizabeth I made wood or stone optional in 1559 and, if wooden, the altar had to be covered with a cloth. High altars were now returned to their original position until the Puritans again brought some of them forward in the seventeenth century. Generally, they remain at the eastern extremity of the chancel; however, in recent years, some churches have been extended and the altar moved to the new part of the building. In addition, progressive ecclesiastical views have led to the altar being brought forward to a more central position in the church. A crucifix flanked by candles usually stands on the altar.

Altar canopy Generally a dome-shaped covering to the altar. All medieval examples were replaced, generally by a reredos, but canopies were revived by Baroque architects early in the eighteenth century. Also known as a baldachino or a tester.

Altar frontal Covering of the west face of the altar, usually a fabric decorated with symbols. Generally covered by the altar cloth.

Altar rail Decorative low screen, usually of wood or iron, protecting the altar and enclosing the sanctuary. Introduced from the Continent shortly after the Reformation when chancel screens were being demolished, to protect the altar from desecration by animals. Their low height was convenient for communicants to lean against and also provided the congregation with a clear view of the altar. Archbishop Laud encouraged the adoption of a single rail between the north and south walls to establish the altar's position. After the Restoration the rail was usually turned at both ends to meet the east wall.

Ambulatory Passageway in a church formed by continuing the aisles behind the high altar.

Anchorite's cell See hermit's cell.

Apse Semi-circular or octagonal extension to a building.

Arcades A wall perforated by arches and supported by columns set in a range. Used to separate aisles from the body of a church or to provide one wall of a covered passageway, e.g. a cloister or gallery.

Architrave Internal or external moulding surrounding an opening.

Art Nouveau Late nineteenth-century style developed on the continent and based on curved, flowing forms inspired by nature. Popular in England c.1900 and adopted enthusiastically by William Morris.

Ashlar Large blocks of smoothed stone laid in level courses.

Aumbry Recess in the wall, usually of the sanctuary, forming a built-in cupboard. Altar vessels, relics and sometimes the Blessed Sacrament (consecrated bread) were kept in them. Most surviving aumbries in London have lost their wooden door.

Baldachino See altar canopy.

Baptistry The area of a church where the font is sited and baptisms take place. Generally the west end of the nave is chosen and frequently its north-west corner.

Baroque Exuberant continental development of the Classical style.

Barrel vault A continuous arch forming a curved roof. Also known as a tunnel vault.

Battlement A parapet indented for defence or observation purposes. Most commonly surmounting a church tower.

Bay Compartment of a building divided by repeated elements.

Belfry The structure housing the church bells; generally an upper stage of a tower.

Bench end Upright end-section of a pew, often decoratively carved. Floral shaped terminals are called poppy heads.

Bishop's chair Chair, usually elaborately carved, reserved for the bishop when he visits a parish church. Most in London are Jacobean and some originally served a secular purpose.

Blind A structure without openings.

Boss Ornamental projection covering the intersection of ribs in a roof.

Box pew Bench seat enclosed by high wooden partitions, often painted white and entered through a door. Introduced to England c.1580, probably from the Netherlands. Favoured by the Puritans but not, as some believe, by Wren. They were allocated by churchwardens and families paid rent for their private pew. Box pews gave protection from draughts and the wealthy sometimes added curtains; a few even had their own fireplace and dog kennel installed. Those who could not pay sat in the galleries or on stools; alternatively they stood in the aisles. Special pews were reserved for churchwardens and the beadle at the rear, the mayor and corporation and the assize judge at the front. The high partitions were removed when the three-decker pulpits were cut down in the nineteenth century; all seating then became free.

Brass Brasses are memorials in the form of effigies or lettering engraved on a brass alloy. They evolved on the Continent early in the thirteenth century. England's oldest figure was made in 1277 and more survive in this country than elsewhere. The English preferred to cut out the effigies and mount them on stone, whereas European craftsmen engraved rectangular plates. It is generally agreed that the finest examples are fourteenth-century work, often with a Decorated-style canopy surmounting the figure. From then on a decline set in, but brasses again became fashionable in the Elizabethan era and remained popular until the seventeenth century when the great Jacobean monuments replaced them. Traces of brightly coloured enamelling have been found on a few brasses but it is not clear what percentage received this treatment. Most brasses are found in the chancels of medieval churches, often removed from their original tombstone; they are an important source of information on the dress and fashions of our forebears. Some churches permit 'rubbing' on application; All Hallows-by-the-Tower, St James Piccadilly and Westminster Abbey have brass rubbing centres where, for a fee, copies from duplicates may be made.

Bread cupboard/shelf Ventilated cupboard in which bread was kept for distribution to travellers and the poor. The bread was distributed at the end of Sunday morning services, which had to be attended by the recipient unless sick. The bread 'dole' existed from medieval times until the nineteenth century and was paid for by a parish benefactor. Sometimes known as a dole cupboard.

Buttress Structure attached to a wall to counter an outward thrust. See flying buttress.

Campanile Bell tower detached from the church.

Capital Top section of a column or pilaster, usually carved with the distinctive ornament of a Classical Order.

Cartouche Decorative panel painted or carved to resemble a scroll.

Caryatid Figure of a woman, her head supporting an entablature. Ancient Greek feature as at the Erectheum, Athens. See St Pancras, Euston Road.

Castellated Applied to a building where all or most parapets are battlements.

Cathedral The most important church in a bishop's diocese. Westminster Abbey is an exception, as it is a 'royal peculiar' not a cathedral. A cathedral is the bishop's seat and no town has city status unless it possesses one. In the Middle Ages worshippers were sometimes persuaded to attend services at their parish church rather than the cathedral.

Censer Trumpet-shaped vessel containing incense. Angels with censers were a popular medieval decorative theme.

Chalice Ritual goblet of gold or silver in which wine is served during Holy Communion. Represents the Holy Grail from which Christ drank at the Last Supper. A chalice engraved on a tombstone indicates that a priest is commemorated.

Chancel The section of a church reserved for the clergy and generally all, or part, of the choir. Its name derives from the early cancelli or low wall which divided the apsed sanctuary from the nave. It usually extends eastward from the nave with the sanctuary at its eastern extremity. Saxon and Norman churches possessed virtually no chancel; only a shallow apse projected from the nave to provide the sanctuary. Enlargement took place from the late twelfth century and the long, rectangular English chancel became established. This was inspired by the rebuilding of Canterbury Cathedral where, for the first time, the monastic choir was moved into the chancel from the east end of the nave. Medieval chancels are frequently out of line with the nave; this is due to orientation problems and does not represent Christ's head leaning to one side during crucifixion as has been suggested. From the mid-fourteenth century chancels became ever larger and aisles were added in imitation of York and Lincoln Cathedrals. The importance of chancels has since varied according to the positioning of the altar.

Chancel arch A large arch in the wall dividing the nave from the chancel. In medieval times the section of wall above the arch was usually decorated on its west side with a Doom (Last Judgement) painting but these were limewashed over by order of Elizabeth I. Generally chancel arches were abandoned in Classical buildings.

Chancel screen Screen that separates the chancel from the nave. In parish churches, generally of wood, but in cathedrals or abbey churches of stone, and then called a pulpitum. Most screens originally had doors that were kept locked, except during services. When Elizabeth I ordered the removal of all roods and rood loft parapets in 1559 many rood screens which stood below were also unnecessarily destroyed and a royal order two years later forbade the removal of those that remained. If already gone, they had to be replaced by new ones. Where there was a stone pulpitum this was usually additional to the wooden rood screen which stood one bay west of it. Chancel or rood screens were introduced in the thirteenth century when the long Early English chancels were replacing their shallow-apsed, Norman predecessors; few surviving examples, however, pre-date the fifteenth century. Archbishop Laud ordered the construction of many screens in the mid-seventeenth century and they were frequently erected in new buildings until 1818, even though Wren and his followers disliked them. Pugin wanted screens kept, but the Victorian insistence on an unrestricted view of the high altar led to the destruction of most; many examples on the Continent were lost for a similar reason.

Chandeliers A popular form of lighting since the Middle Ages. From the mid-seventeenth century brass examples were imported from Holland but

English chandeliers were soon made in a similar style. Few were installed after c.1830 but there has been a limited post-war revival in London.

Chantry chapel Small chapel, usually, but not always, within or attached to a church and paid for by a wealthy benefactor. A chantry was the mass chanted daily for the donor's well-being and, after decease, his or her soul. From the early fourteenth century all had to be licensed and paid for. First recorded c.1235, popularity increased following the Black Death of 1349 when life expectancy was short. Many endowments only paid for the chantry at an existing subsidiary altar within the church and for a limited number of years. Most were founded in the fifteenth century when trade guilds sponsored chapels dedicated to a patron saint, which often occupied an entire aisle. Some larger endowments also paid for colleges and hospitals. Chantries were connected with the theory that prayers could speed the progress of a soul through purgatory to paradise. This was denounced as 'doctrine and vain' by Edward VI's act of 1547 which put into effect the transference of chantry property to the Crown as demanded by his late father, Henry VIII. Some of the income was used to sponsor grammar schools, university colleges and poor relief but much remained in the royal purse. Six major foundations were spared, but none in London, where more than three hundred existed. The chantry chapels, particularly in the larger churches, were generally stripped of all representations of figures and any fitments that might be of value to the Crown; the tombs themselves were not usually removed.

Chapter house Rooms associated with a cathedral or abbey, where important meetings between the dean and canons, i.e. the chapters, are held; in monastic churches, for the abbot or prior to use in a similar way. Most are distinctive, polygonal buildings linked with the chancel.

Charnel house Crypt of a church used for the storage of human bones transferred from the churchyard.

Choir Area of a church used by the (singing) choir; usually the west section of the chancel. To avoid confusion with the singers themselves it may be spelt 'quire'. Sometimes erroneously used to define the entire chancel.

Cladding Material added to a structure to provide an external surface.

Classical Style following those of ancient Greece or Rome.

Clerestory Upper section of the nave's wall which is pierced with windows to provide additional light.

Cloister Covered passageway, generally arcaded. Most common in churches with monastic origins, where four, linked passageways enclose a rectangular, grassed area known as the garth. Used by Benedictine monks for teaching and working purposes; the arcades were then generally glazed for weather protection.

Coade stone Artificial, hard-wearing material resembling stone; invented c.1769 to provide statues or decorative features for buildings. Only the Coade family of Lambeth possessed the secret of manufacturing this material, a secret that died with Elizabeth Coade.

Coffering Recessed ceiling panelling.

Communion table See altar.

Commandments board Boards displaying the Decalogue (Ten Commandments) were set up in churches during the reign of Edward IV but made compulsory by Elizabeth I. In 1561 it was specified that the board should be situated above the altar, i.e. as part of the reredos, but many continued to be fixed to the chancel arch.

Consecration cross In the early days of Christianity in England only the altar was consecrated and the mensa (stone altar top) was inscribed with five crosses, representing Christ's stigmata. Later, the whole building was consecrated, possibly because pagan temples were re-used, and twelve crosses inscribed or painted on different parts of the building.

Corbel Wall bracket, generally of stone, supporting a beam, for example.

Corinthian Greek Classical Order. Columns are slender and their capitals intricately decorated with carved leaves and small spiral scrolls (volutes).

Cornice A projecting decorative feature running horizontally at high level.

Cove Concave shaped ceiling.

Credence table A table which supports the bread, wine and water during Holy Communion. Introduced at the Reformation and championed by Archbishop Laud.

Crenellation See battlement.

Crossing Where the nave, transepts and chancel intersect.

Cruciform Shape of a cross formed by a church plan which comprises nave, transepts and chancel.

Cupola Small domed roof, generally surmounting a turret.

Cusp Pointed projection formed by the intersection of foils (petal-like shapes); a decorative feature common in Gothic tracery.

Dado Lower section of a wall's inner surface. Often protected from wear by a lining of strong material surmounted by a timber dado rail.

Decorated Second period of English Gothic *c*.1290–*c*.1360. Remarkable for flowing window tracery and ornate pinnacles and porches.

Decoration Medieval churches bear little resemblance to their original colourful appearance. Most were plastered and limewashed both externally and internally and practically no internal surface was allowed to remain wthout paint or gilding. Stonework was the building material only; its natural surface was not considered attractive.

Shortly after the Conquest, the Normans painted gaudy zig-zag patterns in red, black and yellow around the internal walls. This fashion was superseded by red lines, imitating the joints between ashlar stonework, and later each 'stone' was decorated with a centrally placed red rosette. Good examples have recently been discovered at Barnes.

The walls of the nave, which was reserved for the laity, were painted with instructional scenes from the earthly life of Christ and the saints. In the late Middle Ages a popular subject facing the usually open south doorway was St Christopher, as many believed that if they saw the image of this saint no unforeseen fatality would strike them on that day. Around the chancel arch there was usually a Doom painting, illustrating the Day of Judgement. Within the chancel, wall paintings depicted heavenly scenes, a popular subject being Christ enthroned. Early churches had small windows and were dark; in order to be visible, therefore, a robust style and strong colours were necessary. From the twelfth century, fresco work (on wet plaster) was employed, but murals (on dry plaster) were always more common. Colours were limited, as some, e.g. deep blue, could only be made from expensive materials. As windows became larger, the importance of stained glass increased and the quality and extent of wall painting gradually fell.

At the Reformation, Edward VI rid churches of most of their decoration; paintings were either removed or obliterated with limewash and religious statues demolished as idolatrous. Practically all ancient wall paintings that exist do so because of the removal of this limewash covering during modern restoration work. In general, however, stained glass windows were spared, presumably because many were difficult to reach and their replacement would have been costly. Edward VI commanded the writing of sentences from the scriptures on the walls that warned against idolatry and thus supported his Protestant views. Cromwell's Puritans found few paintings or statues remaining to destroy and most of their iconoclastic energy was spent, particularly in London, in smashing stained glass. Apart from paintings on a few domes, the Classical style depended chiefly on carving and plasterwork for decorative effect and it was not until the mid-nineteenth century that, with the Pre-Raphaelites, wall painting again became fashionable in churches.

Devil's door Traditionally, the north side of the church was the Devil's side and the north door of the nave, often leading from the baptistry, was occasionally left open so that the evil spirits could leave a child during the christening ceremony.

Dole cupboard See bread cupboard.

Doric Classical order, the oldest and sturdiest. The capitals of Doric columns are virtually undecorated.

Dormer window Window protruding from a sloping roof.

Early English First phase of Gothic architecture in England *c*.1190–1310. Characterized by narrow pointed arches and windows (lancet). In the London area, most Norman chancels were rebuilt, in extended form, during this period.

Easter Sepulchre A stone-canopied recess, usually situated above a tomb chest and set in the north wall of the sanctuary. It represented Christ's tomb and at Easter housed the altar's crucifix and consecrated bread which was placed in a cavity in the breast of a figure of Christ. This effigy was generally made of wood and kept in store for the rest of the year. The Easter Sepulchre was decorated with flowers, candles were lit, and constant vigil kept by parishioners from Good Friday to Easter Monday. Surprisingly, Easter Sepulchres survived Edward VI but were eventually banned by Elizabeth I.

Eave Horizontal edge of a roof overhanging the wall.

Fan vault Ribs of a vault that make a pattern resembling a fan.

Festoon Carved hanging garland of fruit and flowers.

Finial Decorative terminal to a structure, e.g. gable apex. A feature of the fourteenth century Decorated style.

Flowing tracery Succeeded geometrical tracery in the fourteenth century during the final phase of the Decorated style. Intricate curving patterns were formed, similar to the French Flamboyant style which inspired it.

Fluted Vertical grooving.

Flying buttress Semi-archlike structure that directly transfers the weight of the wall to a vertical pier.

Foil Petal-like shape that forms cusping in Gothic tracery. The number of foils, usually three, four or five, are indicated by the words trefoil, quatrefoil and cinquefoil.

Foliated Leaf decoration.

Font Fonts are free-standing bowls supported by a stem on a base and used exclusively for baptism. They were at first square or round but late Gothic fonts usually had octagonal bowls, denoting regeneration as symbolized by the figure eight. Early fonts were usually painted but few surviving examples pre-date the twelfth century and it is probable that most Saxon fonts were wooden. Occasionally fonts were made of lead but the majority are carved from English limestone that takes a polish. In grander churches genuine marble has been used. Fonts are generally placed near the door, signifying the child's entrance to God's church through baptism; however separate baptistries exist in some larger churches, often within a transept, aisle or disused chantry chapel. Zealots vandalized many fonts at the Reformation but Elizabeth I ordered that they should remain. The Puritans also approved of fonts but preferred them away from the west end of the building. In the eighteenth century they were often placed adjacent to the reader's desk at the east end of the nave.

Font cover Covers for fonts, nearly always of wood, were developed to conserve and protect the consecrated water which stayed in them for up to six months. In 1220 it was ordered that they should be locked when not in use, to avoid theft of the water for superstitious practices. Simple flat boards were replaced in the fourteenth century by more elaborate structures, often operated by pulleys. London, particularly the City, is unusually rich in exquisitely carved seventeenth century and early eighteenth century font covers.

Fresco A method of painting on a wall while the plaster is still wet, thus providing a more permanent result than on a dry surface.

Gable Upper section of wall at each end of a building. Generally triangular in shape owing to the slope of the roof.

Gallery Storey added at an upper level, usually arcaded below.

Gargoyle Decorative protruding spout which ejects rain water from the roof of a building away from the walls. Often carved as beasts and demons in Gothic churches. Popular in the late medieval period.

Geometric tracery Early tracery of the fourteenth century Decorated period in a pattern that is regular rather than flowing.

Gothic Style of architecture from the twelfth to the seventeenth centuries employing the pointed arch. Named Gothic as a term of abuse in the late seventeenth century, but not connected with the fourth to sixth century Goths, renowned for their part in the destruction of ancient Rome. Evolved in the great twelfth century cathedrals of the Isle de France and quickly came to England.

Gothic Revival Serious nineteenth century attempt to reproduce the Gothic style.

Greek Revival Buildings designed *c.*1770–1840 in ancient Greek style.

Grisaille Grey, monochrome decoration of walls or stained glass.

Groin vault Intersection of two tunnel (or barrel) vaults.

Hagioscope See squint.

Hammerbeam roof Form of roof construction, popular in the late fourteenth to sixteenth centuries, unknown outside England. Short, horizontal 'hammerbeams' act as cantilevers, thereby eliminating the need for a tie-beam and increasing the apparent height of the roof.

Hatchment Armourial bearings usually painted on canvas and fixed to an oak-framed diamond-shaped board. A black background indicates that the deceased is single or widowed; a black and white background that the spouse survives. Popular from the seventeenth to the early nineteenth century. The hatchment was hung outside the home of a deceased person and then borne in procession at the funeral. Returned to the house, it was later displayed in the church. Some churches retain outstanding collections which decorate their walls and roofs.

Hermit's cell Small room added to a church as a lean-to building. Occupied, in the Middle Ages, by an anchorite who vowed not to leave until death. A small inner window (a squint) permitted a view of the altar and food and drink were passed through an outer window. There was rarely a door and if the hermit wished to leave he, or she, risked excommunication. The cell was normally built on the north side, to avoid excessive heat in the summer. Although anchorites lived in seclusion, not all lived in cells.

High altar See altar.

Ionic Classical Order. Columns are slenderer than those of the Doric Order and capitals are decorated at corners with spiral scrolls (volutes).

Jamb Straight, vertical side of a door or window.

Joinery Woodwork that is fitted in, but not structural to, a building.

Keystone Central stone at the apex of a rounded arch or where the ribs of a vault intersect, frequently elongated to become a boss.

King-post Vertical wooden post that connects the horizontal tie-beams to the ridge of the roof.

Lady Chapel Chapel dedicated to the Virgin Mary. In larger churches this often extends east of the chancel as a retrochoir.

Lancet window Slender window with a sharply pointed arch. A distinctive feature of the Early English style *c.*1190–*c.*1310.

Lantern Small turret pierced with openings and crowning a roof.

Lectern Stand that supports the Bible from where lessons are read. Made of wood or metal, usually brass, they are now movable, but generally face the pulpit in the nave. Since the fourteenth century they have taken the form of a desk or a pelican, but most commonly an eagle, the symbol of St John the Evangelist. The height and speed at which this bird flies is considered analogous to the spread of God's word. Earliest lecterns were of stone and fixed to the north wall of the chancel; a few twelfth century examples survive but not in London. Before the Reformation they always stood in the chancel and supported the gospel or large music books.

Leper window Name erroneously applied to the low window sometimes found in the south wall of the chancel. Never used by lepers; more probably a bell was rung from them at important stages in the mass. Also known as the confessional window or lychnoscope.

Lierne vault Short decorative rib in a Gothic roof vault which connects two main ribs. Introduced in the fourteenth century.

Lich-gate (or **Lych-gate**) Roofed gateway to a churchyard. Corpses rested here awaiting the arrival of the priest for funeral services. Lich meant 'a corpse'.

Light Section of a window filled with glass, i.e. a pane.

Linenfold panelling Wooden panels, carved to resemble material with vertical folds. Popular throughout the Tudor period.

Lintel Horizontal section that spans an opening; generally of stone or timber.

Litany desk Desk at which the reciter of the litany kneels. Situated near the chancel's steps.

Louvre Overlapping boards, fixed at an angle, with gaps between for ventilation. Often part of a lantern.

Majolica Glazed earthenware generally used as decorative tiling. Also known as faience.

Mass dial Sundial that also indicates the time of mass. Always fixed against a south wall. Some Saxon examples have survived in London although not *in situ* and lacking their gnomen (pointer).

Mensa See altar.

Misericord 'Mercy' seat in the form of a narrow surface for resting purposes that protrudes horizontally when the seat itself is tipped up. Monastic in origin, now most survive as choir stalls in larger churches or cathedrals. The supporting brackets are often richly carved with a wide variety of allegorical subjects, frequently grotesque and humorous and usually copied from ancient manuscripts. First recorded c. 1200.

Monuments Christian monuments are known to have existed in the fifth century but they were not allowed inside the church until permitted by the Council of Nantes in 658, and then only within a porch. The earliest to survive in England are eleventh-century tomb slabs of Tournai marble. Coffin lids from the twelfth and thirteenth centuries also survive. Effigies only of royalty appeared from the 12C until the 15C on tomb chests, but soon began to feature as separate monuments. These were always stylized and did not represent a likeness of the deceased. Costume, although accurate, was contemporary with the period in which the effigy was made, often many years after the death of the subject. Materials used in medieval monuments included Purbeck marble, alabaster, wood (rarely) and bronze which was almost entirely reserved for the royal monuments at Westminster Abbey. Recumbent effigies in military dress were made from 1226; from c. 1250 until the late fourteenth century, knights were shown cross-legged but this did not mean that they were crusaders, as many believe. In the late Middle Ages all types of figure were commonly shown with their hands in prayer. From c. 1430 until the seventeenth century, skeletons and shrouded figures decorated monuments, death through recurring plagues and wars being ever present. After the Reformation, the figures' position evolved from semi-recumbent to leaning on an elbow, kneeling, seated, and finally standing. Jacobean alabaster monuments, brightly coloured and of great size, dominate the walls of many churches; additionally, the children of the deceased, frequently a great number, are often illustrated in relief at the base. From c. 1650, marble was preferred to alabaster as a material, monuments became even larger and humility disappeared, with fulsome tributes to the person commemorated replacing praise, or even reference, to the Almighty. However, London in particular was fortunate that Continental sculptors of genius had settled in England, and many of their works are masterpieces. A decline set in as the nineteenth century progressed and gradually the monuments became less ambitious, eventually being restricted in the main to tablets.

Moulding Decorative addition to a projecting feature such as a cornice, doorframe, etc.

Mullion Vertical bar dividing a window into 'lights'.

Mural Wall painting generally on plaster.

Narthex An ante chapel, generally at the west end of the nave, sometimes merely a covered porch.

Neo-Gothic Gothic features used in a light-hearted manner in the mid-eighteenth century.

Norman Romanesque architecture distinguished by round-headed arches and massive walls c. 1060–1200. Most long-established London churches were built or rebuilt by the Normans and several retain examples of their work.

Obelisk Tapering stone shaft with flat sides that evolved in ancient Egypt. Generally serves as an external monument.

Ogee A pointed, double-curved arch, roughly onion-shaped. Popular in Muslim architecture and introduced to England in the fourteenth century as a feature of the Decorated style. It had probably been seen on the crusades.

Oratory Small private chapel.

Order Classical architecture where the design and proportions of the columns and entablatures are standardized according to the Order chosen.

Organ Musical instrument, the invention of which is attributed by legend to St Cecilia, patron saint of music. First appeared in England in the eighth century. Generally stood in the rood loft prior to the Reformation, and later in the west gallery, where most remain. Some, however, were transferred elsewhere when galleries were demolished in the nineteenth century. Many outstanding seventeenth century examples designed by Renatus Harris and Father Schmidt remain in the City.

Oriel window Window projecting at an upper level; designed in the Tudor period. Rare in London churches, but see St Bartholomew-the-Great.

Palladian Style of architecture based on the sixteenth century work of the Italian Andrea Palladio which itself derived from ancient Rome.

Parapet Low solid wall surmounting a structure.

Parclose screen Screen, generally of wood, to a subsidiary chapel.

Peculiar A Church of England church, not directly responsible to the bishop of the diocese. Once, some were answerable to the Archbishop of Canterbury. Now all are 'royal peculiars', directly responsible to the sovereign.

Pedestal Base between a column or statue and its plinth.

Pediment Low-pitched triangular gable above a portico, door or window.

Pelican Bird, always portrayed 'in her piety' suckling her young with her own blood, as it was once believed she did, and signifying Christ's self-sacrifice to redeem mankind. Commonly featured surmounting a reredos or forming a lectern.

Pendant Elongated hanging feature decorating a roof or stairway.

Perpendicular Architectural style peculiar to England. The last and longest phase of Gothic, 1360–1550 (or 1660). Distinguished by large windows divided by horizontal transomes as well as vertical mullions.

Pew Bench seating for the congregation in the nave. Introduced in the fourteenth century; prior to this, the congregation sat on the floor which was usually covered with rushes. See box pew and bench end.

Pier Solid structure supporting a great load, frequently square in shape.

Pietà Carving or illustration of the Virgin supporting the body of Christ after the descent from the cross. Became popular in the fifteenth century.

Pilaster Shallow flat column attached to a wall.

Pinnacle Vertical decorative feature surmounting a Gothic structure.

Piscina Stone bowl, usually fixed within an arched recess in the wall of a church. From this the water used for ritual cleaning purposes during mass was drained directly to the consecrated ground outside. Its existence always indicates that an altar once stood nearby. Most are found on the south wall of the sanctuary next to a sedilia with which it is sometimes linked by extravagant tracery. Towards the end of the thirteenth century, double piscinas were specified by the Pope: one for washing the priest's hands prior to the consecration and the other for rinsing the vessels. This practice ended in the fourteenth century; instead, the celebrant drank the rinsings. Many piscinas incorporate a shelf for resting the vessels which now stand on a credence table.

Plinth Projecting base of a wall, column or statue.

Podium Lowest stage of a pedestal for a column or statue.

Polygonal Many sided, as, for example, an apse, chapel or chapter house.

Portico Classical porch of columns supporting a roof, usually pedimented.

Presbytery Alternative name for the sanctuary within a church, or a residence for the clergy.

Priest's door Small doorway for the priest on the south side of the chancel. Surviving examples now often lead to the vestry but most have been blocked.

Priory Monastic community under the authority of a prior or prioress.

Pulpit Enclosed raised structure approached by steps, from which sermons are preached. The word derives from the Latin *pulpitum*, a raised platform used for recitation. Pulpits were developed in monastic refectories for reading during meals and are first recorded in a church in the twelfth century. At the Reformation preaching declined and to combat this Edward VI ordered that every church must install a pulpit. James I made a similar order in 1603 which is why so many Jacobean pulpits were produced. High three-decker pulpits were made so that the speaker's voice could reach the galleries and he could be seen from the box pews. They became popular at the Restoration and comprised a preaching pulpit above a curate's reading pew and a clerk's pew. Surmounting this assembly was a canopy (or tester) which served as a sounding board to amplify the speaker's voice. Most surviving eighteenth-century pulpits were once three-deckers but cut down by the Victorians when galleries and box pew partitions were removed to open up the view of the high altar. Pulpits were generally placed in a central position until the mid-nineteenth century when they were moved to one side of the nave, at its east end. Most are made of wood but a few stone examples survive. Hour-glasses were often fixed to a pulpit by a bracket from the sixteenth to the eighteenth centuries in order to time the length of the sermon. Some brackets and holders survive in London together with wig pegs which were another fitting of the same period.

Pulpitum In large monastic churches the stone screen separating the chancel from the nave.

Quire See choir.

Quoin stones Dressed stones fitted externally at the angles of a wall to give added strength. Popular in the late seventeenth and early eighteenth centuries.

Reading desk or pew Desk from which the curate read the lesson. Introduced in the reign of Elizabeth I. Usually opposite or adjacent to the pulpit and incorporated with it in a three-decker. Now generally replaced by a lectern.

Rebus A medieval inscription which expressed a name in visual terms that could be understood by the illiterate. Generally made use of puns and popular with the monastic clergy.

Refectory Dining hall, also known as a frater when situated in a monastery.

Reliquary Container for a fragment of a body, usually a saint's, which is venerated. Many became the centrepiece of shrines in the Middle Ages. Pilgrimages were made to them chiefly because 'miraculous' cures were often claimed and they became an important source of income to the church. Due to their superstituous aspects most were destroyed at the Reformation.

Reredos A backing to the altar in various forms – murals, painted panels, carved wood, alabaster, glass or stone. The most popular composition in London is made up of panels with the Decalogue (Ten Commandments) in the centre, flanked by the Lord's prayer and the Belief. Paintings of the law-giver, Moses, and his brother Aaron are also common. Frequently, the Tetragrammaton ('Jehovah' in Hebrew) surmounts the reredos and many City churches feature the pelican in its piety. If there is an altar painting its subject is frequently The Last Supper.

Retable Vertical section fixed either to the rear of the altar or standing immediately behind it. Of stone or wood, generally highly decorated. Used in medieval times instead of, or as well as, a reredos. Ornaments stood on its shelf-like top.

Reticulation Tracery in the form of cusped double ogee shapes repeated in a regular net-like pattern. A feature of the early Perpendicular style. Probably evolved to overcome the difficulty that glassmakers had in fitting the irregular shapes of flowing tracery.

Retrochoir Section of a church behind the sanctuary.

Rib Protruding band supporting a vault; occasionally purely decorative.

Rococo Last phase of the Baroque style in the mid-eighteenth century with widespread use of detailed ornamentation. Few examples are found in England.

Romanesque Style of architecture featuring rounded-headed arches. Popular from the ninth century to c.1200. Saxon and Norman buildings were Romanesque.

Roman numerals Many monuments will display dates given in Roman numerals and the following conversions may be helpful:
1=I, 2=II, 3=III, 4=IV, 5=V, 6=VI, 7=VII, 8=VIII, 9=IX, 10=X, 11=XI, 12=XII, 13=XIII, 14=XIV, 15=XV, 16=XVI, 17=XVII, 18=XVIII, 19=XIX, 20=XX, 30=XXX, 40=XL, 50=L, 60=LX, 70=LXX, 80=LXXX, 90=XC, 100=C, 200=CC, 300=CCC, 400=CD, 500=D, 600=DC, 700=DCC, 800=DCCC, 900=CM, 1000=M, 1500=MD, 1900=MCM, 2000=MM.

Rood Crucifixion scene, generally depicted in wood or stone. Prior to the Reformation a large rood was erected on a beam beneath the chancel arch. The rood or chancel screen stood below. Flanking Christ was the Virgin Mary and St John the Evangelist. Early roods also included St Longinus the centurion, and the Roman soldier with the sponge. By the thirteenth century, lofts were created around the beam to accommodate the choir and musicians. They were decorated with candles and a special rood light, often in the form of a circular chandelier. The entire assembly was brightly painted and gilded, dominating the church. Roods were abolished by Edward VI in 1548 as being idolatrous but many returned with Mary I before again being abolished by Elizabeth I in 1559; this time the rood loft parapet also had to be removed. Rood beams and screens were never abolished and although many were destroyed, some survived until the nineteenth century. Traces of where the beam was fixed and the staircase to the loft exist in some medieval churches.

Rose window Circular window used in Gothic architecture. Its tracery pattern resembles a rose. Introduced in the mid-thirteenth century from France.

Rotunda Circular building, generally domed.

Royal arms These appear in many forms, e.g. carved, painted, stained glass, to symbolize the sovereign's position as head of the Church of England. Began to appear during the reign of Henry VIII, and when Elizabeth I ordered the removal of the Doom paintings above the chancel arch the royal arms usually replaced them. At the Restoration in 1660 Charles II made it compulsory to display them and they remained obligatory until Victoria's reign. Most numerous in London are the arms of Charles II, Queen Anne and the early Hanoverians.

Rustication Use of stonework on the exterior of a building to give an impression of strength. The jointing is always deep.

Sacristy The room in a church where sacred vessels and vestments are kept. Generally used for robing. Also known as a vestry.

Sanctuary Area reserved for the clergy in which the high altar stands. Generally at the east end of the chancel but sometimes elsewhere, particularly in buildings that have been recently reorientated. Alternatively, refers to the freedom from arrest granted in medieval times to a fugutive from justice when inside the church or its precincts, a privilege ended by Richard III in 1484.

Sarcophagus Carved coffin.

Saxon English architecture in Romanesque style pre-dating the Norman Conquest of 1066. Many London churches were founded by the Saxons, generally in the tenth century, but little evidence of their work survives.

Scissor beam Roof construction in which secondary beams cross each other diagonally in support of the main beams.

Sedilia Seating, generally of stone and recessed into the south wall of the sanctuary. Reserved for the priest and his assistants during the singing of the mass. Generally three in number but may vary from two to five. Simple sedilias are formed by a low windowsill but most are decorated with carved canopies, sometimes linked in one design with the piscina to the east. They may be stepped. Sedilias were made redundant at the Reformation but many survive. Reintroduced since emancipation in the nineteenth century in Catholic and Anglo-Catholic churches.

Shaft Section of a column between its base and capital.

Spandrels Roughly triangular areas in a wall, on either side of the curved part of an arch.

Spire Tall pointed structure with flat or rounded sides surmounting a tower. Apparently most medieval towers were intended to be surmounted by spires.

Splays Sloping sides of a window that has been set in a thick wall. Tapers from a small outer to a larger inner opening. A feature of Romanesque and lancet windows.

Springer Section of stone at which an arch begins to curve.

Squint Small aperture through which an unseen person can view the altar without entering the chancel. Also known as a hagioscope.

Stained glass First recorded in the sixth century, the earliest stained glass in England dates from the Saxon period. Colours were added by pot-metal leading during manufacture and initially brilliant blues and reds predominated. A reaction in the thirteenth century, chiefly due to the desire to lighten interiors, led to the substitution of grisaille (grey) glass. Yellow staining was discovered in the fourteenth century and this simplified the addition of crowns, halos, etc. as the surface of red glass could be scraped and the yellow painted on avoiding the need to make a separate piece. Flowing tracery of the late Decorated period made glassmaking difficult because of the complicated patterns formed by the leading; the simpler reticulated tracery of the early Perpendicular style was evolved partly to overcome the problem. This coincided with the development of 'silver stain' which provided particularly brilliant colours, and fifteenth century glass is judged by many to be the finest. Although it seems that much medieval glass was spared at the Reformation, Cromwell's Puritans, particularly in London, smashed a great deal which is why so little survives in the capital. However, St Margaret's, Westminster, possesses an outstanding early sixteenth century east window. Little stained glass was made between the Reformation and the nineteenth century, but the Gothic Revival led to its return. The early work of *Kempe* and the *William Morris/Burne-Jones* partnership is highly regarded artistically. Some post-war stained glass has been made, particularly notable being the work, in London, of *Carl Edwards*.

Stalls Seating in the chancel originally reserved for monastic clergy. Generally provided with desks and now mostly used by the choir. Medieval stalls are often canopied and exquisitely carved. See misericord.

Stations of the cross Fourteen incidents from the sentencing of Christ to the laying of his body in the sepulchre which are depicted by paintings or sculptures around the walls of a church. Popularized in the late Middle Ages by Franciscan monks as an alternative to making the pilgrimage to Jerusalem and following the way of the Cross. Generally restricted now to Catholic and Anglo-Catholic churches.

Steeple Tower, together with its crowning structure, e.g. lantern, spire.

Stiff leaf Foliage carved in a stiff formal manner; a decorative feature of the Early English style.

Stoup Basin for holy water, usually of stone and situated near a door. Worshippers dipped a finger in the consecrated water and made the sign of the cross. Every medieval church had a stoup but they were abandoned at the Reformation.

Stucco Plaster applied to the external face of a wall and painted.

Swag Carved representation of a piece of hanging cloth. Generally incorporates festoons of flowers, fruit, etc.

Sword rest Decorative stands for a Lord Mayor's sword and mace when attending a service in state. Usually of iron but some early examples were of wood. Generally restricted in London to the City churches. The oldest example known was made in 1610 but most post-date the Great Fire. None have been produced since the nineteenth century. Some churches possess more than one; they usually stand at the east end of the nave fixed to front pews or columns and are highly ornamental.

Terracotta Unglazed earthenware used as tiling.

Tessellated pavement Mosaic flooring.

Tie-beam Horizontal main beam in a timber roof.

Tierceron vault Vault comprising intermediate pairs of ribs which meet at an angle and form a star shape.

Tracery Intersecting bars that create a decorative pattern in Gothic architecture.

Transept The area that runs on either side of the nave of a large church forming the short arms of the cruciform (cross) plan. Some larger cathedrals possess more than one pair of transepts.

Transitional The merging of Gothic with Norman architecture *c.*1150–1200.

Transomes Horizontal bars dividing a window into 'lights'.

Triforium Blind passage that runs above the vault of an aisle.

Trophy Decorative carving of military objects.

Tunnel vault See barrel vault.

Tuscan Roman adaptation of the Greek Doric Order.

Tympanum The area between a horizontal lintel and an arched area above.

Undercroft Vaulted room or area at ground floor or basement level.

Vault An arched structure of stone forming a roof. Alternatively, an underground room frequently reserved for internment.

Venetian window Window of three openings, the central taller section having a round-headed arch.

Vestibule Entrance hall or anteroom.

Vestry See sacristy.

Wainscotting Timber lining on the lower section of an internal wall.

Weatherboarding Timber strips fixed to an internal or external wall for protection or decoration. Also known as clapboarding.

Weathervane Often surmounts a church tower or spire, most commonly in the form of a cock, symbolizing Christian watchfulness and the spread of Christ's word to all points of the compass. Symbols such as St Peter's keys or other saints' emblems are also used.

Saints

Many churches in this book are dedicated to the same saint; to avoid repetition, and for ease of reference, brief information about them has been collated. It should be remembered that every church is dedicated to God and any other dedication is secondary. In England it was customary during the Saxon period to canonize, by popular acclaim, kings who had met with a violent death. Although referred to as martyrs none were killed for their religious beliefs. Edward the Confessor was the first king to die peacefully and still be canonised. Papal authority for canonization has been needed since the 12C and no English monarch following the conquest has become a saint, in spite of claims made for Edward II, Henry VI and even Charles I to whom a few churches are dedicated. Accounts of the lives of the saints incorporate some facts with many legends and experts disagree in which category the events related should be placed.

Andrew (first century)
Disciple and brother of Simon Peter. A follower of John the Baptist, Andrew first met Jesus at his baptism. He immediately became Christ's first disciple and introduced his brother. After Christ's death he preached in Scythia and Greece. By tradition, Andrew was crucified at Patras on an X-shaped cross. He is a patron saint of Russia and the patron saint of Scotland whose national flag is St Andrew's cross, which is also incorporated in the Union Jack.
Emblem: transverse cross. Saints Day: 30 November.

Anne (first century BC)
Mother of the Virgin Mary. Allegedly married Joachim at the age of twenty but no offspring ensued. Visited by an angel, Anne promised to dedicate any child to God and Mary was born when she was forty years old. Neither Anne nor Joachim are referred to in the Bible and all information is apocryphal.
Emblem: a door. Saints Day: 26 July.

Augustine (of Canterbury) (d.604)
Prior of St Andrew's monastery in Rome. Augustine was sent, with other monks, by Pope Gregory I to evangelize Britain in 596. King Ethelbert of Kent received him on the Isle of Thanet; his wife was already a Christian and he was soon converted and baptized. Augustine went to France and was made a bishop but returned to England and continued his work of conversion. Ethelbert presented him with land at Canterbury and here he built a monastery with a great church. Augustine, known as the 'Apostle of the English', became the first archbishop of Canterbury.
Emblems: dove, pen. Saints Day: 26 May.

Bartholomew (first century)
An apostle who may also be the Nathaniel described by Christ as 'incapable of deceit', he preached in the Middle East and India. By tradition, Batholomew was flayed (skinned alive) and then beheaded by King Astyages at Abanapolis on the Caspian Sea. A 'gospel' of St Bartholomew has been condemned as apocryphal.
Emblem: flaying knife. Saints Day: 24 August.

Botolph (or Botolf or Botulf) (d.c.680)
May have been Irish or Saxon. He built a monastery at Icanhole in 654. Botolph was renowned for his learning and sanctity. He was the patron saint of travellers and most churches dedicated to him are sited outside a city wall.
Saints Day: 17 June.

Alfege (or Alphege) (c.954–1012)

Alfege left a Benedictine monastery to become a hermit and was eventually appointed Abbot of Bath, Bishop of Winchester and, finally, Archbishop of Canterbury. The Danes captured Canterbury and imprisoned Alfege for admonishing them. A plague struck the town and he was temporarily released to minister to the sick. Alfege refused to pay the 3000 gold crowns demanded for his permanent release and was put to death, probably at Greenwich. There is also a tradition that Alfege was killed on a Danish ship by drunken sailors who pelted him with bones.
Saints Day: 19 April.

Agnes (d.304)

Agnes was a Roman girl who dedicated her virginity to God. Rebuffed suitors denounced her to the Emperor Diocletian as a Christian. She was sent to a brothel but her saintly behaviour gave protection from violation. At the age of thirteen Agnes was beheaded, or, an alternative tradition, stabbed in the throat. She is the patroness of virgins.
Emblem: lamb – presumably as *agnus* (lamb) puns with Agnes. *Saints Day:* 21 January.

Bridget (or Brigid or Bride) (c.450–525)

Born near Louth in Ireland, Bridget became a close friend of St Patrick who had baptized her parents. After taking the veil at a young age she founded and became abbess of Ireland's first convent, at Kildare. The city grew around it and Bridget founded a school of art. Its most famous work, the illuminated Book of Kildare, unfortunately disappeared in the seventeenth century. Bridget is buried at Downpatrick with St Columba and St Patrick her co-patron saint of Ireland.
Emblems: candle, cross. *Saints Day:* 1 February.

Clement (d.c.99)

Baptized by St Peter, Clement, by tradition, was a freed royal slave. Elected pope in 91. The Emperor Trajan banished him to the Crimea. There he converted many prisoners before being thrown into the sea with an anchor around his neck. His letter of rebuke to the Corinthians is one of the most important early Christian documents. Clement is the patron saint of sailors.
Emblem: anchor. *Saints Day:* 23 November.

Cuthbert (d.687)

Cuthbert was orphaned at a young age; for a short time he was a shepherd before becoming a monk at Melrose Abbey. After a period with St Eata at Ripon Abbey, he returned to Melrose as prior and later was appointed prior and eventually bishop, of Lindisfarne.
Saints Days: 20 March, 4 September.

Cyprian (of Carthage) (c.210–258)

Probably born in Carthage, Cyprian, who was initially pagan, became a successful lawyer. Caecilius, a venerable priest, converted him to Christianity c.246 and two years later Cyprian became Bishop of Carthage. He wrote many theological treatises and was a pioneer of Christianity in the Latin world. Although championing the oneness of the church as founded by St Peter, Cyprian came into conflict with Pope Stephen, as he refused to recognize baptism by 'heretics'. During the persecution of Decius in 249, Cyprian went into hiding but was criticized for this and returned in 251. That year he formed the Convention of Carthage which asserted the supremacy of the pope and established terms for accepting the return of lapsed Christians to the church. From 252–54 the plague raged in Carthage and Christians were held to be responsible. Soon, they were required to abandon Christianity and support the officially approved pagan religion, but Cyprian refused and was exiled to Cerubis, a small town fifty miles from Carthage. The following year, all leading church officers were sentenced to death unless they recanted. Again, Cyprian refused and was beheaded on September 14, 258.
Saints Day: 16 September.

Dunstan (c.910–88)
Born of a noble family near Glastonbury, Dunstan was educated by monks and joined the Benedictine Order. St Alfege, Bishop of Winchester, was his uncle and ordained him c.939. After a period as a hermit at Glastonbury he was appointed its abbot by King Edmund and the abbey soon became a centre of learning, Dunstan being a skilled musician and craftsman. He was banished by King Edwy in 945 for reprimanding the new monarch for his licentious behaviour, but returned on Edgar's accession to the throne. High appointments proliferated and Dunstan was made Bishop of Worcester, Bishop of London, Archbishop of Canterbury and papal legate to Pope John XII. During this period he reformed the church and revived the monasteries. Under King Ethelred, Dunstan lost most of his influence and retired to teach at Canterbury's school. He is the patron of skilled metal craftsmen.
Saints Day: 19 May.

Edmund (841–70)
Edmund was elected King of the East Angles in 855 at the age of fourteen. He was captured by the invading Danes at Hoxne, Suffolk, and beheaded after torture.
Emblems: wolf with crown between paws, sword.
Saints Day: 20 November.

Ethelburga (d.c.678)
The daughter of King Anna of East Anglia, Ethelburga was born at Stallington and became a nun. She was soon appointed the first abbess of Barking Abbey, by her brother Erconwald who founded it. Ethelburga died there, a virgin. Her family was most saintly, all her brothers and sisters being canonized: Erconwald, Etheldreda, Sexburga and Withburga.
Saints Day: 12 October.

Etheldreda (or Audrey) (d.679)
Born at Exning, Suffolk, Etheldreda was sister of Ethelburga (see above). When young she married Toubert, a prince, who permitted her to remain a virgin. Apparently the strain was too much and he died three years later! After five years the lady remarried, this time to a young boy, Egfrid, son of King Oswy of Northumbria. Eventually, conjugal rights were demanded but refused. Not surprisingly, the marriage ended and Etheldreda joined a nunnery. She built a convent at Ely in 672 and was its first abbess. Ely's church eventually became the great Ely Cathedral.
Saints Day: 23 June.

George (d.c.303)
Nothing certain is known about George, in spite of his wide and long-lasting popularity. It has been alleged that he was a Roman soldier martyred in Palestine for his Christian beliefs. Legends began in the sixth century and by the eighth century George was already patron saint of the military, being particularly popular with crusaders. The dragon-slaying fable is first recorded in the twelfth century and by the fourteenth century George had replaced Edward the Confessor as England's patron saint. His arms, a red cross on a white background is the country's national flag and, like the transverse cross of St Andrew, forms part of the Union Jack. George is also the patron saint of Germany and Portugal.
Emblem: dragon. *Saints Day:* 23 April.

Giles (or Aegidius) (c.712)
Giles was an Athenian hermit who reputedly performed miracles. A legend is that he went to France, took refuge from King Flavius in the forest and was fed by a deer's milk. Later he saved the animal from hunters by shielding it with his own body. Giles eventually became an abbot and took confession from the Emperor Charlemagne. His shrine was a popular centre for pilgrimages in the Middle Ages. He is a patron saint of cripples and beggars.
Emblems: deer, crozier. *Saints Day:* 1 September.

Helen (or Helena) (c.250–330)

Born at Drepanum, Helen married Constantius, a Roman general who, on his election as Caesar in 293, divorced her. At his death, the Roman troops in York proclaimed their leader Constantine, son of Helen and Constantius, emperor. Constantine (the Great), together with the empire's co-ruler, Licinius, issued the edict of Milan in 313 which permitted Christianity in the empire for the first time. Helen then became a convert, evidently aged sixty-three. She was renowned for her charity and it is claimed that she discovered the True Cross (on which Jesus had been crucified) in Palestine. Fragments of this became coveted medieval relics. She is believed to have been buried at her son's new capital of the empire, Constantinople.

Emblem: cross. *Saints Day:* 18 August.

James (The Greater) (d.42)

One of the disciples, elder brother of John the Evangelist and son of Zebedee. Jesus called the two brothers to follow him at their first meeting on Lake Genasareth whilst they were mending their fishing nets. James was beheaded at Jerusalem by Herod Agrippa I, the first of the Apostles to be martyred. There is a tradition of a Spanish mission, but this is not generally believed. However, it has been claimed that his body was taken to Santiago de Compostela in Spain and this remains a centre of pilgrimage.

Emblems: scallop shell (probably because he was a fisherman), key, pilgrim's staff. *Saints Day:* 25 July.

John The Baptist (first century)

John was born in Jerusalem, the son of Zachary, a priest at the Temple. The child's birth had been prophesied by the Archangel Gabriel, although his mother, Elizabeth, was already elderly. John lived as a hermit in the Judean desert and then, age thirty, preached on the banks of the Jordan that the kingdom of heaven was close at hand. He attracted large crowds, including Jesus, whom he baptized and recognized as the Messiah, calling him the Lamb of God. John was later arrested and imprisoned by the tetrarch Herod Antipus for denouncing his adulterous marriage with Herodias. At the prompting of Herodias, her daughter Salome demanded the head of John the Baptist and he was duly executed. According to the New Testament John was the last of the prophets.

Emblems: head on a platter, lamb. *Saints Day:* 29 August.

John The Evangelist (c.6–c.104)

Born in Galilee, the younger brother of James (see above). Of all the Apostles, John was the youngest and Christ's most 'beloved'. However, the two brothers' volatile temperament earned Christ's appellation 'sons of thunder'. John, the only disciple to attend the Crucifixion, was entrusted by Jesus with the care of his mother. It was, therefore, usual for John to be depicted with Mary on medieval roods. No other disciple escaped martyrdom but John is alleged to have miraculously emerged unharmed from a vat of boiling oil. He wrote Revelations on Patmos and the fourth gospel and three epistles at Ephesus. John evidently lived to a great age.

Emblems: eagle, armour, chalice. *Saints Day:* 27 December.

Katherine (or Catherine) (d.c.310)

In spite of her veneration since the tenth century, nothing certain is known about this saint; all information is, therefore, apocryphal. Born in Alexandria, Katherine was converted by a vision. Bravely, she denounced Emperor Maxentius for his persecution of Christians. She converted philosophers, soldiers and even the Emperor's wife. All were executed and Katherine tied to a torture wheel; this miraculously broke, and she was, instead, beheaded. Her body was taken to a monastery, high on Mount Sinai, and it is said to remain there. Because of this, most churches dedicated to the saint stand on hilltops. The voice of St Katherine was amongst those claimed to have been heard by Joan of Arc. She is the patroness of philosophers, maidens and preachers and, apart from the Virgin Mary, the female saint most frequently depicted in religious art.

Emblems: wheel, lamb. *Saints Day:* 25 November.

Lawrence (d.258)
Born in Spain, Lawrence was a deacon of Pope Sixtus II. When Sixtus was condemned to death, Lawrence sold most of the valuables belonging to the Church and gave the money to the poor. Soon the Emperor demanded the treasures and Lawrence was given three days in which to collect them. In due course, he assembled the crippled, sick and poor, saying 'These are the Church treasures.' Lawrence was seized, bound to a red hot grid-iron and burned to death; his bravery during this ordeal led to the conversion of Rome.
Emblems: grid-iron, book of gospels. *Saints Day:* 10 August.

Lawrence (of Canterbury) (d.619)
Lawrence accompanied St Augustine (see above) on his evangelical mission to England in 596 and succeeded him as Archbishop of Canterbury. He experienced difficulties when Edbald became King of Kent in 616, as the new ruler permitted the return of paganism. Lawrence considered returning to Gaul but in a dream was rebuked by St Paul who lashed him with a whip. On awakening, his back was lacerated and, seeing this, Edbald became a convert. Although the third century St Lawrence is better known, it is probable that some English churches dedicated to St Lawrence in the Saxon period referred to Lawrence of Canterbury.
Saints Day: 3 February.

Leonard (d.559)
A courtier of his godfather, Clovis I of France, Leonard was converted by St Remigius. Refusing the see offered him, he became a monk and later a hermit. Leonard prayed for the Queen during a difficult childbirth; she survived and the grateful King offered him all the land he could cover in a day, riding a donkey. On the land acquired, Leonard built Noblac monastery, around which grew the town of St Leonard. It is alleged that Clovis released prisoners at Leonard's request. He is the patron saint of women in labour and prisoners of war.
Saints Day: 6 November.

Luke (first century)
Reputedly a Greek, born in Antioch, Luke was a physician who accompanied St Paul on his pilgrimages. Allegedly he also painted portraits of the Virgin Mary. Luke wrote the Acts of the Apostles *c*.64 and the third gospel *c*.80. He died at Boetra, aged eighty-four. Luke is the patron saint of physicians and painters.
Emblems: book, palette, ox. *Saints Day:* 18 October.

Margaret (or Martha)
All information is apocryphal. Margaret's father, a pagan priest at Antioch, drove her out following her conversion and she became a shepherdess. Prefect Olybrius was spurned by Margaret and in revenge denounced her as a Christian and she was imprisoned and tortured. During her imprisonment she survived attempts to burn and drown her and made many converts. Eventually she was beheaded – seemingly the only miracle-proof method of execution where saints are concerned! By tradition, Margaret encountered the Devil in the guise of a dragon; he swallowed her, but irritation, caused by the crucifix that she wore, forced him to disgorge her and she escaped. Margaret is the patroness of childbirth.
Emblem: dragon. *Saints Day:* 20 July.

Martin (of Tours) (*c*.316–97)
The son of an Hungarian officer, Martin was forced into the army at the age of fifteen. At Amiens he divided his cloak, giving half to a beggar. That night Martin, in a dream, saw Christ wearing the half-cloak and became a convert. Refusing to fight any longer, Martin was discharged. He devoted his life to missionary work, and in 371 became Bishop of Tours, soon establishing a monastery at Marmontier. Martin's shrine at Tours was a popular centre for pilgrimages. He is one of the patron saints of France.
Saints Day: 11 November.

Mary the Virgin (first century)
Mother of Jesus and the pre-eminent saint. Her divinity and virginity are declared unequivocally in the New Testament. By tradition, she was born in Jerusalem, the daughter of Anne (see above) and Joachim. She was presented in the Temple and made a vow of perpetual virginity. Following the announcement by the Archangel Gabriel that she had been chosen to give birth to Christ, Mary and Joseph married. Soon after Christ's birth, the Holy Family fled to Egypt but returned to Jerusalem following Herod's death. Little reference is then made to Christ's mother in the gospels until the Crucifixion. Mary is said to have died at either Jerusalem or Ephesus at the age of forty-eight. The cult of the Virgin appears to have developed in the twelfth century in England, where Annunciation lilies first appeared, but by the thirteenth century she had become the most important saint throughout the Christian world. Many myths then developed, including that of her Assumption to heaven.
Emblem: vase of lilies. *Many Saints Days include:* 25 March (Annunciation); 14 August (Assumption); 8 September (birthday).

Mary Magdalene (or Magdalen) (first century)
Presumed to have come from Magdala by the Sea of Galilee. Christ cast out seven devils from her, she was converted and became the embodiment of repentant sinners. Mary attended the Crucifixion and was the first to see Christ after his Resurrection.
Emblem: ointment box. *Saints Day:* 22 July.

Michael
Together with Gabriel and Raphael the most venerated of the angels. Captain of the heavenly host that overthrew Lucifer. Many hilltop churches are dedicated to St Michael.
Emblems: dragon, sword. *Saints Day:* 29 September.

Nicholas (*c.*350)
Probably born, of wealthy parents, in Asia Minor. Renowned for his goodness, Nicholas became Bishop of Myra but was later imprisoned by the Emperor Diocletian. What were claimed to be his relics were brought to Bari, Italy, in 1087 and a shrine was built which became popular with pilgrims. Reputedly, Nicholas brought three murdered children to life, or, alternatively, released them from captivity by paying a ransom of three bags of gold. First called Santa Claus in Holland, the name by which he is now known throughout the world, he has since acquired the Father Christmas image of Thor the Nordic god of winter. Nicholas is the patron saint of Greece, Sicily and Russia.
Emblems: three purses, boat, anchor. *Saints Day:* 6 December.

Olav (or Olaf) (995–1030)
A pirate when young, Olav Haraldsson 'the Fat', son of a Norwegian lord, was later baptized in Rouen. In 1013, he helped King Ethelred fight the Danes in the battle of London Bridge. Olav pulled the bridge down as a defensive measure thus giving rise to the nursery song 'London Bridge is falling down', which began as a Norse saga. Returning to Norway, he freed the country from invaders and became king. However, his strict rule led to a revolt and Olav was eventually killed in battle. He was soon venerated and his shrine became Trondheim Cathedral. Olav is the patron saint of Norway.
Saints Day: 29 July.

Pancras (d.*c.*304)
Probably born in Syria, Pancras was orphaned when young and taken to Rome by his uncle; both were converted to Christianity. Pancras was beheaded by the Emperor Diocletian at the age of fourteen.
Saints Day: 12 May.

Paul (d.c.64)
Origianlly named Saul, he was a member of the Jewish tribe of Benjamin, and born at Tarsus, which made him a Roman citizen. Saul, a tentmaker by profession, became a Pharisee and enthusiastically persecuted Christians. However, on his way to Damascus c.35 he had a vision and was immediately converted. Saul preached and eventually met the Apostles in Jerusalem. He carried out three great missions, changed his name to Paul and wrote the Epistles. By tradition, he was beheaded by Nero in Rome c.64 on the same day as St Peter.
Emblems: book, scroll. *Saints Day:* 29 June.

Paulinus (of York) (d.644)
Accompanied Augustine on his mission to England and was made a bishop in 625. Paulinus baptized King Edwin at York, thereby bringing Christianity to Northumbria. Later paganism was revived and Paulinus returned to Rochester.
Saints Day: 10 October.

Peter (d.c.64)
Disciple and brother of Andrew. Originally named Simon, like his brother he was a fisherman on lake Genasareth. Jesus was introduced to him by Andrew and named him Cephus, the Greek for Peter, meaning 'the rock'. Peter denied Christ three times before the cock crowed. He was allegedly imprisoned by Herod Agrippa c.43 but escaped with the help of an angel. Peter is believed to have been beheaded by Nero in Rome c.64 on the same day as St Paul. St Peter's Cathedral in Rome is built above what may be his tomb. The saint is regarded as the keeper of the gates of heaven.
Emblems: key, cockerel. *Saints Day:* 29 June.

Stephen (d.c.35)
Stephen spoke Greek and may, therefore, have been educated in Alexandria. He was converted to Christianity and preached in Jerusalem. Tried for blasphemy, Stephen condemned his persecutors who, in fury, dragged him to the outskirts of Jerusalem where he was stoned. Stephen was the first recorded Christian martyr.
Saints Day: 26 December.

Vedast (or Vaast) (d.539)
Vedast was ordained near Toulouse and instructed Clovis I for his baptism at Rouen. Following missionary work he was ordained Bishop of Rheims in 499.
Saints Day: 6 February.

English architectural styles

Experts disagree on the precise definitions of some styles and periods, and as this affects their time spans, alternative dates are shown in brackets where applicable. It should be remembered that architectural styles always overlap by several years and no precise dividing line can generally be drawn. Dominant styles are shown in bold type.

Period ruled and rulers	Architectural style	Important London examples of churches and their completion dates
Romans	**Roman** 43–410	
Anglo-Saxons and Danes	**Romanesque** 500–1200	
	Pre-Conquest Romanesque or Saxon 500–1066	Kingston (cross) Cheam (Lumley Chapel) St Pancras Old Church, 6C altar All-Hallows-by-the-Tower, 7C arch Orpington, sundial
Normans 1066 William I 1087 William II 1100 Henry I 1135 Stephen	Post-Conquest Romanesque or Norman 1066–1200	Addington, chancel 1080 Harrow-on-the-Hill, tower 1094 St Mary-le-Bow, crypt late 11C St Bartholomew-the-Great *c.*1125 East Ham *c.*1130 East Bedfont *c.*1150 Rainham *c.*1170 Harrow-on-the-Hill, porch late 12C
	Transitional 1145–90	Temple church, nave *c.*1185 Harmondsworth late 12C
Angevins 1154 Henry II 1189 Richard I 1199 John	**Gothic** 1190–1550 (or 1630)	
	Early English 1190–1310	Barnes, Langton Chapel 1190 Harrow-on-the-Hill, transepts late 13C Littleton late 12C Bexley *c.*1200 St Helen Bishopsgate, south transept *c.*1215 Barking, chancel *c.*1216 Temple church, chancel 1240 Coulsdon 1260 Wennington 13C Hillingdon, nave mid 13C
Plantagenets 1216 Henry III 1272 Edward I 1307 Edward II 1327 Edward III	Decorated 1290–1360	St Etheldreda *c.*1300 Northolt, nave early 14C
1377 Richard II *House of Lancaster* 1399 Henry IV 1413 Henry V 1422 Henry VI	Perpendicular 1330–1550 (or 1630)	St Ethelburga late 14C St Helen Bishopsgate (part) 1475 Stepney 15C Hornchurch *c.*1500 Hayes (part) early 16C St Giles Cripplegate 1550

House of York
1461 Edward IV
1483 Edward V
1483 Richard III
Tudors
1485 Henry VII
1509 Henry VIII

	English Renaissance 1528 (or 1550) −1650 (or 1830)	Chelsea Old Church, More Chapel 1528 Stoke Newington Old Church *c.*1560 St Katherine Cree 1630 Wimbledon, Cecil Chapel *c.*1628
1547 Edward VI 1553 Lady Jane Grey 1553 Mary I 1558 Elizabeth I *Stuarts* 1603 James I (Jacobean period)		Charlton: St Luke *c.*1630 St Helen Bishopsgate, fixtures and fittings *c.*1630
	Classical 1622–1847 Palladian 1622–1700	St Paul Covent Garden 1630
1625 Charles I (Carolean period) 1649 Cromwell (Commonwealth period)	Dutch style 1630–1710	St Benet 1683
1660 Charles II (Restoration period)	Wren Style 1660–1730	Most City churches
1685 James II 1689 William III/ Mary II (joint rulers) 1702 Anne		
	English Baroque 1705–31	St Mary-le-Strand 1717 St Anne Limehouse 1724 Deptford 1724 St George-in-the-East 1726 Christ Church Spitalfields 1727 St Mary Woolnoth 1727 St John Smith Square 1728 St George Bloomsbury 1731
House of Hanover 1714 George I 1714 (or 1702) −1830 (Georgian period)		
	Neo-Gothic, or Georgian Gothic 1720 (or 1682) −1780	St Michael Cornhill, tower 1722 St Margaret Westminster, tower 1734
	Palladian Revival 1720–1830	St Martin-in-the-Fields 1726 St Giles-in-the-Fields 1733
1727 George II 1760 George III	Adam Style 1760–1790	

	Greek Revival 1766–1847	St Pancras 1822 Southwark St Peter 1825
1811–20 Regency 1820 George IV		
	Gothic Revival 1824–1900	St Luke Chelsea 1824 All Saints Margaret St 1859 St Augustine Kilburn 1880
1830 William IV		
1837 Victoria		
	Romanesque Revival 1860–1900	St Pancras 1848
	Neo-Wren (or Neo-Queen Anne or Neo-Georgian) 1870–1960	Brompton Oratory 1878
House of Saxe Coburg and Gotha 1901 Edward VII (Edwardian period) *House of Windsor* 1910 George V 1936 Edward VIII 1936 George VI		
	Modernism (or *Functionalism*) 1950–82	
...beth II	*Brutalism* 1960–82	
	Post-Modernism from 1980	Barnes, north section 1984

Designers

Outstanding architects, sculptors and decorators whose work is featured.